LEGENDS' END

As McWade drew near the doorway, he barely heard the doors of a car opening behind him.

Suddenly, two men appeared on his flanks.

"This way, Mr McWade," said the smaller of them. His accent was dark and glottal. He stretched out his palm to show the glint of steel.

McWade tried to turn, but the bigger man took hold of his arm.

"I am expected," said McWade.

Supporting McWade between them like an invalid, the men turned back to their car and urged him into the rear. The man with the pistol slid in beside him.

"Put this on," he said, holding out a black cloth sack that looked like an execution hood. "Now lean over. Head on knees. You are young and limber. It will not be so painful."

A hand seized his neck and pressed him downward. When he had gone as far as he could go, the hand remained on his neck. The car began to roll.

**Also by the same author,
and available from Coronet:**

OUR FATHERS' SHADOWS

About the author

Jack Fuller is the author of four highly acclaimed
novels – CONVERGENCE, FRAGMENTS,
MASS and most recently, OUR FATHERS'
SHADOWS – and works as a journalist in his
native America. A graduate of Yale Law School,
he has reported for the *Chicago Daily News*,
the *Washington Post* and is now editorial page
editor of the *Chicago Tribune*. In 1986 he was
awarded the Pulitzer Prize for editorial writing –
for his leaders on the law.

Jack Fuller lives in Evanston, Illinois with his
wife, Alyce, and their two children.

Legends' End

Jack Fuller

CORONET BOOKS
Hodder and Stoughton

Copyright © Jack Fuller 1989

First published in Great Britain in 1990 by Hodder and Stoughton Ltd

Coronet edition 1991

British Library C.I.P.
Fuller, Jack
    Legends' end.
    I. Title
    813'.54[F]
    ISBN 0-340-53552-0

Printed and bound in Great Britain for Hodder and Stoughton Paperbacks, a division of Hodder and Stoughton Ltd., Mill Road, Dunton Green, Sevenoaks, Kent TN13 2YA (Editorial Office: 47 Bedford Square, London WC1B 3DP) by Clays Ltd., St Ives plc.

Ambition must be made to counteract ambition. . . . It may be a reflection on human nature, that such devices should be necessary to control the abuses of government. But what is government itself, but the greatest of all reflections on human nature?

James Madison, *Federalist* No. 51

Man . . . is a sinner not because he is one limited individual within a whole but rather because he is betrayed by his very ability to survey the whole and to imagine himself the whole.

Reinhold Niebuhr

For my godson, Michael Conway,
and his family

PART ONE

Fisherman and Ross

1

Anyone who had been in government as long as Isaac McWade knew that at a certain level there are only two reasons people begin backing away from you – either they are afraid or you should be.

But it wasn't always easy to tell the difference. The evidence was the same whether people thought you posed a threat to their power or they sensed you were losing yours. Conversations died in your presence. Telephone callers stuck obsessively to the point. Formality crept into hallway encounters that should have been as casual as a nod.

And so when Ross and the delegation left on their mission and McWade felt the corridors of the Old Executive Office Building turning to ice around him, he could not be sure what it meant. Nobody was in a state yet about the Moscow initiative. The information loop remained small and tight within the National Security Council staff. As far as McWade could tell, even Langley was still in the dark, not to mention State and Defense. So McWade's intuition told him the freeze he was feeling had to have another cause.

Michael Ross was big on trusting intuition. If you waited for things to clarify, he said, you would always be behind the curve. But Ross wasn't McWade's only mentor. He had also spent time with Ernest Fisherman, the Agency's chief ferret, and it was Fisherman's view that the only thing a man of the world should trust was his doubt.

This was just one of the differences between Fisherman and Ross. There were so many others that sometimes McWade wondered how they had managed to remain allies for all these years. Before Ross was recruited for the NSC staff, he had come up on the positive intelligence side at Langley, running agents against America's sovereign enemies; Fisherman had served his whole career in counter-intelligence, sniffing out enemies within. Ross was known for his tailored clothes, catholic good taste and precise ability to explain the way things worked; Fisherman was a dumpy ascetic, an oracle, a troll. If Ross's gift was that he appeared the confident embodiment of a strong nation engaged in the world, then Fisherman was the punishing voice of its most secret fears. It all came down to this: Ross made things happen, and Fisherman made them painful.

Advancing McWade's career was one thing they had in common, though, and that was a comfort at times like this when he began to feel others grow cold. He knew it would get worse once the news of the Moscow trip began to leak. Under these circumstances it did not hurt to have friends all over. That was why he had decided it was time to get together with Martin Swain.

It was nearly dark by the time he locked up his safe and left for the restaurant. The last tour buses were loading up along the Mall for the daily evacuation. Stragglers from the memorials moved slowly across the green. A single flag hung motionless in the twilight over one wing of the Capitol, giving proof through the night that the House was still in session.

McWade barely noticed as he rode up Independence in the back seat of a motor pool sedan. The people's representatives could work until dawn for all he cared. There were no bills of interest to him on the Speaker's list, and Swain came from the other side of the Hill.

But as his driver edged slowly forward, McWade squinted past the spotlights until he located the other pole, the one that Congress kept obscure from public view. It stood empty now, but during daylight hours a detail of men hoisted banner after banner up the halyard there. These were distributed to city halls, marching bands, veterans' posts and loyal constituents in every district of the land, each accompanied by an official letter certifying where it had flown, the authentic fabric of our democracy.

When McWade was a boy, his father had been honored with one of these mementos himself. The letter that preceded it had come from a man so important that it traveled all the way from Washington to Manitee Bay on his signature alone. McWade remembered the day the package itself arrived, how his dad had solemnly raised the flag on the tall staff outside their porch then led the family in the Pledge, how that night McWade and his brother had folded it into a tight triangle the way they had learned in Scouts.

That was many years ago, and McWade had learned a lot about the ways of government since then, including what it mass-produces and what it tries to hide. But even now, despite all the darker secrets of state revealed to him at Langley and after, he still had a stab of fondness whenever he recalled the way he had once felt the call of history beneath that flag.

The driver pulled the shiny pool car to the curb near a line of sidewalk vendors selling flowers and leather. They took little notice as he emerged into the heat and hurried to the door of Jacob's Grove.

The restaurant borrowed its name from an arbor the history books said had once shaded the side of the Hill. In another city Jacob's Grove might have been a place where young professionals went to find companions of like mind and sexual inclination. Here it served a different lust.

Once inside, McWade looked for Swain at his usual table, one that guaranteed that he would be noticed by everyone in the place without once having to acknowledge a man he could force to come to him. But tonight somebody else was sitting there. That was odd. Swain ordinarily insisted on a place of prominence. In this town, a person was known by whom he knew and what position he could command; these were the ways he was defined.

McWade gave the maître d' Swain's name, and the man regarded him just long enough to be sure it was all right not to recognize his face. It did not bother McWade that he usually escaped notice, even now that strictly speaking his job did not require anonymity. Once he left the CIA to work for Ross on the National Security Council staff, he was free to be seen and talked about around town, but still he kept his public profile low. It suited him to be a man of average stature and conventional dress, the kind you

11

could see coming and going by the hundreds at National Airport every day of the week. It suited Ross, too, because he was still enough of an Agency product himself that he considered anyone who courted publicity to be simply undisciplined, like a man who could not hold his liquor.

"Perhaps you would care to wait in the bar," said the maître d'.

"I'd just as soon go to the table."

"We will call your name."

"McWade. Isaac McWade."

"Certainly."

It was typical of Swain to make him wait. McWade had known him since college, where they used to pile into somebody's car every Saturday night to go cruising for something to do. Swain was always the first to call shotgun, leaving the others to crowd hip to hip into the back seat while he sat easily in the front. Swain seemed to know exactly what he wanted, even then, and it wasn't so much a matter of where he ended up as where he rode along the way.

The bar was crowded, but McWade found an empty seat at the far end. When he ordered a drink to have some claim on the space, he noticed a familiar figure in conversation down the way, and he turned to the side to avoid catching the man's eye. It was that bastard George Leighton, one of the reporters who had helped hound Ross out of office during the post-Watergate purges.

Like so many of his generation, Ross had built his network of sources in Europe during the chaotic period after the Second War. The take had been so rich that access to it required a compartmented clearance that carried a special codeword, NARCISSUS. Over the years, the operation had given Langley the organization chart of the KGB hierarchy with a name in almost every box. It had blown Soviet deep cover agents and provided a litmus test for defectors. And during the feckless years of détente, it had warned of the Kremlin's hidden designs.

But once the news of its existence began to leak during the early stage of the purges, the NARCISSUS sources started flickering out. Assets disappeared under ominous

circumstances. Then one of Langley's own was assassin-
ated in London – a man named Ben Wheeler, who had
been Ross's principal runner for twenty years. McWade
had first learned of NARCISSUS during his investigation
of Wheeler's death.

The loss of the NARCISSUS sources did not destroy
Ross. It was the relentlessness of his campaign to protect
them that ruined him. He used every bureaucratic trick at
his disposal to slow the disclosures, then finally went to the
Hill and delivered a jeremiad in open session that pro-
foundly embarrassed the new management at Langley.
His dismissal followed quickly. It was summary, public and
utterly without ceremony.

Fisherman had been one of the few survivors who dared
to keep up a relationship with Ross during the years of
exile. They were seen dining together whenever Ross had
business in Washington. At Langley this gesture did not go
unremarked, because it was not like Fisherman to let
himself be seen at all. And when the pendulum finally
swung back and a new President brought Ross on at the
NSC, there were plenty of men in the Agency who wished
they'd had the nerve to break bread with him, too.

Most reporters also eventually realized the error of their
ways and began to treat Ross with renewed respect. But
Leighton was unrepentant. When Ross's career revived, he
dredged up all the sorry history and even made an effort
to link Ross to the Iran-Contra business, which had taken
place during his time in private life. Leighton had failed,
but everyone knew that he had tried. And they were
amazed that Ross never punished him for it. Though Ross
could have made Leighton's life difficult around the NSC,
he did not do so. He was not one to spend a lot of time
looking back. He left the settling of scores to Fisherman,
who had a gift for it.

In the mirror behind the bar McWade saw Leighton
extricating himself from his conversation. He wore a shape-
less tweed jacket over a plaid shirt and knit tie, which was
held down by the chain of his White House credentials. A
long, narrow notepad poked out of his coatpocket, and as

he passed through the crowd he patted an occasional shoulder and bestowed knowing nods.

"Drinking alone these days?" he said when he reached McWade. "Times must be pretty bad."

"Same old thing," said McWade, "preserving this island of human liberty in a hostile world."

"You haven't returned my calls."

"Meetings all day."

"Even when one of you guys leaves the church," he said, "you never quite get over the vows of silence."

"I have so little to say," said McWade.

"We need to get together, Ike," said Leighton. "You owe it to yourself."

"Schedule's pretty tight."

The last thing McWade wanted to do was to give Leighton a chance to poke around for a hint about the Moscow talks. The danger now was expectations, what with all the Kremlin management's soothing words and fresh designs. That was one of the reasons for silence, to keep the pressure of optimism off the team in Moscow — that and to prevent the jealousy of Defense and State from wrecking any chance of success.

"Look," said Leighton, "I know all about your problem."

"You'll have to let me in on it someday."

"I don't want to draw you into this story unless you force me to," said Leighton. "But one way or another, I'm going to write."

"One way or another," said McWade, "you always do." Then he heard his name being called by the maître d'. "Excuse me. I'm being summoned."

"Have your girl call with a time," said the reporter to McWade's back.

Luckily, no one else in the crowd at the bar snagged McWade on his way to the front of the restaurant. And when he reached the maître d's desk, he leaned over and tried to read the names in the book.

"Is there some problem with the reservation?" he asked.

"Telephone, sir. You can take it back there in the office."

The maître d' directed McWade to a small room near

14

the toilets. It must have been used by the manager because the phone sat on a stack of invoices and credit card slips on the metal desk. McWade picked up the receiver and heard Swain's voice.

"Where the hell are you?" said McWade. "You're half an hour late."

"Are you alone?"

"How much longer will it be?"

"I'm not coming, Ike," said Swain. "I'm sorry."

"Are you all right?"

"This is awkward for both of us," said Swain.

"I've wasted a lot of time here in unpleasant conversation with George Leighton."

"You didn't tell him who you were meeting, did you?"

"Your name did not come up."

"Whose did?"

"He was annoyed that I'd been stiffing him," said McWade. "He's been pestering my secretary all day."

"I called your office this afternoon," said Swain, "but you were in a meeting."

"You could have left a message."

"I didn't want to give my name."

McWade came around the desk and lowered himself into the battered swivel chair. The door was open, but the hallway was empty.

"What's this all about?"

"If it was anybody else," said Swain, "I'd just let the guy twist in the wind."

McWade had the sinking feeling that there had been a leak.

"Do you know something about Ross's agenda?" he asked.

"You mean the Kremlin trip?" said Swain. "I'm not talking about that."

"Where the hell did you hear about it?"

"It's all over town, Ike. The *Post* has already been calling around. I got worried when I realized Ross had left you behind."

"Is that why you stood me up tonight?" said McWade. "Because you thought I'd become dispensable?"

"Leighton is onto something. That's why he has been trying to get through to you," said Swain. "And he could only have gotten it from Fisherman himself."

"Gotten what?"

Fisherman did not deal with reporters as a rule. It was one of the few rules he abided by in his obsessive hunt for Soviet agents within the ranks.

"Fisherman thinks there's been a hemorrhage from your office, Ike. He's got the smell of blood in his nostrils."

"What the hell can he be thinking of?" said McWade.

"You know him, Ike. He only thinks about one thing."

"Leighton has already talked to you about it?" said McWade.

"To the Senator. Just this afternoon."

"Who is Fisherman after?"

"I wish I knew," said Swain.

"Did the Senator tell you not to be seen with me?"

"He didn't have to."

2

Leighton was gone when McWade returned to the dining room. McWade explained to the maître d' that there had been a mixup and was offered a table for one, but he declined and moved to the door. It made an unpleasant sucking noise as he opened it.

Outside the air was still hot and sticky. There were no taxis on the street, and all the vendors had packed up their wares for the night. A man and woman swayed arm in arm down the sidewalk. A bum near the corner followed McWade with his eyes.

"Spare any change?" he whispered.

McWade dug into his pocket and came up with a quarter and two nickels. He pressed them into the man's hand, registering the face, the faded fatigue shirt, the baggy jeans and jogger's shoes. He looked just a shade too healthy for the role. His eyes were alert, and he did not look past McWade to find another mark as he might have if he had been as professional as some others McWade had known.

McWade's senses spread out like the quick, mosaic eye of a fly, taking in the movements on the street, the rooftops of the buildings, the lighted windows and the dark ones without shades. The Library of Congress was open for a concert or a reading. For a moment he considered ducking inside, but there was only one exit. A stalker team could simply wait him out.

The closest taxi stand was at the Capitol, but if the House had adjourned, it would be empty. So McWade headed toward Union Station. Sweat beaded on his forehead and gathered in the small of his back as he walked down First Street at a slow and steady pace, as alert as if he were in enemy territory. One of the first things you learned in the Agency was that the most dangerous place in the world was anywhere you thought you were safe.

Ben Wheeler's murder was a textbook example. With NARCISSUS in trouble, he had been grounded in London: no more missions to the Continent, let alone behind the Wall. As a result, he had allowed his boredom to lead him into a rut so deep that he could be found in his neighborhood tube station every morning at the same hour. One day a man with an umbrella jostled him on the platform. He felt the tip striking his calf, a sting of pain. As Ben started after him, the poison took hold. He staggered up the stairs and collapsed on the street.

Ben's funeral was the first time McWade laid eyes on Michael Ross. It was a rainy day, and the services were private. Nobody who was still working under a legend was allowed to attend. McWade watched the burial party from an observation post across from the cemetery. Maybe it was only Ross's physical stature, towering over all the other mourners, but through the fieldglasses, he seemed larger than the event. Something about Ross made him the measure of his surroundings. Fisherman did not show that day. Everyone said it was just like him to play by a fieldman's rules. Ben would have kept his head down, too, they said, if it had been the other way around.

As McWade walked past the high facade of the Supreme Court, a guard was making his rounds. The echo of his footsteps seemed to come around from behind, but McWade did not check his back. It would have been too obvious on the open sidewalk.

By the time he reached the brightly lighted train station, the sweat was cool on his skin. He wasn't thinking of Ben Wheeler anymore, only of getting from here to there. He passed the taxis waiting in line on the ramp and went through the cavernous old building to the Metro station, where he bought a ticket from the machine and rode the escalator slowly down.

There were only a few people on the platform at this hour, so it was easy to find an empty bench. Presently, he heard the automatic ticket-taker thump open and closed, and a man in a polo shirt and khaki pants descended the moving steps. He walked in front of McWade and took up a place ten yards down the way. They did not look at one another.

After a few minutes the train to Farragut Square arrived. It was almost empty, and the man in the polo shirt boarded another car. He did not get off at McWade's station. But there were several who did. And a few of them followed him up the escalator and on toward Pennsylvania Avenue.

It had been a long time since McWade had felt the sensation of someone watching him. It had always made him queasy to think that his movements were being marked, that others might come secretly to know him better than he knew himself.

Or at least better than he had known himself since he left Manitee Bay, where his identity had been as fixed as fate. He had chafed against the certainty then, had yearned to leave Manitee Bay to find a larger cause that would have given his life its own unique meaning and shape. And so when others of his generation turned away from the call of military service, McWade went gladly, believing that the test of war would define him, that in battle the purest elements in him would be distilled.

But the effect of combat had been the opposite. Once he came under fire, he felt as if everything vital was being leached out of him. When he moved through the jungles, he sensed unseen eyes upon him and wondered what they saw. He took hits, the jagged steel proof of sacrifice but not of anything gained. And when he finished his tour, the pull of incompletion tugged at him more strongly than ever before. It did not take long for him to gravitate to the Agency, where they carried on the fight in the shadow of peace and understood what it required.

He trained for Europe, and in the field he proved to be a skilled agent with a gift for impersonation. He used whatever words he needed, lived the legends he had been assigned. Over time the shrapnel scars on his arms faded like old tattoos, the names of men he might have forgotten if they could have been saved. All the boundaries were blurring in him, until he did not know who in the world he had become. And so he was ready to come in out of the field to Langley when Fisherman finally offered him the chance.

But counterintelligence did not give him refuge. The human element still haunted him as he followed the paper spoor of countless secret lives. He had access to the most private details of his subjects' existence, and yet they remained as bloodless as the jargon in the Handholders' behavioral profiles. He tracked them across continents, collected data on their habits and faults, the kind of women they attracted, the money they hoarded or squandered, their unnecessary lies. And yet they only came alive to him in his sleep, sometimes demanding that he identify himself, sometimes speaking in tongues.

Of course, he did not confess this to Fisherman any more than to the Handholders during the annual psychological vettings. But when Ross came to him with the proposition that he move over to the National Security Council staff, he leaped at it.

"I wouldn't think of holding you back, Isaac," said Fisherman.

"The word is out that you may have arranged this," said McWade.

"There was bound to be speculation."

"Is it true?"

"I am often given too much credit," Fisherman said.

Going to work for Ross was a deliverance. He was a difficult man to work for, driven and demanding, with as little taste as Fisherman for personal intimacy or the exchange of praise. But he had a manner that made you want to be on his side, just as Fisherman made you hope he would never go against you.

As McWade had done before when he found a man who seemed to be in touch with the larger interests, he gave his loyalty without reservation, as if he thought this was the way of the world. Although nakedly ambitious acquaintances like Swain sometimes accused him of submitting too easily to the agendas of others, by every measure McWade had done very well for himself. In the next term, the National Security Advisor was expected to move over to head up State, bringing the Deputy along with him. Ross, who had earned unprecedented access to the President as chief of the Soviet and Eastern European section, was in line to take over the NSC. And McWade was all but assured of rising behind him.

But if Swain was right, Fisherman was threatening all that. McWade's newfound sanctuary was under attack. Suddenly he was back among the unseen eyes, the unanswerable voices, the names that had replaced his own.

When he reached the 17th Street entrance to the Old Executive Office Building, he fished out his identification and strung it around his neck then signed his name in the book, glancing at the lines above to make sure no one else from the staff had returned after dinner.

"Hot one out there," said the guard.

"Good night to stay inside."

The long, empty corridor stretched out before him. His heels ticked on the polished floor. Before going to his office he had to make a preliminary stop, if only to give himself a plausible reason for returning late. He moved straight through the building and crossed over to the West Wing, where he was obliged to sign another visitors' book.

The Situation Room was inside the first doorway past the guard. It was much smaller than might have been suggested by its name or the stakes men played for there, just large enough to accommodate a long table where they spread out maps under a low, overhanging fixture that lighted every acre of disputed terrain. Outside the conference room, a communications detail kept a twenty-four hour vigil in a cramped foyer.

"Anything come in?" he asked at the desk.

"Nothing to worry about," said the Navy lieutenant on duty. He handed McWade a few pieces of salmon colored teletype paper, still curled from the roll. McWade took them into the Situation Room and flicked on the light. The messages were routine. He initialed each page. In Moscow there had been no surprises.

Outside the White House again in the heat, McWade glanced up at the high, moonlit facade of the Old Executive Office Building, its ornate detail haunted by shadows.

There were no lights on in the NSC suite. He crossed over and rode the elevator up. The door of his office was double-locked, and when he got inside he saw that the cleaning ladies had already been through to collect the unclassified trash. The heavy, wooden door eased shut behind him, and as his eyes got used to the darkness, he made his way to his desk.

He sat down and switched on the little lamp, which left the corners of the office in darkness, making the room seem even larger than it was. His secretary had straightened and sorted the papers, checking to make sure he hadn't left out any classified documents when he locked up the safe. If she had been on duty now, she would have wanted to record his calls in her meticulous daily log. He was glad she had gone home, because he had one to make that he did not want written down.

The open line was a risk because of the microwave monitoring. He would have used the scrambler phone except that traffic on those circuits was automatically noted. Just to put in a cutout, he dialed the Agency's general number and had the operator switch him through to the right extension. The phone rang again and again, but McWade was patient. He knew Fisherman's habits. The man always worked at night.

McWade had also learned early on that no one was so close to Fisherman as to be immune from his attentions. He had discovered that when he presented the case against Randolph Bourne.

According to the folklore of the Agency, Bourne had given up a finger to the Nazis in occupied France rather than reveal to them where Fisherman was hiding. There might have been others in the Agency to whom Fisherman owed as much as he did to Bourne, but McWade did not know of any. And so he hesitated to push the matter at first. But the evidence that Bourne had come out of his forced retirement to work for the Libyans became stronger and stronger. Then Bourne left his calling cards all over a terrorist bombing in Beirut. Two Americans were killed. McWade had to act.

When he went to Fisherman, the old man was sitting at

his cluttered desk, his elfin head almost obscured by the stacks of files. There was nothing of the man of affairs about his quarters, none of the usual photographs of presidents and DCIs, no paintings from the Smithsonian, no diplomas or plaques. There weren't even any maps on the wall because they did not show the geography Fisherman was interested in. It was less an office than a cell.

As McWade entered, Fisherman looked up with eyes that seemed to have been born weary. McWade presented the file without comment, the analysis of the way the bomb had been built and planted, the Israelis' reports, the photos of the man shot fleeing the scene. Fisherman silently flipped through the documents until he got to the photographs.

"I suppose the bullet was a .38," he said.

McWade doublechecked the ballistics report and confirmed.

"Randolph was always very hard on his errandboys," Fisherman said, tossing the file back across the desk. "With his bum hand, he doesn't trust his aim with anything but his old police special. Poor Randolph would do anything for you except alter his signature."

It took Fisherman less than a month to track Bourne down and lure him back to the United States. He made a point of being present when the Sisters made the arrest. The two men were said to have greeted one another like kin.

McWade waited motionless in semi-darkness at his desk overlooking the White House, clutching the receiver, until the ringing finally stopped and the line went hollow. There was no greeting; Fisherman made a point of never speaking the first word.

"Do you have a minute?" said McWade. Still there was no sound, not even a breath. "Did I catch you in the middle of something?"

"I wondered how long it would be," Fisherman said at last.

"I've been hoping to have an excuse to get out to see you," said McWade. He did not say the word Langley. The eavesdroppers keyed on proper nouns.

"You must be very busy."

"Yes."

"I thought perhaps you had forgotten us."

"Not much chance of that."

"I am glad to hear it," said Fisherman. "We feel quite neglected these days."

"I wouldn't say that either of us has exactly gone unnoticed," McWade said, using the ambiguities of open code to make a reference both to Leighton and to anyone less visible whom Fisherman might have deployed.

"Men of your experience have great powers of observation."

"You taught me all the tricks."

"Almost all," said Fisherman. "Tell me, how is your beautiful friend?"

McWade admired the way the old man introduced a tension and then relieved it by introducing another.

"I'm afraid she may be feeling neglected, too," he said. "I haven't been holding up my end lately."

"She is a bright woman. I'm sure she appreciates your position."

"You let so many personal things slide," said McWade.

It was perhaps an odd thing to say to Fisherman, who had no private life whatsoever, so far as anyone knew. Unmarried. No family to whom he acknowledged any bond. No friends outside of Langley and damned few even there, if friendship meant anything deeper than respect for what he might do. And yet McWade had always felt that Fisherman had singled him out for a special relationship. Not that Fisherman ever said so directly, of course. McWade was only able to infer it by using the techniques Fisherman taught for recognizing the vulnerability in any man.

"Love and work," Fisherman said. "Conflicting loyalties. I've seen many men damaged because they were torn."

"There should be a brief respite," said McWade, "with Ross away."

"Is that commonly known?"

This carried a tone of a rebuke, but it might only have been because McWade had slipped and used the name.

"It's in tomorrow's papers," said McWade. "Surely you were told."

"One hears so many things," said Fisherman.

"Usually only what he is meant to hear," said McWade. "It is all a matter of how much credence to place upon it."

Conversations with Ernest often seemed to be about several things at once, some apparent, others covert.

"I hear you've been taking an interest in our operations," said McWade.

"I am always concerned to know about your progress, Isaac," he said.

"They say you are pursuing certain doubts."

Fisherman gave a short, sibilant laugh.

"I suppose that is always a safe assumption," he said.

McWade switched the phone to his left hand and flexed the right one to work out the cramp.

"Perhaps it is inappropriate for me to be talking to you about this at all," he said.

"Who can say what is appropriate and what is not?" said Fisherman. "I have never been able to find the rules that govern such matters."

"The rule of appearances."

"We know," said Fisherman, "how appearances can deceive."

"I'm in a delicate position."

"Your position makes you a valuable asset," said Fisherman, "just as I knew it would."

Was that an offer of recruitment? For the record McWade made his response impersonal.

"I think you would find a good deal of cooperation here if you sought it," he said.

"Are you speaking for yourself?"

McWade hesitated.

"I believe I have the latitude to speak for my organization," he said. "Don't you?"

"It is easier for me," said Fisherman. "You see, I have no ambitions."

"I don't think that's the issue."

"Isn't it?"

"I'm only thinking about how to minimize the damage," said McWade.

"Have you consulted your superiors?"

"I don't think that would be advisable," said McWade. And then, again for whatever record would be made of the conversation, he added, "I think that can wait."

"This must be quite awkward for you," said Fisherman.

"I don't intend to be disloyal," said McWade, suspending the word across all its possible objects.

"The ancients believed," said Fisherman, "that one had first to be true to himself."

This was no time to debate philosophy, but it was a little more complicated than Fisherman made it out to be. McWade had always located himself in relation to others. To be true to something, you first had to know what it was.

"I have a great deal of respect for both you and Ross," said McWade.

"I do not place much stock in personal loyalty," said Fisherman. "The underlying interests are always so much more dependable."

"It is possible that all our interests are the same."

"That would be quite a remarkable coincidence."

"We all have aspirations," said McWade, "or had."

It was all right to show a trace of irritation. After all, Fisherman could not expect him to be eager to commit himself. The man once had ambitions of his own.

"It is an interesting question who poses the greater danger," said Fisherman, "someone who wants everything or someone with nothing to lose."

"I didn't meant to suggest . . ."

"Ambition countering ambition. That is the usual way the genius of our system is described. But you mustn't be misled. Ambition does not tell you what is right and what is wrong."

"You've never needed much guidance there," said McWade.

"One can always use assistance."

"I am ready to be of whatever help I can," said McWade. That was as far as he was prepared to go.

"One must be careful not to get ahead of oneself," said Fisherman. "The tongue can be too eager."

"That's the one thing I don't understand," said McWade. "Why did you talk to Leighton?"

"If there is only one thing you don't understand, I suppose I should envy you."

"He isn't making much of a secret about where he is getting his information."

"I don't think my peril is great," said Fisherman.

"If you want to make a formal inquiry," said McWade, "I'm sure you would get as much cooperation as you need. I think that will go for Ross as well."

"An embarrassment of riches," said Fisherman.

And with that he abruptly rang off.

McWade held the phone to his ear as the line sputtered and went flat. Then he gently laid it in its cradle. He had not learned anything about the object of Fisherman's attentions, but at least he was sure now that the game was real. He had positioned himself as carefully as he knew how. He did not think of this as an act of bad faith toward either man; he was only trying to clear up whatever misunderstanding existed between them. He could not believe that either was capable of malice. Confusion, perhaps, or misplaced zeal. But not malice. He thought he knew that much about both of them. Fisherman would probably have said that to know this was to be twice blessed.

3

With the knob of the front door of his townhouse held tightly in his hand, McWade pushed with his knee at the spot where the wood was warped. The quickest way to spring it was with a sharp kick, but he did not want to disturb Sarah. When the sticking point gave way, McWade stepped inside. Then he pushed the door shut again and engaged the locks. It relieved him to say goodnight to the stalkers. He had given them nothing to show for their efforts, unless they tried to make something out of the circuitous route he had taken home.

After finishing with Fisherman he had called the house and gotten no answer. He couldn't reach Sarah at the law firm either. So he worked awhile longer then drove past her office just in case. Her windows were dark when he got there, and he made a quick U-turn and went back the way he had come.

Even if the stalkers reported it as an attempt to elude them, Fisherman would know better. Sarah's place of employment was duly noted in Langley's vetting files. There had been no need to be furtive about their arrangement when he was with the Agency, and even now that he was in a more visible position, no one raised any questions about their living together without the benefit of marriage. This wasn't Manitee Bay.

In fact, here it might have been the subject of more gossip if he hadn't had some attachment. In Washington everyone seemed to make assumptions about sex and power. They were generally thought to be reciprocal, though as Fisherman put it, if power is an aphrodisiac, it is like Spanish fly; the itch gets worse the more you try to scratch it.

Quite a few men ended up like Ross. Divorced for years, he had long enjoyed the seductive comforts of political society with one elegant woman after another. Lately, it was

Emma Baron. He had attended many embassy functions with her over the past couple of months, and they had even flown off on a short holiday during the Congressional recess. To McWade she seemed an odd choice, not nearly as glamorous as some of the others Ross had gone out with, just a little too hard. But she did give the impression of being as worldly as Ross, perhaps even quicker than he was to judge people's motives as cynically as they judged her own. This much could be said for Emma: like Ross, she was completely at home in the world of men.

McWade took off his suitcoat in the front hallway and hung it on the hook. Then he pulled down his tie and rolled up his sleeves. The lights were on in the living room. He thought he heard Sarah moving inside.

"It's me," he said. There was no response.

When he stepped into the doorway, he froze. A man was watching him from the couch.

"Welcome home," the man said.

McWade was about to retreat. But then he saw it was safe to stand his ground.

"Fisherman sent you," he said.

The intruder apparently thought McWade had told a pretty good joke. It was the only time McWade had ever seen Richard Harper laugh.

"I suppose you could say that he inspired my visit," said Harper.

"You're lucky Sarah didn't hear you and call the police."

"She let me in."

"What did you tell her?"

"I was surprised when I saw her without you," said Harper. "A woman like that shouldn't be left alone at night."

McWade went to the stairway and looked up toward the bedroom. It was dark.

"It isn't like her to let a stranger in," he said.

"Actually," said Harper, "we'd already been formally introduced. At Ross's swearing-in. You would have been pleased how careful she was tonight. She asked for identification. You've trained her well. One never knows who is out and who is in."

29

"Are they noting that on the Agency's IDs now?"

"I told her we had business. She offered to wait up, but I said that wasn't necessary. She was really very poised, considering how much I must have startled her when I approached her at the door."

"If you have business with me," said McWade, "you should call at the office."

At one time Richard Harper had been one of the Agency's most promising young men. Then something happened to his career. He was withdrawn from the operations side and given a supervisory position on the analytical end. On the organization charts he still looked like a significant player, but to insiders he was little better than a paper shuffler. He might as well have worked at the Smithsonian.

The National Security Council did do some business with him, though, especially when it came time for threat assessment, so there were proper channels by which Harper could have made his views known. And if he had been blocked, there were also improper ones that would not have left him so exposed. He wasn't exactly the kind of man you would expect to invade a person's home at night. At Langley they said he always looked so well-pressed because he rarely exposed himself to heat.

"I think you will forgive the unorthodox nature of my visit," Harper said, "when you learn what it is about."

McWade went to the old oak icebox and poured himself some Scotch neat. He chose a chair across from Harper, which put the coffee table between them.

"Let's get on with it," he said, taking a sip of the whiskey and putting the glass down on a coaster decorated with a Chinese ideograph.

Harper picked up another coaster and turned it between his fingers.

"I didn't know you had been posted in Asia," he said. "It seems we have quite a bit in common."

"Sarah picked those up somewhere."

"As you may know, I spent quite a few years in Japan and Vietnam."

"I thought you were on the Soviet end."

"It's all the Soviet end," said Harper. "At least that's always been Ernest's view."

He put the coaster down and adjusted the lay of his collar and the integrity of his crease.

"It's usually a mistake to think you know Fisherman's mind," said McWade.

"Yes," said Harper. "I remember the first time I went to him for advice. He was quite gracious. I made the mistake of listening to him."

"You didn't come here to discuss your regrets."

"Hear me out," said Harper, and there was more authority behind it than his position would have suggested. "You see, I have had considerable experience with Ernest. I thought that under the circumstances I ought to share it."

"Maybe at some point you could tell me why."

Harper leaned forward, spreading his hands on the table before him.

"When was the last time you spoke to him?" he asked.

It would have been easy for McWade to have bridled, to have said that he was not in the habit of allowing himself to be interrogated by rogue agents. He would have been well within his prerogatives simply to have thrown the man out. But that was not how McWade played it. He took the path of least complexity, which was simply to lie.

"It's been months," he said.

"That surprises me."

"Maybe you don't understand my role at the NSC."

"In fact, I've made quite a study of it recently."

"Fisherman used to be my boss," said McWade. "He isn't anymore."

"He is a dangerous man."

"One of many," McWade said.

"More than most," said Harper. "I know how he works. Perhaps more intimately than you do. You see, I have been on the other side of Ernest Fisherman. I have learned what he can do to those he has chosen to oppose. Though you may not realize it, I was not always the figure of contempt you see before you. Not until I got crosswise with Fisherman."

31

"What does that have to do with me?"

"I believe he is after Michael Ross," said Harper. "And you are his instrument."

Harper delivered the warning flatly, like a briefer giving a situation report.

"That's absurd," McWade said, sipping his drink. "They think alike."

"Ernest has a supple view of the world."

"I don't see anything that would make them enemies."

"To have enemies implies feelings of which I'm afraid Ernest is not capable. You cannot hate unless you can love."

"Spare me the poetry."

"A remark worthy of one of Ernest's students," said Harper. "Poetry is just the most graceful form of lying. Isn't that what he says?"

"He appreciates the art in all its forms."

"Look into it for yourself," said Harper. "Find out why he has been investigating the collapse of the NARCISSUS net."

"NARCISSUS was a long time ago."

"He has the files in his office. Ask around. You'll confirm what I say."

"Whatever is going on at Langley is out of my jurisdiction now," said McWade.

"You are right, of course, to suspect my motives," said Harper, and he stood up abruptly and straightened the sleeves of his jacket. "I invite you to look into that, too. You will find it quite instructive, I think. There is a moral in it somewhere, and it has to do with Ernest's willingness to use and destroy any tool that presents itself to his hand. Ask about the operation that Ernest called CONVERGENCE. Ask what happened to the unfortunate Jerry Birch."

Harper stepped past McWade toward the door.

"If you're afraid of Fisherman," said McWade, "shouldn't you be careful about being seen?"

Harper seemed to take some satisfaction in that.

"Careful of Fisherman?" he said. "Ernest and I go back a long way. We know what to expect from one another."

After McWade let him out, he locked up and finished his drink, which now tasted like cold metal on his tongue. Then he mounted the stairs as quietly as he could.

He may have shuddered as he undressed and slipped in between the sheets. Sarah may have felt the sweat of his hand when he rested it on her side. But she did not acknowledge his touch, and it was just as well. Feelings welled up in him that he was not sure he could control, cold, brutal feelings that belonged to Joseph Leggatt. Their intensity surprised him after all the years. Leggatt was supposed to be dead.

4

The bright green digits of the clock slowly came into focus. McWade stared at the dot of the colon as it blinked off the seconds, then he turned his face to the pillow.

It was his habit to be first to rise, and it always gave him pleasure to see her beside him, breathing easily, her eyes softly closed. Then to invade the dream by touching her shoulder or kissing her cheek and to wonder what strange thing she might have made of him in her sleep – a secret lover, a demon, a protector in the night.

McWade rolled over and extended his arm, but the blanket was flat. For a moment it was as if he were falling. His muscles tightened and his eyes snapped open. Sarah was not there.

He slid to the side of the bed where she had been. The sheets were cool, but her smell was on them, and he breathed it in.

When he had first met her, he had been back in the country for less than a month. The adjustment had not been going well. He was having trouble when he had to introduce himself or sign credit card slips. And whenever he spoke, he had the feeling that his voice was much too loud. Sometimes when someone came into the office he would turn on a recorder he kept hidden under some papers on his desk. Later he would play the tape, just to hear himself and see if he recognized the sound.

The Handholders told him that this was not an abnormal reaction for a man who had lived a cover as long as he had. It did not concern them that he found himself doubling back as he drove home from Langley or inventing mnemonics for the license numbers of cars in his rearview mirror. This was not paranoia, they said. You know the joke: even a paranoid has enemies.

The best thing to do, they said, was to get out and around. Let yourself be known. You might even find it amusing. And so he forced himself to spend evenings in public places. At first he just went to the little, hidden spots where Agency people gathered to tell war stories and get drunk in the company of men who had heard them all. Then he ventured out into the singles bars, but he did not like the feel of them. They reminded him too much of Leggatt's haunts in Copenhagen and Amsterdam. He was supposed to be beyond that now. So he began to look up old acquaintances around Washington, reviving friendships he had made before he began taking on his secret lives.

One of the first people he contacted was his company commander from the First Cav. Now a colonel stationed at Fort Meyer, he had a nice place in Arlington, two lovely children and a wife. It was at one of their dinner parties that McWade met Sarah. She was a friend of the colonel from way back before he got his nomination to the Point. All that she and McWade had in common was being out of place in the midst of men united by the conventions of arms.

After dinner the colonel took him aside and said that they had originally invited another woman whom his wife thought would make a perfect match, a brilliant young analyst from the SecDef's office who specialized in technical intelligence. Sarah was a stand-in, the colonel said, when the other woman fell ill. Hell of a good person, but she knows absolutely nothing of the trade. Beautiful, said McWade. Stunning, said the colonel, in a certain kind of light.

This was exactly the light in which he saw her that evening. Thin and athletic, she wore her blonde hair short and parted so it was easy to set back in place with a casual sweep of her fingers when it fell across her forehead as she laughed. She could easily have been distant and inaccessible if she had wanted to. But it was as if she did not realize how desirable she was.

That first evening McWade spoke to her almost entirely in asides as the officers talked about promotion lists and

35

other forms of combat. She did not seem at all guarded, except when one or the other of them made a remark about the soldiers and they had to keep from laughing out loud. Somehow she made him feel as if she had known him for a very long time.

But as the evening was coming to an end, he realized that he did not know her last name. When the others moved toward the door, he hung back with her and said he hoped it would not be too forward if he asked to see her again.

"Too forward?" she said. "My God, I haven't heard that kind of thing for years."

"I've been away," he said. "Is it appropriate to ask you for your phone number?"

"They're in the book," she said. "Both of them, office and home."

"I feel a little foolish saying so," he said, "but I'll have a hard time looking it up if you don't remind me of your full name."

"Sarah Hawley."

"I'm . . ."

"Isaac McWade," she said.

"Embarrassed," he said.

"Well don't be," she said. "They've told me all about you."

"They have?"

"Even your war record. Naturally, they thought I'd want to hear about that."

"It was a long time ago."

"The colonel has a lot of respect for you," she said.

"I'll call you, if that would be all right."

"I hope so, Isaac," she said.

"Everyone uses Ike."

"I like Isaac. It sounds so unquestioning."

"My father was at Normandy," he said. "I would have been a Dwight if he could have been sure of the right nickname."

"Goodnight, Isaac," she said, and she touched his hand.

As McWade drove home, he played his conversation with Sarah over and over again as if he had captured it on a hidden mike. He had been much too careful, of course, but better to have seemed a little old-fashioned than to have stiffened up like a man who is not at liberty to disclose. No longer bound by a cover, he had to recreate himself. And to make a legend, you first had to know what it was supposed to accomplish, the legend's end. Now that part of it had become easier. He simply wanted to be the man he had been, a person she would warm to, because after meeting Sarah he felt as if he had suddenly recovered someone he thought he had lost: the awkward, thrilled and earnest boy from Manitee Bay.

He wondered what she would have made of his other legends. Colorless George Perkins, for example. He was not exactly a dashing fellow, and his missions were all routine. He was damned near invisible in his tattered sweaters and faded shirts; this, of course, was his greatest virtue as a spy. Anthony Rogers had much more style, since he had to travel in certain circles during McWade's time in the London station. Sarah might have found him a little too well-made. But she would certainly have respected the sheer competence of Bravo Three, which was the callsign McWade had used to identify himself on the field radio in the jungle, bringing in artillery and air, wheeling his unit around to engage the enemy and concentrate the fire.

There was one figure McWade was sure a woman like Sarah would have found repellent, but fortunately he did not think he would ever have to reveal him to her. Leggatt lay safely buried with all the other terminated legends somewhere in the HUMINT files.

McWade called Sarah the day after the colonel's party. They got together for dinner that night and talked about many things but very little about themselves. Over the next few weeks, they saw one another whenever she had time. Slowly, he worked his way around to telling her vaguely about his business, but she had already figured it out.

"You were so reluctant," she said, "that I knew it had to be either that or the tobacco lobby. And you don't smoke."

Perhaps because she had seen through him so easily, he began to wonder whether he had missed something about her. Another man in her life. There were just too many evenings when she could not see him, too many gaps in his knowledge of her that his imagination rushed in to fill.

He took to driving past her place on nights when they were apart. Sometimes he saw lights. When the windows were dark, he waited a distance down the street until she came home. She was always alone, but that did not satisfy him. The next step was a rolling surveillance. It wasn't easy without a backup car, especially on Washington's tricky traffic circles, but he managed to keep up with her. All he learned was how much time she spent at the law firm where she worked.

Then one night they went to a film, a mindless thriller one of her colleagues had recommended. When they came out of the theater, she took his arm and held it tightly, as if she were cold or unsteady on her feet.

"You must hate movies like that," she said.

"I couldn't tell the bad guys from the good."

"They make it out to be so sinister," she said.

"You get used to it," he said. "You get used to anything."

"It must have been terrible, the sense that someone was always watching you."

"Better that than having them there and not knowing it."

"Is anyone that good?" she said. "I mean people have an instinct."

"Do they?"

She glanced over her shoulder. He laughed.

It was her idea to pick up some Chinese at a carryout and take it back to her place. When they got there, she sent McWade to the living room while she set the table. The only evidence of his presence in her life was a book he had given her. It stood with many others on a shelf.

"Dinner's ready," she said. "I wasn't sure about the candles."

They lit her face nicely. She had put out chopsticks for both of them. He picked his up and clicked them together.

"Very authentic," he said.

"I've never learned how to use them properly," she said.

He went around behind her and took her hand.

"You hold one steady on the bottom like this and the other like a pencil. There you go."

"I'd like to go to Asia sometime."

"I'd like to take you there. Europe, too. Or am I being too forward?"

"You could show me all your favorite spots."

Not all of them, he thought. Leggatt's would not be suitable for a woman without regrets.

"We could find better things to do," he said.

"I really ought to know something about that side of your life," she said, "at least what attracted you to it."

"My father wanted me to become a lawyer."

"But you wanted adventure."

"Maybe I was afraid of the risks."

"Don't be patronizing."

"No, it's true. When you're an advocate, you have to stand up for something."

"That part is easy," she said. "You take the position that's given to you. It doesn't matter who you really are."

"Who are you, Sarah?" he said, and though he was smiling, the question was the most serious one he knew.

"Maybe just the sum of what I want," she said.

"Then we have something in common after all," he said, "because what I want is you."

She put down the wooden chopsticks, arranging them carefully on her plate so that she would not have to meet his eyes. Her silence was unbearable.

"What are the other men like?" he asked.

"Oh, Isaac. Is that what you think?"

"I've been trained to discover secrets," he said.

"There isn't anybody else," she said. "Hasn't been for a long, long time."

"I'm sorry," he said.

"Well, don't be," she said. "We've both been too careful."

She stood and went to him.

"I was only trying to be proper," he said.

"And me thinking you were just so shy."

She put her hands on his shoulders, holding him there, at the distance of her outstretched arms.

"Maybe that, too," he said.

She kissed him then. It wasn't the first time, but it was as surprising as if it had been. And he did not care about Anthony Rogers or George Perkins or any of the others. They were nothing more than onlookers now. When he kissed her again, they were gone.

"We've been making it pretty complicated, I guess," she said.

"Wary. Self-conscious."

"Nobody's watching," she said.

"How can you be certain?"

He did not know exactly how they reached the bedroom, who was leading, how they had suddenly become so sure. He just remembered the way they stood before one another naked for the first time, how perfectly awkward she seemed under his gaze, how that stirred him. And he remembered that when they made love, she said his name, the name he had been born to, over and over again.

The memory and the tingle it caused subsided and McWade rolled to his back in the empty bed. Her pulled himself upright and went into the bathroom. The shower revived him, the water splashing hard against his face. When he was finished, he pulled a suit and shirt out of the closet. It didn't matter which; they were all about the same.

He was going to have to keep Sarah in the dark as he tried to work out this problem with Fisherman and Ross. She hated being in competition with the hidden side of his life. As he tied his tie, Anthony Rogers stared at him from the mirror over the dresser, eyes of the London station, revealing nothing.

When he reached the bottom of the stairs, he heard paper rustling in the kitchen and saw through the doorway her hand where it rested on the counter. He may have paused on the last step, but not for long.

"Hello," he said.

She peeked around the corner.

"I hope I wasn't supposed to wake you," she said. "I wasn't sure how late you were up with the mystery guest."

He kissed her, but it was only a gesture. Already he felt himself becoming remote.

"I figured you'd gone to work already," he said.

"There was nothing urgent."

He went to the refrigerator and got out a package of English muffins then split one open and put it into the toaster oven.

"I guess I owe you an explanation," he said.

"More than one," she said.

"Swain was worse than usual last night," he said, joining her at the counter. "Full of dangerous gossip."

"He must have gone on and on."

McWade buttered his muffin and took a bite.

"Actually," he said, "I had to stop back in the office before coming home. That's what delayed me. I tried to call."

She put the paper down.

"I suppose you have witnesses," she said.

He wiped his greasy fingers on a paper napkin.

"I guess you decided to work late, too," he said.

"Is that what that awful man told you?"

"Swain?"

"The man who was here to see you last night."

"He said he had surprised you."

"He must have been sitting there in the car watching the house all night," she said.

"I'm sorry, Sarah," he said, moving back to the stove. He touched the side of the kettle. It was still hot. He poured the steamy water into a cup and floated a teabag on the surface. When he picked up the saucer, it trembled, but not enough for her to notice. "If I'd coordinated better I could have given you a lift home from your office. I must have just missed you."

He set the cup down and stretched, feeling her eyes on him. They made his every move seem false.

"I didn't like that man being here."

McWade dunked the teabag until the water was richly colored, pulled on the string and dropped the soggy mess onto a plate. He wiped his fingers on a napkin, then pulled the front section of the paper from the bottom of the pile.

41

"I'll tell you how much Richard Harper knows," he said. "He told me I should be careful about letting you out at night alone." He expected her to smile, and persuaded himself that she did. "I let Harper know that I didn't care for any of his advice."

"You aren't going to tell me what it was all about, are you."

"Conspiracies within conspiracies," he said. "More of the same."

"He seemed so serious," she said, "the way they used to be when you were still at Langley and got those terrible calls."

"They're still there," he said. "They haven't changed."

"But you have, haven't you?"

"I'm not going back," he said. "Don't worry."

"It's just that it had been so long," she said.

She took the paper from him and folded it to the story about Ross's secret trip.

"And then I saw that," she said. "I wondered why you stayed behind."

"To have some time with you," he said. "I thought we might be able to get away."

"You sacrificed a trip to Moscow for that?" she said.

"I'm hopeful about stealing some time away. Guardedly optimistic," he said. "That would be the operative phrase."

"Do you think it was wise to let them go off without you?"

"Ross wanted someone running interference here," he said.

"I was sure there'd been trouble."

"They also serve who stay at home."

But no matter how calm a front he put up, he could tell she sensed the danger.

"What's wrong, Sarah?" he said.

"He frightened me, that's all."

McWade pushed the papers aside and reached across to touch her hand. She did not withdraw it.

"Harper was way out of line," he said. "I told him so."

"It was like being a criminal or something."

"He isn't interested in you," said McWade. "That isn't what it was all about."

"What was it then?"

He chose his words carefully so that he did not deceive her any more than necessary.

"He's got a fight on his hands at Langley," he said. "He wanted to get me on his side."

"That's all?"

"That's all."

"I don't like the way those people do business," she said.

"It won't happen again. I promise."

"You mean I don't have to worry about my secrets being discovered?" she said, and for the first time that day she was able to make it seem like a joke they shared.

5

His secretary had a message waiting for him at every checkpoint: The President wants you immediately.

McWade received each summons with a nod. He did not show surprise or excitement. He simply marched through the Old Executive Office Building and across to the West Wing, retracing his steps of the night before, this time without mental reservation or purpose of evasion.

On the way to the Oval Office he stopped at the Security Advisor's suite to see if anybody knew what awaited him. The woman who kept the NSC's schedules was pacing in the tiny outer office, a sheaf of classified files clutched to her chest.

"Where in hell have *you* been?" she said.

"I need to talk with him a minute," he said, leaning toward the Deputy Security Advisor's door.

"The President got impatient," she said.

McWade stepped back down the hall and looked around the corner toward the Oval Office to see whether by some miracle the Deputy was still out there on hold. But the only person in view was the Secret Service man, and he blended right into the wall.

"I'll be down in the Situation Room," McWade told the scheduler.

"He was pretty irritated," she said.

The narrow hallways of the West Wing weren't like those in other public buildings, no high, ornate ceilings or broad expanses of marble. At the beginning of the administration 't had been like a freshly decorated home, but now it had become just a touch shabby, lived-in. And as he moved to the stairway, he could not help but recall the times as a boy when he had slouched back to his room after disappointing his father by something he had done or failed to do.

When he reached the Situation Room, the rumble of a

crowd made it seem as if he were stepping into an arena. The sound came from speakers mounted over the teletype machines.

"Press briefing at State," said an Air Force major behind the counter.

"I'll need to see the cable traffic from Moscow," said McWade.

He signed for the documents and began to read the longest dispatch. It was stunning. Suddenly he understood the reason for all the excitement. The Soviets had wasted no time in getting to the point. What was more, Ross had foreseen their move. The thing was breaking cleanly, just as he had predicted it would.

"Ladies and gentlemen," said the spokesman at State in his most measured briefing voice, "I have one announcement."

The crowd noise began to die down except for the scrape of chairs as tardy correspondents took their seats.

"An American delegation led by Charles Simpson has arrived in Moscow to hold discussions at the Foreign Ministry level."

That had certainly been the plan, but as Ross reported in his cable, the party chairman himself had presided over the first lunch and laid out the proposal.

"The mission was to be secret," said the spokesman, "but as you know, there has been an unauthorized disclosure. The Secretary regrets that it has become impossible to hold negotiations on a confidential basis without the grave probability of compromise."

"Jim," said a voice, "are you saying the American people don't deserve to know when their representatives are out there cutting a deal?"

"I am not prepared to discuss the substance of the discussions," said the spokesman. "But I will say this: there has been no deal."

He spat out the final word as if it were a piece of bad fruit.

"Jim . . ."

"If you'll allow me . . . The delegation arrived yesterday at noon, local time. The first meeting took place today,

45

and the exchange ranged over matters of mutual concern. The discussions have been broad and candid . . ."

Which by the commonly understood code meant that they had been pointless and a half a millimeter deep. But that was not how McWade would have described the meeting set out in Ross's cable. Dramatic. Even historic. Or if it were for public consumption, he might have stuck to understatement and called the talks significant and substantive. Never candid. Not with the Soviets.

"Why isn't the Secretary leading the delegation, Jim?"

The spokesman must have turned from the podium or started speaking into his bow tie at that point because a few words were lost to the microphone, swallowed up in the white noise of cynicism.

". . . division of labor. The Mideast situation is at a critical point, and the Secretary has chosen to put his maximum efforts where the most can be achieved."

"They're going to be talking about where this leaves his influence," said a reporter, already tinkering with his third paragraph, the one that counted up the personal gains and losses.

". . . would be mistaken to assume the Secretary does not fully concur in this approach," said the spokesman. If the Man was listening upstairs in the Oval Office, he would get a pretty good laugh out of that. State concurs with the President. Damned decent of him.

"Mr McWade," said the major, turning to him with a phone to his ear. "The President's meeting is breaking up now."

McWade left the cables on the counter and bounded back up the stairs. The Deputy was just coming down the corridor, lost in the gravity of the moment. When he saw McWade, he took a little hop in his step and said, "Jesus H. Christ."

"That good?" said McWade.

"We're heroes, Ike. Except to those who think we're the villains. Come on in. Let's get our ducks in a row."

Before long, nearly everybody outside the White House was taking shots at the Soviet proposal and trying to enlist men on the inside to join their cause. State's reasons for trying to discredit the discussions were simple. It considered the NSC, and particularly Ross's section, a den of cold warriors who lacked the delicacy to bring off anything of lasting significance. Not to speak of the all-important matter of process, by which State meant getting its hands on everything. The priests of arms control did not like amateurs meddling in matters theological. On the other side of the river, Defense was worried that the bargaining strategy had not been adequately staffed out. In other words, the Pentagon didn't want anybody swapping its toys. And the generals were known to be worried that Simpson and Ross had gone soft, that they were too interested in the President's political needs to appreciate how much damage an era of good feelings could do to the Defense budget on the Hill.

Outside of a small circle in the White House and NSC staff, the Soviet proposal caught everyone by surprise: deep offensive cuts, phaseout of multiple warhead missiles, defensive systems research and testing, single-track negotiations to include theater forces and conventional arms, with French and British participation at the table. The give, especially on the defensive side, was remarkable. And it set the stage for the first significant arms control breakthrough since Reagan cut his modest theater weapons deal.

In the endless interagency meetings examining intentions and options, this approach had received little attention. Ross had made sure that McWade put it on the agenda, but the other representatives had been so confident that it was purely hypothetical that they let his proposed response go by virtually without amendment.

Because of this, there was really very little that needed to be done with the Moscow cables except to put the options paper into the language of presidential instructions with a few slight wording changes to bring it into line with the vodka-soaked enthusiasm with which the Soviets had made their proposal. The President, of course, would have a final crack at the document.

"Maybe we ought to move immediately," said McWade.

"He's solid," said the Deputy. "We'll stick to the timetable."

The plan was to make sure the delegation stayed locked up in conversation for at least four days so that the initiative would appear credible, regardless of the outcome. Ross had asked the Soviets for time to hold consultations on what he had toasted as an "exciting opening". The Soviets had been so pleased with his wording that they magnanimously granted him forty-eight hours.

But just because everything was going according to schedule did not mean there was no work to be done. First of all, McWade had to take to the telephone to put out the word to the press on how the Moscow trip had come about. He did not have a chance to give much thought to what Fisherman was up to, so when Leighton called, McWade had his secretary put him off.

The first skirmishes came from State, which wanted a National Security Council meeting. It began nicely enough with a call from the Secretary's counselor. Very informal, of course. Just thought I'd give you a ring, Ike, to feel out the possibilities. Let's get this thing back on course and avoid a lot of problems downstream. McWade reminded him that they had already worked out a contingency plan. You remember it, don't you? I think it struck you as fairly remote at the time. The counselor was polite. He acknowledged that State had misread the field. You hid the ball, Ike. Congratulations. But now it's time to get together. We're on the same team, after all. McWade promised to get back to him, but of course he never did.

Then the Deputy called to say that the Undersecretary had escalated the matter by paying a personal visit.

"It was not cordial," said the Deputy.

"I don't see any point in trying to resolve this at our level," said McWade, and under the circumstances the Deputy did not bridle at the way the first person plural raised McWade up or brought the Deputy down.

"It's out of our hands," said the Deputy. For the moment they were equals, the way any two men are when the joke is on someone else.

The next move belonged to the Man, and he was not subtle about it. His press secretary delivered the stroke at the daily briefing of the White House press corps.

To counter State's cautious reading of the signals from Moscow, the press secretary announced that there was every reason to believe that the stage was set for a conceptual breakthrough of the first order. Those were McWade's words, and it pleased him that they had made it through all the filters.

When the wire services moved the lead of a story quoting White House sources to the effect that State was playing the role of spoiler and didn't speak for the administration on this matter, the Secretary exercised his prerogative to talk directly and confidentially to the President. But it might as well have been a conference call, because within minutes everyone on the White House staff knew all about it. The Man tried to settle him down by expressing undying confidence and telling him the anonymous source wasn't speaking for the President. The upshot was that by late afternoon, nobody was speaking for anyone, and everyone was yammering away all over town. Ultimately even the Defense Secretary got on the line to join in the push for a meeting, which had become a make or break issue. Careers rode on it. Letters of resignation were discussed.

The group finally convened in the Cabinet Room late that afternoon. Defense won the competition to be last in before the President. State had come with two more in his party than the invitation allowed, but nobody made a fuss over it. The Man appeared a minute after the others had all found their seats, and a minute after that came the camera crews and pool reporters for the allotted ninety-second photo opportunity. As long as the gathering was under the lens the atmospherics in the room were as fresh as that one wonderful day in September when the summer sky finally lifts, the wind blows off the haze and you can see little clouds scudding high against the blue.

A tall woman from the press office kept the clock, and when the last second had passed, she began herding the photographers and film crews out of the room.

"Mr President," shouted a pool reporter, "are you ready to make peace with the Russians?"

"Well, by golly, it's a lovely day for it," he said, grinning like Huck Finn in a business suit.

Once the gaggle was gone, the room fell silent. Defense pulled off his glasses. State slipped his down low on his nose. They sat on either side of the President, with the Vice President's spot left empty just in case he should take time off from his busy schedule to join them.

"Well," said the Man at last, "I guess you've all heard the news."

State had taken the brunt of it, so he stepped in to lead things off.

"There's been," he said, "a certain lack of . . ."

"Hank," said the Man over his shoulder. "Don't forget to lay on the flight for Hilary's friend."

"It's all . . .," said an aide.

"Communication," said Defense, replacing his glasses now. "We've been flying in the dark."

"Chopper leaves for Andrews at nine," said the aide.

"The need to speak with a single voice," said State.

"Let's make sure there's a little group to see her off," said the Man.

"I'm disturbed by the regrettable haste, Mr President," said Defense.

"What's your hurry, George?" said the Man. "Hell, over there it'd be the middle of the night now. Getting their beauty rest."

"Sleeping it off," said State, who had been there himself a time or two.

"Vodka dreams," said the Chief of Staff.

"Triple strength Maalox is what they need," said the Man.

"Preparation H to help them outsit the Russians," said the Chief of Staff.

"Why don't you send them some," said the Man. "A CARE package."

"I'll have it done," said the Chief of Staff.

"We'll want to make sure the Speaker is kept informed," the Man said to no one in particular. McWade and several others jotted a note.

"Ought to think about the committee chairman, too," said the Chief of Staff.

"Maybe we'd better get our own act together first," said State, and though it was a bit abrupt, it did serve to jar things back to the matters at hand.

"Do we need to review the bidding?" said the Man.

"Hearts or clubs?" said Defense. "That's the question."

"We can have it all," said the Man. "The whole damned deck."

The principals had received the draft of the negotiating orders. Copies were on the table before them, each one numbered and code word stamped.

"Preliminarily," said Defense, "I see a number of technical problems. Maybe we all should have a little time."

"Hell, George," said the Man, "you were the one who asked for the damned meeting."

"Coordination," said Defense. "The Joint Chiefs will have to get in the boat."

"They'll just start squabbling over who gets to build it."

"What I'm afraid of . . ." said State.

"Everybody knows what that is," said the Man. And it was easy to be amused no matter where you were allied because even State allowed himself a smile.

"I'm worried we might be going down a road to nowhere," said State when the chuckling subsided.

"There are a couple of people I'd like to name ambassador there," said the Man.

"The single-track approach is going to bog down," said State. "The French won't want anybody else to do the talking."

"The French may prove dispensable," said the Chief of Staff.

"Not their warheads," said Defense. "The Russians will want to count them. That is obviously their strategy."

"This isn't exactly a new trick for them," said State.

"They'd count China against our totals if they thought they could get away with it," said Defense.

Meanwhile, the Man decided to settle another matter with his staff.

"In and out, but I'm not staying for an hour and a half of screeching violins."

"I can keep it under an hour," said an aide, consulting his watch.

"Figure out something," said the Man. "After all, how many divisions does Beethoven have?"

The others were pushing ahead without him, glancing over from time to time to see if he was paying attention, holding off with their most telling points.

"What concerns me, Mr President," said Defense, "is the risk of globality."

The word caught the Man's fancy. He leaned forward and put his elbows on the table, and his face was as sweet as honey in a trap.

"I miss something?" he said.

"Opening the door to an argument for counting rules that bring in our systems based in the rear."

"The world is round, George," said the man.

"And it has at least two sides," said Defense.

"Us and them," said State, with a certain amount of disdain.

"Forward and rear," said Defense. "That's clean. That's easy to verify by national technical means. But we could pick up on their idea of umbrella negotiations, vertically but not horizontally inclusive."

"I'm afraid I have to agree with George on this one," said State. "If we accept the Soviets' proposal as the working document, we might never get the French and British out."

"I'm not sure," said the Deputy, "that if we looked closely at the horizontal option we wouldn't find that it was not without advantages."

The Man looked at him as if he had just spoken a riddle.

"You're gonna have to learn not to be so emphatic," he said.

The conversation lagged for a moment, and a young White House political type stepped in to display his acuity by counting the Senate, as if they already had a treaty and were about to send it up.

"There may be some virtue in extended talks," said Defense.

52

"The Senate won't wait," said State.

"Maybe the Senate will have to," said Defense. "They aren't going to cut the President's budget when he's nose to nose with the Russians over the bargaining table."

"It didn't take long for you two to break ranks," said the Man. "Charlie, tell me one thing. Do you smell a rat?"

Down at the other end of the table the Director of Central Intelligence opened a file jacket as brightly colored as Christmas morning under the tree. He had a reputation for keeping his own counsel until he was asked.

"I never underestimate the deviousness of the Soviets," he said.

"Here we go," whispered the Deputy. "The wild card."

"You sound a little envious," said the President.

"For the record," said the Director, "we are completely satisfied at Langley that we can do the job within the appropriate constraints."

"Did everyone get that down?" said the President.

It was gentle, but it was enough to make clear that even the Director wasn't immune to the Man's wit. That always made it easier for the others to accept the decision when, as he often did, the President went the Agency's way.

"Certain points are rather obvious, I think," said the Director. "The Soviets still harbor the notion that they can divide the alliance. And it must be admitted that if the Europeans begin negotiating for themselves, certain differences of interest would become very sharply defined."

The President had turned in his direction, but he was not looking at him. He was staring up at the far end of the room, where sunlight streamed in upon the hearth and Lincoln brooded above the mantelpiece in a shadow.

"That is a political judgment," said the Director. "But before making it, I think there are other factors to be considered. The Soviet leadership has just gone through a five-year military planning drill, and it was the stage upon which much of the succession struggle was played out. There were compromises, gentlemen, and these arrangements form the basis of the new chairman's power. He is not likely to undo them lightly."

"But the initiative was theirs," said Defense.

"There are, of course, external reasons for giving the appearance of movement," said the Director, and the Man underlined the point.

"We've got Congress and they've got Germany," he said. "Maybe they'd like to trade."

"They know that the period of conflict allowed us to get the support we needed to rearm. They'll surely want to change this dynamic."

"I guess you're saying they've got Congress, too," said the Man. "Poor bastards."

"If we reject them," said the Deputy, "it will play right into their hands. But patience. With time we'll have leverage. That's the judgment we're getting from the team in Moscow."

"I'd have to defer to Ross on that," said the Director.

The Man leaned forward on his elbows.

"I thought Ross was working for me now," he said.

"We all are," said the Director.

"Some more than others."

"He has proven instincts."

"You fellas from Langley sure do stick together," said the Man. "Why don't you spread that glue around a little?"

There was laughter from everywhere around the table, because silence would have been a confession, and it was every man for himself.

As the amusement settled down to a murmur, McWade kept his eye on the Director. After delivering his unequivocal endorsement of Ross, the dapper intelligence chief sat silently with his hands resting on his papers, as if he were holding his place. Fisherman had never trusted the Director, so it was not surprising that he had cut his boss out of his move against Ross. Until Ross had talked him out of it, the Director had wanted to be the one who finally forced the old man to retire.

"It is my understanding," said State, "that we have another day to prepare a specific reply." He held up his copy of the draft. McWade noticed that it was already marked up like a schoolboy's theme.

"You fellas can work out the details," said the Man.

"If you're wedded to the approach . . .," said State.

"I only married once, and that was to a woman," said the Man.

"The basic thrust, though," said the Deputy.

"I may have one or two questions," said Defense.

"We want to be straightforward," said State.

"Not necessarily," said the Deputy.

The President glared at State.

"Nobody's gonna doubt your manhood, John," he said.

"It's not mine I'm worried about," said State. Then he realized that he may have stepped over a line. "What about the delegation? Laboring mightily to produce a mouse."

"The delegation concurs," said the Deputy.

"Shouldn't we aim for something definitive?" said State. "At this stage, clarification is going to look like acquiescence."

"Time," said the Deputy. "The matter of time."

"I pay them to cool their heels," said the Man.

That ended the meeting. The Deputy set up a working group to refine the wording of the questions in the draft. The President stood up and went to the door. The official photographer slipped in and shot a picture of each man close to the President on the way out. McWade and the Deputy deferred to rank and waited until everyone else had gone through the line. The President held them back until all the others had cleared the hallway and then flicked his own aides away with a shake of his head.

"Looks like we've got 'em on the run," said the Man when the three of them were alone with the photographer in the big room.

"We'll catch the Russians by surprise," said the Deputy.

"I don't mean the Russians."

"State won't give up," said the Deputy. "They'll be back at it tomorrow."

"Don't give an inch," said the Man. "Here. Let's get one with the three of us."

The strobe caught McWade awkwardly trying to step past the President and the President holding him firmly in place. The next day, McWade knew, a print would appear on his desk with a signature straight from the automatic pen, a moment of history recorded, something to put up in his office if he ever decided to cash in his chips and go into private consulting. But McWade wasn't thinking of retirement. He had work to do, a different sort of history to examine, the kind that was not written in the book of days, whose face did not smile down from any wall.

6

It was only a few miles from the Cabinet Room to the bar they called Fortune, and the way was cluttered with franchises. If you landed there a little drunk and didn't know where you were, you couldn't have guessed from the surroundings. It might have been any state of the union, north, south, east or west. An Arby's, a Pizza Hut, a Taco Bell. One nation, indivisible.

For some reason, nobody had ever thought to put the utility lines underground in this part of Arlington, and they helped give it the look of an industrial park whose industry had fled. The bar itself stood all alone between two parking lots. They said Blackie owned the lots, too, because he always liked to have a clear field of fire.

The pavement was bumpy and perpetually under repair. McWade drove slowly. He wasn't worried about the stalkers. He didn't need an excuse to spend an evening at Fortune. The stalkers could certainly supply their own; they had probably spent time there themselves.

He pulled into the paper-strewn lot and parked his car. A narrow walkway cut through some low, scraggly bushes and brought him next to the building. There were no windows at the side or rear, and the front glass was painted black with gold letters. It might have been a palmist or a bookie joint.

The only sound came from an air conditioner grinding away high up under the eaves. The smell of whiskey poured from it, along with the aroma of stir-fry oil that carried McWade back to another time and place, as distant from the White House and Langley as the interval between intention and act.

Blackie had stationed himself at the small counter up front. The light was dim, and from the ceiling hung a slowly turning fan. The bar accommodated only four stools. Across from it stood three tiny, round tables that could have used refinishing. If you didn't know Fortune's secret and blundered in off the street, you would have wondered how it ever made a go of it.

Instead of a mirror, the wall behind the bar was hung with several large contour maps, their legends obscured by two rows of bottles. The maps were marked off into grid squares, but the terrain wasn't familiar to the untutored eye. To recognize the pastel swirls as highlands and rain forests, you had to have been there and used the coordinates to call in fire.

A television stood on a platform mounted high in one corner, but it was not turned on. A multi-band radio huddled in the corner of the counter, its dial aglow. The music tonight was Latin; it faded in and out of the static.

"He's not here yet," said Blackie. His chest and arms strained the fabric of a khaki safari shirt. There was no telling exactly how old he was, but it was clear that some of the years had been very hard.

"You heard from him?" asked McWade.

"Like I told you," said Blackie, "he's a regular. Unlike some others I could name."

But, of course, Blackie would never say the names aloud.

"Rufe used to be as punctual as an accountant," said McWade. "It was one of his few weaknesses."

"You can wait in the back if you want," said Blackie. "You remember the way."

"It hasn't been that long."

"Ever since you started showing up in the papers."

"I didn't realize anybody noticed," said McWade.

"It could ruin a man, a thing like that."

McWade had gotten his introduction to Fortune from Rufus Stockwell, the man he was hoping to meet tonight. Initially, Blackie had not seemed impressed by the fact that they had worked together in Europe. To him, European operations were like a job in a bank. But he perked up when Stockwell mentioned the war. No, McWade had said with some irritation, he wasn't Special Forces. He had commanded American rifles – straight leg infantry.

Blackie had just said, "Fuckin' grunt," and awarded him entrée to the business end of the joint.

The magnet-locked door that Blackie controlled from behind the bar opened onto a catacomb of private rooms where parties as large as a platoon or as small as a sniper team could go, unhindered by the requirements of discretion, to savor old lies. Each room was decorated differently, representing some of the benighted provinces in which Fortune's clients had operated. Beyond them lay a common area, more than twice as large as the front bar. It was draped with odd-looking unit flags from battalions that did not exist on any official order of battle, photographs of armed men, black and white and yellow, and the dead.

McWade took a place in one of the wooden booths as the doors of the kitchen swung open and Lan came through them carrying two steaming bowls of vegetables in a tangle of fine egg noodles. She was a Cambodian girl Blackie had picked up somewhere along the way. He had also brought home two others, a North African Moslem who had lost the modesty of a veil and a Hmong so stunted that she looked like a child. Everyone assumed that Blackie kept all three of them as wives as well as servants. That would have been in keeping with the prevailing idea of Fortune, which was to recreate as authentically as the law would tolerate all the perquisites of the secret wars.

Lan was small and shy. She dressed in silk pants, sandals and a white, collarless blouse. Her hair was covered by a checkered cloth like the ones the peasant women wore to shade themselves from the sun. Her face was marked by the pox, and a sharp scar slashed up her right arm, disappearing into her sleeve. They said Blackie had found her wounded. They said her baby had been killed. The pale, jagged gash on her arm showed the traces of Blackie's makeshift first aid, but the wound had apparently healed strong. She did not favor that side at all.

"You drink tonight?" she said.

"Scotch rocks," said McWade.

"Eat now too?"

"Later," he said. "I'm meeting someone."

"Blackie say you beaucoup important man now."

59

"Tee-tee."

"Number one."

"Number five on a good day," he said. "It's a big world out there."

"*Dinky dau*," she said in the Vietnamese slang the soldiers had brought with them across the border along with their weapons. It meant weird, insane. In that place, it had been a term of mutuality, if not affection.

She shuffled away and returned quickly with his drink. It surprised him that she had remembered him from when he was first back in country. He had not come to Fortune often, and when he did, he might even have reverted to the crudeness of Leggatt. He had been drinking heavily then, just to try to get to sleep.

McWade was still nursing his first round when Stockwell arrived. He wobbled over to McWade's booth and sat down as unceremoniously as if they had been meeting here every day.

"Slumming, eh?" he said.

Stockwell was a portly man, and he did not move quickly. He had obviously started elsewhere; alcohol reddened the wings of his nose. But this man could surprise you if you weren't careful. Quite a few on the other side had underestimated him, maybe one or two at Langley as well.

"It's been a long time, Rufe," said McWade.

"I'm available, chum," said Stockwell, "if you've got work."

"That bad, is it?"

Stockwell did not look as if he was down on his luck. He dressed in outdoorsman's clothes, but they were the kind that came dearly from Eddie Bauer or Bean. The rings on his fingers were gold.

"Hey, Dolly! You gonna get a man a drink or what?"

"I thought maybe they'd called you back by now," said McWade.

"Out once and you're out for good."

"Ross made it back."

"Friends in high places."

"There've been a lot of changes."

60

"My chinamen are gone," said Stockwell. "Fisherman's the only one from the old school still around."

"Have you seen him?" asked McWade.

Lan put a full tumbler on the table and Stockwell gave her ass a little slap. Blackie allowed just so much and no more, and Stockwell was a man who always went at least up to the line.

"I see a lot of people," he said. "They come looking for me. It's getting so I can't even go into my favorite gin mill without somebody waiting for me there. I'm a regular celebrity. Like whatsisname. Phil Donahue."

"You don't have enough hair, Rufe."

"But all the dollies love me anyway," said Stockwell.

"They can't take that away from you."

"Took everything else."

"That's not the way I heard it," said McWade.

"You can't believe everything you hear."

If Stockwell had learned anything about McWade's part in the decision to put him out on waivers, he had never given any indication of it. Whenever anybody asked, he blamed the Handholders. They were the ones who wrote him off after he went for a very obvious piece of bait. She was young and hard, and she set him up so well that to get him back the Agency had been forced to trade away an East German deep cover agent they hadn't finished sweating yet. When Stockwell came out of the Hungarian prison, the marks were still on him. But he insisted that he hadn't blown a single cover. At Langley, they didn't dare believe him, of course. They rolled up all his nets. And when they looked at the pictures of the woman, everyone agreed that she had come overpriced. Then the Handholders' report came in. It wasn't overly technical. It simply said that Stockwell had lost control of his dick.

McWade had fought for his retention as long as he could, but Fisherman would not compromise. He said that when a man crosses the border there is no passport to bring him back. In the end McWade accepted the Handholders' evaluation and argued that Stockwell's problem was service-related. At least he was able to make sure Stockwell was taken care of as far as money. Since

Stockwell was willing to go quietly, nobody wanted to quibble. They even held a small dinner in his honor at Fortune. Fisherman was the principal speaker. He called Stockwell the best of a breed. You mean best breeder, someone shouted. Stockwell was man enough to laugh.

"You're not drinking."

"Slacking off, I guess," said McWade.

"Dolly, get us another round, won't you, love?"

"Getting old," said McWade.

"Bring back old Joe Leggatt. There was a man who knew how to have a good time."

"May he rest in peace."

Stockwell reached across the table and ran his thick fingers over McWade's lapels.

"Fancier uniform now," he said. "It must get kind of squirrely up there where you are, if you're looking up old buddies after all the years."

"Something came up," said McWade. "It's unofficial, I'm afraid."

"I'm deniable."

"If it comes to denial, we're both in trouble."

"Must be pretty tight then," said Stockwell, and for a moment his eyes were almost clear.

"Maybe," said McWade.

Just then a commotion broke out in the opposite corner of the room. A voice soared out over the kitchen din. "I don't give a shit who the little prick works for now." McWade turned and saw a big man break free of the restraining arms of a companion and stamp across the floor. When he reached Stockwell he leaned down on the table with both fists. He was a little drunk and unsteady on his feet, but his size still gave him a certain amount of authority.

"What're you drinking with this cocksucker for?" he demanded.

"He's buying," said Stockwell. "Sit down, Turk. Join us."

"I don't drink with errand boys."

"Remind me," said McWade. "What exactly did I do to you?"

Turk did not deign to address McWade directly.

"The sonofabitch busted my buddy," he told Stockwell.

"Ike McWade was a right guy," said Stockwell, "while he lasted."

"I mean his boss. Fisherman. He took Randolph Bourne down."

"Somebody had to," said Stockwell.

That seemed to set big man back for a moment, making the matter even, two against one. In the meantime, Turk's companion had come up next to him, speaking the voice of sweet reason.

"You make trouble, Blackie'll have your ass for sure," the companion said.

Turk stood up to his full height.

"You tell him to tell Fisherman . . ." he said to Stockwell.

"That you're gonna get him someday, right?" said Stockwell, grinning. "You'll have to get in line, my friend."

Turk accepted that and let himself be led out of the room. When he was gone, Stockwell took a long pull from his glass.

"It wasn't Fisherman," said McWade. "I took Bourne down myself."

"I know," said Stockwell.

"He was working for Khadafy. Setting off bombs in Beirut. The case was solid."

"Fisherman's usually are," said Stockwell.

"I didn't even know the guy," said McWade.

"I guess that makes it easier," said Stockwell. "Dolly, get your ass over here. We're ready to eat."

McWade wasn't hungry, but he ordered something anyway. Stockwell told Lan to bring him the usual.

"Look," said McWade. "Bourne had gone over the side. He was selling his country."

"It happens," said Stockwell.

"Working for that butcher."

"You take whatever work you can get, I guess."

"I'd have done it to anyone, even you Rufe, if you'd pulled something as stupid as that."

"There are plenty who blame Fisherman," said Stockwell. "They get drunk and say things they shouldn't. Smart ones don't say a thing."

"But they know what happened to them."

"Yeah," said Stockwell. "They know."

A group of men got up to leave and gave McWade and Stockwell a good looking over as they passed.

"What about Richard Harper?" McWade asked when they had cleared the door.

"He don't know as much as he thinks he does."

"He have a problem with Fisherman?"

"He's still inside, isn't he?" said Stockwell.

"You mean there's no bad blood."

"I mean Fisherman never got him. But that don't mean he didn't try."

Lan brought the food, and Stockwell pushed away the chopsticks and went at it with a fork.

"I love this shit the way she makes it," he said.

"Harper paid me a midnight visit. He wanted to give me a friendly piece of advice."

"Once an asshole, always an asshole, chum," said Stockwell.

"What does he have against Fisherman?"

"He's a scared little man," said Stockwell, and his voice dropped down. "Fisherman knew that."

"What do you hear?"

Stockwell put away some more hot, spicy beef and fed the fire with whiskey. Sweat broke out on his brow.

"That dolly sure can cook," he said. "Burn your damned tongue out of your mouth."

"This doesn't go any further than me, Rufe."

Stockwell put down his fork and wiped his face with his napkin. Then he leaned forward and let out a soft hissing sound between his teeth.

"I may be in a jam," said McWade.

Stockwell wadded the napkin in his hand and then tossed it off to the side of the table, where it slowly unfurled.

"They say Fisherman burned one of Harper's boys," he whispered.

"I don't get it."

"The stupid sonofabitch went and killed himself. Nice young kid named Birch. Army type. Harper took it hard."

"Fisherman was leaning on this guy?"

"Set him up is what I hear."

"How?"

"They say he got the kid to meet with Kerzhentseff. Heard of him?"

"The one they call Zapadnya," said McWade.

"Mean bastard," said Stockwell. "Harper didn't even see it coming. See, he was in the trick bag himself. He had a bet down on Birch, so when the guy started looking like he had turned, Harper was in trouble. I'll tell you what he did, Ike. He tried to have it both ways. He didn't stand up. He didn't go a hundred per cent. He left the kid hanging out there. And he didn't even know what it was all about until it was too fucking late. That's the kind of guy he is."

"What was Fisherman after?"

"Way a lot of people figure it, he didn't give a shit about Birch. He was out to get Harper."

"And Kerzhentseff just played along?"

"Looks that way."

"Fisherman made the arrangements?"

"Maybe he had help."

"Who?"

"You ask interesting questions," said Stockwell. The fire was beginning to ebb in his cheeks, and he returned to his plate to stoke it up again.

"You always seem to have the answers," said McWade.

"Not all of them."

"What's your guess?"

"I can't give a name." Stockwell put down his fork. "But Fisherman was running this thing with Birch on the sly. He wouldn't have used anybody in the Agency."

"Dangerous move for Fisherman."

"He was pure gold in those days. Nobody could touch him."

"So he found somebody on the outside and had him set the Russian up. Had to be somebody with a few resources."

"Guy doesn't lose it all when they put him out to graze," said Stockwell. "If he's smart he keeps his hand in because he never knows when somebody's going to come along looking for him to do a little business again. Unofficial, of course. Deniable."

Stockwell gave McWade the grin.

"I don't figure Kerzhentseff," said McWade. "He's not the type to let himself be used."

"I'll ask him about it next time I see him," said Stockwell.

"Why didn't Fisherman go for somebody easier?"

"Way I understand it, Kerzhentseff had dealt with Birch before. Ran him in Tokyo when our boy was with a pretty sensitive communications unit. I don't know all the details. But apparently the Russians made the approach and Harper heard about it. He recruited Birch to double against the Russian. And the way it ended, Langley marked it up as an ironclad operation. Something very big."

"Harper mentioned CONVERGENCE."

"That was the name Fisherman gave it. The word I heard was BLACKBODY or some damned thing."

"But this was later."

"Much later. Here in Washington."

"And Birch was just bait."

"Bait for Harper, not Kerzhentseff. Harper took it and didn't even feel the hook. Birch was in the middle. Until he went to a hot sheet joint one day and cut his wrists."

"You think Harper finally saw the way it had played. That's why he hates Fisherman."

Stockwell took the last swallow out of his glass.

"Harper wants to get you to go against Fisherman," he said.

"Something like that."

"Stay away from him," said Stockwell. "That's my advice."

When Lan came by, Stockwell took her around the waist and pulled her close,

"How come Blackie's such a lucky guy?" he said.

Lan smiled, and for a moment she was almost beautiful.

"You ever get tired of him," said Stockwell, "you just give me a call."

"Something make you happy tonight, Mr Rufus," she said.

"Whiskey," he said. "Old friends. A little action."

Lan moved away, and Stockwell watched her cross the floor.

"I can't pay," said McWade. "I don't have a budget."

"What do I need money for? This one's on Langley. The pension covers my overhead."

"They say Fisherman's got the NARCISSUS files tucked away in his office," said McWade. "I want to know why."

Stockwell put down his fork and rubbed his greasy fingers across the tablecloth.

"You're asking me to run a job against Fisherman?" he said.

"Not exactly. For now I just want you to get what you can on the street. There's got to be talk, a thing like that."

"I'll tell you what I already hear," said Stockwell. "I hear he's asking questions about how Ben Wheeler died and why nobody paid a price."

"That was my case," said McWade.

"Looks like he might be running a job on you, my friend."

In other circumstances, McWade might have felt the need to feign anger or at least surprise. But this was Rufus Stockwell he was talking to.

"He gets around to everyone," said McWade.

"Sooner or later."

"You in with me?"

"Why not."

McWade took the money out of his wallet and laid it on the table.

"If you need to get in contact with me . . .," he said.

"I'll find a way."

"So long, Rufe."

Stockwell stood up.

"I'll give you two minutes," he said, "then I'll follow. Just in case the Turk's out there waiting to continue the conversation."

"Covering my ass again."

"Somebody's got to," said Stockwell and slapped McWade sharply across the shoulders to send him on his way, like a coach putting his best boy back into the game.

PART TWO

Joseph Leggatt

7

When Stockwell told him Fisherman had disinterred the
files on Ben Wheeler, it threw McWade back to part of his
career he preferred to keep buried. It had been a time
when he had almost lost his way, and it had not helped
matters that he had been coming straight off home leave
with his mother and father when he first heard what had
happened to Wheeler. He had been as unprepared for
what was to come as he had been when he first left Manitee
Bay to train for the secret wars. It had seemed a sacrilege
to perform the death rites under someone else's name and
then to fashion a lie that lay over the facts of the killing like
a shroud. Where he came from, kindness was the only
excuse for not telling the truth about the dead. But that
was a different place, and in it he had been a different
man.

The town of Manitee Bay stood on the bluff above Lake
Michigan like a sentry, its back to the rolling farmlands to
the west. It was big enough to be the county seat but
isolated enough to have retained much of its character
against the relentless march of sameness that had spread
across the land.

On his way into town at the start of his home leave
McWade had driven past the schoolhouse where he had
spent the first eight grades. The walls were still free of
graffiti, the yard immaculate, not a candy wrapper or soda
can in sight. The houses along Main all seemed freshly
whitewashed, their lawns weeded and trimmed along the
walks, their porches warmly lighted against the dusk.
When he saw the treasured old flag from a distance, he
knew it was flying for him, just as it had the day he
returned from the war.

He had been shamed by it then. He had remembered
his mother's story about the homecoming in '45, the

71

bunting on the light poles, the profusion of banners and welcoming signs. But on that cold day in '71, there had only been a single flag, and it had seemed like an accusation.

"Take it down, Dad," he had said even before he had changed out of his uniform. And though his father had not fully understood the reason, he had done as McWade asked.

Once McWade had settled on a career in the Agency, the flag had become less of a burden. And if he winced this trip when he saw the colors billowing on the high staff on the lawn, it was only because the banner drew attention to his arrival and raised certain questions about the nature of his current duties.

Every time McWade returned home, his dad felt obliged to apologize for how much the town had changed, as if this would make his son seem constant, a measure of the flux. Why, even the old Palladium moviehouse was boarded up now, he said. The kids had to go to the drive-in or the Quonset hut over in Shelby. When McWade was a boy, they had gathered in the Palladium lobby on Saturday night, boys and girls arriving separately, then pairing up to sneak into the balcony, which was always roped off, probably for just that purpose. The girls had worn slacks or shorts with zippers on the sides, and it had been glory to touch the cold metal with your fingertips.

One day after he had been back for more than a week, McWade took the rental car and drove out into the country, the baseball game from Milwaukee on the radio. He didn't keep up with the standings anymore, but whenever he was at home, even after the Braves had left and the only game in the state was strictly minor league, he got back into baseball again the way he had when he was a boy and Hank Aaron was a god.

He swung through dairy country and then back to the lake. Up north there were still quite a few stretches that remained uninhabited. This was where he had always gone to be alone, sometimes sitting for hours just listening to the hush of the waves. The lakeside woods were safe and confining – the boughs a ceiling, the needles a soft

72

carpet beneath his feet – except for the water that stretched out to all the faraway places a boy would rather be.

The woods were also good when you did not want to be alone. In Manitee Bay you always had to be careful about a girl's reputation. Young people were warned sternly against holding hands on the street. But this did not mean they buried all their yearnings. They simply learned the virtue of furtiveness, and there were plenty of secluded spots along the lake where virtue could be rewarded.

But McWade had always held himself back. On beds of pine needles, with damp, chill air prickling their skin, the girls tried to domesticate him through the miracle of their lips and fingers. McWade took them only so far and no farther. And on Sunday mornings in church, when he saw Saturday night's companion in the choir, her white dress billowing up his imagination, he had nothing to regret.

Late in his junior year when the test scores started coming in, they confirmed that he had it in him to go wherever he wanted. College. Law school like his father. Then he could come back and inherit the leadership of the town. But he knew that if he was ever to find out who he really was, he would have to leave the town behind; he would have to carry the family name into the larger world in order to discover what it meant. By the time he graduated he had already seen what it stood for here, the nature of the responsibility and, quite precisely, the price.

It was a short drive from the forests along the lake to the spread that used to belong to Fred Granger. Granger's troubles had not come to light until McWade's second to last summer in Manitee Bay, but the tale itself had begun much earlier, long before McWade was born.

The way his mother told it, Granger and McWade's father had not been particularly close until the war. Three years separated them in school. But when the state had decided to raise its own division to get ready to fight the Axis in Europe, they had been among the first volunteers. Neither of them talked much about it afterwards, at least in company, though McWade could remember hearing their voices outside on the porch at night, laughing or not laughing, when he was supposed to be asleep.

When they came home from the service, they began dating the Rubensholm sisters. And they were both in a powerful hurry to get on with it. The two couples were married in a single ceremony the summer after their first year up in Madison on the GI Bill.

They started to have families right away, and when they graduated, Granger returned to Manitee Bay. But Mc-Wade's father was determined to get his law degree, and so for three years the couples were separated from each other. By the time McWade's parents returned, Granger had already made a success of himself. He introduced them to golf and tennis, loaned them the money to build their home and superintended the construction himself.

The Granger spread was just outside town, and when McWade reached the access road, he was surprised at how overgrown the shoulders had become. Uncle Fred had always kept them mowed like fairways, just as he made sure his automobiles were waxed as deep as a mirror and the big old farmhouse was painted as white as a Sunday shirt.

McWade pulled off the gravel onto two dirt ruts worn into the weedy lawn. The house looked as though it hadn't felt the touch of a brush since Aunt Lorraine sold it. An old tractor sat rusting next to the shed, and nobody was going to move it soon because it had been cannibalized for parts. He climbed out of the Pontiac and walked around to the side lot where he could see the rundown barn and a bunch of chickencoops somebody had slapped up out of cratewood, all gray and smelling into the wind.

McWade was sorry to see the place so rundown, sorry the way he might have been about the fact that the rains had not blown in on time and a drought had stunted the crops. His father had been a man in the middle who had simply done what he had to do. And the only thing McWade blamed himself for in Fred Granger's fall was having failed to see it coming.

Of course, he had noticed all the hushed conversations, the shaking heads, the silences when he entered the room. But at first he had thought they were talking about him. Only when Aunt Lorraine showed up one day with the girls and a car full of suitcases did he begin to understand what was going on.

Uncle Fred was seeing another woman, and he did not even take the trouble to lie about it anymore. "The man says he has needs," Aunt Lorraine said. McWade had to look away in embarrassment because he was old enough to know what those needs felt like and young enough to think they were supposed to abate with age.

It seemed that Uncle Fred's frequent business trips were not all business. He did have call to go to the insurance company's regional office in Madison from time to time for conferences. But he had also taken up with a woman there, one he had known in college. McWade's father had known her, too, and he assured Aunt Lorraine that she was not serious competition, not serious anything as he remembered, as stupid as a hen in the rain. This did not do much to comfort Uncle Fred's lawful wife.

Finally it was decided that the best thing for Aunt Lorraine and the girls was to get out of Manitee Bay. Uncle Fred came up with the money to establish her in a house in the next county, beyond the reach of tongues. At the time, nobody thought this would be much of a financial strain on him. To all appearances, his insurance and construction businesses were going strong.

After Aunt Lorraine and the girls had moved away, Uncle Fred began showing his face at the McWade house again. It was tense at first, McWade's mother behaving so godawful polite that you might have thought she was entertaining a banker who'd come to foreclose. Uncle Fred did not make things any easier by employing schnapps against his defenses, which tended both to make him confessional and to dilute his penitence. But McWade's father kept things peaceful enough that McWade had no inkling that his father had set into motion a process that would eventually bring Uncle Fred crashing down.

There was no outward sign of what was afoot. With Uncle Fred, McWade's father was more than cordial. The two of them sometimes sat outside for hours, talking about the past. Though McWade's father always steered the conversation away from the sinkholes of remorse and incrimination, he did encourage Uncle Fred to stop seeing the woman in Madison, and Uncle Fred assured him that he would. In fact, he sometimes seemed to nurture a sodden hope that he might be able to put it all back together again.

But as it turned out, Aunt Lorraine had a deep streak of vengeance in her. Beneath the Christian rectitude seethed a mighty wrath. She had discovered precisely what Uncle Fred had been up to all these years to pay for his secret pleasures. And before she left him she had copied out the most damaging entries from his second set of books.

The only person she showed them to was McWade's father, not only out of kinship, but because for more than a decade he had served as county attorney. It was part-time work, a civic duty he undertook on top of his law practice and the management of the store. He had no honorable choice once she brought the evidence to him but to make sure the case she presented was pursued.

This was why he had been so reluctant to open himself to Uncle Fred's admissions. He did not consider it fair to take advantage of Uncle Fred's whiskey candor. Thinking back on it, McWade had to respect the way his father handled the situation. It could not have been easy for a man who believed so deeply in loyalty. But the law, he often said, was no respecter of persons. Though that was supposed to be its greatest virtue, in a small world like Manitee Bay it was hard, very hard.

Once McWade's father had documented the basic facts, he took himself out of the matter by calling in a special attorney from out of town and presenting him with the dossier – the receipts for insurance policies that Uncle Fred had failed to forward, the records showing the inferior materials he had put into the county roads, the corners he cut on the new firehouse. Eventually the United States Attorney was brought in on the case, too, because it seemed likely that Uncle Fred neglected to report to the IRS some of his fraudulent receipts. And McWade began to understand the way a lie could corrupt everything. It had to be defended by other lies, which themselves had to be embellished, and on and on. There was no end to it. A lie altered the whole universe. And when it began to be challenged, it collapsed in on itself like a building succumbing to flame.

When Uncle Fred realized what was happening to him and why, at first he raged against McWade's father and spread vicious rumors about him and Aunt Lorraine. The town was not deceived, but still the scandal became the talk of the sweetshop, the topic of every haircut conversation, the subject of the preacher's Sunday warnings. Uncle Fred went into seclusion on his farm. Nobody saw him, let alone sought out his side of the story. Nobody even inquired whether he was sick or well. Nobody, that is, except McWade's father.

At first it was difficult, but McWade's father visited the farm regularly, bringing provisions and news. McWade often went along for the ride because his father did not like to drive alone at night. Sometimes Uncle Fred was furious. Sometimes he was pathetically grateful. It all depended on the level of alcohol in his blood.

When Uncle Fred was lucid, McWade's father urged him to make a clean breast of it, to sell the farm and settle up.

"Hell, man," he said. "We've been through worse, you and me."

"We didn't have anything to lose back then," said Uncle Fred.

"We thought we did at the time."

Uncle Fred reached over to the tumbler and took a long, bitter pull.

"I can't fault you, Bill," he said, tears welling up in his eyes. "But I feel like I've been ambushed." The tears overflowed now, regret and anger together, the pain. "And you never said a thing. I saw you every day. Every damned day."

The grand jury brought in an indictment after a few months, and the arraignment was set. McWade's father found a good attorney to handle the defense and took it upon himself to guarantee the fee.

Then one night McWade heard the fire bell clanging in the dark.

"My God!" his mother cried. "It's the store!"

77

"You stay here," said his father as he rushed outside, McWade and his brother right behind.

As soon as they reached the corner, they could see that the store was in no immediate danger. The fire was across the street. Flames shot out of the upper windows where on idle afternoons they used to be able to see Uncle Fred sitting with his feet on the sill.

They all helped the volunteer firemen that night, the brothers manning a hose together, bathing down the nearby roofs. But nothing could save the main building. Finally the walls collapsed. The insurance agency was a total loss.

At dawn McWade's mother came down with blankets and hot coffee. The volunteers excused the boys from helping to reroll the hose. Father and sons gathered in the doorway of the store out of the wind.

"Did anybody think to go out and get Fred?" his father asked the firechief. They could not have phoned, of course, because the line had been cut off when Uncle Fred failed to keep up with his bills.

"Tried," said the chief.

"You look in the barn?"

"Expect we might find him in there," said the chief, lifting his smoke-blackened hand to the fallen timbers, ashes and broken glass.

McWade's father sent the boys home and stayed to help search the wreckage. When he finally returned, he sat down at the kitchen table and ran his sooty fingers through his hair.

"It'll have to be a closed casket," he said.

"Lorraine doesn't want a funeral," said McWade's mother. "The expense of it."

"I hope she has pockets in her shroud," he said. But then the mood flared out and his eyes sank to the tabletop. "I'm sorry, Ethel. He was my friend."

"Maybe you should make the arrangements," she said.

"I already have."

Fortunately, nobody could prove that Uncle Fred had intentionally set the fire. The best explanation, based on physical evidence, was that he had passed out drunk and dropped a cigarette on some papers on the desk. The lady who regularly cleaned the office reported that two days earlier she had taken one look at the place and just walked away from it. There were files all over, she said, and empty bottles on the floor. Dead soldiers, she called them. In the end the insurance company had to pay double indemnity on the one policy that Uncle Fred had made sure had never lapsed.

In the aftermath McWade's father talked about resigning as county attorney, but he never actually did it. McWade wondered what purpose he himself might find to inspire him to the same grand and painful sense of duty.

From the old Granger spread, McWade drove directly back to town. He stopped at the store, but his father was out, so he crossed the street to the sweetshop for a bite to eat.

They had done the place over, and he hardly recognized it inside. The booths were now padded and covered with vinyl. In the old days they had been solid wood, and as the boys told their tales of daring over cherry Cokes and malteds, they squirmed against the seat backs, which were as hard and uncompromising as the truth.

The two pinball machines that used to be in the back were gone now. McWade had been forbidden to play them until he turned twelve, but once he came of age, he spent hours perfecting his wrist action and his sense of how much he could jar the thing before it called a tilt.

Where the old fountain used to rise from the counter in a swirl of shiny chrome like a car straight off the lot, the counterman now drew drinks from a plastic machine. And the ceiling, once a byzantine effusion of plaster flowers and heraldry, had been lowered and fitted with acoustical tiles.

When he had settled in a booth away from the window, the young waitress took his order. On the table, the mat showed a map of Wisconsin decorated with drawings of Indians, deer and jumping fish.

"Aren't you Ike McWade?"

McWade looked up, but the woman's face was turned away from him as she wrestled a wriggling boy out from behind her.

"Richie, this is Mr McWade. Ike, this is my son."

The boy couldn't have been more than seven years old. He finally overcame his shyness and stuck out his hand. McWade took it then looked up again at his mother.

"Julie," he said. "Julie Marks."

He was standing now, and he took her hand to shake it. She leaned upward and gave him a peck on the cheek. He wanted to touch the wet spot with his fingers, but he had sense enough not to.

"I didn't know you were back in town," she said.

"I want a cheeseburger, Ma," said Richie, "and fries."

"We've heard all kinds of things about you," she said.

"Ma!"

"Just a second now, Richie. You go find a booth."

The boy was obviously not satisfied with this arrangement. He moved a step or two and then stopped.

"Here, Rich," McWade said, sitting down and scooting over to make room. "Why don't you come join me."

But it was the boy's mother who slipped in beside him, maneuvering Richie across the table and straightening his placemat with her fingers.

"I thought you were overseas somewhere," she said.

"On and off," he said. "This is home leave. I mean, I'm still overseas. Well, you know what I mean."

She seemed pleased by his nervousness.

"Not the Army still," she said.

"No."

"I didn't think so," she said, shaking out her hair with a gesture he had seen a thousand times before. "I saw your picture in the paper with your uniform. That was years ago. You didn't seem comfortable in it."

"You're not supposed to be," he said.

The waitress put a burger in front of him and slipped the little newsprint check under the heavy plate.

"You want to order now, m'am?" she said. It made him suddenly feel his age.

"Richie will have a cheeseburger," she said.

"Here," said McWade. "You take mine. The young man is obviously in a mighty big hurry. Are onions all right?"

The boy slid the plate over without objection. McWade had to smile. You always had onions at the sweetshop, everyone did, so you never had to worry about having them on your breath.

"Give me just a little taste of them," he said. They were warm on his lips, a kiss. Julie reached over and took some, too. Richie pulled the plate closer and surrounded it with his arms to fend off any more raids.

"I'll just have a Coke," said McWade.

"No burger?" said the waitress.

"That's all right."

"I'll have cola, too," said Julie. "Diet."

"So," said McWade.

"Where do we start?" she said.

"Ketchup," said Richie.

"Here," said his mother, reaching back into the next booth for the squeeze bottle. Her jacket fell open as she stretched. The fabric of her blouse strained against her breasts.

"How many kids is it now?" he said.

"Just Richie. He's a handful all by himself, aren't you, Richie?"

"Ma," said the boy, retreating to the corner of the booth.

"And you, Ike? You have kids?"

"I'm not married."

"You always knew exactly what was right for you and what wasn't," she said.

When they had started going together in high school, Julie was a sophomore and he was already a senior. She drew him out slowly after Fred Granger died, when everybody else was walking on tiptoes around him, whispering. For a long while she did not even tell anyone she was serious about him. He was like an older brother, she said, which caused him to take quite a ribbing from his buddies.

But after a while, he began to see their names together on the notebooks of other sophomore girls. Ike + Julie. Sometimes framed by a heart. It upset him, being mapped out there for all to see. But he could not blame Julie for what the others did.

Then one day he came upon her in the library. Her back was to the door, and she was working with a pencil and paper. A book was open before her, but she was not looking at it. He came up behind her softly and was about to say hello when he saw what she was doing. On the paper was a column of words in her soft, careful hand. Julie McWade. Mrs Ike McWade. Mrs Isaac F. McWade. He turned and left the room. Though he never mentioned it to her, something went out of him when he saw the names on the paper, something taken that was not yet his to give.

"Can we go now, Ma?" said Richie, stuffing the last of the fries into his mouth. She reached over to wipe it with a napkin, but he slipped away.

"In a little while," she said.

"Come on, Ma. Let's go."

"Don't pay any attention to him," said Julie. "He's just in a mood."

"Am not."

"Well, sport," said McWade, "I bet you're a Brewers fan."

The boy turned back to his food and mumbled something.

"He doesn't get much man talk, I'm afraid," said Julie.

"You're . . ."

"Divorced," she said. "I don't think you'd have known him. I met him in Appleton. I gave up school to get married. I guess I was pretty naive."

McWade sipped his Coke and then took a drink of water to wash away the cloying aftertaste.

"I went back and finished after the divorce," she went on. "It took a few years, but I did it."

"Always the brightest in the class."

"Aren't you nice to say so?" she said. "Hear that Richie? Your mother isn't so dumb after all."

"Julie," he said because he didn't like the idea of being her measure after all these years.

"I'm working now," she said. "Just part time. Some tutoring and a little needlework. Your father takes some on consignment. Maybe you've seen it in the store. Samplers and tea cozies. Very corny. It must seem pretty dull around here."

"I kind of enjoy coming back."

"You always had a special kind of fire in you."

"All those onions," he said.

"I never thought I'd see you again," she said.

"Well, I'd better be going," he said. "I promised my mother I'd take her to visit some relatives."

He made a move and she hesitated before sliding out to let him go.

"Maybe we could get together again later," she said.

"I'll be around," he said.

"Why don't you come over for dinner?"

"I think my parents have my meals all booked up."

"Then afterwards."

"I'll have to see what they have planned."

"Good," she said. "I'm going to be out tonight. At a PTA meeting, of all things. But I'll call you tomorrow."

"Sure," he said. "That would be fine."

He picked up all three checks, added them up in his head and dropped a single bill on the table to cover them.

"I want to hear all about this job of yours," she said.

"So long then," he said, this time preempting her by leaning down to graze her hair with his lips.

"Tomorrow, Ike," she said as he left her.

But he did not wait for her call. He was gone shortly after dawn. It was a simpler matter to tell his parents he had been summoned to Washington for a meeting than to try to explain that he was once again fleeing from the capture of his name.

8

The woman behind the counter tapped a key on her terminal and watched the screen, her fingers drumming on the counter next to the ticket which showed him already booked on the flight.

"That's odd, Mr Rogers," she said. "This machine just doesn't seem to want to . . . Wait. . . . Well, finally."

Relief softened her face to the expression the airlines liked to advertise.

"Smoking or non-smoking?" she asked.

"Non."

Anthony Rogers sometimes took a mild cigar, but that was prohibited on airplanes. And anyway McWade did not feel the tug of habit coming back to him yet. The time in Manitee Bay had left McWade and Rogers worlds apart.

"Window or aisle?"

"Window is fine."

She touched a few more keys then wrote something on the ticket folder and handed it to him.

"I'm sorry for the confusion, Mr Rogers," she said. "The computer has been having an identity crisis today."

He passed through the security arch without alarm. When his briefcase slid off the conveyor belt from the X-ray, he lifted it and opened the lock. The numbers of the combination were set to the date of his mother's birthday, which helped him remember when to send a gift and card. He took out the Rogers passport from his breast pocket, put it in the briefcase, then snapped the lock shut again and went off to board his flight.

Strictly speaking, it was not necessary to travel under a cover, but if you punched in and out under the same name, there was no dangling record. This was one of the routines McWade had picked up when he was assigned to London station, also known as the Nest, though at first his assignments were so drab that caution was hardly necessary. As the junior man he had drawn all the worst duties: administrative matters, paper chases, little overseas errands that nobody much cared about. He might not have been able to survive the boredom if it hadn't been for Ben Wheeler.

McWade had first met him one morning at the dull modern building where the Agency leased space. It was a fair distance from the Embassy in one of those bland neighborhoods of concrete and glass that had sprung up after the war. He was waiting in the lift when into the lobby came a thin, rakish fellow in tennis garb. McWade thought he must have been one of the dentists the Agency allowed to occupy the lower floors. But when McWade punched the button for seven, the other man simply watched the light pop on and did not make a move.

"What floor?" McWade asked.

"Same as you, I trust."

"Are you sure?" said McWade.

The man had a presence, smooth enough to get a diamond right off your finger and leave you feeling grateful that he had deigned to shake your hand. The door of the elevator slowly closed.

"It's a secret," said the man.

"Pardon?"

"What I'm sure of, Mr McWade, and what I doubt."

"You know my name."

"Yes."

"I don't know yours."

"Advantage to the service," said the man.

Then the doors opened and he stepped off the elevator and turned into the corridor, racket on his shoulder, whistling a tune from a show that had just crossed over from New York.

It did not take long for McWade to learn that Ben cut quite a figure whatever clothes he wore or name he traveled under. Slight in build, maybe half a head shorter than McWade, he was much more imposing than this might suggest. It was as if the lines of age had given his whole being an upward aspect, like a feather or a flame.

He invited McWade to his club a few days after their first encounter. When they were ready to be seated, he introduced McWade to the headwaiter as Anthony Rogers. As far as McWade could tell, he just pulled the name out of the air. The headwaiter mentioned that the Winchester Rogerses had been members of the club for six generations, and Wheeler looked at him as if the man had just accused his companion of being mongrel bred.

"They hate it when a Yank is more of a shit than they are," Wheeler said when they were settled at a secluded table. He pulled a tin of little Dutch cigars from the breast pocket of his blazer and fired up, inhaling the thick smoke and letting a little wisp escape his lips.

"Who is this Rogers exactly?" asked McWade.

"That's up to you," said Wheeler. "But I'll tell you this: you'd be well advised to make sure he shares your tastes."

McWade examined the incriminating tips of his fingers and then smoothed out the crease in the white linen.

"Don't rule out pleasure," said Wheeler.

"He might find himself a little awkward in intimate situations. A gentleman usually leaves his name."

"Langley only insists that the ladies be vetted. They do it quite decently, you know. They wear the rubber glove. The Agency understands men's needs," Wheeler swept his hand toward the elegant old room, "in extremity."

He gave generously of his advice that evening. And in the weeks that followed McWade got together with him at the club whenever Wheeler was in town. McWade looked forward to their conversations keenly, because otherwise his routine was unbearably dull.

Occasionally he traveled to the Continent on some errand or another, always going as timid, forlorn George Perkins. No excuse for adventure there. No sense of the larger mission either. The Agency designed its operations the way a marine architect designs a warship, each unit sealed off by bulkheads so that if the vessel took a hit, the damage could be contained. This left McWade feeling utterly cut off, and he yearned to taste again the camaraderie of danger and common purpose that he had known during the war.

For the time being, though, he had to settle for a substitute, the jaded fellowship of boredom. As Anthony Rogers, he began knocking around the Fleet Street pubs with a crowd from the American news agencies, mostly desk riders like himself, men who had lost their legs or nerve.

One evening while he was listening to a photographer exaggerate the joys and terrors of Angola, Bob Reynolds of the AP joined them with an unfamiliar young woman in tow. It was hard to miss her, because her red hair was a flash of wildness in the drab, smoky confines of the pub. She caught McWade watching her and did not reward his glance. She was obviously used to being looked at. Once Reynolds had established her at the bar, he drifted off to gloat over a string of beads he had gotten in Beirut, full of the wireman's pride in a three-minute edge. It was quite clear that the woman did not share his excitement. In fact, the monologue seemed to exclude her so completely that McWade moved over to introduce himself. She did not show any particular gratitude for his company, but she did tell him that her name was Jane Kurling and that she did her reporting on a freelance basis, if he knew anybody who had work.

"It's not my line, I'm afraid," said McWade. "I'm in tangible exports."

"Tony's stuck in the marmalade trade," said a UPI reporter.

"Anything sweet to the tongue," said Jane.

It didn't take long for McWade to learn the reason for her bitterness: ignorant editors, the bastards, who wouldn't know talent if it came up and punched them in the nose, which it would certainly do if it had any self-respect.

"You're too young to be so angry," he said.

"I don't know what age has to do with it," she snapped.

McWade decided it was probably better just to let her brood. But a little bit later, when Reynolds left without her, she began to relax. So McWade tried again to draw her out. As he did, he found himself attracted to her anger. Or more precisely to the flashes of wit and fragility behind it. Just to see if the hidden side was the genuine one, he suggested that what she needed was a good long laugh.

"You're kidding."

"I know just the place for it," he said.

It was a short walk to the Mermaid Theatre on the river. They had no trouble getting seats in the stalls. The farce was full of mistaken identities, men passing for women, bedroom hijinks in which sin had no chance against the fun. When it was over, she agreed to have a drink with him at his flat. And it struck both of them as perfectly hilarious when they found their way into one another's arms. It was all a wonderful joke on somebody, like the cuckold in the play, though they couldn't say precisely who that some-body was.

As soon as he reached the office the next morning, he reported his encounter. Nobody saw any obvious prob-lems. Her father, it turned out, was a wealthy man, well known in London. Ben Wheeler was the only one who took the matter at all seriously.

"If you have any real feeling for her," he said, "you'll want to hold a lot back."

"Because otherwise I might have to betray her some-day," said McWade, grinning at the archness of it.

"Because you already have," said Wheeler.

It might have been more difficult to keep his distance if it hadn't been for the freelance assignments that took Jane out of England for weeks at a time. In a way, they were defined by absence, by what was withheld. This was the dirty secret of the era of clean sex. It gave freely what once had been guarded, but drew back when it came to bestow-ing anything more intimate than flesh. This lent their relationship a tantalizing quality. For a long time, neither of them let themselves risk being overwhelmed by feelings they could not control. But sometimes when they were together, he did give her glimpses of what was really in him. To let her discover him this way was like the touch of hand to thigh in the balcony of the theater in Manitee Bay.

They developed a comfortable routine during these first months, dining together frequently and then spending the night at his place or hers, separating early in the morning to get ready for work. They did not merge their wardrobes. This was one of the lines they held.

Meanwhile, Jane's work situation improved, and as it did, she was willing to take a greater chance on affection. On his side, McWade retreated into the character he had created. In fact, he became so settled in his role as Anthony Rogers that it startled him when someone on the inside addressed him by his childhood name. He was Rogers to his barber, Rogers to the cleaning lady, Rogers in Wheeler's club. McWade was someone out of the past, and Rogers looked down on him with cool detachment, on the rare occasions when he took the trouble to look at all.

As time went on, he found himself being given more responsibility at the Nest. He was still an inside man, but with Jane's erratic schedule, at least that meant he was almost always available when she was. Then suddenly everything changed.

Even before the station chief called him in, McWade knew about the problem they had been having in Czechoslovakia. It had been a delicate matter, extracting Greenfield from the hospital in Prague after his coronary without blowing his cover. The cable traffic had been intense, with Langley in an awful state over salvaging the net and the station chief muttering about how little there was left to save.

When the rescue mission was concluded, the chief informed McWade that he was the one who would inherit the mess.

"Are you ready, Ike?" said the chief.

"I guess I'm supposed to say yes."

"Greenfield had been letting things deteriorate. I should have cut him a long time ago."

"How extensive is the net at this point?"

"Maybe a dozen active in country. Most of them are in about as bad shape as Greenfield. It's a challenge, Ike," the station chief said, staring past McWade out the smudged casement window into the gray London drizzle. "You're going to find yourself away more than you've been used to."

"That won't be a problem."

"I would think you would want to cover your comings and goings a bit more securely than you have in the past."

"Are you telling me to break it off with the girl?"

"Not at all," said the chief. "I'm only showing you the horizon."

"Will I be able to talk to Ben?"

"Of course."

"Maybe he can hold my hand on the first operation."

"Sorry," said the station chief. "Too much exposure."

"You're not saying Ben is known."

"We can't afford to have Ben compromised, in case you run into difficulties."

Whether by accident or design, Wheeler was in town at the time. McWade asked him if they could get together at the club. Wheeler surprised him by inviting him to come by his flat instead.

Wheeler's quarters turned out to be on the small side, but the address was good. In the living room every surface was crowded with exotic objects: an ivory opium pipe, gold inlaid boxes, ashtrays made from artillery shell casings, geodes and silver mugs. McWade picked up a mirror in a busy, painted frame.

"Sherlock Holmes said the mind is like an attic," said Wheeler. "If it becomes too full, one cannot retrieve what one wants. When I put an object out on display, I find that this gives me relief from the recollections associated with it. It makes for a crowded mantelpiece and a neat, untroubled mind. The only problem is that it puts all my regrets on display."

Wheeler went to the sideboard and poured drinks from crystal decanters. McWade picked up a nautilus shell and turned it in his hand. It had been cut to expose the graceful curve.

"That was given to me in Geneva just after the war," said Wheeler.

"It's a beautiful piece."

"The woman who gave it to me said it was like history, spiraling outward, as fixed as a logarithmic table. She was a Marxist."

"Your adversary?"

"There had been common interests at one point. But that had changed. I told her I thought the shell was like deception, doubling and redoubling, carrying all the weight of the past as it grows."

"She deceived you?" said McWade.

"It's rarely as clear as that," said Wheeler, handing him a glass. "I simply had to assume that she would."

"Did you love her?"

"No more than was required." He took the shell from McWade and replaced it on a shelf. "So," he said, "you are about to have an adventure."

"I'll need a new cover."

Wheeler picked up a fancy wooden box and began to manipulate its sliding panels, turning it this way and that, flicking the slides in and out with his thumbs. Within a few seconds the top came off.

"What do you keep in there?" asked McWade.

Wheeler handed it over. There was nothing inside.

"A diversion," he said. "You always want to construct a legend with as many layers as possible. And at the center . . ."

"Neat and untroubled," said McWade.

"The situation in Czechoslovakia," said Wheeler. "You'll have to be able to move about in the lower circles. Our people there are not exactly well-placed."

"So I've heard."

"Any ideas?"

"I was thinking perhaps of Rogers, international trade."

"Too obvious," said Wheeler. "How is your Czech?"

"Just passable."

"That's all right. You are not meant to be a cultured man."

"Who then?"

"Someone with a past. A man trying to escape."

"Won't that draw attention?"

"Sleight of hand," said Wheeler. He took back the box and closed it with a few lightning movements. "Draw the eye to one and pick the pocket with the other. A man with a grave weakness. To give them confidence that you are more to be disdained than feared."

91

"Drugs?"

"You have to be able to live your vice, remember. How about a woman?"

"That's not considered a weakness anymore, is it?"

"They are more puritanical than we are. Perhaps you had an unfortunate episode some years ago. Yes. The girl died. Killed herself. You drove her to it. You probably drank too much. Got a little rough. They may be watching, so you have to leave the impression that nobody would trust you. Least of all us."

"What takes me to Prague?"

"It is where the girl was born."

"I'm drawn there," said McWade.

"Compulsion to repeat. They'll understand that. A chambered nautilus."

"But how do I earn my living?"

"Something you can do anywhere. A writer perhaps."

McWade balanced his glass on his knee. It was cold through the cloth.

"That's a little high profile."

"A writer of junk," said Wheeler. "For the pulps. Under a variety of *noms de plume*."

"What kind of junk?"

"Stories. Articles. Gunplay and abusive sex. It doesn't matter. You'll write whatever anybody's willing to buy."

"Are you going to christen me?"

"I'll leave that up to you," said Wheeler. He lifted his feet to a hassock and relaxed back into the cushions of his chair.

"The clothes don't fit me too well," said McWade.

Wheeler shifted in his chair and put his hand to his collar as if it had suddenly begun to bind.

"I've never lived a legend so unpleasant," he said, "that I couldn't find the essential elements in myself. This one is easy, my friend. He is a shit to women. That's in every man."

The next day McWade went to a second-hand bookstore and searched the shelves until he found in a collection of sea stories the name he was looking for. Leggatt. Joseph Leggatt.

Over the next few weeks he worked on the role with the help of Rufus Stockwell, who was to be his backup man in Prague. Stockwell already knew the net and the city. But he wasn't going to be making any formal introductions. His job was simply to watch McWade's flanks and to show him the back way out in case the mission went bad. "Don't look for me, chum," he said. "I'll be there."

As the day of his departure approached, McWade found it more and more difficult to conceal from Jane his anxiety. He became irritated at her smallest lapses. He took the opportunity of mentioning it whenever she was late to meet him. He cut her off when she went on too long about some editor's slight. He could not tell her of his mission (she thought he was preparing for a selling tour), but he wanted her somehow to appreciate the stakes he was playing for. And so he found himself putting their very relationship at risk, as if to say: What I'm about to do means as much to me as you.

He was surprised by Jane's reaction. As he escalated his demands, she met him with an attempt at genuine empathy that was all the more touching because he knew that it was doomed to fall short. It was as if she sensed what was missing between them, and it drew her like a void. Only much later did he realize who had really come into play during the last days before his mission to Prague. Wheeler had been right. McWade had already found the beginnings of Joseph Leggatt deep within himself.

He made the crossing by train. When the border guards came through, he felt the way he had the first time he had fired a rifle at another man. Even though he had the sanction of his state to do this thing and call it duty, still as he moved across the frontier under Leggatt's false papers, it was as if some profound, universal law were being violated. And when the train reached the outskirts of Prague and he got his first glimpse of the city from the window, it was a medieval vision of punishment. Under the gray, reclining sky, the spires poked up like a bed of nails.

The city that presented itself to him as he passed beneath the train station's faded red banners bore little resemblance to the place he had come to expect as he drilled with Stockwell on the routes of contact and evasion. To reach the hotel he had to pass through some of the older sections of town, and he was not prepared for the gothic menace of their charm. The quaint streets pressed in on him; the winding cobblestoned ways became a premonition of flight and pursuit.

He passed right by his destination at first. It was a nondescript building, and the doorway was only marked with a small, corroded metal plate. The lobby was long and narrow, bare except for a few worn chairs at the far end. The walls might once have been paneled from the look of the trim, but now they were covered with an accretion of paint. A stairway rose on the right, wide enough to accommodate six abreast to the first landing, and the steps were covered with a worn oriental rug.

An elderly clerk in a tattered sweater stood behind the counter across from the staircase. McWade greeted him stiffly and offered to pay in hard currency. The desk clerk demurred, showing no interest in the nationality of man or money. But he did accept payment in advance in the flimsy bills that McWade had purchased at the official rate at the train station. Then he handed McWade a key, which was attached by a short chain to a heavy piece of metal the shape of a bell to prevent guests from comfortably carrying it off.

The upper floors were more rundown than the lobby, the hallways narrow and shadowy. McWade ran his hand over the rough walls until he found a light switch. When he pushed it, he was plunged into total darkness. So he pushed it again and then moved from door to door squinting at the numbers until he found the one that matched his key. The door opened onto a shabby little cubicle whose window looked out over a patched expanse of roofs. Their angle was steep, and they did not look all that sturdy, but it still gave him some comfort to know that he had one possible avenue of retreat.

The only furnishings in the room were an iron bed, a straight-backed chair and a rickety desk. The walls were covered with paper that had to date back to before the war. Water spots bloomed near the ceiling like something alive.

McWade opened his typewriter and set it up, placing his traveling bottle of Scotch next to it. When he lay down on the bed, he kept on his coat and stared at the ceiling, the typewriter, the bottle of whiskey that bisected the angle made by his feet. He did not sleep. Even on ambush in the jungle it was easier to nod off. There, he knew who he was looking for and who was looking for him. Here, he wasn't even sure about himself. Soon it was the dinner hour, time to give Joseph Leggatt his debut.

Not far from the hotel he found a tavern and restaurant that looked about right. From the outside it was plain and uninviting. Inside, the air hung heavy with the smell of beer and frying meat. The waiters all wore short black jackets and white aprons beneath that looked as though they might have been cut from tablecloths that had become too stained to launder clean. When McWade ordered a drink, it was brought by a youngish woman with hard features and a wary eye. She took payment after every round.

He drank enough to give Leggatt's boorishness a reason then forced himself to make advances toward the barmaid. She did not rebuff him until the manager intervened.

The sausage tasted better than it looked. The whiskey was raw in his throat. He did not state his name, but only because nobody gave him the opportunity. If others came inquiring, he wanted to be remembered. Just to make sure, when he rose to leave, he made a point of tipping over a chair.

The next morning, it was no effort to look like a man of whom nothing would be expected. The whiskey had not been good, and he awakened with a dry mouth and pounding head. He hauled on his pants and put shoes on his sockless feet, then padded down the hallway to the common bathroom, which smelled of mildew and urine. In the little, black-streaked mirror over the rusty washbasin, his eyes were bloodshot. He splashed water over his face and hair. It fell back to the basin gray from the sooty air. Suddenly the door opened and a young woman appeared.

"Can't you see?" he snapped in Czech. "It's occupied."

"Excuse, please," she replied.

He grunted and closed the door, engaging the latch. After a moment he thought better of it and swung the door open again. But she was gone. Leggatt would have made something of such an encounter. He cursed himself as he emptied his bladder. Too damned slow on the uptake. The toilet made a rude noise when he flushed it. Somebody pounded on the wall.

"What do you want me to do, eh?" he shouted. "Piss into the sink?" That was better. Leggatt scowled back at him from the glass.

Later, when he went downstairs, the woman was in the lobby. This time he gave her a good looking over, and she was not so bad. Nice little body. Decent ankles. He gave her a nod as he left, and she regarded him with a certain amount of curiosity.

The Charles Bridge was closed to traffic to protect the ornate stonework from the pounding of wheels. Any tourist might have been expected to go see it. The air was wet, but not enough for an umbrella. He cupped his hands and lighted a cheap cigar. The smoke was harsh, and it made him cough. He leaned on the cold railing and shivered as he looked out into the haze over the river, footsteps crossing behind his back. He did not know who was the spotter: the butcher in his bloody whites, the sullen teenaged boy, the old lady with a babushka who caught his eye from a distance then looked away. He held a magazine in his hand where it could be seen. Several people glanced at it, but that meant nothing. An American publication was an oddity here. When the appointed time had passed, he returned the way he had come.

For the rest of the morning he wandered. The mist turned to rain, and he ducked into an arcade. A kiosk inside sold greasy sausages in paper; the smell of spice and flesh did not whet his appetite. The shops did not interest him either until a window full of toys caught his eye.

McWade went inside and pointed to familiar items on the shelves behind the counter. From a distance they looked like lovely Scandinavian woodcrafted vehicles and the durables of Fisher-Price, things his niece and nephew might like. But when the shopkeeper brought them out, he was disappointed. They turned out to be shoddy imitations. The wood of the toy train made in the GDR was soft and the paint sloppily applied. The eyes of a doll almost closed as the shopkeeper tipped it backward, but not quite all the way. One lid stuck in a ridiculous baby wink. He thanked the woman and left.

Here and there he made inquiries about the family he was supposed to be looking for. Nobody had much information. This was no surprise, since the family was chosen precisely because all its members were dead. But one kindly old fellow in a shoe repair shop did show some sympathy, and so McWade told him part of his story: the girl who had perished, the message she had left for him. He did not need to confess his guilt.

When he returned to the hotel, he picked up the key at the desk and, because it might be expected of a man making inquiries around town, asked if there had been any messages.

"Those who stay here do not often receive calls," said the clerk. "Of course there was the girl."

"The girl?"

"Another guest. She asked your name."

"Interesting," said McWade.

"Better to try the streets, Mr Leggatt."

"What room is she in?"

"Number 42. But at the moment she is out."

McWade handed the man a small bill for his trouble.

"Tell her Mr Leggatt would be pleased to make her acquaintance," he said. "By the way, what time is the parade?"

The man looked up at the clock behind him.

"You'll make it if you hurry."

"What is the best way?"

The clerk drew a little map on the back of a piece of scrap paper. McWade watched but did not listen. He knew the route and exactly where he was to stand.

"Have you ever been to one of our spectacles?" asked the clerk.

97

"It is my first time in Prague."

"Everyone turns out to see who is on the podium and who is not," said the clerk. "Unfortunately, my job makes me exempt from this solemn patriotic privilege."

McWade left him and walked quickly toward the designated intersection. He pushed his way to a spot within sight of the reviewing stand. Everything appeared stark and preternaturally clear, the way it did in combat when the rounds came hissing in close and the field of battle flashed with the light of fear. Even in the surge of the crowd he saw faces as singularities, every one of them a possible threat.

Seven old men stood on the platform, seven overcoats, seven mufflers, seven matching hats. On the street, wave after wave of soldiers marched past, followed by artillery pieces and tanks. Banners flashed crimson against the sky. Whenever the seven lifted their arms, the audience gave a rough approximation of a cheer.

The parade was almost finished when an old woman with a babushka reached his side. She was one of the people who had passed him on the bridge. Sloppy tradecraft. She should not have risked two such contacts in a single day.

"When will they let us cross?" she said.

"Are you in such a hurry, Grandma?" he said.

"My bag is heavy," she said, lifting it slowly to her waist.

"Let me hold it for you."

The seven men looked out over them with eyes that were blank with power. Who else was watching, lining them up in the crosshairs of their sights? McWade was quick in slipping the envelope into the bag. It carried an introduction and further instructions as well as some money. Several policemen stood within a few yards of them, gazing at the self-propelled guns.

When the last of the parade had passed, the woman took the bag back from him.

"Here," she said, drawing something from her pocket. "Have a candy for your kindness."

She pressed it into his hand and then shuffled away.

"Good day, Grandma," he said, unwrapping the paper

and popping the bitter chocolate into his mouth. Then he slipped the paper through a slit in his pocket into the liner of his coat. He did not see Stockwell. The crowd was full of invisible men.

After stopping off for a beer to settle his nerves, he returned to his room and took out his typewriter. Six pages of a story had been prepared in advance. It was about a man and a glamorous woman stranded in a jungle after a plane crash. Her high fashion clothes turned out to be biodegradable, and the principal element of suspense concerned how long it would take before they rotted through and exposed her beautiful breasts to his longing gaze.

McWade threaded a fresh sheet onto the roller and typed a few memorized lines. Then he fished the candy wrapper from the liner of his coat and spread it out next to the typewriter. The letters and numbers were written in a steady hand, surely not the grandmother's. He deciphered the message in his head and then, using a trashy paperback he had brought along as his template, he coded it into the next several lines of text. This did not make for a very good paragraph. But it fit well enough with the others. He was satisfied with the way the seams were joined.

He put the wrapper into his mouth and chewed it until it was soft enough to swallow. Then he wrote a few more pages from the outline prepared for him in London, stacked up the manuscript and returned the typewriter to its battered case.

There was a train out of Prague that evening, but as much as he wanted to catch it, this was not the script for his exit. He was to wait through a second night unless he had cause to think his cover had been blown, in which case he was to signal Stockwell, who would lead the emergency retreat. Of course, he had no reason to suspect anything. The discomfort he felt was just the stomach's response to danger and all the unfamiliar fare. And now he had to subject it to dinner again, one last appearance for the invisible men.

As he reached the staircase, he heard a door open behind him.

"Luck strikes twice," he said, the alien words awkward on his tongue.

It was the woman, dressed now to show a bit more leg.

"In a better place than this morning." She seemed shy about it, as if she was forcing herself to be a little bold.

"I barked at you," he said. "Morning is not my best time."

"Evening is better?"

"Maybe I can make amends."

"You don't have to."

"At least introduce myself."

"Yes," she said. "I am Zofia Medera."

"And I'm Joseph Leggatt," he said. "But you know that already, don't you?"

"Excuse me?" she said.

"The desk clerk downstairs," he said. "You were asking after me."

She looked away.

"It's all right," he said. "If you hadn't asked about me, I would have asked about you."

"I do not know why I did," she said. She was smiling. McWade was surprised how easily Leggatt found words that worked on her.

"Were you on your way to dinner?" he asked.

"Yes."

"It is a shame for a pretty young woman to eat alone."

He took her gloved hand and noticed a slight tear in the fabric. He brought his lips to the place where her flesh showed through. She did not try hard to pull away.

"You make me a little afraid, Mr Leggatt," she said.

"But it pleases you," he said. "You will join me."

"I suppose there is no harm."

He let her hand drop as they moved to the stairs, but she stayed close enough to let him know he had established something. For McWade it was as if Leggatt had passed a test.

"You are English," she said when they had reached the street.

"American by birth," he said. "But rootless now."

"That seems very sad."

"Freedom," he said.

She had some ideas about where to go to dinner, but she let him lead her to the place he had gone the night before.

The manager gave him a look as they entered. But he need not have worried. McWade had something to drink, but not enough to set him off again. With Zofia his manner was attentive, even charming.

They talked about the parade, the crowd. Though it was not required of her, being transient, she too had gone to watch. In her village they had only seen that many war machines once before, and that was different. That was 1968.

"What brings you to Prague?" he asked.

"I am looking for a job."

"I thought maybe it was a man."

"Oh, no, Mr Leggatt," she said.

"I imagined an unsatisfying affair, one you had to get away from."

She put her knife and fork down gently on the plate and gazed at the swirls of gravy and grease.

"There was a boy," she said. "He was so young. A child. But that was not the real reason. I could have stayed."

She was quite young herself. Her dark eyes rested easily on him, as if she did not yet fully appreciate the danger of men. Except for her olive complexion with its hint of the gypsy, she could have been a girl from Manitee Bay. Not a farmgirl, though, for her wrists and arms seemed too fragile to have done heavy lifting in the barn. But just as fresh and open as the girls of his boyhood, the girls of sun and air.

After she finished eating, she took out her pocketbook. He would have none of that. He paid the check and told her he had a bottle of good whiskey back in the room.

"Scotch," he said. "The real thing. I bet you've never tasted it."

"You travel well provided for," she said.

"I like my vices," he said.

Once they were in his room, he poured two tumblers. Then he sprawled on the bed. She took off her coat and sat down sideways on the chair in front of the desk.

101

"What is this?" she asked, touching the stack of papers.

"A story I am working on for a magazine."

"What is it about?"

"Do you read English?"

"No."

"I will read it to you."

The words were all simple enough, but his Czech was not smooth. He had to ask her help on some passages, and she seemed embarrassed at the coarse phrases he drew from her.

As he came to the paragraph that hid his message to the Nest, he read on without hesitating – the woman's body, the man's growing lust, the menace of the jungle stripping away all inhibition. And when he reached the place where the writing stopped, he arranged the manuscript and placed it square with the corner of the desk then wet his throat with drink.

"It is a very erotic story," she said. "How will it end?"

"I haven't decided," he said. "It all depends on the woman."

"She would be afraid."

"And excited," he said. Leggatt was perfectly sure of himself. But at the same time, from somewhere deep came the doubt. She was too easy. She had gone out of her way to push herself on him. She could not be what she said she was.

"I'd better be leaving now," she said. "Thank you for the whiskey. It was lovely."

"Have another," he said, rising.

"Thank you, but I really should go."

"Stay," he said. The force of it stopped her. "Come here."

She hesitated, but then she obeyed him. Leggatt did not have to move a step.

"It isn't right," she said.

McWade almost overcame Leggatt and released her. It was not so much the infidelity as the bitter way with which he knew it would be carried out. But before he had time to back away, Zofia Madera reached up and touched his face.

"I need to get ready," she said.

"I will do that."

He drew off her clothing slowly, touching the sensitive flesh. When she was naked, he guided her onto the bed and stood there, still fully dressed. A chill went down her flesh, and it thrilled him.

"Warm me," she said.

He leaned over and stroked her, surprised to find that she was ready for him.

"Now," she said. "Please hurry."

He was excruciatingly slow with his own clothes. And when he finally reached her, she arched against him.

"You're no farmgirl," he said as he entered her. "You're a whore."

"No."

She heaved up, as if to throw him off. But he would not let her. Instead, he caught her hands where they pushed against his chest and stretched them high over her head, pinning them there as she struggled.

"Who are you?" he demanded.

"Please stop."

But he did not until he could tell that she was at the edge. Then, when he was in complete control of himself and of her, suddenly he withdrew.

She clung to him, tried to get him on his back. He would not allow it. Instead he pushed her down to where she did not want to go.

"Show me what you want," he said.

"I can't."

"Then get out."

She yielded to him, and it was clear that she knew exactly what she was doing. It did not matter who she was or where she came from; she had been to this place before.

She tried to finish him that way, but he withdrew again and moved above her. She let out a tiny cry. He did not allow her to help. He needed to take his pleasure now by force, so he locked her arms behind her and held her fast.

This was not simply Joseph Leggatt, working out his compulsion for a dead woman in anger and remorse. The disgust he felt was not only because Anthony Rogers had broken faith. The bedsprings bucked beneath them; the sheets hissed, burning, against their skin. And he could almost hear the little wooden slides of an empty magic box flicking this way and that.

Later, he awakened and saw that she was up looking at the pages of his story again, studying the raw, alien words she had said she did not comprehend. He closed his eyes again so she would not see him watching.

In the morning he told her he was leaving the country. She touched his shoulder and asked him to stay. But he said this was not possible. It was remarkable that she wanted more of what he had given her, that she did not seem at all hurt or ashamed. He felt a confusing rush of emotion. If he gave in to it, he knew he would end up trying to make it up to her, to introduce her to the side of him that was not Leggatt, could never be. She must go, he said, because he needed time alone to finish his work. She tried to entice him, but it was no use. He had to cast her out.

The end of the story came easily and inevitably, the man and woman making love before they died. On his way to board the train from Prague, McWade posted the manuscript to an accommodation address in London as a hedge against trouble at the border. But there was no trouble. His papers held up, and as he crossed back over to the West, he felt as if he had been unjustly acquitted of a crime.

When he reached Amsterdam, he made contact with Stockwell at the place they had arranged. The cover was thin, a chance meeting of old friends in a busy public park. It would not have fooled anyone's mother, but if somebody was on their tail now, it meant that their legends had already failed.

Stockwell was feeding crumbs to the birds as he waited, getting them to perch shyly on his knee. McWade greeted him expansively. Stockwell flung the last of the scraps in a wide wedge on the lawn. The birds wheeled up away from him and then settled down again.

"Leggatt, you old prick you."

They embraced, slapping one another's backs.

"What the hell are you doing here?" said McWade.

"Passing through," said Stockwell. And that much was true. He had another assignment away from the Nest, and this was why they had arranged the rendezvous on the Continent to exchange notes.

"Let's have a drink," said McWade. "You still drink, don't you?"

"Does a bear shit in the woods?" said Stockwell.

Of course it did. That was one of the ways you stalked it.

As they walked, distant now from any intruding ear, Stockwell congratulated him on his success.

"They weren't on us," he said. "We came and went like the wind."

"I wasn't even sure you were there," said McWade.

"You want me to give you a description of the dolly you took to dinner?"

"You saw her?"

"Quick work, chum. She wasn't half bad."

"She came on to me," said McWade. "I had to stay in character."

"You don't have to apologize."

McWade stopped. They were at the center of a wide, rolling lawn now, a hundred yards from anyone.

"Did you recognize her?" McWade asked.

"You got in her pants, didn't you?" said Stockwell. "Hell, just go take the shots."

They moved on again, hands in pockets, kicking an occasional stone as they went.

"She showed an unnatural interest in my writing," said McWade.

"That junk?"

"I found her looking through the manuscript."

"You smell a honey trap," said Stockwell. "Well, relax. What counts is getting away with your dick."

McWade stayed only one night in Amsterdam. Stockwell wanted to hit the bordellos, but McWade declined. It wasn't required now. Stockwell seemed disappointed, and McWade felt cleaner somehow.

But when he reached London and heard Jane's voice again, he had to face up to what he had done. She reached him by phone at his flat, where he had gone to drop off his

105

bags and get out of Leggatt's shoddy clothes. She caught him while he was still half in costume, and as they talked he struggled to get into a proper pair of pants.

"It was a dreadful trip," he said. "Money's tight. Damned dollar and American interest rates. Nobody wants to put up a nickel on the come anymore."

"I missed you," she said.

"I just this minute walked in the door."

"It wasn't an accusation, Tony."

"Accommodations in Brussels got all screwed up. I ended up staying in somebody's spare room."

"It must have been a trial."

He realized he was overdoing it, but the story he made up was a kind of justification, as if to say: Don't think I enjoyed myself. Whatever I might have done, it was as terrible for me as it was for you.

"I'm afraid I'm going to have my work cut out for me now," he said.

"Will I get to see you?"

"Our pricing is all wrong. Somehow I'm going to have to get the head office to see that."

"I almost got killed, Tony," she said softly.

"I'm sorry?"

"It wasn't just to get your attention," she said. "It's true. I had to be evacuated under fire."

"Somebody was shooting at you?"

"The camp I was visiting came under Israeli attack."

"My God, Jane. Are you all right?"

"The jets came in low. The noise, Tony. I'd never heard such noise."

"Look, I'll come over as soon as I can. Maybe we can have dinner or something. Think of a place."

"Here is fine."

"Look, I'm sorry. I didn't know."

"I've been calling every half hour," she said. "I got back last night. And I've needed you so."

He drew back from that.

"Give me a couple of hours. Should I call?"

"I'll be here. Some of my pictures have moved already on the AP wire."

"I imagine Reynolds fixed that up for you."

"It wasn't a favour," she said. "They were good. And so was the money I got for them."

"Then I suppose it was all worth it."

"Don't be that way, Tony. It was frightening. It really was."

"Maybe I'm envious."

"I'd rather you be jealous."

"Maybe that, too. A man can't tell what comes into a woman's head at a time like that."

"I held the thought," she said.

McWade was not sure whether it was he or Leggatt who rewarded her with a lusty laugh.

Back at the Nest, he gave the station chief a fill on what had happened in Prague. He was hesitant when he came to the encounter with the woman. But the chief was altogether pleased with the success of his contact with the existing net, and he may even have seen some possibilities for Zofia Madera as well.

"You played it the way you had to," he said. In the field of intelligence, necessity was always a complete defense.

But Wheeler was more critical. He leaned on his hands at the edge of the desk and shook his head as McWade told the story.

"It isn't melodrama," he said. "You didn't need to wail and beat your breast."

"I didn't write the part."

"I'm not talking about the woman in the hotel room," Wheeler said. "I'm talking about your search for the Povich girl's kin. Don't you think you might have overdone it?"

"Leggatt's a guilty drunk," said McWade. "He's not exactly the soul of understatement."

Wheeler sat down and turned to a cabinet beside the desk.

"Make them work for what they get," he said as he spun the dial of the lock. "Let them find out your story for themselves. They're more likely to believe you if you hide the things you want them to know." He opened the heavy steel door, rolled a drawer open and withdrew a box of cigars.

"I wanted to establish my motive," said McWade.

Wheeler handed McWade a cigar and then held the lighter out to him.

"You should have left them puzzled," he said. "Like a child who is convinced he is slow-witted, they distrust anything they understand too easily."

"You're saying I made a botch of it," said McWade, turning the tip of the cigar in the flame.

"Perhaps they will think a trained man would be more shrewd," Wheeler said. "Only an amateur would go around telling merchants his life story."

The cigar was rich on McWade's tongue after the cheap ones he had been smoking.

"It's a subtle craft," Wheeler went on, "this life in the theater."

After leaving him, McWade stopped off at the Czech section to look at the albums. He described the woman to Frank Lemke, who had been watching Eastern Europe from safely across the Channel for two decades.

"Doesn't set off any bells," said Lemke, handing over the book. "Young bird, eh? She might be new."

"Clever woman," said McWade. "Knew her business."

"That good was she?"

"Of course, I was a little bit distracted."

"Hellish thing," said Lemke, "to have so much on your mind."

McWade looked through the photographs, page after page. None was even close.

"I'll write up a description," said McWade, handing back the book. "Maybe somebody will get a line on her."

"It's bloody cold out there," said Lemke. "I understand."

That evening as he rode the Underground to Jane's flat, he could not seem to pull himself together. Too many things had changed at once, on her side as well as his. Anthony Rogers was as distant from her adventures as a man could be and still read the same morning papers. But Leggatt understood her feelings perfectly and knew how to take advantage of them. As for McWade, all he knew was regret.

As soon as she let him inside her door, she threw her arms around his neck and kissed him.

"*Newsweek* is going to run my colour pictures," she said. "The cable came just after I talked to you. Isn't it wonderful? Champagne and caviar all around."

"Do they pay that well?"

She let go of him and stepped back.

"I didn't even ask," she said.

"You didn't tell me you were going to be in danger," he said. It came out sounding as wounded as if she had done to him what he had done to her.

"You were so preoccupied," she said.

He thought he heard an edge of resentment.

"Next time," he said. "I'll have to assume the worst."

"I'll lie, you know."

"And I'll see through it."

"My cunning lover," she said.

Then she led him to the couch and sat next to him, one leg tucked up under her on the cushions.

"Tell me about your trip," she said.

"My boss thought I accomplished more than I thought I did," he said.

"Then we both have something to celebrate."

"Separation," he said.

"Tony," she said. "Please don't."

"And the pleasure of reunion."

She kissed him and turned into his arms. Her body slid smoothly beneath the silken wrapper.

"It takes some getting used to," he said, lifting her back away from him. "Your thrilling new life."

"Am I too eager?" she said, but lightly now. "A soldier coming back randy from the wars."

"There's time."

"When the jets came in," she said, her hand moving flat above the cushions, like a shadow across the landscape, "they drove off every other feeling. I think it was the purest sensation I've ever known."

"Fear," he said.

"Only afterwards. At the time it was a feeling of absolute clarity."

"The mind works that way," he said. "That's how it protects itself."

"You do understand, don't you?" she said.

"From what I've read."

All of a sudden the lies seemed to cross with the truth. She leaned over and kissed him again. And when they made love that night, he was hard and demanding. She rose to him, and he met her. Or Leggatt did. It made no particular difference who.

9

It did not take long before McWade began to fear Leggatt's success. The guise of his flaws became a strong force in McWade's life and work. Within a matter of months he was well on the way toward rebuilding the Czechoslovakian net. He found and isolated the quislings, recruited new faces and put the ancient retainers on pension. One of the first who had to go was his initial contact in Prague, the old woman in the babushka who had met him at the military parade. It quickly became clear to him that she had lost the vital sense of fear and was endangering everyone else in the net. To get her to retire quietly, McWade had to be very firm. He was not exactly ruthless; for a man like Leggatt ruthless is an awfully demanding word.

McWade's trips to the Continent meant that he spent a good deal of time apart from Jane. He would be away for weeks on end, and when he returned, as often as not, she would be off somewhere herself, covering the strife that she had come rather cheerfully to call her beat. By now she had become quite skilled at getting in and out of trouble spots. But when she talked about it, he could tell she was holding back. He yearned to boast to her of the frontiers he had penetrated. But that was Leggatt's life. It had to be hidden. Whenever he slipped and showed something he shouldn't, Jane responded to him, and he struggled to push his double back out of sight. It was as if McWade's old self had become the legend and Leggatt the man behind the mask.

Whenever he was in London, he tried to recover the simplicity of their early days. They often went to the theater and afterwards stopped by the Fleet Street pubs, where old associates like Bob Reynolds and Tom Segal regaled them with tales of adventure and told her how radiant she looked. She told them she owed it all to Tony

Rogers, but he knew better. It was not predictability that made a woman glow. She only shone when Leggatt had made an appearance in their bed.

McWade's trips to the other side were far less complicated than his time at home. At least in the field Leggatt's sins were in the nature of duty, women with access to information because of the jobs they held or the other beds they shared. The only one who had no clear operational purpose was Zofia Medera, and she was the one who obsessed him.

Whenever he returned to Prague in the months following his first visit, he had made a point of trying to find her. He inquired at the hotel where they had met, but to no avail. The address she had written down on the register was not in the countryside where she had said she grew up. And when he went to check it out, he found that it belonged to a baroque church with hundreds of stone angels glaring down from the facade.

If the invisible men had been following his inquiries, they could have easily concluded that Leggatt simply wanted to renew his pleasure or deepen his shame. The real motive, of course, was as unsentimental as the stories placed in pulp magazines by Leggatt's literary agents in the Nest. He wanted to confirm that Zofia Medera had been on assignment, just as he had been, that what they both did had nothing to do with love. It had been a pure act of war.

Meanwhile, the dissonance between the two sides of his life was becoming intolerable. When he was with Jane, he became jealous of Leggatt. And she became bored. He could not tell her what it was that made him so distracted. As far as she knew, the stakes he played for were no more than a tick up or down on a balance sheet, nothing that could not be measured either in dollars or pounds at the prevailing rate of exchange.

Then McWade saw an opportunity to rid himself of his double for good. A retirement in the Nest left an opening at the head of the desk that had responsibility for operations throughout the Eastern Bloc. McWade's principal disadvantage was his lack of experience in counterintelligence, but on the plus side, he was on good paper with Langley thanks to his recruitment of a colonel in the Czech service.

That mission had gone off with textbook precision. Leggatt had met with the man several times in third countries, arranged for him to be vetted and interrogated by the house skeptics and then sent him back doubled. But then suddenly the colonel passed an emergency message through Milos Norakova, his cutout, that he wanted out, and fast. He had reason to believe that he'd been sold by somebody at the Nest.

McWade had arranged an exfiltration route in case Leggatt ever got in trouble in Prague, and he sent word back to the colonel through Milos to make his way one week hence to a spot along the Austrian border where he had purchased for hard currency and the favors of a soft woman an option on the inattention of a guard.

The colonel made his exit without a hitch. But when they debriefed him, he did not have any specific information about who inside the Nest might have been turned. All he knew for sure was that a certain Georg Havel had been deployed to the Czech Embassy in London. There was only one reason for posting a man like Havel: he must have had a line on somebody.

"Probably a Brit," said the station chief. "I'm afraid you may have overreacted, Colonel. We don't tell our allies who we own in Prague. Thrice burned and so on. They've had a pretty sorry track record. It was a Brit who coined the term 'mole', you know. From sad experience."

The colonel persisted. They wouldn't use Havel against an Englishman, he said. The man's father had for many years served in the Czech delegation in Washington, and so Havel had been educated in the States like a native. He'd taken a degree in American studies at Yale, the colonel said gravely. His mission in life was to penetrate the CIA.

"Well, that would be quite a problem for us," said the chief, making a show of amusement. "Now that you've bolted, how much time would you say we have to catch the inside man before he bolts, too?"

The colonel paused for a moment and then simply looked at his watch.

It took the stalker team several days to locate Havel. At first he seemed to have vanished, and there was speculation that he had already made his exit. Then he reappeared at the Embassy. He did not set foot outside again until the morning he went to Heathrow and took a flight east, and there wasn't even enough evidence to have the Brits put a hold on him at the gate.

"He was out of pocket long enough to warn his contact," said McWade.

"It's possible," said the station chief.

"That means the inside man is probably going to split, too."

"At least if he runs we'll know who he is," said the chief.

"Let me try to stop him," said McWade.

"Go ahead, Ike. Make yourself indispensable."

"I thought I already was."

The station chief tamped down his pipe and shook his head. He was not a man who handed out compliments freely, because even encouragement had a price.

"Counterintelligence is a hard business," he said. "Look at Ernest Fisherman."

"Never met the man," said McWade.

"He'd tell you not to make any assumptions. They'll blind you."

"If it were us," said McWade, "we'd roll up the whole net at the first whiff of compromise."

"They do not share our sentiments, I'm afraid."

"Maybe Havel was trying to milk the last drop out of him."

"Or else a mission of reassurance. The colonel didn't have access to the inside man's identity. They would be more than justified in concluding that Havel was the only one blown."

"You're saying they pulled him so he wouldn't compromise others," said McWade.

"A source inside the Agency isn't somebody they'd want to lose. Bring him out and they'd just have to pay him a pension and listen to him squawk about the way he's being treated."

"Did I mention that the colonel wants to speak with you about the heat in his flat?" said McWade.

"See what you have to look forward to as you move up?" said the chief.

"I'm sure there are compensations."

McWade's first step was to run through the roster of the Nest to determine who was out of town during the period between the colonel's departure from Prague and the evening the stalkers picked up Havel returning to the Embassy. The length of Havel's disappearance made it seem likely that the meeting had taken place outside London.

The list of absentees from the Nest was not long: Mike Sanders, Robbie Duquense, Fred Tapper and Sharon Gilley. Discreetly, McWade checked into each of them and determined that they had all be on trips planned well in advance of the colonel's message that he wanted out.

"That leaves you without a suspect," said the chief.

"I haven't played out every string yet."

"What is it you see exactly?"

"Same thing you do," said McWade, meeting his eyes across the desk, "a man who is trying too hard."

He was not ready to elaborate, but while he was looking over the roster for unexplained absences, he had stumbled upon an unexplained presence.

Sidney Dorsen had been due to go on a vacation a few days after the colonel crossed the border. But he had cancelled his holiday at the last minute and gone to some length to create a paper trail establishing his continuous attendance in London.

Dorsen had been in the Agency a good deal longer than McWade, recruited straight out of Columbia during the time when the course in the humanities at certain colleges was a kind of trade school for the secret life. He had been posted in various spots around the world, most recently Bonn, specializing in economic intelligence, a regular growth industry thanks to the oil cartel. At the Nest he had continued to work on the analysis side, the consummate desk rider, bright but not especially cunning, a man without a flair. There were plenty of men who had more to

115

sell than Dorsen did, but he was still in a position to do some damage.

McWade had worked with him from time to time when one of the members of his net came up with something of a financial nature that needed massaging. He had never been too careful about Dorsen; there hadn't seemed to be any reason. McWade had always found him pleasant and methodical, an individual with steel habits who was not likely to change his loyalties any more than his travel plans.

It was a simple matter for McWade to establish that Dorsen's work had not required him to cancel his holiday in France, where he went each year to sample the wines and replenish his cellar. In fact, he had just finished a major project on the effect of OPEC's price increases on Poland's balance of payments. He had booked the trip through one of the Nest's vetted travel agents and had lost a substantial amount in deposits when he decided to postpone it. The reason he gave, in a note to personnel that was not strictly speaking required, was that a friend with whom he had planned to travel on the Continent had been called away on business. When McWade ran down the inns involved, he found that Dorsen had always taken single accommodations and that no one else had parallel reservations.

But these were minor inconsistencies, not a bill of particulars. So McWade began to track back over Dorsen's movements. The cancellation of the trip had come on a Monday, the day after the colonel disappeared in Prague. Subsequently, Dorsen had made his whereabouts known at all times. There were an uncommon number of business dinners throughout the period, all documented through items on his expense account. In fact there was a record somewhere in the files for every day except the Sunday before Georg Havel reappeared in London. At first this shook McWade's confidence. If Dorsen were the inside man, this was a time for which he would be most interested in having an alibi. Then McWade discovered that Dorsen had gone out of his way to account for that day on the calendar as well.

Tod Holtz was the dayside duty officer on weekends at

the Nest. McWade called on him one quiet Saturday and asked him at the outset to promise he would hold the nature of the inquiry in confidence. A thing like this could ruin a man, he said. You see, questions had been raised about Dorsen's sexual inclinations.

"Which direction?" asked Holtz.

"It's a very delicate thing," said McWade.

"I'd never have guessed old Sidney was a pile driver," said Holtz. "But why come to me? I'm a married man."

"It might be a case of mistaken identity," said McWade. "Somebody reported seeing him in a compromising position in a leather bar in Paris on October 26. Before going any further I wanted to make sure he wasn't here in London that day."

Holtz opened a drawer and pulled out a sheaf of papers. "I think maybe old Sidney's manhood just got a reprieve," he said. Each sheet had a date on the top and a list of names below it. "Sure. Here it is. I got a message from him that day."

"What kind of message?"

"He apparently called just after I went off duty. I found it on the machine when I played the tape the next morning, but I remember that when I ran into him in the office, he told me to forget about it."

"Happily for him, you didn't."

"He said he had called to see if anything had developed at the OPEC meeting over the weekend. He was sitting on a report and getting worried he might have to update it. Case of the nerves, he said. I remember thinking that if all he had to worry about is whether he'd have to rewrite a few paragraphs, he must be a pretty lucky guy."

"I guess he is," said McWade.

"Why?"

"He didn't call from Paris, did he?"

"He left his home number."

"Who else did you hear from on the 26th?"

"The usual shit. Guys with lines out who wanted to make sure nobody was calling May Day. Section chiefs covering their asses. And, of course, the anal compulsives who call in with a number every time they go out for a pint."

117

"Any peculiar calls?"

"Pining queens asking for Sidney, you mean?"

"Wrong numbers. Fishing expeditions."

"Just one. A little before I went off duty. But nothing like the week before when some jerk kept calling and hanging up. Just around the time I was trying to clean things up to leave. Must have rung me up a half a dozen times. Made me late getting home to the kids."

It was at this point that McWade got permission to secure Dorsen's phone records from the Brits. Dorsen lived a fair distance outside London, so the printout had a record of charges for all calls to the Nest. And on it McWade found what he hoped he would: several calls to Holtz's number on the Sunday previous, but not a one on the 26th.

"The week before he was checking out Holtz's schedule, preparing an alibi for his meeting with Havel," McWade said when he laid it all out to the station chief. "He wanted to be able to get his call on the answering machine as early as possible so nobody would know he had been away all day at his rendezvous. But he had to be sure Holtz had gone off duty, because he didn't want to run the risk of a return call. You see, he didn't make the call on the 26th from home. He made it from wherever he had gone to see Havel off."

"You're way beyond the data," said the chief. "Maybe he was just down the street at a pub or with some lovely having tea."

"I can't prove he's the inside man," said McWade, "but I can prove that he went to considerable lengths to prove that he wasn't."

The chief lighted his pipe, and a cloud of heavy Turkish smoke rose before him. He followed it up to the ceiling with his eyes.

"It's worth working him," he said finally. "But I'm afraid the Czechos aren't going to risk contact again right away."

"No. But Dorsen might," said McWade. "I want you assign him to a project with me."

"You want to run a game on him."

"Give him a look at something and see what he does with it."

"You have something in mind?"

"Young Milos Norakova has been wanting to bolt through the same channel the colonel used. He's convinced that Prague's in such a state about the colonel's defection that it's only a matter of time before they bring him down."

The station chief put his pipe in an ashtray and leaned forward across the desk. "I would hate to have to use live bait," he said.

When the conversation was over, McWade wrote a memo to file which was as fair to the gist of the station chief's remarks as such documents usually are. It said the chief had agreed to the reassignment and had expressed certain reservations about how to set the trap. But he had not denied permission. Silence was almost as good as consent.

It took several weeks to line up all the elements and give Dorsen time to settle into his new position. Meantime, Jane was between assignments, and so McWade was able to spend every evening with her. He wanted it to be a prelude to the better times ahead, but it did not work out that way. Every detail of the setup obsessed him as he let Dorsen discover that somebody else was going to cross the Czech frontier and where. He took pains to make Dorsen think the Brits had gotten wind of the plan so that he would not be afraid that when it was compromised, the process of elimination would leave him out there all alone.

Meanwhile, as McWade elaborated the deception step by step, Leggatt began taking over the operation. It was Leggatt who did the cold and ruthless plotting of the trap, Leggatt who spoke the lies to Dorsen, Leggatt whom McWade counted on to have the selfish drive to carry it through to the end.

At home with Jane, though, McWade submitted completely to the discipline of his trade. Leggatt was banished, except when he watched over their lovemaking and ridiculed him for not having the nerve to push her past the point of resistance.

119

"I don't know what's wrong with us," Jane said.

"Overworked. Too damned busy to relax properly," said McWade. "It'll get better."

"Will it?"

"I'll make sure."

"I'm not sure it's something people can control," she said.

Finally the day of Milos's escape attempt came. Dorsen had known the place and time for better than a week, long enough to pass the word. They did not have him covered, for fear a surveillance might scare him away. And they did not want to have any more people involved than absolutely necessary. The experiment was as clinically controlled as human hands could make it in a septic world.

Jane insisted on dinner that evening, even though McWade told her it would have to be early and brief. As soon as they sat down at their usual table at the Ivy, she told him she was confused and hurt by his behavior, which she said had been deteriorating ever since she started getting good assignments, as if he were punishing her for her success.

"I won't let you turn me against my luck," she said.

It made him angry.

"I've supported you right down the line," he said. "When have I complained?"

"You don't do it that way, Tony," she said. "You just aren't there for me anymore. We don't share anything. You aren't there now. You're a million miles away."

The actual figure was much less, but he did not correct her with the precise distance to the Czech frontier.

When he returned to the Nest, the balloon had already gone up. Signals Intelligence was reporting a heavy volume of coded traffic from the sector of the border where Milos was told to cross.

"What the hell's going on, Ike?" asked the duty officer. "You'd think they were going to war."

"We've got trouble," said McWade.

"You're running an operation, aren't you?"

"Keep me informed."

"It would have been good of you to have given us some

warning. If you were trying to insert somebody, you'd better get out the black bunting. Looks like the poor bastard walked right into a snare."

Before long the reception team reported that there had been a lot of shooting and that Milos had never shown. McWade ordered them out of the area immediately because soon the Austrians would be swarming around the noise.

When the station chief arrived, McWade gave him a full briefing on the way the crossing incident had gone down.

"We think Milos is probably dead," said McWade.

"That would be a blessing."

"They may also have gotten the border guard we paid."

"Who knew about this, Ike?"

"Only Dorsen."

Something flickered across the station chief's face.

"A tragic accident," he said. "But at least some good may come of it. Chance's economy."

McWade, of course, did not force him to assess the economy of intention, the balance of means and ends. These things were best unspoken, left to the torment of secret dreams.

In short order it became clear that as far as Langley was concerned, the consequences of the border incident had been unambiguously positive. When Dorsen was sweated, he disgorged a surprising amount of useful information. Eventually it was decided to leave him in place as a conduit for disinformation. He was to be run by McWade, who for the purpose of this operation reported directly to Fisherman. To facilitate his new role, McWade was promoted to the position he had wanted. And that meant he was through operating in the field.

"It's a pity to lose Leggatt," said the station chief. "All the girls will miss him."

The station chief turned out to be prophetic. As soon as Jane returned from her trip to southern Lebanon, she announced that she had decided it was time for them to stop seeing one another. It was over, she said. There was nothing left.

He tried to talk her out of it with promises that he now

felt he might be able to keep. A change of circumstances at work, he said. The pressure is off. Far less travel. He had wanted to surprise her because he had arranged this all for their benefit when he realized that something was going terribly wrong.

But she was unshakable, and when he tried to explain why it would be different from now on, he could feel the words coming off his tongue as heavy as lies. She said there was someone in him that she could never love. He wasn't sure which one it was.

The only person McWade felt he could talk to about it afterwards was Ben Wheeler, and he did not offer much solace.

"You should be thankful it ended so well," Wheeler said.

"I lost her."

"But at least she will never hate you," said Wheeler, "because she never knew who you were."

10

The descent into Heathrow was slow and bumpy on the return flight from McWade's home leave in Manitee Bay. Little lines of water fluttered nervously across the window. Surrounded by dense, lint-colored clouds, he could find no sign of earth or sun. McWade hated to fly.

Since taking the inside job at the Nest, he hadn't needed to as much as before. The work pretty well tethered him to his desk: memos, action plans and reports that never seemed to sate Fisherman's appetite for detail concerning other men's lives. Not that he found any of this tedious. Since capturing Dorsen, every task was an ordeal in which he felt he had to purify himself of all ulterior ends. Having finally broken free of his hated double, he did penance by flaying away every layer of the self that he had saved.

"If you want to become a saint," said Ben Wheeler, "you're in the wrong business."

Wheeler was ready to listen to McWade. He said he had seen things like this happen to men many times before. But he did not give an inch to McWade's remorse.

"Nobody cares what you wanted," he said. "Langley doesn't believe in conscience. That's one of the fringe benefits. The firm takes responsibility for your qualms the same way it picks up your dentist bills."

Wheeler had had a fair amount of time for conversation during this period because his travels had also, for some reason, been sharply cut back. McWade wondered whether this might have had something to do with the purges. In Manitee Bay he had read about them in the papers every day, thirty years of secrets being blown for no apparent reason except the country's morbid curiosity and instinct for self-punishment.

Wheeler had never given McWade a hint what he was about or whether he felt any vulnerability. McWade was sure that if Wheeler ever were called upon to defend publicly what he had done, he would choose disgrace rather than violate the code of silence. But the one thing McWade never gave a thought to was physical danger. Wheeler had always seemed larger than life, and so it was easy to think he was larger than death as well.

The jet finally broke through the clouds, and the ground below was the color of cold coffee with cream. When the wheels touched down, McWade relaxed in his seat. He forced himself to swallow, but it only opened one of his ears. Not until the stewardess released the cabin door did the pressure in his head give way, like a vacuum can sniffing open.

He cleared customs quickly with nothing to declare and emerged into the waiting room where Steven Greene was pacing and consulting his watch. As McWade approached him, it was like going toward a mirror ground to flatter. Ten years younger than McWade, Greene was about the same size and build, big across the shoulders, square of head and frame, straight hair pulled evenly across the brow. From the look of them they might have been cousins, but the resemblance was purely accidental. Greene had been born to a family of distinction. His ancestors had been bankers, Cabinet members, heroes in war. He was much surer of himself than McWade had been at his age. And like so many of his generation, he had not made peace with time. He was impatient to demonstrate the qualities that, because he believed they were bred into him, he was utterly confident he possessed.

"Good of you to come," McWade said, handing Greene the lighter of his bags.

"It wasn't my idea."

They walked briskly into the car park, Greene in the lead, making no allowance for the extra weight McWade was carrying.

"I hope everything went well," said McWade.

"Let's just say I'm glad you're back."

"You could have done worse than working for Lemke."

"Bastard pulled my security file as soon as you were

gone. He would have had me fluttered if I hadn't complained to the chief."

They reached the pool car and put the bags in the trunk. McWade got in on the passenger side.

"You might as well give me a fill," he said as Greene pulled out of the space.

"Gossip first?"

"Save the best to wake me if I doze."

McWade pulled the lever that lowered the angle of the seat back. His head on the padded rest, he closed his eyes like a man waiting for the drill.

"A lot of nothing from the operational nets," said Greene. "Top Hat is excited about troop movements on the frontier. He thinks it's 1968 all over again."

"How old were you then?"

"Langley's been pushing for more out of East Germany. You should see the taskings. We'd have to have the whole leadership wired."

"It's because of the purges," said McWade. "They're hurting for sources now."

"That's the gossip. I was getting to that."

"It's going to be a problem."

"I mean why everyone is scrambling to pick up the slack," said Greene. "It seems that your friend Ben Wheeler's lost his legs."

McWade hauled himself up wearily.

"Is that what you think?"

"Hangs around the Nest like a senior statesman."

"The leaks came from Washington," said McWade.

"Everybody knows you'll stand up for him."

McWade eased himself back. If you wanted to discredit a man's analysis, the surest way was to claim he was blinded by friendship. Loyalty counted against you in the Agency, if its object had a Christian name.

· When they reached the Nest, the offices seemed vaguely unfamiliar: things out of place, shadows in the corners, the wrong shade of paint. He put his bags away in the closet and sloughed off his suit jacket. Then he tested his memory on the lock of the safe and found the numbers still there under his fingers. Lemke had left his desk in good order. There were a few unclassified cables awaiting his action. The pending file from the safe was also mercifully thin.

"Stiff upper lip, old sport," said a voice.

When McWade looked up, Lemke was standing just inside the door. At one time he might have affected the British clichés as a joke, but after so many years in the Nest, this had advanced beyond parody. Gone native, the younger men said; he's attracted to the Brits for the quality of their cooking and their women, all those plump, lovely glands.

"Looks like you've made out all right without me," said McWade.

"We're going to have to have a word about that young batman of yours," said Lemke, tugging up his pantleg to protect the crease as he lowered himself onto the couch. "Mr Greene has a rum sense of subordination."

"We'll have to be sure to discuss it one day," said McWade.

"He's a royal pain," said Lemke.

"I thought you admired the Queen."

Just then the phone buzzed, and McWade picked it up. There were no pleasantries. The station chief's voice was urgent.

"Better come see me," he said. "We've got trouble."

McWade rang off. "I've been summoned," he told Lemke, as lightly as he could. But when the chief used the word trouble, he did not mean annoyance or a petty squabble in the ranks. A problem was grim. Trouble was the next closest thing to war. These principles of understatement governed conversation in the Nest. Picking up the slang of the soccer graffiti that splashed the walls of Brixton, everyone called them "London rules".

The chief's secretary was on the phone when McWade entered. She directed him into the inner office with a flick of her hand.

"It's Wheeler," said the chief. His glasses were off, and his eyes seemed dark and sunken without them. "They've hit him."

McWade stopped a few paces from the desk, but when

the station chief spoke again, his voice seemed to come from a great distance.

"The call came in a few minutes ago. It looks like they took Ben Wheeler down." He picked up a scrap of paper from his desk, then dropped it. "You'd better get to the hospital, Ike. He's been asking for you."

"How bad is it?"

"The doctors aren't saying. But Ben thinks he's finally bought the farm."

McWade took hold of the back of a chair. Wheeler did not believe in exaggeration either. He despised melo-drama. This life in the theater. London rules.

"Who did it to him?" McWade demanded.

"We'll want to reciprocate."

"What does Langley say?"

A look of disgust came over the chief for a moment. Then he brought it under control.

"I haven't communicated with the wise men yet," he said. "I wanted to be able to tell them you'd be handling it."

"I'll need some backup."

It did not matter to McWade now that he had personal reasons. In the Agency, this kind of revenge was right-eous, an act of faith.

"Who do you trust?" asked the station chief.

"What about Greene?"

"Is he ready?"

"Was I?" said McWade.

Wheeler was unconscious when McWade cleared the police guard outside his door. A bottle of colorless liquid dripped slowly above his head, the fluid passing down a transparent tube into a needle taped to his tennis arm. On the screen of a black box next to the bed a thin green line blipped irregularly.

A nurse bustled in and began checking the equipment.

"You're the other American," she said.

"Yes."

"He's been asking."

"By name?"

"Yes," she said.

"What name?"

She put down a bottle of fluid and looked at McWade as if he were the one showing symptoms.

"Why, Rogers," she said. "Anthony Rogers."

McWade allowed himself a small breath of relief. At least Wheeler's mind was still alive enough to lie.

"Where is the wound?"

"You'd better talk to the doctors about that."

"Is the bullet still in him?"

"I'm sorry, Mr Rogers," she said. "It's all very strange."

He pulled a chair up next to the bed. A pallor had already crept into Wheeler's face. His eyes darted behind the lids. Suddenly his hand spread wide, as if to fight a cramp, then it curled up like a spider touched by a flame. His eyes came open. At first there did not appear to be any recognition. Then he whispered something. The nurse moved up closer.

"Leave us," he said.

She hesitated.

"It's all right," McWade said.

With a certain show of reluctance, she moved out the door. McWade closed it after her.

"Turn my head so I can see you," Wheeler said.

McWade moved it gently with both hands, like a fragile crystal sphere.

"In the tube station," said Wheeler. "Only saw the bastard's back. Bowler hat. Umbrella."

"The weapon?"

"I assume," said Wheeler. He stiffened, the pain shooting through him.

"Shall I call her back?"

Wheeler waved the idea away. Then his hand went slack again on the sheet.

"Something touched my leg," he said. "Just a pulling, like a paper cut. Tried to go after him. Platform started to give way. Had to hang on to something. Shit works fast."

"What does?"

"That one from Radio Liberty. What was his name?"

"You can't be sure it was the same toxin."

"He didn't last a day."

Wheeler's eyes closed and another shudder passed over him. A small sound crossed his lips. McWade stood up and moved to the door.

"Wait," said Wheeler. "It comes and goes."

McWade sat down again and touched Wheeler's hand. It was cold and dry.

"Who was it, Ben?" he said.

"I've made a lot of friends."

"But why now?"

"The NARCISSUS net," said Wheeler.

"Is that what they called your operation?"

"Until it went bust. You've figured out that much, haven't you?"

"I haven't been in the loop."

"The loop," said Wheeler, and when he tried to curse, it turned into a wracking cough.

"You'd better rest now," said McWade.

"Read the files," said Wheeler.

"Who can give them to me?"

Wheeler swallowed, blinked. Took a breath.

"Ross," he said.

"But if NARCISSUS has been blown . . ."

"Find out why," said Wheeler. "Man with the umbrella. Man who sent him."

"What did they think they'd gain?" said McWade.

Wheeler's eyes fastened on McWade's and did not move.

"Somebody needed to prove something," he said at last, and it was as if this simple deduction had taken all his strength.

"To make it look like NARCISSUS hadn't turned him, you mean," said McWade. "Somebody scrambling for cover. Give me names, Ben."

But he got no help, for Wheeler had sunk into another troubled sleep. Or perhaps, McWade thought later, he might have feigned it with his last draught of will, because speaking the names aloud was forbidden, even on the lip of death.

When Wheeler opened his eyes again, more than an hour later, he began to ramble. His mind was no longer right. He talked about the men he had corrupted, the lives lost, the figures he had worked for: Donovan, Dulles, Fisherman, Ross.

By nightfall the words had become slurred beyond recognition. And then they stopped. McWade left the hospital briefly to get Greene to work researching the death of the man from Radio Liberty and any others whose murders followed a similar pattern. By the time he returned to the bedside, Wheeler had lapsed into a coma. Shortly after dawn, it ended.

At McWade's request the Brits put a heavy press on all known Soviet and Eastern European agents. They tightened up at the airports and other points of exit. During the first twenty-four hours there was no unusual movement. The smug bastards were behaving as if they had nothing to fear.

Around the Nest, the betting was that it had been the Bulgarians, who were the Soviets' favorite choice for thug work. When the pathologist's report came back from Langley, it confirmed that the toxin was a Soviet specialty. But the KGB was selective in its use; there were only a half dozen documented cases in all theaters.

McWade gained access to the station chief's limited NARCISSUS materials and spent days poring over them. He was astonished at how important Wheeler's operation had been in its prime. The take had been prodigious, everything from advance warning of East German harrassment along the Berlin corridor to a report of what the Soviets would have been willing to trade to forestall our deployment of multiple warheads during the negotiations on SALT I. There were many names in the documents — some of them obscure figures serving as KGB menials in embassies around the world, others as prominent as Andropov, Kerzhentseff and Shaliatan. But the sources were never revealed. They were identified only by coded designations. Even the station chief could not say who was TANGO, who was LARYNX, who was ROGUE. To get that information and the names of dozens of other, more minor figures, they had to gain access to Ross's files.

An operation like NARCISSUS was so sensitive that the chain of command went directly from the case agent in the field to a single supervisor at Langley and from him up to the Director. The documents received no circulation. Everything from sources to funding was kept utterly opaque to the usual processes of review. Radical compartmentalization of this sort was at odds with command and control, which was why only the most trusted individuals such as Michael Ross were chosen to coordinate black projects. The only other protection was Fisherman, whose suspicions were catholic. But even as Fisherman's agent, McWade could not get into the central NARCISSUS files without seeking formal clearance from the DCI.

What came rocketing back from Langley was not approval. Instead, McWade received an urgent cable reporting that Wheeler's name and photograph had appeared in a publication called *CounterAttack* a week and a half before the hit. *CounterAttack* was described as a virulent little magazine printed in Arlington, Va., by a left wing group that had seized upon the purges to publish as much damaging information on the Agency as it could collect. There was plenty to fill its pages, what with the leaks that were springing up all over Capitol Hill and the confessions of ex-agents who had gotten religion as soon as the weather changed. *CounterAttack* made a specialty of collating information from multiple sources to come up with lists of Agency men and women operating under cover. Langley already attributed one death in the Mideast to a revelation in the magazine.

When the next packet came from Headquarters, it included the offending copy of *CounterAttack*. It was printed on cheap newsprint, so the photograph of Wheeler was smudgy and blurred. Even so, McWade could identify the location, not a block from the Nest. From the angle, it appeared that the picture had been taken at street level. Ben was dressed casually in a sport coat and open-collared shirt. He might even have noticed something; he had that look. Not fear, exactly, just a kind of recognition. Or perhaps it was only the sun in his eyes.

As time went on, Langley hardened its theory about the killing, and its attentions turned inward. The issue of *CounterAttack* with Wheeler's photo was dated two weeks before the murder. A message to all stations had apparently been drafted, warning the compromised agents. But it had gotten stalled somewhere in the bureaucracy. The DCI opened an internal inquiry to find out who had dropped the ball.

McWade could not figure out why Headquarters was so committed to the *CounterAttack* explanation. It made little sense to assume that the Soviets had gotten their information from magazines, and even if they had, that still did not explain why they had chosen Wheeler to hit rather than one of the others *CounterAttack* had compromised. Though he did not have any evidence, McWade thought it much more likely that the Soviets had planted the revelation in *CounterAttack* to throw Langley off the track when the hit went down.

From the sketchy NARCISSUS files at the Nest, McWade tried to work out a chronology, putting together the substantive reports with all mentions of Soviet officials by name. He pulled the folders on all the Soviets to determine where they had been serving and what they might have known. If he had been dealing with a man less clever than Wheeler, this might have given him some hint of which had been a secret source. But Wheeler had disguised every reference. McWade could find no pattern in the intelligence attributed to TANGO, LARYNX and ROGUE. All three seemed to have operated in the European theater at least some of the time, but beyond that there was no relationship between the information they passed on and the biographies of the Soviets who might have provided it.

To McWade's disgust, the DCI flatly refused to reveal the identities behind the codenames. When the station chief appealed for reconsideration, he received a strongly worded cable accusing him of trying to shift the blame for his own failure to Headquarters. In the current political climate, the DCI wrote, this was not appreciated. London station was invited to leave off chasing our own assets and get to work finding who used the *CounterAttack* information to locate and kill Ben Wheeler.

Through all this, young Greene was undeterred. By

sheer persistence he located a number of people who had been on the subway platform at the time of the attack. They gave him vague and contradictory stories, from which he pieced together a more complete – if less reliable – description of the man in the bowler than Wheeler had provided.

McWade gave Greene plenty of leash, and it did not take long before he came up with something more definitive.

"I've seen him," he said, bursting into McWade's office. "I've seen our man."

"Where?"

"A Bulgarian Embassy driver. I've been watching him. Here."

The Polaroid snapshot was no clearer than you would expect, but it did bear some resemblance to the rough details the witnesses had provided.

"Have you shown this to any of the people who were on the platform?"

"They didn't rule him out."

"Not enough."

Though McWade later regretted it, he did not pull in anyone senior to give Greene depth. There were reasons, of course. Greene would have made an unholy fuss about it if he had. And at the time, the Nest wasn't exactly awash in idle manpower. Every available agent had been thrown into the effort to find substitutes for the NARCISSUS sources. It was one thing for the station chief to let McWade pursue his hunches; it would have been quite another to put more resources into a cause that seemed to be going nowhere. So McWade simply gave Greene the wink and let him run against his man however he saw fit. Meanwhile, McWade continued to work his way through the files.

The more he studied the data the more perplexed he became. Checking the reports against the log of Wheeler's travels, he found that the two did not correlate. The overseas trips were often long enough for Wheeler to have gone anywhere in the world to make his contact. The first hop was always to Paris or Rome, but there Wheeler changed his cover and disappeared into the anonymity of

133

the airlines' careless flight manifests. At times, Wheeler sent flash messages to Langley during periods when he had been in London for weeks, as if he had picked up the information over whiskey and cigars at his club.

McWade went to the Brits to get a calendar of Soviet comings and goings during the times in question. By way of mutuality, he mentioned the Bulgarian lead Greene was pursuing.

"Interesting," said his British counterpart.

"What do you know about him?" he asked.

"Afraid we might be straying into forbidden territory."

"Unofficially," said McWade.

"Frankly, I can't keep up with all the names."

The British log of ins and outs did not reveal anything of much importance. During some of Wheeler's most fertile periods in London there was almost no Soviet movement, in either direction. McWade began to believe that Wheeler came back from his overseas missions with a bag full of goodies and then doled them out a little bit at a time. In a dishonest man, this would have been a way to justify his expenses and avoid too much time on the road. But Wheeler would have had another purpose. McWade toyed with the idea that all the key NARCISSUS sources were a single man and that Wheeler had held back information to obscure this fact. But none of this got McWade any closer to the assassin.

Then one day he got a call from the Brits, and the message about the Bulgarian suspect was discouraging. When McWade tried to contact Greene with the news, the young man was nowhere to be found. McWade left him a message and returned to his flat where he poured himself a tumbler of Scotch, then another.

The telephone awakened him well past midnight. His head was pounding as he picked up the receiver. He did not turn on the light.

"Mr Anthony Rogers, please."

"Speaking."

"Are you acquainted with a man called Steven Greene?"

"Yes, of course."

"There's been a bit of a ruckus, sir. Quite unfortunate all round."

"What happened?"

"We found him in an alley. He was in a, well, in rather a state. Perhaps you'd better come to the hospital, sir."

"Right away."

"And, sir. I wonder if you might bring a change of clothes with you for Mr Greene if that wouldn't be too much bother."

When McWade arrived at the hospital, the emergency room was empty except for an Indian family huddled in a corner. The nurse summoned a police officer when McWade identified himself. As the officer moved across the room he glanced at the family with all the benign concern of a representative of the Raj.

"Mr Rogers, I presume," he said, extending his hand, one white man to another.

"Has he been admitted?"

"That won't be necessary. As I suspected, he is more rattled than injured. Here, follow me."

He led McWade into a wide corridor. On one side there was a long admitting desk staffed by two tired clerks, on the other a series of small examining rooms. The officer stopped at the last one. A white curtain was drawn across the doorway. The officer parted it.

There sat Greene on a simple wooden chair. He was dressed in a hospital gown, his hands holding it down over his knees. a stark white bandage angled across his forehead. A mighty shiner blossomed under his left eye.

"You're quite a sight," said McWade. The young man looked away.

"He hasn't been very helpful, I'm afraid," said the officer. "Insisted on speaking to you first."

McWade laid the suitbag on the examining table.

"I hope these will fit," he said.

"I assured him that he did not need a solicitor," said the officer.

McWade took him by the arm and led him back into the corridor, closing the curtain behind them.

"I'm not an attorney," he said. "We're colleagues. We work in the same firm."

"It would be helpful if we could get a statement. We don't like visitors to our city to be mistreated . . ."

"Of course."

When McWade went back behind the curtain, Greene had gotten into the pants and was buttoning the shirt with fingers that looked painfully swollen. He turned his face to the corner.

"Give me your other clothes," said McWade. "I'll pack them away for you."

"They're gone."

"No matter," said McWade. "We can have them picked up tomorrow."

"He stole them," said Greene. "He left me naked."

With that, he finally lifted his head. His expression was painful, more shame than anger.

"Who?" said McWade.

"I followed him into an alley. He jumped me from a doorway. Clipped me on the back of the neck with something hard. I went down."

"The Bulgarian?"

"I'd let him see me," said Greene, lowering his voice and glancing at the curtain.

"We'll work out a story," said McWade.

"I thought I could make him panic."

"We should have had a backup."

"I must have blacked out on the pavement because when I woke up he had stripped off my clothes. I tried to stand up. He knocked me down again. Kicked me. Then . . ."

"Give the police some kind of a description and be done with it," said McWade. He was touching Greene's shoulder now. The young man twisted away from him and sat down again.

"I never laid a hand on the sonofabitch," said Greene.

"Don't worry about that now."

Greene stood up again and went to the mirror above the sink.

"Goddammit!" he said, and he slammed his palm against the metal bowl. It rang like a muffled bell.

"Everybody gets blindsided sometimes," said McWade.

"Not like this," said Greene. "Not what he did to me."

"The Bulgarians are animals," said McWade.

"I was curled up on the concrete. I thought he would never stop kicking me. When I looked up, he had unzipped himself. I hurt too much to do anything about it."

Greene glared at McWade, and it was like an accusation.

"He pissed on me," he said, "and I had to let him."

Eventually Greene repeated part of the story to the police officer. He did not reveal the Bulgarian's name, of course, or the circumstances of their encounter. And he left out the most demeaning part.

McWade held back, too. He did not tell Greene the worst until the next day at the Nest: the Bulgarian wasn't their man. When the Brits ran a check on the name, they had discovered that he had not arrived in the country until three days after the murder.

"He must have doubled back to establish an alibi," said Greene.

"They were on him abroad," said McWade.

"He tricked them."

"I'm afraid we've come up empty," said McWade.

Greene refused to accept his failure. He wanted McWade to file a report fingering the Bulgarian as the hit man. He wanted to volunteer to roll him up and turn him over to the Brits. But it was no good. The best McWade could do was to keep the details of what happened in the alley out of the official reports.

Within days, Greene had applied to the station chief for a change of assignment. He did not even come to McWade to say goodbye. McWade thought he understood, but he wished Greene had been able to talk to him about it. He might have been able to persuade him that shame was inappropriate in intelligence work, that if you hid your face, you would never be able to see.

With his assistant out of the action, McWade had to pursue whatever he could salvage from the investigation by himself. He prepared a list of queries for Langley, which the station chief forwarded without endorsement. Weeks went by without a response.

"Maybe it is time to put the case aside," said the chief.

"I have to make a report," said McWade.

"Tell Langley what it wants to hear." The chief stood up at his desk. "Bureaucrats," he spat. "When the Chinese called us paper tigers, that is what they must have meant."

"I don't even see the motive," said McWade. "When was the last time the Soviets hit one of our fieldmen?"

"They would have to have a powerful reason."

"If they started killing ours, they'd have to expect us to respond in kind," said McWade. "Mutually assured destruction."

"It doesn't make sense, Ike. But I don't see where to go from here. We don't have a target, and Langley doesn't have the stomach for escalation in the midst of a purge."

"It isn't right to bury Wheeler this way," said McWade.

"Someday somebody will exhume him," said the chief. "Fisherman if nobody else. He's the keeper of all our corpses. If you want to know when the time is ripe, keep your eye on Fisherman."

But McWade refused to call it quits, and within a week he received an odd message directly from Langley. It came in a plain envelope, inexpertly typed. When he opened it, he saw that it was signed by Michael Ross.

By this time, Ross was under attack for his refusal to cooperate with the Congressional committees. It was even harder now for him to leave Washington than it was at the time of Wheeler's funeral, and yet he was coming to England for the sole purpose of talking to McWade. We understand, Ross wrote, why you are troubled by what happened to Ben Wheeler. Before you pursue it any further, perhaps I can put your mind at ease.

They met a week later. Under Ross's instructions, McWade told nobody at the Nest before driving to Bath. It was high tourist season, so the ruins were aswarm with Americans. He followed a guide through the underground chambers, where the invaders had taken the waters two millennia ago. He touched the moist, stone walls and gazed at the empty, ancient pools. At one point the dark excavation opened to the light. Statues of centurions were silhouetted against the brilliant blue sky. Suddenly he noticed Ross standing beside him. Neither of them said a word.

When the tour was over, McWade followed Ross through the Pump Room and onto the street. At a careful distance he pursued the tall figure down the long avenues where rows of Georgian houses rose like castle walls. Finally, Ross entered a park. A band concert was about to begin. The bells of the tubas and trombones gleamed in the sun. Ross put some coins into the hand of a gray old fellow at the edge of the lawn and took the loan of a canvas chair, which he set out in a distant patch of shade. McWade queued up behind a group of ladies in floral dresses and obtained a chair for himself.

Ross did not give any sign of recognition as McWade approached him. And he made no effort to help as McWade struggled to figure out how to unfold his chair. By the time McWade was ready to sit down, the band had tuned up and launched into its first march. It was loud enough that McWade had to lean over to make himself heard.

"You came a long way," he said.

"We thought we owed it to you," said Ross.

"I haven't been getting much cooperation."

Ross stared off toward the bandstand and spoke directly into the music so that McWade had to strain to hear the words.

"You've been in an untenable position," Ross said. "It could not be helped. There were some who assumed that you could be induced by frustration simply to give it up."

"He was my friend," said McWade.

Ross turned to him.

"And mine," he said.

"I'm afraid that without Langley's cooperation, I am at a loss," said McWade. "If I knew the NARCISSUS sources, I might be able to proceed."

"At a time like this," said Ross, "it is all we can do to keep those names buried."

"We're talking about one of our own here."

"We had hoped that we would not have to burden you with this," said Ross. "We know the way you felt about

Wheeler. Many of us had worked with him ourselves, so it was with regret that we had to take the steps we did."

He handed McWade a manila envelope. When McWade began to open it, Ross touched his hand.

"Not now," he said. "I want you to read it carefully and then destroy it. I do not want its contents revealed to anyone else. There is no use tarnishing a man's reputation when there is nothing to be gained from it. And I needn't mention how eager certain parties in Washington would be to get hold of another weapon to use against us. I trust that once you have digested this material, you will see fit to consider the matter resolved."

"You aren't saying that Langley had something to do with what happened," said McWade.

"Nothing of the sort," said Ross. "Now, if you excuse me, I am going to make my exit. I think you should suffer this lovely concert for a while longer before getting up to go yourself."

"How can I contact you?"

"I don't think that will be necessary," said Ross.

He stood up and lifted his chair, which he folded with a minimum of effort, then walked off along the edges of the crowd as stately as a lord.

When McWade returned to the anonymous B and B room he had taken, he felt a fever coming on. He wrapped himself in a blanket from the bed and sat down at the tiny writing desk on an uncertain chair. Stiffened in every muscle, he was dizzy as he opened the envelope. It was not easy to read the document, which was a blind Xerox with all identifying marks carefully masked. The light in the room was no good, and his eyes burned.

When he was half a page into it, a chill went through him and he did not know whether it was the illness or the words, because the memorandum made the case that Ben Wheeler had been playing both sides.

The circumstantial evidence was contained in an analysis of Wheeler's spending habits, which could not be accounted for on the basis of his salary. It seems that he liked the ponies and was well known in the casinos. And in this pursuit he was no luckier than any other man. Over a period of two years, he had dropped more than a hundred thousand dollars, according to estimates that McWade had no way of challenging. The money had to have come from somewhere.

But the file on Wheeler went beyond speculation. Ross had run a game on him, and he had lost that one, too. The setup was of a common type, not too different from the one McWade had used on Sidney Dorsen.

A few months before the killing, Wheeler had cabled Ross to clear a NARCISSUS meeting. Acting upon his suspicions, Ross had ordered Wheeler to cancel. A major series of arrests and expulsions was about to go down at the Soviet UN Mission, Ross reported to him, and it was too risky to have any of the NARCISSUS sources in contact. Ross made sure he gave Wheeler all the suspects' names. The setup was complete.

Langley did not put a tail on Wheeler. Ross respected the man's moves too much for that. Instead, he simply waited. And sure enough, Wheeler disappeared. That was not unusual. Since he reported directly to Langley, the people at the Nest did not keep track of him, and Ross had never demanded that he punch in and out. But this time, he was carrying a marker. Within a week, the men in the UN Mission had been recalled to Moscow. There was only one explanation. Wheeler had turned.

Apparently Ross was still debating whether to run Wheeler in place or to burn him when the assassination closed the issue off. The implication was that once NARCISSUS began to leak, Wheeler was a dangerous man to the Soviets. He was vulnerable, and he might have disclosed everything if the pressure became great enough. The Soviets killed him not because of what he had done against them but because of what he had done on their behalf.

McWade wanted to deny it. His head was throbbing and a silent refusal rose in his throat. But there was no way he could refute the evidence that Ross had laid out. He put the document back in the envelope and never looked at it again.

The next day he was well enough to drive back to the

141

Nest, where he shredded the incriminating papers and filed a short cable acknowledging his failure to find Wheeler's killers and acceding to Langley's theory about *CounterAttack*. The file was officially closed and put away in the dark place Langley kept for mysteries it wanted to remain unsolved.

All McWade kept was a single sheet of paper on which he had written the names of everyone who had been touched by NARCISSUS. From the Agency there were Ross, the DCIs, a few others. Then there were the Russians NARCIS-SUS had one way or another fingered. The names filled most of the page. And at the bottom he had written on a single line: TANGO, LARYNX, ROGUE.

He kept this document in his personal file from assign-ment to assignment. Years later, it was still there in his safe, yellowed by the acids of age. He was no closer to understanding its meaning now than he had been the day the station chief told him to be patient. Keep your eye on Fisherman, the chief had said. It was really very funny, looking back on it, because now Fisherman was watching him.

PART THREE

Loyalties

11

The most immediate problem was to fight the eerie feeling that Fisherman was everywhere, which was precisely the illusion a magus needed to create. But at least McWade knew how hard it was to put the bell to a man, even when the Agency did the surveillance with all the resources at its disposal. And it was McWade's guess that Fisherman was operating on his own, with whatever he had on hand. The Moscow talks were too critical and the Director too loyal to the President for him to have authorized Fisherman to make a move on Ross at a time like this. If the Director had even an inkling, at the meeting in the Cabinet Room he surely would at least have covered himself. It would have been a simple matter for him to have quibbled with a point or two of Ross's assessment, to raise a few unresolvable questions, just a grace note here and there so that if Ross ultimately did go down, the Director could show that he'd had reservations all along. Instead, he had gone out of his way to ally himself with Ross, right down the line.

But even though the Agency wasn't a problem so far, when State began to whine about the premature disclosure of the trip and the President called its bluff by bringing in the Sisters to find the source, McWade had to wonder whether Fisherman hadn't somehow arranged it as cover for his own investigation.

Until the Sisters came into it, McWade had still hoped he could get away for a long weekend with Sarah. There wasn't much he could do in Washington once Ross finished up the substantive discussions in Moscow until Rufus Stockwell came up with some information, and he thought that maybe a little time away would give him a chance to figure the angles better than he could standing at their crux. But then he received a call from Inspector George Watling and learned that, since the Man himself had issued the order, the Sisters weren't going to indulge in the usual period of bureaucratic delay. McWade had to break the news to Sarah that their plans would have to be postponed.

He could only explain the half of it, of course, hinting at the connection between Ross's success in Moscow and State's ridiculous effort to get the NSC to wear the hairshirt for the unauthorized disclosure.

"Somehow I'll make it up to you," he said.

"It wasn't just for me."

Watling showed up right on time. McWade had forgotten to clear him past the guards, and FBI credentials worked no magic at the doors of the Old Executive Office Building. The White House grounds were like a separate principality at the heart of the capital, a Vatican. The inspector had to wait with all the supplicants in the lobby until the formalities of his audience were concluded by phone.

"Sorry for the inconvenience," McWade said as he showed the stocky, red-faced man into his office. "I wasn't sure you'd want your name printed out on all the morning lists."

"You guys slay me, you know?" said Watling, pulling at his collar.

McWade led him to the sitting area in the corner away from the windows. Watling's eyes wandered around the big room.

"Can I get you some coffee?" McWade asked.

"Decaf if you have it."

McWade buzzed his secretary from the console next to his armchair and then sat back.

"The real stuff gives me the jitters now," said Watling. "Wife says it's bad for the ticker."

"So," said McWade, holding out his palms as if to show he had nothing hidden, "to what exactly do I owe the honor?"

"You knew of the Moscow trip in advance," said Watling.

"I handled a lot of the details."

Betty knocked before coming in but did not wait for an

invitation. She set out the china cups with the presidential seal.

"It had been in the planning stage for about three months," McWade went on.

"Not in front of the girl," said Watling.

She quickly laid a paper napkin beside each saucer and hid her annoyance until her back was turned to the inspector. McWade gave a wink to her scowl. When she was gone, Watling picked up his cup by the rim.

"This instant?" he asked.

"I think so."

"It's pretty good. You know the brand?"

"Am I under oath?"

"Look," said Watling, noisily setting the cup back down again, "I can make this as hard as you want it."

"I guess I'm just not used to being on the receiving end."

"Everybody gets his turn," said Watling, and there was a note of empathy in it, as if this man had been in the dock himself. "By the way, did we ever work a case together? Something clicked when I pulled your file."

"Were you in Division Five?"

"Still am," said Watling.

"They're calling this a security matter?"

"What the hell else would they call it?"

"Maybe just the way things work," said McWade.

"You don't take this matter very seriously, do you, Mr McWade?"

"I've got nothing to hide."

Watling sipped his coffee, then he pulled out a notebook from his breast pocket.

"It's been my experience that guys who have been in the Agency have trouble leveling," he said.

"I assure you, I've gone straight."

Watling opened the notebook to a fresh page and laid it out flat on the coffee table.

"We might as well get started," he said, printing McWade's name and the date and time in neat block letters at the top.

"When did you first get involved in planning the trip to Moscow?"

"I'm not sure how far I'm supposed to go."

"Maybe you didn't see the memo," said Watling, opening his attaché case, which held a few thin file jackets, an extra notebook and half a dozen plastic pens clipped neatly to the divider. He drew out a single sheet of paper and slid it across the coffee table, its front edge lifting like a wing.

"At Langley you learn certain habits," said McWade as he glanced at the Chief of Staff's initials beneath the terse order to cooperate.

"I know all about Langley's habits," said Watling. "They want you to think they're a bunch of nuns."

"They think highly of the Bureau, too," said McWade. "That's why they call you the Sisters."

"Never mind what we're called," said Watling.

McWade took a sip of coffee and put the cup back on the saucer with a steady hand, just to demonstrate that he could.

"I was in on the arrangements from the beginning," he said. "It all got started when Ross had his first stroll with the Soviet *chargé d'affaires* in Rock Creek Park."

"You were covering it?"

"We had men on the hillsides," said McWade, "but they stood off a good distance. They were only there to make sure the other side stayed back, too. Ross and the Russian were to have the park to themselves. They could have been communing with nature for all anyone could prove."

"Sounds like a screwy way to do business."

"Maybe I thought so myself, until it started to show results."

McWade stood up and got a calendar off his desk.

"The first meeting was in March. They got together periodically after that. By the middle of May the idea of talks in Moscow was beginning to look firm."

The initial conversation had been on a lovely spring day, too early yet for flowers, but the buds were out, a pointillism of fresh, innocent green. McWade only caught sight of the two principals briefly from time to time as they emerged around a corner on the bike path or set off across a wide expanse of lawn with their backs toward McWade's vantage.

The Russian walked slowly with shoulders so stooped that it looked as though he were examining the ground for coins. Ross himself stood erect, one hand in a pocket, the other making sweeping gestures that seemed from a distance to indicate all that was at stake. Their talk lasted better than an hour.

When Ross returned to the office afterwards, McWade used the day's correspondence as an excuse to join him in his office and fish for news. But at first Ross did not volunteer any. He simply went through the letters McWade had prepared for him and had him redo nearly every one. As McWade gathered up his papers, Ross began jotting some notes on a legal pad. He did not look up until McWade had reached the door.

"Goronov isn't a subtle man," Ross said, "but he's a survivor. That tells you something."

McWade returned to his place before the desk but did not sit down because he was not sure Ross wanted him to.

"It tells you Goronov knows his own interests," McWade said.

"Doesn't go off freelancing," said Ross.

McWade put down the papers. He sensed that Ross had been pursuing a similar line of thought and wanted to hear it played back to him.

"A man of modest ambitions and a taste for the comforts of life in the West," McWade said.

"But a time comes when any man will stand up," said Ross, and McWade was sure he was testing the thought by challenging it. "He's got to figure that he knows more about the Americans than any of the men above him. Look how long he's been at it. And now he's got an opportunity to make something happen, to go down in the history books."

"Or find himself written out of them," said McWade. "They aren't like us."

"That's what they want you to think," said Ross. "The New Soviet Man. But Goronov would have done all right no matter where he was born."

"A man like him wouldn't lift a finger without explicit authorization," said McWade. "It takes a certain kind of

149

person to thrive on theology. In Moscow the high priests run the government. Here they only run the courts."

Ross seemed to appreciate that, so McWade took it a step further.

"You can see the difference in the reasons people change sides," he said. "When a Russian defects, it's because he's lost his faith. But Americans don't turn because of ideology. They do it for a price. Fisherman always said a society gets the traitors it deserves."

"Ernest has an explanation for everything," said Ross, with a certain amount of impatience. "Was there anything else?"

McWade saw no need to give Watling all the details of this conversation or any that followed. The deeper origins of the Moscow meeting had nothing to do with the investigation of the leak.

"I need to know everybody with access," said Watling.

McWade buzzed his secretary and told her to bring in the list he had prepared. It was typed on plain bond paper, one column, in order of rank. When she had closed the door again, Watling asked, "Her name on this?"

"I didn't include secretaries," said McWade. "You can talk to her, but I think you'll just be wasting your time."

"It's all the same to you, isn't it?" he said. "How I waste it, I mean."

"This whole thing is pointless as far as I'm concerned."

"Tell it to the President."

"Maybe I should have."

"Nobody likes to object to leak investigations. Makes them look like the leaker," said Watling. "That's why the damned things always end up in our laps."

He put the list into his attaché case and flipped a page of his notebook.

"Let's see if I understand your position," he said. "You say that since you went to all this trouble to keep the thing quiet, why would you turn around and blow the whistle."

"Something like that. The whole point was to avoid the situation where each side postures to make the other look like the heavy. That's why we held everything tight."

The preparations were kept completely in house. Ross

150

formed a small working group, including McWade, to staff out the options. The President gave his enthusiastic go ahead. There was no significant dissension among any of those in the know. The secret united them like co-conspirators.

"I imagine Simpson might have been feeling a little neglected," said Watling. "It sounds to me like Ross was edging him out."

"You have to understand the way Ross operates," said McWade. "From the outset, he made it clear that Simpson would lead the delegation if the Moscow trip could be arranged. Simpson is a team player. That's what makes him such a strong candidate for Secretary."

McWade watched to see whether Watling was picking up on the equation, who would move over to State, who would move up and who would move out.

"Which one's the candidate, again, Simpson or Ross?" he asked.

"Simpson," said McWade. "At least that's been the talk."

"These were the only people involved throughout the planning stage, then," said Watling, touching his attaché case where he had filed away the names.

"Until we got to the last stage, laying on the aircraft and so on. Then the circle got considerably larger. But that wasn't until a couple of weeks before the trip."

"What about State?"

"The President called the Secretary when the plane landed in Moscow. He apologized for waiting so long and said he thought somebody on the staff had taken care of it earlier."

"Defense?"

"They might have realized a little sooner than State if their early warning systems were working. After all, the Air Force owned the plane."

"No alarms went off, though," said Watling.

"Not until after the delegation was on its way."

"I suppose Defense could have tipped off State."

"All I know is that the *Post* didn't run the story until after the President made his call," said McWade.

He was relieved that Watling wasn't interested in pursuing

the private talks in the park, which were Ross's most vulnerable point. There had always been a danger that the Soviets or somebody else would make some wild claim about his undertakings and he would be powerless to offer any rebuttal but his own word. It was altogether likely that the President favored the odd arrangement precisely because he could scuttle it at any time and blame it on rogue behaviour on the part of Ross.

Yet the same things that created the danger gave Ross an unheard of measure of control over the interpretation of what had been said. This was perfectly consistent with Ross's style. He had a reputation for dominating the analysis of the international field of play – the conflicts, the personalities, the underlying interests. He could navigate all the jealousies and strained alliances with subtlety and nuance. And yet one element had absolutely no part in his analyses, whether he gave them in public, before the President or in the privacy of his office with his most trusted aide. He never revealed his own ambitions. They were so muted, so complex, so extraordinarily well disguised, that even McWade could never quite be sure how Ross was positioning himself and to precisely what end.

"One thing has me a little confused here," said Watling. "You claim that the NSC was buttoned up, but the news stories had a lot of details. Even about the walks in the woods."

"If you go back," said McWade, "you'll see that they didn't come out the first day."

"First day. Second day," said Watling. "Our marching orders are to find out where all of them came from."

"There's an easy explanation for the later stories," said McWade.

"Which is?"

"I put the information out," said McWade.

Watling looked as though he might be ready to read McWade his rights.

"Some of that was classified, you know," he said.

"I'd better get you a copy of the contingency plans," said McWade. "In the event of a leak, I was authorized to give

152

out the background on a not-for-attribution basis. That was the script, and the Man signed off on it."

Watling smiled.

"Looks like you have your ass covered," he said.

"Galvanized, I'm afraid."

The inspector closed his notebook.

"You deal with reporters a lot, do you?" he asked.

"Only when I have to."

"How about before the trip?"

"Nobody so much as called," said McWade.

"You have any ideas?"

McWade picked up a State Department directory from the end table next to the phone and slid it across the table.

"Start with the As," he said.

Watling stood up.

"I may have to get back to you again as this thing develops," he said.

"Any time."

"As you know, the inquiry is confidential."

"What is it they say about second marriages?" said McWade. "A triumph of hope over experience."

The day was humid, but McWade walked to his appointment rather than sign out a pool car and driver, which would have left a paper trail. He removed his jacket as soon as he stepped into the heat. There was plenty of time, so he walked slowly and made sure no one was at his back. When he hit the park, he hugged every stretch of shade. A sax player honked out an angry rhapsody near the statue of Lafayette, his instrument case open before him to collect tributes to his rage. McWade gave him wide berth, then crossed over to the Hay-Adams, where he stopped to pick up a cigar. When he left again he did not notice anybody waiting for him. He did not care whether Fisherman had eyes on him this trip. It would only cause trouble if the Sisters learned of his destination, and the Sisters were considerably easier to see.

By the time he reached his destination, he was sweating. He was pleased that an elevator stood waiting in the lobby, with several passengers already inside. That meant nobody watching the control panel could be sure which floor was his. When the doors opened on nine, McWade stepped into a small waiting room where a receptionist was busy clipping a newspaper.

"I'm here to see Mr Leighton," he said.

The woman punched up a number on her phone and said, "Guy here to see you, George."

The arrangements had not exactly pleased the reporter. He would have preferred a fancy lunch, but he had grudgingly acceded when McWade explained that he could not afford to be seen in public just now.

"Welcome to the nerve center," Leighton said as he came through the inner door.

McWade followed him inside. Piles of press releases and documents littered rows of gray metal desks. On the walls hung old campaign posters, photographs of recent Presidents caught looking like fools. A few people were working at computer terminals or talking on the phone. They barely looked up at him as he passed.

"Back here, Ike," said Leighton, leading the way into the bureau's library. In one corner stood a small refrigerator with a coffee pot on top. The refrigerator was secured with a lock.

"You want something to drink?" said the reporter.

"No thanks."

"Mind if I have a soda? Maybe it'll satisfy my hunger pangs."

"If you want to go out later and put me down on your expense account, I won't deny it," said McWade.

"Hey, I'm an honest guy."

Leighton pulled out a key and opened the refrigerator then withdrew a single can of diet cola.

"Cleaning ladies'll rob you blind," he said, snicking open the top. "Now what's the big deal that you can't break bread with me?"

"Just being careful," said McWade.

"It's the fight you're having with Langley, isn't it?"

"First I heard of it."

Leighton tipped the can to his lips. A little soda ran

down his chin and dripped onto his tie. Leighton wiped it with his thumb.

"We going to have to go through all the foreplay?" he said. "I thought when you called you were ready to do business."

"Maybe I can help you. Give you some guidance. Steer you in the right direction. But first I've got to know what you've got."

"So you can lag it to one of your buddies at the *Times*?"

"I'll be straight with you," said McWade. "Publicity doesn't do us any good right now. But if we're going to get it, I'd just as soon it came from you, and I'd just as soon you got it right."

"Protecting my reputation," said the reporter.

"Protecting mine."

That seemed to please Leighton. He leaned over and put the soda can on the rug next to his chair then eased back and hung his knee over one of the arms.

"The word is that Langley's after your ass," he said.

"Mine?"

"Collectively speaking," said Leighton. "What I know is that Fisherman's got something started. I want to know what and why."

"You've talked to him?"

"I have a lot of sources," said Leighton.

"Maybe your sources are trying to use you."

"Hey," said Leighton, "it's like getting laid. You give a little, you get a little."

"Just as long as you know who's screwing who."

Leighton gave a little smile. Then it passed.

"Tell me about this big operation Ross had going," he asked.

"I can't say anything more about the negotiations than what's already been out. Sorry."

Leighton flicked away the notion of discretion as if it were a fly.

"I'm talking about when he was still in the Agency," he said. "Back before the purges. That's what it's all about, isn't it?"

"You're going to have to do a little better than that," said McWade.

The reporter obviously did not like showing his hand.

"Let's not fuck around, OK?" he said. "I know about NARCISSUS. I know that it was blown. Did Ross have a hand in that?"

"Times sure do change," said McWade. "Back during the purges when Ross tried to protect our sources and methods you guys accused him of covering up."

"Way I understand it, some people got killed."

"Ross was trying to contain the thing. That's what got him in trouble. He had his finger in the dike."

"Then why is Fisherman so interested in him?"

"You tell me."

"What was NARCISSUS? A person? An operation?"

"A name on a file," said McWade. "Maybe you should try to get Fisherman to show it to you."

"Forget about me and Fisherman," said Leighton.

"Here's my problem," said McWade. "Except for what you're telling me, I don't have any evidence of his interest. And the way I see it, you don't have much either."

"I've got the CIA investigating somebody on the National Security staff. That's a hell of a story, my friend."

"But maybe you can't even name the name," said McWade.

"Don't have to. And if I don't, you all get dirtied up."

"For all I know, Fisherman might be after me."

"Were you in on NARCISSUS?"

"I didn't say that," said McWade.

"It isn't you," said Leighton. "I've got that much solid. Otherwise do you think I'd be talking to you about it?"

"I have a hard time following what you guys call your principles," said McWade.

The reporter let out a laugh.

"Look," said McWade, "Fisherman stuck by Ross when you and all the others were running him out of town. And Ross stood up for Fisherman when the rumor had it that the new Director wanted him retired."

"Well, there's bad blood somewhere."

"I'm telling you as plain as I can," said McWade. "It isn't the CIA that's been nosing around our shop."

Leighton picked up on it immediately. And McWade did not even feel obliged to feign a look of regret for having let something slip. The reporter had been around long enough to understand that nobody in this town told you anything he did not want you to know.

"Then who is it who has been nosing around?" he asked.

"I've got to be sure you'll cover for me," said McWade. "This isn't widely known."

"Check my references. Hundreds of satisfied customers."

"We didn't even talk, right?"

"Ike McWade?" said Leighton. "Who's he, that new guy at Justice?"

"OK," said McWade. "The Sisters have a leak investigation going. They're interested in the disclosure of the Moscow talks."

"You're shitting me."

"I had a visit from one of them just this morning."

"Maybe Fisherman's behind it," said Leighton. "Maybe he set the Sisters on you just to see what they could smoke out."

"That's a little farfetched."

"He'd get the Bureau's take, wouldn't he?"

"Not routinely."

"You worked for him. You know how he operated."

"He can get what he wants," said McWade.

"So he sits back and lets the Sisters act as his cutout."

"You've got a hell of an imagination," said McWade.

"Hey," said Leighton. "Nothing surprises me anymore."

12

Leighton didn't draw an Agency connection in his story about the leak investigation. But he did ask a lot of questions before going into print, and that gave McWade a small victory. The Sisters were so concerned about the suggestion that they were fronting for Langley that the FBI Director issued an Airtel strictly limiting dissemination outside the Bureau.

This, of course, did not prevent public speculation about who told the original tale, and the consensus seemed to be that State had done it to sabotage the mission. There was no official comment, unless you counted the President's ambiguous remark at a press conference that the American government is a vessel that leaks from the top. And by the time Ross started back from Europe, where he had stopped off to brief the Allies, the flap had pretty much gone away.

Even if McWade hadn't leaked the story of the leak investigation, it would have been hard to sustain any campaign to discredit Ross in the face of the rush of exciting reports from the Moscow delegation. Ross had anticipated every Soviet move. And across the table, the Soviets had a sixth sense, too. They pushed hard until they reached the limit of what Simpson and Ross were authorized to accept, but for once they did not try to muscle beyond it.

Reading the cables, McWade thought he sensed an authentic change in the atmosphere. For the first time since SALT I, both sides seemed willing to discuss the fundamentals of the strategic equation. And unless something knocked the process off track, it seemed possible to reach agreement on deep mutual cuts. This was especially important now because with technology relentlessly driving toward greater precision in warheads, the land-based missiles of both superpowers were becoming more of a threat to each other's arsenal and at the same time more vulnerable to a disarming first strike. All the slack had been taken out of the trigger.

It was difficult for McWade to keep his optimism about the Moscow talks from coloring everything else. And as the days passed without a further word about Fisherman, he began to wonder whether the rumors of his intentions hadn't all been some kind of enormous misunderstanding.

As the talks drew to a close, the pressure on the Washington end eased. All the essential decisions had been taken, and it was just a matter of waiting until Ross returned. McWade saw a window of opportunity, and Sarah was able to rearrange her schedule to get through it with him. A night in Williamsburg was not the get away they had been hoping for, but they needed something. Or at least he sensed that Sarah did.

As they drove down, he told her as much about what had been going on as he could. A lot of it had come out already in one place or another, but he knew it would be fresh to her. She was not as attentive to news about his work as she once had been.

"I know I've been distracted," he said. "I haven't been there for you the way I should. But the stakes are enormous. *Glasnost* on the bilateral level. For once the Soviets are more open in private than in public."

"Let's not even think of it tonight," Sarah said. "Wasn't it in Williamsburg that George Washington warned about entangling alliances?"

"I don't think so."

"Well he should have," she said. "Everybody needs someplace where the world leaves them alone."

The declining sun shone amber through the trees as they approached the restored colonial village. The only downside of the Williamsburg Inn was that sometimes you ran into people you knew. It was a special favorite of the people at Langley. The archaeological aspect drew them, the idea that history became habitable once its secrets had been aged in the earth.

Fortunately, there were no familiar faces in the dining

room. They even risked an hour in the parlor common room, where Sarah played Mozart and Bach for him on the lovely old grand that sounded like a full orchestra compared with the little upright they had at home.

"You've been practising," he said.

"I've tried to spare you."

"I guess I've given you a lot of solitude lately."

"No entanglements here. Remember?"

"You are my one and only liaison."

"Then maybe we ought to think about liaising."

It was not like Sarah to take the initiative this way, and she seemed surprised at how bold she sounded.

"Am I being too forward?" she asked.

"Live dangerously."

"Well, all right," she said.

He thought he heard a note of hesitation in it, but maybe it was just the awkwardness that had once made him feel so secure with her. Still, when they made love, it was strangely urgent, as if she were trying to reach something hidden and reveal it, something lost to time. He could not tell whose secret it was, hers or one of his.

In the morning he woke before her and waited in the stillness, watching her eyes darting beneath the lids. He wanted to be part of her dream, but he felt excluded, as if she had not found what she had been looking for the night before. Of if she had, would not dare look at it in the light. He was willing to try again, to see if he could overcome the tug of inhibition that held him back from her. Had it been Leggatt he had been afraid of again, just as he had been in London when he was struggling to hold his crude double in check? There was no reason to worry now. Sarah had never been tempted by Leggatt, and since London, neither had he.

When she stirred, he touched her shoulder. She opened her eyes and looked past him to the bedstand clock.

"It's sinfully late," she said.

"It's never too late for sin. We were in quite a mood last night."

"All the ghosts that haunt this place."

"Dead patriots," he said.

"Shall we try to raise them again?" she said, just before the phone next to the clock began to ring.

He picked it up and heard his secretary's voice. There had been another cable, she said. The Deputy wanted him back ASAP because there were some final details to attend to.

"You told them where we'd be," said Sarah.

McWade sat up in bed and replaced the phone in its cradle.

"I always do," he said. "I have to."

"Of course you do."

Ross's homecoming was to be kept low-key in the interest of preserving whatever shreds of comity remained in the administration's foreign policy team. The arrival was not publicly announced. McWade and the deputy security advisor were assigned to do the honors at Andrews Air Force Base and transport the party by car.

It was one of those summer mornings when the price of coolness is a thick, engulfing fog. McWade checked in at the office briefly and then climbed aboard the caravan. The traffic groped along the whole distance. Just as the limos reached the base, the weather lifted a little, and the plane was able to touch down on schedule before the fog closed in again.

A special kind of fatigue sets in at the end of a long overseas mission. The traveling party showed the effects as it slouched down the steps. But then came Ross, looking as if crossing international borders only energized him. As he set foot on earth again, he seemed ready to plant or seize a flag.

The Deputy stepped forward to greet Simpson formally as he emerged from the plane after Ross reached the tarmac. McWade, the practised aide, hung back a pace or two.

"Congratulations," he said when Ross picked him up on the way to the cars. "It should have been a hero's welcome."

Whatever disappointment Ross might have felt at the modesty of the official reception, he sloughed it off. He had learned to live without public glory during his years in the Agency, accepting instead the narrower compensations of inside influence. The morning intelligence briefing was his *People Magazine*, the discussions in the Oval Office his turn on the cover of *Time*.

"We've got a lot to straighten out," he said.

"I think you'll find the groundwork pretty well laid," said McWade.

"I'm talking about the damned leak investigation."

"Oh, that," said McWade. "The Man was just having a little fun with State."

As they reached the second limousine in the line, Ross stopped.

"This isn't the first time one of his practical jokes backfired," he said.

"We weren't even touched," said McWade.

"He's got to bring State around. Otherwise it's going to be guerrilla war. I thought you might be bright enough to see that."

"Bringing in the Sisters was not exactly my idea."

"We're going to have to stop this thing."

"Too late," said McWade. "The word's already out."

"So I heard."

Read that: Not from your cables. McWade had not thought it useful to trouble him.

Ross let McWade open the car door for him. By the time McWade ran around to the other side, Ross was already on the phone.

"Set it up for eleven," he said. "We're briefing the President at ten, so it might have to slide . . . Sure, sure . . . Whatever the sonofabitch wants."

"Maybe you ought to give yourself a little time," said McWade. "I didn't book anybody in today."

"She told me."

It wasn't necessarily a rebuke for a principal to assert control over his own schedule, but McWade felt a sting in Ross's tone.

"I thought you might need to do some work in-house," McWade said.

"You've taken charge, I see."

"The docket is clean," McWade said. "I'll set up whatever you want."

"State's sending Potter over stalking. I hope you agree that I have to entertain the visit."

The car began to roll slowly, letting Simpson's driver set the stately pace.

"The networks have been calling about putting you on the Sunday shows," said McWade.

"It ought to be Simpson," said Ross, "or better yet, the Secretary."

"State would only throw smoke."

"Not if we put him out front."

"Everybody knows he was dealt out of the game," said McWade.

"I guess you've got your work cut out for you," said Ross.

McWade took it as a vote of confidence, being delegated the job of fashioning the public lie.

"You think Simpson would go along with putting State in the spotlight?" McWade asked.

"When he sees the President wants it that way."

"The Man's been undercutting State at every turn."

"I guess I have some work to do myself," said Ross.

McWade handed him a copy of the President's schedule for the day. Simpson and Ross were on with him as soon as they reached the White House, and there were several other windows during the day in case Ross wanted to slip in alone.

"You have to admit," said McWade, "you'd be the best salesman."

Ross turned in his seat.

"You pay too much attention to TV, Ike," he said. "It affects your judgment."

Ross never shied away from personalizing an argument. As he liked to point out, history is written by and about men. The key to his success was his skill in playing upon the quirks of those who held the decisive measure of power. If they had a weakness for luxury, he supplied it, for a price. If they yearned for the good life for their people, he threatened it. And if they liked to see their faces on the screen or had an undue affection for the sound that issued from their throats, he let them talk themselves into line. The devil's bargain was to grant a person's fondest wish. For Ross the *ad hominem* was not a fallacy. It was the way of the world.

The red tail lights of the lead car were like homing beacons in the fog. The traffic had thinned out, and so they moved at a decent clip. Ross did most of the talking on the way, fixing priorities, testing out avenues of approach that might be used to woo the skeptical elements on the Hill, getting McWade up to speed on what needed to be done.

When they reached the White House, the iron gate swung smoothly open and the guard gave a respectful nod as they passed through. Simpson darted out of his car and into the West Wing. There was no question of McWade participating in the meeting with the President, so he picked up Ross's extra briefcase and headed toward the Old Executive Office Building.

"Ike," Ross called. McWade returned to the car. "Emma is planning a small dinner party tonight. She wanted to be sure you and Sarah could come."

"Sarah will be delighted," McWade said.

"Seven thirty for cocktails. My secretary will call with directions."

McWade did not need them. Ross had apparently forgotten, but McWade had been favored with Emma's invitations twice before. Her events were so dazzling that he did not take it as particularly significant that he had been lost in the glare.

A daunting pile of pink message slips awaited him in his office. Betty had arranged them with the ones from the most important people on the top.

"I didn't know what to make of this one," she said, handing him a note that simply said Miss Johnson and did not include a number.

"Did she say what it was about?"

"She called herself a friend of a friend."

"Who did she say was the friend?" asked McWade.

"Somebody named Leggatt. She said you'd know."

McWade wadded the message slip up and dropped it on the corner of the desk. Then he permitted himself to meet his secretary's eyes. The message had to be Stockwell's way of signaling that he had something to report.

"Was there anything else?" McWade said.

He was in a hurry to find out what Stockwell was up to and why he had chosen to bring the hateful name into it. But before slipping out of the office, McWade called Sarah to tell her about the party. She was not enthusiastic, but she said she would meet him there.

"It's not as promising as a night at Williamsburg," he said, "but it doesn't hurt your practice to be seen in that kind of crowd."

"On your arm," she said.

"There are bound to be some interesting people to talk to there if you want to avoid me," he said.

"Let's make it a date rather than an obligation, Ike."

"Nobody there will care about me anyway. It will almost be like being alone together."

"All that romantic talk of diplomacy and power."

"Who's up and who's down."

"We're going to talk ourselves out of it," she said.

He switched the phone from his right hand to his left and began jotting down a list of things he had to do when he returned to the office.

"Are you there?" she said.

"Yes," he said. "Somebody's buzzing me."

"Sometimes I don't know for sure."

Fortune was not open for customers when McWade arrived. Lan let him in through the kitchen. It was cleaner than he would have guessed, every counter bare, with woks and iron implements hanging over them from hooks.

Blackie was in the dining room dressed in olive drab boxer shorts and T-shirt. Before him on a table was an old adding machine, a metal cashbox and a clutter of letters, bills and receipts.

"The king is in his counting house," said McWade.

"We're closed," said Blackie.

"I'm looking for Rufe."

"You see him here?"

"How would a man contact him who needed to in a hurry?"

Blackie reached into the cashbox and tossed a quarter across the table. It spun for a moment, then came to rest.

"Call information," he said.

"He tried to reach me. I wasn't in the office."

"Missed connections," said Blackie. "They'll fuck you up every time."

"If you see him, tell him I came looking."

"You might try the zoo."

"When?"

"Give him about an hour."

"Any place in particular?"

Blackie stood up and scratched his belly through the GI cotton.

"By the pandas," he said. "Ever since Korea Rufe always had a soft spot in his heart for the Chinese."

By the time McWade fought his way through the traffic and found a place to park, it was nearly eleven thirty. He made a quick circuit of the zoo, slipping into the small mammal house along the way. When he got out the other end he queued up at a refreshment stand and watched to make sure nobody emerged behind him. By the time he had gotten to the front of the line and bought a Coke, the only people who had come out were a small boy and his exasperated mother.

When McWade reached the pandas, he found Stockwell throwing peanuts. He would take one from the little bag and fling it overhand with a lot of shoulder behind it and a snap of the wrist. None of the missiles actually hit the animals, but it wasn't for want of trying. McWade came up next to him and leaned on the rail. Stockwell wadded up the bag and hurled that, too.

"We're going to have to use a better system," McWade said. "From now on we'll signal by the London book."

"We might as well walk," said Stockwell. "I'm out of ammunition."

They moved lazily as McWade ran down a list of signs

166

and countersigns. Children raced around them. Up ahead a lost balloon rose slowly above the trees. A little girl gazed up at it sadly until her mother bought her another, which she promptly set free.

"Well, what have you got for me?" said McWade.

"Been real quiet."

"Fisherman's biding his time."

"He must think he's going to live forever," said Stockwell.

"You don't think he's given up, do you?"

Stockwell stopped at a bench and sat down, glancing right and left like a man who enjoys watching people in their natural habitat.

"He's awfully interested in Ben Wheeler, the way I hear it."

"You told me that already," said McWade. "You didn't say why."

"He's been around to see some of the old crowd from the OSS."

"Maybe it was just nostalgia," said McWade.

"He's been asking about Wheeler's habits. What he did on his own time. Like he was vetting the poor bastard. A guy deserves better, once he's dead."

"What's he looking for?"

"Jesus, it's hot out here," Stockwell said. "Let's go in somewhere."

The closest building was the reptile house. Enormous snakes lay curled up against the glass. The room was dark and muggy, and it had the scent of urine and rancid food.

"We're going to have to let him make a play," said McWade.

"What does Ross think?"

"I haven't talked to him about it."

"You're not sure of him."

"Just me and thee, Rufe," said McWade. "And like the man said, I'm not so sure about thee."

"He knows though."

"Does he?" said McWade.

"Guy like Ross? He's wired."

"He hasn't said a thing."

"Maybe he's not so sure about thee either."

"Are you?"

They moved through the reptile house and out again into the heat.

"I don't know which is worse," said Stockwell, "the stink or the fucking sun."

He led McWade to the aviary where their words were covered by an echoing din of song.

"I got a little something on Ross," he said. "But I don't know if it adds up to anything."

"A lot of guys at State are taking shots at him," said McWade.

"Look, if you just want to save his ass, count me out. I don't owe anybody enough to take a side."

"I wouldn't ask you to," said McWade.

"I hear Ross was the one who set up Richard Harper's boy."

"The kid he told me about the night he showed up in my living room? The one who killed himself?"

"When Fisherman wanted to put the squeeze on Birch, he apparently called Ross and had him get word to Kerzhentseff."

"Kerzhentseff must be a pretty accommodating guy."

"Wouldn't you have been interested?" said Stockwell.

"What was the pitch?"

"All I know is what a guy I know heard later from a defector. The story the defector told is that Ross led the Russians to think he was pissed at the way he'd been treated during the purges."

"And Birch looked to Kerzhentseff like a go-between."

"That's the tale."

"It's hard to believe Kerzhentseff really figured he'd be able to get to Ross."

"What did he risk? He exposes himself one time, and from then on it's just some poor wretch from the Embassy motor pool who has to take all the chances."

"And when Birch gets caught . . ."

"His great pal Harper runs away from him. Birch is the man in the middle, caught in contact with the KGB. He doesn't know who's who anymore. He has nowhere to turn. So he checks into a cheap motel and kills himself and the whole thing fades away."

The noise was getting on McWade's nerves. He began to edge toward the door.

"When did this defector appear?" he asked.

"Year ago. Maybe two."

"After Ross was back in the fold."

"You're thinking maybe Kerzhentseff sent the defector to piss on Ross because Ross had played Kerzhentseff for a sucker," said Stockwell. "That was the reading the thing got at Langley. Ross just laughed it off, they say."

"Kerzhentseff isn't the only one with a reason to go after Fisherman and Ross," said McWade. "Richard Harper was an even bigger sucker. The Birch thing sunk his career. That's what you're saying."

"Don't get me wrong," said Stockwell. "I'm not saying a thing."

They left the piercing chatter of the birds and circled back toward the gate.

"I'll lag behind," said Stockwell. "Give you fifteen minutes to clear."

"Good of you, Rufe," said McWade. "But from now on don't signal me with that Leggatt business. Guy deserves better, once he's dead."

"What Leggatt business?" said Stockwell.

"The woman on the phone," said McWade. "The one you had call my office. Who was she, Rufe?"

"Nobody I know," said Stockwell. "I thought you were the one who came looking for me."

"You mean that wasn't one of your dollies?" said McWade.

"It must have been a secret admirer, my friend."

13

Emma Baron's street was growing fashionable around her. Of course, the big old houses along it had always had a lot of charm, and Emma would have been the last person to point out that it wasn't until she started entertaining that their prices began to outpace the curve. She didn't have to. Everyone knew. In Washington, real estate was politics by the quarter acre, a matter of finding your place and then relentlessly improving it.

Every window in her home was brightly lighted, and this made it seem more imposing than its neighbors, though some of them were in fact a good deal more grand. A man in a tuxedo opened the door when McWade rang the bell. Inside, another accepted his umbrella. Emma herself stayed back several paces. Ross's secretary had said the dress was to be informal, but Emma had stretched the definition to its limits. Her long white gown made her the most striking woman in the place.

"Isaac," she said, extending her hand and drawing him forward for the obligatory kiss on the cheek. "We were beginning to think there had been a crisis."

"All is well," said McWade.

"I made Michael promise that nothing would delay him tonight short of total war."

Sarah stood across the room near the fireplace, her arm resting on a low mantelpiece beneath a towering oil of a former attorney general whom Emma counted among her ancestors. Beyond her, a double door led to the windowless dining room where the place settings sparkled amber in dusky light like crystals left by a glacier. McWade started toward her. She saw him and took a step to open a place for him in the circle. But before he reached her, he spotted Fisherman in the far corner, locked in conversation with Ross.

170

Fisherman noticed him, too, and gave a nod. It would have been a confession of weakness for McWade not to have faced the man. So he turned to Sarah and lifted one finger to beg her pardon. He did not wait to see if she gave it.

"So," said Fisherman, "now it's to be a *ménage à trois*."

McWade took his hand, and the grip was steady without being especially firm.

"And to think we're here to celebrate the cause of peace," said McWade.

"You know I'm not concerned with causes," said Fisherman, "only with effects."

"Ernest would be the first to tell you," said Ross, "that peace is the common enterprise on his side of the river, too."

"Peace through knowledge. Peace through strength. Peace through commerce and contact," said Fisherman, as if the word was wearisome to repeat. "Peace can justify almost any course a man might choose to pursue."

"You shouldn't be so hard on our pieties, Ernest," said Ross. "They're good for morale."

Fisherman gave a little bow of acknowledgement.

"What are your views on that, Isaac?" he asked. "Do you think it is always useful to say what others want to hear?"

"If you'll excuse me," said Ross, "I have duties. Why, I haven't even said hello to your lovely partner, Ike."

"Neither have I," said McWade.

"We don't want her to feel excluded."

When Ross stepped away, McWade was trapped. He put his back to Sarah to avoid her impatient glances.

"I was surprised to find you here, Ernest," he said.

"You seem to have become quite settled in your expectations," said Fisherman.

"When you leave the trade, you start to lose your edge."

"A consequence of love and security, I suppose." Fisherman exchanged his empty wine glass for a full one from the waiter's silver tray. "Your drink is Scotch, isn't it?"

"Just some soda water," McWade told the waiter. "With a twist to make it look like gin."

"Sober fellow on such a festive occasion."

171

"It doesn't seem to be the kind of company in which you'd want to free your tongue."

Fisherman raised his glass to that and took a sip.

"It was really very thoughtful of Mrs Baron to include me," he said.

"And quite a rare achievement for her to have you accept. They'll be talking about it tomorrow."

"But think of what they might have said if I had declined."

"I thought you wanted your doubts to be known," said McWade. He watched for any gesture of recognition, but tonight Fisherman wasn't giving anything away.

"I suppose that when a man gets old enough to begin imagining how he will be remembered," said Fisherman, "he risks becoming vulnerable to the desire to be understood."

"George Leighton is a strange one to entrust with your reputation," said McWade. "Most men just write their memoirs."

"I would need a sycophant as attentive as Boswell," said Fisherman. "Do you know of one?"

But before McWade had to answer, relief arrived in the person of the House Minority Whip.

"Talking shop?" he asked.

"Ernest has been thinking of writing his autobiography," said McWade.

"Now that would be something to read," said the congressman.

"Actually," said Fisherman, "I have been going back lately and trying to reconstruct certain moments. Just to see how they hold together this many years after. Nothing as grand as history, mind you. That is not for us to write."

"Hell, Ernest," said the congressman. "If you don't write it, a hundred years from now those boys are still going to be trying to figure out what you fellas have been up to."

"Of course, nothing I wrote would circulate," said Fisherman. "It would remain on Langley's closed reserve. I would hate to expose those who have thought they have known me to the truth and vanity of my failures."

"There you go twisting things again," said the congress-man. "All the wise men say that success is vain and failure noble. Well, dammit all, Ernest. We're modest folks, you and me. We don't want to be noble."

His belly shook with laughter, and he clapped Fisher-man on the back with his open palm.

"I hope you won't forget your contemporaries," said McWade.

"It would be an interesting exercise," said Fisherman.

"What would you say about our host?"

Fisherman paused. McWade detected a glimmer of respect for his daring.

"I suppose I would say that Michael Ross is a true patriot," said Fisherman, "one in whom national interest and personal ambition have burned with a single, bright flame."

"A damned fine epitaph," said the congressman.

"Would it serve as your own, Ernest?" asked McWade.

"I have never been able to find the happy convergence," said Fisherman, "that sustains great men like Ross."

The congressman liked that so much that he drew one of his colleagues over to share it, and McWade was able to make a retreat. But before he could reach Sarah, he was cut off by a woman from the *Post*, who said she wanted him to meet her husband. She introduced him by his job description, everything but the GS rating.

"Who was telling me about you the other day?" she asked.

"One of my many detractors," said McWade.

"Were you really a spy?"

"Are we on the record here?"

"It's a party," she said gaily. "There's no record. Only gossip and luscious innuendo."

"Then you shouldn't believe everything you hear."

This obviously pleased her. She laughed, taking his arm as she did. Her husband did not seem to mind, but McWade noticed Sarah eyeing them from her spot near the fireplace.

"It's a fascinating group, don't you think?" said the woman from the *Post*.

"A peculiar one," said McWade.

"Simpson isn't here. Nobody from State either. Very intimate."

"Simpson had another commitment," McWade suggested. He did not want the guest list reported as a snub. "And I understand the Secretary is hosting something of his own."

"How very convenient," said the woman.

"In fact," said McWade, "it is very inconvenient. State has the lead in the arms negotiations, you know."

"Does it now?"

She showed no particular interest in the line he was dutybound to advance. In what the journalists liked to call the marketplace of ideas, harmony always went at a discount; you could hardly give it away.

"It's sweet of you to try to protect Simpson," she said.

"He was invited. I'm just telling you what I know."

"And I know for a fact that he went home to bed. Jet lag. He doesn't have Ross's stamina."

"I didn't realize your beat was personal fitness," he said.

She did not take offense. She simply touched his arm again and said, "I'm interested in every part of the anatomy of power."

That finally got a rise out of her husband.

"Margaret," he said. "You're shameless."

"Here," she said, handing him her glass. "Get me a refill, won't you? I feel a wave of decency coming over me."

When her husband left, McWade maneuvered her into the circle where Sarah stood silently. After the introductions Margaret asked Sarah what she did, and when that did not provide an explanation for her presence, who she was with.

"I came alone," said Sarah.

"Actually, we're together," said McWade.

"Ike didn't tell me it was going to be a reunion," Sarah said.

"Ernest Fisherman you mean," said Margaret. "Isn't that precious. He's somebody you just never see."

"Until it's too late," said McWade.

Margaret touched him again, and Sarah was not amused.

174

"You ought to go introduce yourself, Margaret," Sarah said.

"Do you know him, too?"

"I suppose he knows me better," said Sarah. "He's had me investigated, hasn't he, Ike?"

"Not recently."

"Are you a risk?" asked Margaret.

"I haven't the faintest idea," said Sarah.

"Will you walk me over, Ike?" said Margaret. "You won't mind, will you, Sarah?"

Fisherman's conversation with Simpson's deputy perished mid-sentence when they saw the woman from the *Post* drawing near. As soon as she moved in and began touching Fisherman's hand, McWade took it as a formal transfer of responsibility, freeing him to ease away. But before he could get back to Sarah, the Deputy snagged him.

"We have to talk," he said.

They moved into the empty dining room away from the crowd.

"Who the hell decided to invite Fisherman?"

"Don't look at me," said McWade.

"It was a stupid thing to do."

"They've known each other for a long time."

"Fisherman's being cut," said the Deputy. "Ross is a fool to try to stop it this time."

McWade looked back into the parlor where Emma Baron had graciously interposed herself between Fisherman and the woman from the *Post*.

"I thought Fisherman's lease had been renewed," said McWade.

"He's not being dumped. He's being bled. They're ripping his budget, cutting his staff."

"He'll try to make an end run. That's why he was so cozy with the congressman."

"It's a hell of a time for Ross to give him a big, public kiss on the mouth," said the Deputy.

"What's behind it?"

"The Director is tired of the Agency feeding on its own

flesh. And it's not worth a fight. We need Langley with us on the bigger things. Ross will understand."

"Fisherman can raise a lot of dust."

"Not if everybody's wetting on him."

The lock didn't exactly click open to reveal all the hidden jewels, but a few of the tumblers did drop into place. If Fisherman was able to come up with something on Ross's own operation, nobody could touch him for fear of being accused of a coverup. The counterintelligence budget would have to be restored. And Fisherman would look pure as hell because everyone knew Ross had been his protector, his friend.

"He'll go after somebody," said McWade.

"It's a showdown, Ike," said the Deputy. "The Director isn't going to budge. We'd have to run right over him to save Fisherman's ass. And if we do that, we'll have the Agency ringing end of the world alarms about Soviet intentions every other day. You think we could hold arms talks under those conditions?"

"Don't underestimate Fisherman."

"Just talk to Ross. Explain the facts of life to him."

Emma Baron appeared in the doorway, an apparition in flowing white.

"This just won't do," she said.

"We've been conducting a little business, Emma," said the Deputy.

"I'm obviously going to have to change the seating arrangement," she said. "I can't have you near one another or you'll make yourself total bores."

"Maybe you could put me next to Sarah," said McWade.

"She's much too charming to waste," said Emma. "Now why haven't they brought out the shrimp?"

As she swept toward the kitchen, McWade turned to try once more to warn the Deputy about Fisherman's methods. But the Deputy had already returned to the parlour and attached himself to a conversation. He was laughing quite convincingly, considering.

When McWade got home, he was surprised to find the house dark. He had been waylaid at Emma Baron's door by the woman from the *Post*. Just to make sure she didn't have the wrong spin on anything, he had toyed with her for better than a half hour after Sarah got impatient and left. So he was ready to find Sarah waiting for him with a bill of particulars about his neglect.

"Sarah?" he called.

He stopped at the table in the hall and flipped through the mail. Nothing but catalogues and bills. In the kitchen he poured himself a Scotch. To get ice out of the freezer, he had to rearrange the boxes of Lean Cuisine. When he had finally extricated the metal tray, he twisted it until it gave a gnashing crack. A couple of cubes fell to the floor and skated into a corner. He picked them up and ran them briefly under the tap before dropping them into his glass. Then he slid the depleted tray back onto the rack and closed the freezer door.

Sarah always lectured him about refilling it with water: a lawyer's idea of mutual obligation. If they both did their duty, neither would ever be caught short. This was one of the differences between them. She believed in rules and he in covert operations.

After taking a single sip of Scotch, he set his glass down on the counter and dialed her office. The whiskey stung his tongue and cleared away some of the sour taste of cigars and dinner wine. The line buzzed again and again. Of course she was not there. She would have told him if she were planning to stop downtown. He replaced the phone on the hook and took another drink. The emptiness of the house opened out around him, the hush of the air conditioner, the buzz of the refrigerator, the tick of the kitchen clock.

When he went to the living room window and parted the drapes, the street was deserted in both directions. Nothing moved. He let the curtains drop and slumped into the big old chair. He must have nodded off there, because when the door sprang open, it startled him.

"I was getting worried," he said as he rose to meet her.

She let him embrace her for a moment then pulled away and set the double locks.

"I went for a walk at the Tidal Basin," she said. "I needed some air."

"It was a rotten night for you."

"The whole cast of characters, each with a claim superior to mine."

"Bankrupt," he said. "I understand how you feel."

"Do you?"

He took her hand and led her to the couch. She let herself down onto it, but she was tentative, poised on the edge of the cushion, ready to move away.

"I needed to work things out, Isaac," she said.

"I would have gone with you."

"It was better alone."

He touched her shoulder with his fingertips, but beneath the thin cotton, her flesh was inert.

"There's been a lot of pressure lately," he said.

He waited for her to ask about it. He was prepared to lay out the more open elements. She would have been quick to see the implications, the opportunities and the risks. But when he looked at her, she turned away.

"I don't like what's been happening to us," she said.

"This too shall pass," he said.

It annoyed him that she didn't even give him the benefit of the doubt. The worst he could fairly be accused of was not giving her enough time. And everyone in Washington lived that way.

"It's not right," she said, "the way we've been."

"It hasn't been all that terrible, has it?"

She must have heard an echo of his irritation, because she turned her face to him and it was suddenly very hard.

"Maybe not for you," she said.

He stood up and let his hand slide off her shoulder, his fingers trailing across her hair like a bow across the strings.

"I think I've lost my way here," he said. "I'm not sure I know what we're talking about."

She looked at him as if he had just trapped himself in an implausible lie.

"I haven't appreciated your checking up on me," she said.

"Checking?"

She did not speak at first. It was an old inquisitor's trick, to use silence like a hot iron against the flesh. He waited her out.

"Have they told you interesting things," she finally said, "the men who have been following me?"

"Where did you get that idea?"

"When that awful man came here."

McWade took her face between his palms and gently turned it toward him.

"You're imagining it, Sarah," he said.

"Don't patronize me."

"If they were really on you," he said, "you'd never see them. Not unless you were trained."

"I know what I've seen and felt," she said.

"Sometimes what you feel colors what you see," he said. "You're trembling. Believe me, Sarah, it's only your imagination. It isn't real."

"I'm not crazy," she said. "You must think I'm awfully weak."

"It can happen to anybody."

"But why? There has to be a reason."

He had a dozen to give for his own anxiety. And every one of them was real. But the question he could not answer was this: what did she have to fear?

"It's late," he said. "We have all day tomorrow to talk about it. It'll be easier when we've had some sleep."

McWade let her go upstairs alone while he checked the doors and windows, rinsed out the glass and turned off the lights. When he had finished, he paused outside his study then thought better of it and hurried up to the bedroom. She was under the covers already, lying on her back, gazing at the ceiling.

He finished in the bathroom quickly and climbed in beside her. She was not yet asleep, though her eyes were closed now. As he leaned over to kiss her, he rested his hand on the soft curve of her belly and then let it move to her hip. She shifted her weight away from him. He pushed himself up on one elbow and let his lips graze her forehead and temple.

"I wouldn't be any good tonight," she said.

179

He let himself down on his side of the bed.

"It's all right," he said.

"You're angry."

"Tired," he said. But something was rising in him, an ugly presence he thought he had rid himself of long ago.

"Goodnight, Ike," she said, and even though the sadness in her voice enraged him, he had sense enough to be still.

Before long he could tell from the rhythm of her breathing that she was deep asleep. When he slipped out of bed, he avoided the creaky board in the floor and stepped around to her side. As he stood there watching, her head moved on the pillow as if she were denying something in a dream. He closed the door quietly as he left the room and moved back downstairs.

In his study his hand felt for the light switch, which by a carpenter's error was behind some books on a built-in shelf. The sudden glare stung his eyes. He shut the door behind him and in the same motion engaged the button lock.

Strictly speaking, the pages he had brought home should have been kept in a safe. Written in his own hand, they were not marked with an official classification stamp, but they derived from documents that bore the highest security designation. Top Secret plus a special code word for compartmented access. The word was NARCISSUS.

He lifted his briefcase to the desk and flicked the numbers on the cylinder. The latch came open under his thumb. He had never told Sarah the combination, and she had never asked. But he had often been careless. She might easily have seen it lying open next to his desk and noticed the numbers to which the cylinder was set. And it was not difficult to pick a standard lock like this one. Anyone with a few hours' training could have done it.

Inside his briefcase, the documents were neatly arranged. He checked the order of the file jackets and manila envelopes. They were just the way he had left them, but even an amateur would have known enough to replace them correctly. He found the file he was looking for and pulled it out. Gently lifting one corner of the cover, he slipped a letter opener in and slid it slowly along the edge until it hit a sticking point. Satisfied, he pushed the blade through the tiny clot of glue that held the file shut. It was a simple trick to check for searches this way, but now he was glad he had taken the precaution. With the jacket spread before him, he ran his finger over it until he found the rough spot. Holding it directly under the desk lamp, he inspected it. Nobody had applied a second dab of glue.

McWade relaxed back into his chair. His breath was shallow but his hands were dry. There was no reason to review the notes he had made during his investigation of Wheeler's death in London. He had brought them home only because he did not want them in the office safe. Too many people had access there.

Just because Sarah had not tampered with the material didn't mean that she hadn't been in contact with someone. She showed all the classic symptoms: the accusations that acted as denials, the undirected fear. He knew these signs all too well. He had detected them often in himself.

He wanted to believe the most innocent explanation. Maybe Harper had asked her some questions and she had answered, not thinking of what damage she could do. And only later did it dawn on her that she had been subtly turned against him. She was afraid to tell him, afraid to find out exactly what harm she had done.

But that just didn't fly. If it had been as simple as a conversation with Harper, she would have mentioned it that first morning. It had to be something more. He tried to remember whether at the party she had shown any unusual awkwardness around Fisherman. No, she had been perfectly cordial and proper with him. It had been a strain, but it always was.

Worst case. What did she know? All she could report were his comings and goings. She might have said something to Fisherman's agents about Harper's visit. But McWade had to assume the old man knew all about that already. Fortunately for both of them, when it came to anything that mattered, she was in the dark.

McWade opened the drawer and took out a bottle of Elmer's. He put an almost invisible spot on the file jacket just a few inches from the first then closed the cover, pressing it with the heel of his hand. When it had set, he put everything away and turned the cylinders of the lock on his briefcase to another number he would remember just in case someone fooled with it and was sloppy enough not to set it back right. He did not think she was cunning enough to recognize the mnemonic, so he felt free to use a number that should have meant something to both of them – the date years ago when they had first met.

14

The faraway ring of the telephone saved him from a nightmare of capture and interrogation. His eyes snapped open, but he did not know where he was – London, Langley or somewhere behind the Wall. A rush of panic went through him. Who he was depended on where he was. Even now.

But then the elements came back to him: the light on the blinds, the digits of the clock, the faraway sound of the phone ringing in the kitchen, the curve of Sarah's body next to him under the covers. She did not stir.

He rolled out of bed, dizzy and sour of mouth. The phone persisted, and he wobbled downstairs to get it. Damned White House operators.

"Hello," he said. The whisper caught in his throat, and he coughed.

"Mr McWade?"

It was a woman's voice, but it didn't seem right, too dark and distinctive. At the White House they liked them to be as uniform as new dollar bills.

"It's awfully early," he said. "This better be good."

"I will leave you to be the judge of that."

"Who is this?"

"We met in Prague."

He took the phone from his ear for a moment to listen for movement upstairs. The house was silent. He stretched the cord until he stood in the far corner of the kitchen, facing the wall.

"We met through Joseph Leggatt," she said.

His grip tightened on the throat of the phone. He heard the sound of breathing through the receiver and realized that it was his own.

"Mr McWade?" she said.

"Yes," he said. "I'm still here."

183

"There is someone else, isn't there?"

Her English was accomplished, but the inflection was alien, as if she had practised it with others for whom it was also a foreign tongue.

"I'm alone," he said.

"That is good. You see, I am very afraid."

"Yes," he said. "Of course."

The connection broke.

"Hello?" he said. "Goddamn it. Hello?"

"I must pay more coins," she said. The line gagged as she dropped them in.

"Do you have some way of identifying yourself?" he said.

"Can you remember the day of the great parade?" she said. "All of Prague was in the streets."

"Yes," he said. But the voice on the phone was too young. His contact that day had been a grandmother.

"The hotel," said the woman. "You read me a strange, exciting story."

"Who put you up to this?"

"You don't remember me," she said.

"What do you want?"

"To see you," she said. "Today."

She delivered the demand without a waver of emotion.

"Maybe you'd better tell me why."

"You say where and when," she said. "I have something you will want. And I'll want something in return."

"How much?"

"Money is of no use to me," she said.

He heard footsteps above him, the sound of an opening water tap.

"Are you here in Washington?"

"I will be wherever you tell me."

It was a risk to talk openly on an unsecured line. But he had no choice if he wanted to see her. He gave the instructions once, quickly. She did not ask him to repeat them. She was a professional; he was quite certain of that.

"What time?" she said.

"Eleven o'clock. Wait no later than eleven fifteen. I will

184

be in a brown Toyota automobile. Do you know what that looks like?"

She gave a short laugh.

"I have studied all of your American customs," she said.

Sarah came down the stairs and into the kitchen. He turned to her from the corner as if he had nothing to hide.

"It will be good to see you again, Joseph," said the woman. "Perhaps you will find my story as interesting as I found yours."

"All right then," he said, his tone suddenly brisk and businesslike. "It can't be helped."

Sarah watched him as he crossed the room and hung up the phone.

"They got an early start this morning," she said.

"I'm sorry if I woke you."

"I couldn't sleep anyway," she said. "Thinking about last night."

"It was a terrible party."

"I mean the way I acted." She pulled a stool from under the counter and sat down, her arms bundled around her. "I don't know what I was thinking about."

"It happens," he said.

"We need to settle down," she said. "We'll spend the day reading the Sunday papers, things in black and white."

"I have to go into the office, I'm afraid," he said. "Something's happening apparently."

She came off the stool and went to the stove. Her back was toward him as she rearranged the pots and pans with a certain amount of clatter and then turned on the fire under the kettle.

"Can't you let it happen just this once without you?" she said. "Tell them there's been a family emergency."

"I can't lie to them."

"Maybe you won't," she said. "But don't say you can't. You could if you wanted to. You've been trained."

It stung him to hear her put it so bluntly. He went to the sink and drew a glass of water. It did not wash the taste from his mouth.

"Someday maybe I'll be able to tell you what's been going on," he said.

"Do whatever you want."

"They own me."

"They own us both."

It was early enough that the streets were all but deserted. Still, McWade used the one-ways and narrow alleys to make absolutely sure there was nobody following. Eventually he pulled into a McDonald's and found the pay phones. He dialed the number from memory and let it ring for several minutes before Stockwell finally answered.

"Yeah," said the phlegmy voice.

"Bob?"

"Who?"

"Is Bob Hawkins there?"

"You got the wrong number, buddy," said Stockwell.

"Isn't this 248-0602?" The last digit was the signal for where he wanted to meet. The three preceding it gave the interval in minutes before the contact should be made. It was comforting to McWade to be working by the London book again.

"Not even close," Stockwell growled and then hung up.

McWade ordered breakfast and carried the styrofoam containers to a booth near the windows. A few other people drifted in as he ate, but nobody to worry about: harried dads with their kids, men in workclothes, older women alone. When he was finished, he checked his watch, picked up the empty coffee cup and the rest of the trash and dropped it in the wastebasket. Then he went to the phone and dialed Stockwell's number again. There was no answer.

Outside, the traffic had picked up a little, but McWade wasn't especially concerned about it. He drove straight to the bridge over Rock Creek Park and left the car a half block down the way. The exit ramp had a decent shoulder, but he didn't have to walk on it. There were still no cars coming off the parkway at this hour.

Stockwell was up ahead, leaning wearily against a tree at the spot where the bike path veered away from the road.

"For a guy who isn't paying," Stockwell said, "you sure do make unreasonable demands on a man's time."

"We've got a problem," said McWade. "The woman who called my office mentioning Leggatt."

"Somebody playing mindfuck," said Stockwell. "Amateur Handholder. The world's full of them."

"She called again this morning."

"I can't stand squirrely women."

"She said her name was Medera."

"Nice name. Like the wine."

"From Prague. My first time out. You remember."

"The one you picked up? I remember thinking, well, maybe this doofus isn't as slow as he looks."

Stockwell pulled out a package of French cigarettes from his safari shirt and lighted one. The acrid smoke made him cough.

"I always thought I'd been set up," said McWade.

"Take it from me, pal. When they really do you, you know you've been done. They explode through the bedroom door yelling, 'Gotcha!' or words to that effect. And the next thing you know they're hauling your bare ass into the street while the sweet little thing is cadging herself a smoke."

"Now she suddenly shows up here," said McWade.

"Escaping to freedom. Looking for a better way of life."

"With my name and phone number in her pocket."

"Resourceful," said Stockwell.

"I'm supposed to meet her this morning."

Stockwell stubbed out the cigarette against the mossy trunk of the tree and then pushed himself upright. When he began to walk, McWade followed him.

"You aren't authorized," said Stockwell.

"Not if she's what I think she is."

"You tried to run that down once, didn't you?"

"There wasn't any record. She never surfaced in the files," said McWade. "They can't very well call it consorting with a known foreign agent, can they? I went out of my way to ascertain."

"They can call it anything they want, chum," said Stockwell.

"But from my point of view."

"Fisherman isn't exactly famous for trying to see it through other people's eyes."

A whir of early bikers passed.

"What's my move, Rufe?"

"You asking what I would do?"

"Maybe you just want out."

"A good looking woman calls me out of the blue. Wants a secret rendezvous. You can count on it, chum. Rufus Stockwell definitely would take the bait."

The little park was crowded with folks who got their thrills by hanging around the edge of the runway as the big jets came roaring down. Families had set up charcoal grills and picnic baskets in the sun. Fathers lofted frisbees high into the wind as if they were trying to bounce one off the silver underbelly of a plane. Across the narrow stretch of water, heat waves rose on the tarmac, and a few solitary men and women stood at water's edge, spaced like birds on a line, watching the spectacle of gravity and lift.

McWade pulled into the parking area and left the engine on to drive the air conditioner and block out some of the deafening noise of the jets. It was still a few minutes before the rendezvous time, and she would not expose herself any longer than necessary. He was vulnerable, but she was more so. Or at least she would behave as though she were. For all she knew, he had reported the contact already. Unless, of course, she had been briefed on the precise nature of the spot he was in and knew that for once in his life he was operating outside the chain of command.

A flash of red darted at the edge of his mirror. He turned and saw a shiny Camaro turn in his direction and cruise slowly down the line. It carried rent-a-car plates, Maryland issue. The sun flared off the glass, but he was pretty sure there was no one inside but the driver. He forced himself to look away and check the highway and beyond. The traffic was moving at a brisk, steady pace. There was no reason to retreat.

The woman wasted no time in making contact. She walked along the grass at the edge of the lot, idly glancing into every car. He had to admire her poise. He leaned over and swung open the passenger door. Without a moment's hesitation, she slid in beside him.

"I hope you cleared your path," he said, using her language, just as he had the first time.

"I think I am clean," she said.

She had not changed much over the years. A girl from the provinces, a little unsure of the ways of the city. But her face had matured, grown harder. No one could sustain forever the legend of innocence.

"Are you wired?" he asked, in English now.

"No. And you?"

"It's my country. I don't have anything to fear."

He put the car in gear and pulled onto the highway.

"I am confident, too," she said. "My people know nothing about this."

"They usually know more than they let on."

"I'm special," she said. "I have always been special."

"The grace of the KGB," he said.

She replied with a smile of complicity.

"They were the ones who assigned me to you in Prague," she said. "It was a test. I was to evaluate your weaknesses."

There was enough of the legend left in him that he did not register the shock of it. He was quite confident that he showed nothing at all.

"And what did you tell them?" he asked.

"That Leggatt was a cold, cold man. You see, I really believed I could get you to stay."

It would not have been difficult for the Soviets to have made the Leggatt connection once McWade had come out into the open and taken the NSC job. In fact, Langley had corrected against this very likelihood. The Czech operation had languished once McWade left the Nest, so it was not so very costly simply to roll it up before the formal announcement of McWade's appointment. But if the Soviets had compromised him from the very beginning, that would be another matter. It would cast doubt on everything he had achieved as Joseph Leggatt in the field.

McWade had reached the beltway, but he was beginning to get nervous about the traffic. Too many cars, all in a line. They moved at a steady fifty-five, so it was difficult for

McWade to know whether anyone was on him. He pulled off at the next ramp, slowing down to the posted twenty-five. Nobody took the exit with him.

"Maybe you'd better get on with it," he said. "I don't know what you told your keepers, but I can't imagine that we have a lot of time."

The ramp deposited them on a drab, commercial strip rimmed by low buildings and a few scrawny new trees.

"It doesn't matter," she said.

"You may have an exaggerated impression of how special you are."

"I am not going back."

He pulled off into the parking lot of a small shopping center: a Safeway, a video store, a Venture and a theater with three screens, one of them marked with an X.

"Where do you intend to go?" asked McWade.

"I am counting on you."

"You want to defect?"

"It is a word with so many ugly meanings," she said.

"I'll have to get you with the right people."

She stared out the windshield at the lines of parked cars and the gaudy window displays.

"I will not talk to your friends at Langley," she said.

"That's going to be a problem," he said. "The Agency will insist on debriefing you. They will have to be involved."

"Not the man called Fisherman," she said.

"I worked for him once. You must have known that."

"I need your word."

"You will be protected, given a new identity. We have ways."

"It is not enough," she said. "That man is death."

McWade put his hands on the empty circle of the steering wheel and took up the play first on one side and then on the other.

"He's not an easy man to exclude," he said.

"Do you know a safehouse?" she said. "I will tell you everything. Then you will know why it must be done as I say."

It did not take long before he found an anonymous place along the highway, a survivor of the days before the

Interstate, when this was the main thoroughfare north and south. The motel formed three sides of a rectangle around a gravel yard. A few cars sat in the lot. In front of each door stood a single lawnchair fastened to the concrete walk by a rusting chain. The sign along the highway said, "Vacancy". It was painted on.

McWade told her to stay put while he went inside to get things set.

The woman at the desk in the office pulled a Walkman off one ear and gave him a card to sign.

"How long do you want the room for?" she asked.

"The night," he said.

"High roller," said the woman. "That'll be twenty-eight bucks. Up front."

He pulled out his wallet and gave her a twenty and a ten. This was strictly a cash transaction, and the name on the registration card had no official history: Fred Granger, Madison, Wis.

"Number six," said the woman, handing over a key and two singles. "It's over on the other side."

"It have TV?"

"Color," she said, "just like it says on the beautiful rainbow sign. Air conditioner works, too, if you give it time."

"Anybody in the adjoining rooms?"

"We look full to you?"

"The noise, that's all," he said. "We've been on the road sixteen hours. The wife and I need a little rest."

"Whatever turns you on," said the woman, glancing outside at the District plates on his car. Then she slid the earphone back into place.

McWade crossed over to check out the room before pulling up the car. The only window faced the lot, and there were no interconnecting doors. He switched on the TV and raised the volume. It was one of the Sunday news interview shows. The picture wasn't very good.

The air conditioner was mounted high on the wall. A smear of condensation had mottled the plasterboard beneath it. When he turned the switch to High Cool, the picture on the TV narrowed to a squint for a moment as the motor strained. The Secretary was saying something about the lengthy process of analysing the Soviets' proposals in detail. Ross had been right: he lost all the leeway once they got him under the lights.

McWade put his hand up to the vent. The air was tepid and damp. But at least the noise would help cover their voices.

When he went back outside, she was waiting dutifully in the car, all the windows rolled down.

"It's OK," he said as he got in and drove across the gravel.

When he unlocked the door of the room for her, she stepped inside and touched the threadbare floral spread on the bed.

"We will be here how long?" she asked. It was not a complaint. They had both known places just as bad, and for some purposes all places were the same.

"You will stay here until I can get things straight," he said.

"I am not afraid to be alone."

He closed the door and slid the chain lock home.

"This has been a surprise to you," she said. "I thought you knew, even in Prague."

He pulled a chair to the center of the room, and she lowered herself to the edge of the bed.

"I had made certain assumptions," he said.

"I hope you are not so terribly disappointed."

"This time you tell me a story."

It turned out to be a short one. She did not waste a word.

"Joseph Leggatt is back," she said.

"Leggatt is dead."

Yet even as he said the name, he felt the old one reasserting himself, lust and anger rising, seeing this woman again, and this time knowing it was not innocent, had never been.

"He has been reactivated," she said. "He has been seen."

"What are you talking about?"

"In Europe. Asking questions."

"You have spoken to him?"

The Secretary was making his closing comments on TV. McWade did not even turn his head.

"Others have," she said. "I have only seen his picture. He

192

has been asking questions about one of your people, the one you called Ben Wheeler."

"He's dead, too."

"They questioned me when they found my report on you in the files. They were angry with me. They thought I had failed."

"And yet they sent you here."

She stood up and paced the worn shag carpet. Her fingers worried the strands of her straight, black hair.

"They showed me a photograph. It wasn't you at all. He was younger. I told them to find the ones who had followed us that night and ask them."

"They didn't make a photo of us?"

"It was a mission of no great operational significance. They did not in those days waste their precious film. But the men who had seen you with me must have remembered your face, because the inquisitors did not ask me about you again."

McWade rested his hands on the arms of the old chair. It was only to control them, because everything in him wanted to lash out.

"Maybe they expected you to contact me," he said.

"That was my decision," she said.

"You tell such insulting lies."

She did not flinch at this. She stood with her back to the door, palms flat against it.

"I am capable of it," she said. "But if this is hard for you, it is because it is the truth."

"They aren't known for being so forgiving."

"They do not know enough to blame me. They do not realize that I knew exactly who you were, even then."

"You want me to believe that you covered for me?" he said. "I suppose it was out of love. Or maybe you were smitten by my prose."

"Because those were my orders."

"Orders?" he said.

"From Ben Wheeler," she said.

It took a long time to draw from her all the details, the way she had come to be recruited by the Soviets and then went to work for Ben Wheeler, whom she had then known only as Paul. She would have told the story from beginning to end, but he did not allow it. He interrupted, took her back, probed for any sign of contradiction. He did not want to believe a word of what she said.

She told him about her father. He, too, had hidden his contempt for the invaders in obsequiousness, the Slavic revenge against all masters, to ruin them with deference. And when she came of age and was approached by the KGB, he had introduced her to his secret and his contacts.

During her training period in Prague, Wheeler had passed her a message about the arrival of Joseph Leggatt. She was simply to report any indication of Soviet interest. She did one better, arranging to cover him herself. It was not so difficult. The Soviets wanted her debauched, sexually committed to their cause, and Leggatt was a convenient instrument.

After she filed her negative report, that was the last she heard of it, except for the lewd jokes among the oafs who had listened to the tapes from the hotel room.

Once she had proved herself to the KGB, she received various assignments, first in Czechoslovakia and later in Western Europe, where she traveled on a British passport given her by her Soviet handlers. She met Wheeler several times face to face, and he made promises to her about freedom. She depended on them, because she loathed the life she was leading. Her greatest yearning was to extricate herself from duplicity, she said, and become whole again.

But then suddenly the link to Wheeler was broken. He did not contact her anymore. No one passed her lists of new drop sites. She had no choice but to serve the Russians and wait for the call to come again.

It was not until years later, when she was interrogated about the false new Leggatt, that she learned Paul's true identity and confirmed that it had been death that had cut him off from her. And though the information she gave the sullen KGB inquisitors proved exculpatory, she realized that the time had come to flee at the first opportunity.

"Which they conveniently provided," he said.

"You are right to be doubtful," she said. "I cannot tell you what they had in mind."

"Maybe that you would lead them to me."

"You were not so difficult to find," she said.

He started to reach for the telephone, but she stopped him.

"That man," she said. "He will kill me."

"That isn't the way he works."

"Then why did he send out a man as Joseph Leggatt? He wanted to put me in danger. This person, this boy he is using, he is not careful the way you were. He is known to everyone. Fisherman must have wanted it that way. He knew they would check the name against the files. He knew they would find me there."

"Maybe the boy is someone else's," McWade said.

"When they interrogated me, they asked about Fisherman. They accused me of working for him."

McWade moved away from her and went to the window. Parting the drapes, he looked out at the dusty lot.

"There are others we could contact," he said.

She came up next to him and touched his hand.

"Please," she said.

She was close to him now, and he remembered how obsessively he had inquired after her in Prague. They had probably found that amusing. It must have corroborated her evaluation of him as a fool.

"Did you know the project Wheeler worked on?" he asked.

"Only what he told me."

"The code name?"

"It was called DANCER. Is that what you mean?"

He seemed to recall that this was one of the designations in the NARCISSUS file, one of the insignificant ones that he had not even bothered to record in his notes.

"You must think you know something that makes him afraid," he said.

She sat down on the bed again and leaned toward him as if the sound of the television and the rumble of the air conditioner were not enough to cover what she was about to disclose.

"After Paul was killed," she whispered, "I heard that he had been sacrificed."

"Set up?"

"The order came from your side, not mine. I didn't know whether to believe it until the KGB questioned me. But from what they asked, I could no longer doubt it. It was true."

"But why?"

"Somebody had been doubled. The word to kill Wheeler came from above."

"Fisherman. Is that what you're saying?"

"One evening I went to dinner with one of them from the KGB. He got drunk. He began to brag. That was the way he always acted when he wanted to take me to bed. He said we had a man at Langley, a man of influence. It was that one who wanted Wheeler dead."

"The hit order came from Moscow?"

"Kerzhentseff," she said, standing up and touching him again. A chill went from her hand to his. "It was Kerzhentseff who arranged it, on behalf of the American."

"Fisherman would have had no reason."

"Reason," she said. "You have gone beyond me now. I am too powerless to pretend to know a reason."

And as she stood there, her breast lightly grazing his arm, she was more opaque to him than ever. He could not account for her story. It was improbable, absurd. But the chill was not. He almost trusted the chill.

"I'll take care of you," he said.

"That man," she said, "he does not believe in defectors. If you turn, the KGB trainers say, Fisherman will never give you peace. Look at what he did to Schaliapin and Nogorny and the traitor Kirov. He will claim you are pulling a trick. He will accuse you of still working for us. Face it, they say. You shall always work for us. Until you die."

McWade touched her face. There were no tears.

"Everything will be all right," he said.

"I came to you because I hoped that you might have remembered," she said, "that once you might have felt something."

"I worked for Fisherman," he said again, this time to steel himself.

"Yes."

"But still you came to me."

"Ben Wheeler trusted you," she said. "And I trusted him."

"So did I," said McWade.

When she leaned her face upward to kiss him, he let her. Then suddenly the thought gripped him. He had become Leggatt's cuckhold, Leggatt's fool.

"It was never anything," he said. "We were both for others."

She held to him and whispered, "You searched for me afterwards."

"To give them a laugh, because when they laugh they do not doubt so much."

"I wanted you to find me," she said. "But, of course, I knew you never would. They did not think you were worth my time." She withdrew from him slightly, but only to take his hands. "Now I have found you. Come."

"No," he said.

She turned her face away, but her voice suggested anger, not shame.

"Then it was only Leggatt," she said. "A filthy vile storyteller. Nothing more."

"Don't leave this room," he said. "Latch that door and don't open it for anyone but me. I'll use his name."

"I'm the one who has been wrong," she said.

"You'll get what you want," he said. "But it may take some time."

"My name is Teresa Kostka. That is how they will know me in their files."

"They will only know what I tell them," he said.

She did not move from the bed as he went to the door. But when he was outside in the heat again, he heard her engaging the locks, just as he had ordered her to do.

15

McWade found Ross at Emma's house and told him everything, beginning to end, including his conversations with Fisherman. Ross was furious. His voice rose. McWade closed the sliding doors of the parlor and suggested that it might be best to go somewhere more secure.

"Security!" Ross shouted. "You're in a hell of a position to lecture me about security."

"Fair enough," said McWade.

"You held out on me."

"So as not to cry wolf."

"So you could run to Fisherman."

"To sound him out."

"Playing the middle," said Ross. "Who the Christ do you think you're working for?"

"That's never been a question," said McWade.

Ross went to the shelves and gazed at the lovely, unread leather volumes, his back to McWade.

"You fouled the nest," he said.

"Look, this is pointless. We've got a problem here."

"You've got a problem," said Ross, "and I've got you."

If they were up against Fisherman, he'd want them divided like this; he'd be counting on it.

"You can cut me any time," said McWade. "I'll give you my resignation." He went to the antique, leather-inlaid desk and took a sheet of paper from it. "I'll cite personal reasons."

Ross finally turned.

"Leave off the date," he said.

McWade signed his name in a bold script at the bottom. When he handed the document over, Ross read it quickly and then folded it in thirds to fit in his breast pocket.

"Very eloquent, Ike."

"Proof of my loyalty."

"I hope I won't have to use it," said Ross. "It would be a shame to lose you."

"Maybe you'd better talk to Emma," said McWade, "in case she heard the commotion. It wouldn't do any good for the word to get out."

"She's always discreet."

At least as long as it served Ross's interests to be. But if he ever had to exercise his option, the process would begin with gossip. It would go through the network like a flash message. McWade is on the outs. They have had words. Ross upbraided him for meeting some mystery woman. Tried to protect him in the beginning. Wanted to straighten out the mess. Ross has always been supportive of his subordinates, they would say, loyal to a fault.

"The question is where to go next," said McWade.

"It isn't easy, given her demands," said Ross. "You think she's adamant?"

McWade heard music coming from another room, a radio tuned to a classical station.

"She's terrified," he said.

The piece was a Chopin prelude, dark as rain.

"That makes things rather awkward," Ross said.

"We could run her ourselves," said McWade, "you and I."

Ross crossed the room and picked up a wooden box from the coffee table.

"When are you supposed to get back to her?"

"She'll need food."

Ross turned the box over, and his fingers deftly flicked the panels this way and that until it was open. He withdrew a cigar.

"It would be a mistake to leave her hanging too long," said McWade.

"Maximum pressure, minimum information," said Ross "It stinks of Fisherman, doesn't it?"

"Or someone just like him."

Ross seemed to savor the possibilities as he worked open the end of the cigar between his fingers.

"Have you dealt with Kerzhentseff before?" he asked.

"I know his reputation. But I don't see what his play would be."

"That's been the secret of his survival," said Ross, turning the cigar slowly in the flame of a match. "You always have to assume that he has set out a snare. They call him Zapadnya. The Trap. I've always been amused by the way he uses the French transliteration of his name. There's vulnerability there somewhere, but I'm afraid nobody has been able to find it."

"Maybe he's trying to manipulate the arms talks," said McWade. "Bring down the process by discrediting you."

Ross was concentrating now, moving in a familiar element, oxygen firing him, smoke rising from his lips.

"I'll need a few hours," he said. "What's your situation?"

"I can spend the afternoon at home."

"Sarah will be there?"

"She's no problem." McWade turned toward the window. "She is unaware."

"You may have to move rather abruptly."

"Sarah is used to emergencies."

Ross picked up the wooden box again in both hands.

"I'm sorry," he said. "I should have offered you a cigar."

"Ben Wheeler had a piece just like that," said McWade, taking the box when Ross offered it. He ran his fingers over the finely carved figures. "He would go through the elaborate motions of opening it and then show you that there was nothing inside."

"Like the perfect legend," said Ross. "He gave that demonstration to a lot of new men over the years. I prefer to use his box to hold something."

"He gave it to you?"

"It was recovered from his flat after he was killed. I suppose that strictly speaking I should not have kept it. But I wanted something to remember him by, and there were no heirs."

McWade tried to work the slides to close the top again, but he could not find the pattern.

"Here," said Ross. McWade watched him as he pushed the wooden pieces about in their grooves until it was once again secure, then handed it over. The trick was in knowing when to move the slides halfway. It took McWade less than a minute to expose the cigars again. He took one out and put it into his pocket. It was a much better brand than Leggatt usually smoked.

"I wish Ben were with us on this," said McWade. "I still find it hard to believe that he had turned."

"A moment of weakness," said Ross. "I suppose it was fortunate that he died before we lost sight of all his strengths."

"What could Ernest be thinking of, dredging all this up again?"

Ross drew on his cigar and found that it had gone out.

"He will use whatever comes to hand," he said.

"Wheeler was his friend," said McWade. "It's hard to believe he ordered him hit."

"Everyone liked old Ben," said Ross.

McWade had to assume that Ross would build a firebreak before sending him back against the woman. Under ordinary circumstances, the way to do this was to report the contact through channels. But then you lost control. The asset became common property, with everyone in on the tasking and, more importantly, the take. So McWade figured that Ross would probably allow him to act on his own for a time and would involve only a few others in the most peripheral way. This would give him the opportunity to spread the risk, learn what the woman had to offer against the threat of Ernest Fisherman and still retain the ability to deliver McWade any time it became necessary.

McWade did not find that particularly menacing as he drove home, heedless of the mirror now except when he had to stop abruptly at a light. In fact, it was a relief to have finally cast his lot. He had laid out everything he had, holding nothing back – except for Stockwell's involvement, and that was a matter of honor. He was no more willing to compromise Stockwell than he was to turn against Ross.

It was odd the way his loyalty had become a secret virtue. Ross could not count on it, and Sarah had no idea of the temptation he had just withstood with the Czech woman. Somehow everything had gotten reversed, like a photographic negative. He was working again in a place where darkness stands for light. The Handholders made a joke about it. The spy's unconscious, they said, is a sunny, smiling clime where all men are brothers and all women revered. It takes enormous energy, they said, to bottle up these subversive thoughts so that they do no harm.

Sarah was working in the living room when he arrived home. She had put on one of her jazz tapes. A half-empty wine glass stood on the end table next to a stack of correspondence and a yellow legal pad.

"You're overworked," he said.

"The world is safe again?"

"For the moment."

"Was it war or a natural disaster this time?"

"War is a natural disaster," he said. "Where are the newspapers?"

"In the kitchen. I waited for you. Then I got tired of waiting and read them."

"You don't have enough faith," he said.

"How much is enough, exactly?" she said.

The papers were spread out on the counter, front sections buried beneath the Sunday fluff. He retrieved the substantial parts and then went to the refrigerator. The wine he had put there to cool for dinner was in front, only a few inches left in the bottom. He poured himself a plain soda and carried the wine bottle to the living room to refresh her glass.

"Heavy hitting this early in the day," he said, withdrawing the cork.

"And you so perfectly sober."

"I hate to tell you this," he said, "but I might have to go out again later."

"Of course," she said.

He sat down next to her on the couch and she slid over, giving him more than enough room.

"Is there anything I can do to get back in favor?" he asked.

"Maybe we'd better just leave it alone."

She put down the legal pad and took a sip of wine.

"It can't be helped, you know," he said.

202

"You can't help being conscientious, and I can't help being a bitch."

He laughed because he thought she was making a general statement of causes, but then his smile vanished. Her hands covered her eyes. She was weeping.

"Sarah," he said.

"It's so banal," she said. "Anything I could say at this point."

"You don't need to explain."

"You don't even know, do you?"

"Know what?"

She wiped her eyes with a napkin. The mascara had run, making her look bruised.

"I've been seeing someone, Ike."

"About us?"

"Not a therapist. He's a partner in the firm. A tax attorney. Dull, normal. He loves me, Ike. He goes out of his way."

"How long?" he demanded. For some reason it seemed important to get the details, the full situation report: dates, places, the words they used.

"The night that man was here waiting for you," she said. "I was sure you had sent him. I'd been seeing John for about a month, but I was actually relieved when I thought you'd discovered. I wanted to think you were having me followed. I wanted you to be so jealous that you'd go to any length. But that wasn't it, was it? It was only business as usual."

"He came to warn me, Sarah. He came to tell me that I was in danger."

"I tried to believe that you cared," she said. "But you didn't even notice. You didn't even ask where I was at night."

"I guess I thought I knew," he said. Confessing his credulity was more painful than if he'd had to say he had been untrue.

"Oh, yes," she said. "At first it was flattering that you trusted me so. I had brought you in from the cold, you said. My poor, lost soul who did not even know what it

203

meant to let himself be loved. But then I began to realize that you don't value anything you're sure of."

"Where did you go with him? His apartment? Or was it some hotel?"

"When it mattered, you didn't care."

"What's the man's name?"

His voice was cold, Leggatt's voice.

"You won't do anything foolish, will you?" she said. "You won't try to hurt him?"

He did not answer her. He simply turned away. It wasn't her lawyer friend he hated. The man he most loathed was rising, furious, from within.

"I'll leave the keys tomorrow," he said, "after I've taken out my things."

"Where will you go?"

"We'll have to redo the lease in your name. Somebody in your office can arrange that, I suppose."

"Isaac," she said.

But he was already on the stairs, going up to pack.

"I didn't want it to end," she said. "You have to believe that."

He stopped on a middle step. Maybe there were certain words that she wanted from him now. Maybe if he said them they could try to find a way. But another's words were on his tongue.

"It doesn't mean shit what I believe," Leggatt said.

McWade carried only a single bag and his briefcase into the Jefferson Hotel. The others he left in the trunk of his car. Tomorrow he would have his secretary call around to find a more reasonable place. For now, though, he had to get himself situated quickly. And then he had to contact Ross.

"I'll be at the office in twenty minutes," he said. "Any developments?"

"Patience," said Ross. "She has nowhere to go."

McWade hung his extra suit and shirts in the closet then made a quick, professional search of the room. This was not absolutely necessary, but still he looked in all the obvious places for a microphone – under the lampshades, above the doorframes, at the edges of the rug. It was just a matter of discipline, old habits returning. As he left the room, he inserted a small corner of paper just above the lock. Any decent bag job team would notice and replace it, of course. He only put it there as a calling card, an announcement that he was back in the game.

He walked to the White House, suit jacket slung over his shoulder, his pace slow and steady in the heat. The old Soviet Embassy loomed up across the street – its roof strung with antennas like a barbed wire frontier – a gray, shuttered monument to secrecy and power. Americans tended to think of the building's boarded up windows as an acknowledgement of the Soviets' weakness and paranoia. But his service in the clandestine wars led McWade to see the dark fortress on 16th Street as a statement of the Soviets' advantage, an insult and a boast.

When he reached his office, the telephone was ringing. He flung his jacket and briefcase on the couch and picked up the receiver.

"Ike? Are you all right?"

"Fine," he said.

"I wasn't sure," said Sarah. "I was worried."

McWade switched the phone to his other hand and lowered himself into his chair. He pulled out his handkerchief and wiped the plastic where it had become wet and slippery from the sweat of his hand.

"Don't trouble yourself," he said.

"Do you have somewhere to go?"

"The operators here can always reach me."

"I might need to talk. There are things I should have said."

"I guess there usually are, Sarah."

"I mean my real feelings."

"I understand."

"But I don't," she said. "Not yet."

"You've only had a couple of months."

Sarah fell silent. McWade was ready to break the connection cleanly, but something held him back. It was as if the betrayal had created an obligation, the debt the loser at the table had to pay before he could walk away.

"We were slow at the beginning," she said. "Can't it be slow now, too?"

"Any way you want it."

"I'll pretend you mean that," she said, "that you're giving me time to figure things out."

"I'll pretend, too."

"Call me if you want to talk," she said. "I'll be here alone."

"You don't have to account to me."

"Only to myself," she said.

"Alone," he said. "That's what it means."

McWade put the phone back into its cradle and stared at the unlighted buttons on the console. There were things he could do to take himself away from his purposeless anger as he waited for Ross to give him the word. He lifted a stack of unclassified material from the in-box and began leafing through it. Then he put it back and went to the couch.

From his briefcase he withdrew a few old, fragile sheets. Back at his desk, he spread them out before him, smoothing each one beneath his palm. The afternoon light came in over his shoulder and shone on the fading names, which were listed in an order that once had meant something. Now the connections had all been forgotten, and the relationships were even more obscure than they had been when he had first written down the words. NARCISSUS, TANGO, LARYNX, ROGUE. Kerzhentseff, Andropov, Dulles, Helms, Ross. DANCER was not among them. It had seemed to have little significance, back then.

He ran through the permutations, all the possible alliances and uneasy ententes. But it was only an exercise. The combinations were infinite, especially when for the purposes of the drill you cleared your mind of loyalties. And it was not even necessarily a matter of finding the traitor, which was hard enough for a man who had just proven that he had lost his instinct for betrayal. In this case a higher order of duty might have to be factored in; the interests of nations were broad enough that they could cover all manner of personal designs. Fisherman's budget. Ross's advancement. Kerzhentseff's instinct for survival. It did not take a Handholder's training to realize how a man could see his self-interest as the equivalent of the greater good — sovereign imperatives embodied in human form, like ancient Gods descending to seduce the mortals and call it grace. Only Ben Wheeler's taste for the gaming tables did not lend itself to the grand excuse. And that did not help narrow the list of possibilities; Ben was not a player anymore.

When the phone buzzed again, it startled McWade. He took a breath and punched into the line.

"That was quick," he said, thinking it was Ross.

"Guess again," said Stockwell.

"I was expecting a call."

"He's in the boat then?"

"He's been informed."

"That takes care of you."

"You're covered, too."

"I thought I didn't exist."

"You are a figment of my imagination," said McWade. "Unless the damned thing suddenly gets real. Then I'll put you entirely out of mind."

Stockwell did not ask for a stronger vow. A promise was never worth more than you paid for it, usually less.

"What about the bird?" he asked.

"That's still pending."

"Instructions to follow?"

"Precisely."

"You could have found her a nicer rookery," said Stockwell.

"You've been there?"

"I've made a study of hot sheet joints in my time, and this one is off the bottom of the charts. It reminded me of the place Harper's boy Birch met his end. You do that for effect?"

"I thought it would be safe," said McWade. "I didn't expect anybody to be tagging along."

"Thought you might need backup."

"That wasn't in the plan," said McWade.

"I hung around until I got tired of watching the Casanovas come and go. You want me to go back and sit on it some more?"

"Maybe you'd better."

"OK, pal," said Stockwell. "Don't look for me. Remember? I'm the Invisible Man. I won't even fucking be there."

McWade put away the NARCISSUS notes and sat looking out onto the West Wing roof and the lawn. The TV crews were set up for the nightly standups, and McWade watched the correspondents getting ready – combing their hair and powdering the glare from their noses and brows. It wasn't too long before Ross finally called to give him the word to go, no more than the time it takes for a man to review his life and examine every error.

Ross did not explain all the details of the arrangement. He simply told McWade to babysit the woman until morning. By then there would be a reception committee waiting, he said, tailored to suit her. The Sisters would be represented, but not by anybody she would recognize. When McWade questioned the delay, Ross took it as a personal challenge.

"You had other plans for the evening?" he said.

"You know I'm not talking about my own convenience," said McWade.

"Then don't second-guess me, Ike. Get as much out of her as you can. I want to know exactly what she is going to say."

"They'll know I've sweated her."

"I've already given them a reason for waiting. Your previous relationship with her. They think it has some promise."

Or else Ross had told them that he needed time to bring McWade to his senses. *The man is making demands, and I don't know whether they're hers or his.* That would put Ross in a strong position no matter how the thing turned.

"And, anyway," said McWade, "it's my ass."

"Yes it is," said Ross.

McWade took a taxi back to the hotel, where he packed a change of clothes in his briefcase and then called to the front desk to have his car delivered to the door. However vulnerable it left him, he was more than willing to spend the night with the Czech woman, and there was more to it than duty. He needed to strike at Sarah some way, meeting betrayal with betrayal, repaying hurt with hurt.

After clearing his path, he drove south through the Virginia suburbs. On either side of the highway, where it intersected the beltway in a maze of concrete and steel, apartment buildings rose like cinderblocks set end on end. The few trees that had been planted here were blighted, as if the soil had been seeded with salt.

He drove past the motel once just to see if anything had changed. There was only one car in the gravel yard. It was parked along the row of rooms opposite where he had left her, a flashy old Pontiac with Ohio plates and an oath to Jesus stuck to the bumper. As he circled to return, he looked for Stockwell, but the man was good. He was nowhere to be seen.

The gravel bit the underbelly of his car as he turned into the lot, and the wheels skidded slightly as he applied the brakes. The sun was getting low now, but because of the haze there were no shadows. Hot air rushed in as he opened the car door and stepped outside.

Her window was dark. He knocked twice and said the name he had once gone to such hateful lengths to abandon. He could not tell whether there was any movement inside because of the clatter of the air conditioner. He knocked again. There was no answer.

"It's Leggatt," he said again. Then he turned the key in the lock and stepped inside.

The room was dark except for a shallow line of light on the shag by the window.

"Are you asleep?" he said, feeling his way toward the bed.

When he reached it, he felt a lamp upended from the nightstand. He set it right and flicked it on.

The room was a wreck. Bedclothes were strewn on the

floor, empty drawers pulled open, the telephone cord ripped from the wall.

The bathroom door was closed. He rushed to it, afraid of what he might find. But when he flung it open, it was all right. She wasn't dead. The woman was gone.

PART FOUR

Doubled

16

The Hastings was a perfectly acceptable address for a man on the way into town. But for someone who was already established to take a room there was a sign that he was probably on the way out.

The furnished apartment house was a plain 1950's building nestled among the more ornate old places the House of Representatives used as annexes for its less influential staff. In the morning the birds sang in a big old tree out back. McWade stared down from his high window into the leaves and saw cardinals flying up from the ground to perch on its limbs. They cast strange shadows in the angling light, and from above they were crimson apparitions – lost souls or devils on the wing.

It was futile to try to go back to sleep, even though there was no particular reason to rise. He crossed the room to the refrigerator, which stood along with the stove and sink in an alcove behind a dusty louvered door. When he opened it, he saw that he was out of milk and muffins.

The refrigerator door closed with a sucking sound as he went to the night table and retrieved a smudged glass. The smell of diluted Scotch rose up to his nostrils. He had taken to buying half gallons so that it was hard to judge how much he consumed each evening. But who was keeping track?

At the sink he poured out the pale liquid left by the melted ice then ran the glass under the tap, which groaned and sputtered as he turned the spigot. The water did not cut his cottony thirst.

A battered, black-clad short-wave radio stood on the counter next to the sink, veteran of all McWade's campaigns since the war. It was able to pick up everything from Radio Moscow to the Beeb's World Service, but now he left it tuned to a local station. When he switched it on, the announcer was giving a rundown on the traffic.

After rinsing off his face at the sink and drying it on a dish towel, he pulled on the shirt and slacks he had worn the day before. The news came on. He did not bother to shave.

The Moscow opening still dominated the headlines. Today it was a report of a commentary in *Pravda*, which the oracles were reading as encouragement. McWade could not help thinking about the gloss he would put on the Soviet remarks if anyone asked. The rigors of office had already softened into nostalgia. Nobody was interested in his opinions now that Ross had put him on unpaid leave pending an investigation of the disappearance of the Czech woman; all they cared about was what he knew and when he knew it.

He did not turn off the radio when he left the room. As he walked to the elevator, he could barely hear the murmur of the announcer's voice running through the public events of another day of which McWade had no official part.

Outside, the air was already thick and sticky. It stung his eyes as he squinted into the morning glare. The sidewalks were busy with people marching to work. McWade stayed close to the storefronts, as invisible as a street person. He was not eager to run into anyone and have to put up the double front of his pride and fall.

When he reached the little grocery, he ducked in and stood for a moment just inside the door, breathing the fresh, honest smell of citrus and spice. He did not take a cart, because his list was short. He bought his provisions day by day. Muffins, juice, instant coffee, cold cuts: breakfast, lunch and dinner.

Rather than risk returning by the crowded thoroughfare, McWade took the long way back, past the renovated old row houses. He kept his eyes on the sidewalk, a step at a time now, his horizon no more distant than the length of his stride. He did not see Swain crossing the street until it was too late.

"Jesus Christ, Ike," Swain said as he angled in front of him. "You're a mess."

"It's kind of early for me these days," said McWade.

Swain stopped a few paces short.

"I heard what happened," he said.

"Are they still whispering my name?"

Swain looked at his watch. "Let's have coffee," he said. "I've got an hour before the hearing. Simpson's up this morning. But I suppose you knew that already."

"I wasn't consulted."

"That bad, is it?"

"I think I'll take a pass on the coffee," said McWade. "I'm not exactly fit to be seen."

"Do I look worried?" said Swain. "Your stock isn't that low yet."

"Nice of you to say so."

"Hey," said Swain. "How long have we been friends, anyway?"

But, of course, friendship wasn't part of the calculus. Now that McWade was officially on the outs, the risk to Swain was minimal because everyone knew that the oversight committees made it their business to find the angry man. And from McWade's side, there was some advantage in getting Swain straight on the cover story because Swain was in a position to spread it around.

The restaurant was one of those places that catered in the morning to singles who took their croissants on the run. The waiter did not seat the two of them prominently, and for once Swain did not raise a fuss.

"They're saying it was a falling out with Simpson," he said. "Something about a leak."

"Is that the word?"

"Some think you got on the wrong side of Ross."

"Officially I'm on leave."

The waiter brought coffee in two oversized mugs.

"I warned you, didn't I?" said Swain. "I told you something was going on."

"It doesn't have anything to do with that," said McWade. "If it did, do you think they'd be keeping me on the roster?"

"Fisherman works his miracles in strange ways." Swain sipped his coffee and then added another package of artificial sweetener. "I might be able to help, if I knew for sure what I was dealing with."

McWade hid his disgust behind the rim of the mug.

"The dutiful way to put it," he said, "is to say that Ross had no choice."

"I thought sure it was Simpson. He's not a standup guy."

"The decision was unanimous. They couldn't take a risk just now with the arms talks about to go critical. They put me out on waivers."

"How about money?"

"I have a little put away," said McWade. "I'm not exactly living high."

Swain pulled off his suit jacket.

"The heat," he said as he hung the jacket on the back of the chair. "Where did it come from exactly?"

McWade did not have to improvise. His part was scripted on all the essential points, those that had already become public and those that had not yet slipped out. Like any accomplished legend, it rested on a foundation in the truth. And as for appearing troubled, he did not have to pretend; Leggatt was showing himself again. The details of McWade's removal were different from what they were being made to appear, but the underlying fear and anger were real for anyone with eyes to see.

"The Sisters," he said.

"You're under investigation?"

"It sure looks that way. They think I blew the whistle on a leak investigation."

"That story of Leighton's?"

"They're talking about putting me on the lie box," said McWade.

"Ross is? No wonder you're furious with him."

"Who said I'm furious?"

"You don't have to issue a press release," said Swain. "Look, do you need a lawyer?"

"My attorney has left me."

"I heard about that. I never did like the bitch."

216

To McWade's surprise, the word touched him at a place his cover did not reach.

"It just didn't work out," he said.

"She picked a hell of a time."

"That part wasn't her fault. It was coincidence. Things coming in twos."

"I thought it was threes."

McWade gave a stoic laugh, because that was the manliest form of self-pity.

"They're serious about the lie detector?" asked Swain.

"They've got me convinced."

"The Senator might be interested in pursuing that."

"Momma didn't raise her son to be a civil liberties case," said McWade. "I've been fluttered before."

"Can you beat it?" Swain was a pragmatist, and this was the operational definition of innocence. "I know a lawyer who's pretty good at this sort of thing."

McWade shook his head.

"You can't just lie down, Ike."

"I'm not sure posture has much to do with it."

When they got outside, Swain put his suit jacket back on.

"We ought to get together for dinner again soon, huh?" he said as he fixed the show of his cuffs.

"You haven't put me on indefinite leave pending further inquiries?"

"Hey," said Swain. "All for one and one for all."

"When do you want to do it?"

Swain was already stepping off toward the Senate side of the Hill. He stopped and pulled out his pocket calendar, then he put it back into his jacket.

"I'll call you," he said. But he did not ask for a phone number.

When McWade passed the front desk at the Hastings, the young woman behind it did not look up. The elevator was slow, and the building was quiet now that everyone who still had work had gone off to it. Once he reached the hallway, he listened for his radio but did not hear a sound. It was too early for the maid to have come through and turned it off. He slipped his key into the lock, turned it and gave a swift push.

"Gotcha!" said Stockwell, his finger cocked and aimed.

McWade did not flinch. He just leaned over and lifted the grocery bag, which gave way at the bottom. The milk carton bounced, and a juice can rolled into the room.

"Make yourself useful, Rufe," he said.

"Nice digs," said Stockwell, touching the screwtop of the half gallon bottle of Scotch. "Very homey."

"I wasn't expecting company."

"Needs a woman's touch."

McWade got the groceries onto the counter then put a pan of water to boil on the stove and rinsed out a couple of cups. They remained brown at the bottom even when he dug at the stain with his fingernail.

"You want some breakfast?" he asked.

"Never touch the stuff," said Stockwell.

McWade tore at the cellophane wrapper of the muffin package.

"It wasn't very bright of you to come here," he said. "They may be monitoring the ins and outs."

"It's a big place," said Stockwell. "I know some ladies who live here, if you call this living."

"When Fisherman is sitting on a place, he doesn't usually miss a thing."

"Look," said Stockwell, "I'm sorry the broad at the motel got away from me. It must have happened while I was off calling you."

"It wasn't your fault," said McWade. "Whoever snatched her knew what he was doing."

"Made me there first, you mean," said Stockwell. "Saw me driving away. I must be losing my touch."

McWade turned on the broiler and slipped a muffin in to toast.

"Shit!" he said.

"You get burned?"

"Forgot margarine."

"You look a little fuzzy, chum," said Stockwell. "I've been worried about you."

McWade removed the muffin from the broiler with his

fingertips then tossed it from hand to hand until it cooled. When it was ready, he took a dry bite. Then he put it down on the counter, spooned some coffee into the cups and poured in the boiling water. He handed Stockwell one of the cups and switched the radio back on, turning the dial until he got some music then putting the volume up.

"I'm going away," he whispered.

"Where?"

"Somebody set me up."

"One guy against all of them. It can't be done."

"I'll need eyes on Fisherman while I'm gone," McWade said.

Stockwell pointed to the radio.

"You worried he has ears?" he whispered.

"Worst case," said McWade.

"I talked to McWade sure," said Stockwell. "I heard about his troubles. Tried to get him to calm down. But he was buzzed out. I didn't know what the fuck he'd try next."

"There you go," said McWade. "Now all you've got to do is get word to Harper. Tell him he was wrong when he came to me that night. It wasn't Fisherman who was on my ass at all. It was Ross."

Stockwell turned his palms upward and looked at them as if right had become left and he couldn't even write his name.

"I'm missing something," he said.

"Don't you think I owe Harper an explanation?"

"Forget Harper. He doesn't mean anything at Langley anymore. Harper's just a scared little shit."

"This morning I passed the word that the heat is coming from the Sisters," McWade whispered. "That'll get back to Fisherman, too. Everything will. Stories on top of stories. And in all of them I'm the guy in the vise."

Stockwell sipped his coffee.

"You really don't look so swift, you know," he said. "That for show too?"

"It's the waiting," said McWade. "But tomorrow I'm gone."

"You gonna say where?"

"You don't want to know." McWade leaned down and tore a corner off a magazine then wrote down a number.

"That's in London. A message service. The box will be in the name of Fred Granger. Clear it every day."

Stockwell contemplated his stubby fingers again, scraping a little dirt from under one of the nails.

"I'd feel better if I thought you had some backing," he said.

"I've got you, Rufe," said McWade.

McWade had to stretch out his final preparations to make them fill the day. He could have simply called the Riggs Bank from a pay phone to confirm that the money had been deposited in his account. But instead he took the Metro downtown.

As it turned out, Ross must have taken care of the transaction in cash, because when McWade asked about a withdrawal, the bank did not give him the usual runaround about the time it took to clear a check.

He did not know where the funds came from. Ross did not have a black budget, so he must have made a bogus claim on the office account. Ever since the Iran-Contra thing, the NSC had been tight-assed about money, but McWade was not concerned about it. If the mission turned out decently, the expenditure would be more than justifiable. If not, then handling the books would be the least of their problems.

McWade could not complain about the setup. The legend was spreading nicely, near and far. Though McWade's troubles had not been considered important enough to make the papers, Ross had made sure the word of his fall from grace was all over town.

When he had finished his errands and packed his bags, McWade took a decent meal on Ross's budget. Afterwards, back in his room, he poured a Scotch, but only one. He turned the radio to an overseas band and relaxed to the soft, unintelligible phrases. It did not take long until, for the first time in weeks, McWade dropped off into the deep and dreamless sleep that his mother used to call the sleep of the just.

17

Once McWade reached London, Ross's plan for him was to draw the imposter Leggatt into the open and try to get some idea of what Fisherman was using him for. The debacle with the Czech woman made it clear that the old man had not given up his game. But his moves were magnificently oblique. McWade did not know whether Fisherman had deployed the woman or snatched her. He did not know whether this new Leggatt was meant to attract him or to frighten him away. But he did know what he had to do: Joseph Leggatt haunted him, and he had to put the ghost to rest again.

Ross thought the best way to find the imposter was for McWade to get back into the role himself. One Leggatt was trouble for the other; they would eventually draw together like positive and negative charges. So for days McWade prowled the pubs where the emigrés congregated to eat spicy sausages, drink stout and trade rumors of the past. He made indiscreet inquiries in many languages and complained bitterly: somebody had stolen his identity. The old Eastern European men listened with empathy; his rage was as real as their own and perhaps just as doomed.

A few claimed to know of a man called Leggatt who was involved in some dark operations that straddled the Wall. He was a big man, wasn't he? No, said McWade, just about my size. He lost his eye in Malta, they said, or perhaps that was someone else. One man held out his hand and displayed the concentration camp tattoo. Only the devil, he said, keeps a registry of who is who.

When his inquiries did not produce results, out of desperation McWade began visiting his old haunts along Fleet Street. In those circles he could not put himself forward as the real Leggatt. He had to be Tony Rogers again.

"Where the hell did you disappear to?" asked Tom Segal, now the London correspondent for *Newsweek*. It was as if McWade had been gone a matter of days. "Bloody disappointing to see you. We made up such lovely stories. Some said you were a spook. I took the cheerier view. I was sure that you were dead."

"I've been moving around quite a bit," said McWade.

"Well mate," said Segal, "buy me a pint and I'll give you some bad news."

He ordered two, and McWade fumbled with the coins, heavy and awkward in his fingers.

"I guess you've heard about Jane," said Segal.

"It's been quite a few years."

"I never could figure your dropping her. If it'd been me, I'd have kept my finger in."

"What a lovely sentiment," said McWade.

"I always kind of liked the broad," said Segal. "She did some pretty good work for me at UPI. It was a perfect fit. She didn't need money, and we didn't have any."

"She still in London?"

"Making a pretty fair go of freelancing. But I guess I'm still enough of a purist to think a writer ought to stay away from the wrong elements."

"Who's that exactly? I mean, from your vantage at the bottom of the barrel."

"The spooks, Tony," said Segal.

McWade took an exaggerated look over his shoulder and came back laughing.

"You seem to have a fixation," he said.

"I'm not making this up, mate. The guy she's sleeping with doesn't keep many secrets about what he is."

"A real spy does not advertise," said McWade, taking a long pull of beer. "He's an ordinary Joe who likes his pint."

"Like I said, there have been certain conversations about that," said Segal. "But we all decided you weren't the type. You're the kind who keeps his expenses in a notebook, down to the shilling. Makes everybody else look bad."

"How much were these beers again?" said McWade.

Segal lifted his mug and set it down again, making interlocking circles of moisture on the bar.

"Look," he said, "I'm worried about her."

"Do I know the guy?"

"He says he was around before, back in your day I mean. But nobody remembers. Jane took up with him a few months back. She wasn't otherwise engaged at the time."

"Still pining away for me."

"Don't flatter yourself, mate. She's pretty much made the rounds."

The pub was beginning to fill up now that the local deadline had passed. McWade finished his beer and did not suggest another.

"She'll take care of herself," he said. "She always has."

"I'm telling you, mate," said Segal. "This guy is going to trash her career. The editors back in the home offices may not have gotten wind of it yet, but around here, Joseph Leggatt is a joke gone stale."

McWade pushed his empty mug away from him.

"Is that what he calls himself?" he asked.

"I wish somebody could do something."

"You want me to talk to her?"

"It might do some good."

Segal came up with the address so easily that McWade had to figure he had done some surveillance there himself. The flat was a few blocks from the Lancaster Gate tube station. Sitting on it was easy from a pub down the street.

The very first evening, he saw her. After she entered the vestibule of the flat, he marked time until the lights in an upstairs window popped on. Third floor front. It overlooked the park. A pricey view. The imposter had resources. Even with budget problems, Fisherman was not scrimping. A few minutes later the lights went off again. She emerged from the front door, sweeping her long hair back over her ear. A taxi pulled up quickly. She had never had difficulty attracting a man's eye.

In the days that followed, McWade had to limit the occasions of his vigils to avoid becoming too much of a fixture in the pub. Meantime, he stayed away from the other public places where he had previously been showing himself. Now the advantage went to surprise.

It was on a Wednesday that he saw her enter the flat with an overnight bag and an armload of groceries. That was promising, because he had not yet caught her sleeping there. If she was planning to tonight, that probably meant she expected the man to return.

McWade settled in near the pub window and ordered another half pint.

"Is it the top 'alf or the bottom you'll be wanting?" asked the barman.

"I like to sip my beer," said McWade.

"A constitutional infirmity? Or are you just by nature a moderate man?"

"Let's throw caution to the winds today, Jack. Give me both halves."

He was still at work on it when a car pulled up and parked across the street from the flat. The man inside leaned over. McWade could not quite make him out for the reflection. Then the door swung open and the light illuminated him.

McWade placed his hands flat on the bar. He recognized the figure in the car. It was his partner in the Wheeler investigation, Steven Greene.

"Something the matter?" said the barman.

"The sky," said McWade, not raising his eyes from the street as the imposter crossed. "Looks like rain."

"Oh, yes," said the barman. "That must be 'orrifying to a man such as yourself."

"You're a shrewd one, aren't you, Jack?"

"Wet and dry's my business."

"I thought I saw somebody I knew from years ago."

"Mr Leggatt there?"

"Is that his name? I must have been mistaken."

" 'E's a Yank like you," said the barman. "You see him now and again with a lady friend. She's a fair one."

224

"My eyes aren't what they used to be."
"Will you have another then? To sharpen them up?"
"Does he ever come in here?"
"The Yank you don't know, is it?"
"That's the one."

18

McWade left without collecting his change and went around the block to approach the apartment from the opposite direction and avoid the barman's notice. He wondered whether Steven Greene had learned anything from being caught out and pissed on or whether he was still a sucker for surprise. It was obvious that he had learned nothing about loyalty.

As McWade drew near the doorway, he barely heard the doors of a car opening behind him.

Suddenly, two men appeared on his flanks.

"This way, Mr McWade," said the smaller of them. His accent was dark and glottal. He stretched out his palm to show the glint of steel.

McWade tried to turn, but the bigger man took hold of his arm.

"I am expected," said McWade.

Supporting McWade between them like an invalid, the men turned back to their car and urged him into the rear. The man with the pistol slid in beside him.

"Put this on," he said, holding out a black cloth sack that looked like an execution hood. "Now lean over. Head on knees. You are young and limber. It will not be so painful."

A hand seized his neck and pressed him downward. When he had gone as far as he could go, the hand remained on his neck. The car began to roll.

McWade tried to follow the route by dead reckoning, but the angles and turns were too much for him. Under the shroud he was hopelessly lost. Soon the darkness turned him in on himself, a perfect loop, enclosed. It was like a microphone picking up its own sound through the speakers, amplifying it over and over as waves of panic fed on themselves.

Finally the hand lifted from his neck.

"Sit up now," said a voice, muffled by the cloth.

He unfolded himself slowly, waiting for a blow that did not come. The cushions of the seat received his back.

They drove for what seemed like hours in silence before the driver whispered something to the other man and the car slowed down. McWade listened in vain for any sound that might locate him. The driver made a sharp turn, pressing McWade against the door. He felt the lever against his forearm; it was locked.

The car bounced along a rutted road now. McWade imagined a dirt path stretching through the trees. A window opened and the air rustled the coarse fabric of the hood. He leaned into it, trying to find the smell of the earth, the scent of water. But the thing that blinded him also killed this other sense. He could only get the smell of his sweat, the onions he'd had for dinner, the heavy vapor of the beer.

After a few more minutes the car rolled to a stop and the engine went silent. A door opened. A hand grabbed his arm roughly and hauled him out.

"Careful," said a voice. "Zapadnya would not want us to bring this one in damaged."

A hand pulled his arm sharply.

"One step up. Now a turn and three more."

They were inside now. He could feel the stillness of an empty room.

"Come on," said the voice. "Move!"

McWade counted his steps. Ten paces and then another halt.

A hand grasped McWade's and placed it on a cool, wooden banister. Climbing the stairs in the hood, McWade could have been mounting a scaffold, except for the thick carpet underfoot.

"Keep going," said a voice. "You are almost there."

When he reached the top, the guiding hand turned him and led him a dozen paces before turning him again. After only a few more steps, he was brought to a halt. A door shut behind him.

"I'll relieve you of the hood now," said a new voice.

227

Suddenly McWade was bathed in light. He brought his hands to his eyes, stunned by what he saw.

"Will you be requiring dinner, sir?" said the man standing before him.

The room was done in exquisite taste: a four-poster bed, a heavy armoire, an armchair and a large leather-inlaid desk. The paper on the wall was delicate and fresh. The carpet was a light, becoming blue.

"I can offer you a very nice scallopini of veal," said the man. "Fresh broccoli. A light chef's salad to start."

He wasn't more than five feet tall, with a wispy monk's ring of hair around his balding head. The gray vest and black bow tie he wore could have been part of a formal uniform, and his shirt was severely starched.

"Where are the others?" McWade asked.

"They won't be troubling you further, sir."

"Unless I try to leave."

"We flatter ourselves to think you will come to appreciate the accommodations," said the man.

"Where am I exactly?"

"In one of our finer rooms, sir. You may be sure of that. Now, shall I bring you the veal?"

"I've already eaten."

"Your nightclothes are in the drawer," said the man. "The bath is right through there. I believe you will find everything you require."

With that he let himself out.

After the footsteps had receded, McWade tried the door and found the precise limits of civility. When he pressed his shoulder against the wood, there was not a lot of give.

The windows proved to be shuttered from the outside and locked. The bathroom had a shower, just like at his hotel. On the sink lay a basket of soap and toilet articles. He rinsed his face and ran a comb through his hair where it had been flattened down by the hood. His shirt and jacket were badly wrinkled from his contortions in the car. He took them off and put on a terry cloth robe he found folded on top of the bath towels.

When he was finished cleaning up, he went back to the bedroom and pounded on the door. There were footsteps outside. He pounded a few more times before the door finally opened.

"No need to get agitated, sir," said the little man.

"You wouldn't have valet service, would you?" said McWade. "I seem to have made a mess of my jacket and shirt."

"If you leave everything at the door when you go to bed, we'll have it ready by morning. Will there be anything else?"

"A drink."

"Certainly. It's Scotch, isn't it?"

"A double."

"Will Glenlivet be suitable?"

"With ice."

"It does seem a pity, this American taste for the cold."

"How long am I going to be here?"

"If you look in the armoire, you will find a selection of books and recent periodicals. There's a radio on your night table. I'm sure you will find your stay relaxing. I dare say some of our guests rather hate to have to leave."

In the days that followed McWade became accustomed to impeccable service. Meals came on a linen-covered tray, the food handsomely displayed on bone china with a decent selection of wine. He ate at the desk alone, listening to the restrained enthusiasm of the BBC. The books in the armoire were all nineteenth century and quite long.

On the third evening of his captivity, he summoned his keeper to remove the dinner tray and bring the customary snifter of VSOP. When the door opened, McWade did not look up from his book.

"I trust you have not been abused," said an unfamiliar voice.

Before he stood up, McWade put a slip of paper into the book to mark his place.

"It has been very restful, Mr Kerzhentseff," he said.

The Russian took a cigarette from his pocket. One arm hung lifeless at his side. But this did not stop him from deftly striking a match.

"To what do I owe the honor?" asked McWade.

"Forgive the delay in my arrival. I cannot travel as freely as I would like. And you moved more quickly than I had expected. Will you join me downstairs?"

McWade followed him down the hall past a line of lovely hunt prints. There was no sign of the guards. The parlor to which Kerzhentseff brought him was done up even more nicely than the bedroom. Whoever had decorated it must have had a substantial budget. All the pieces looked genuine and quite old.

"We have much to accomplish," said Kerzhentseff.

"It's your meeting."

"Yes it is."

Kerzhentseff was much smaller than McWade had pictured him from the photographs in the files. And the cameras had not begun to pick up the intensity of the man, the fine-edged features and the sense of purpose. Seeing him in the flesh, it was not difficult to understand why Fisherman might have taken an interest in this man.

Kerzhentseff gestured McWade into a chair and then took one opposite.

"So you have had a falling out with your employers," he said.

"You have interesting sources."

"We have followed your career for some time. You rose well beyond what I would have predicted. And then suddenly you were gone."

"On leave," said McWade. "A well-deserved rest."

The fingers of Kerzhentseff's strong hand each lifted in turn and then fell in a slow, silent arpeggio.

"We do not mean to do you any harm," he said.

"I suppose you are going to say it depends on me."

"Not precisely," said the Russian, and it was clear that he operated on narrow tolerances.

"The men who brought me here," said McWade. "They were quick to show me a gun."

"Merely a reminder. A half-measure. Nothing more."

"What is it you want?"

"An opportunity," said Kerzhentseff, "for us and for you."

"*Glasnost*. Hands across the sea."

Kerzhentseff seemed to accept that as the beginning of understanding, a cynic's détente.

"I think we can arrive at some points of mutual advantage," he said.

"You've gone to a lot of trouble."

"We did not want to contact you openly. It wouldn't do to have you traced to us. The terrible bigotry of your great democracy."

"You don't think Fisherman had eyes on his boy?"

"When a man puts out bait he does not run the risk of watching it."

"Spoken like a true hunter, Zapadnya."

Kerzhentseff did not acknowledge the name.

"Let me worry about Fisherman," he said. "Your problem is Michael Ross."

McWade was surprised that it came so directly. He had expected the approach to be more subtle, eliciting first a small betrayal, then another, until he was too entangled to extricate himself. That was Fisherman's way.

"I'm under a shadow," said McWade.

"Perhaps I have the means of lighting your path."

"I don't see it, I'm afraid."

"You must bring him down," said Kerzhentseff, as abruptly as a falling star.

"Fisherman is the man you want to see," said McWade. "He's been all over Ross's case."

Kerzhentseff pulled out another cigarette and lighted it with a snap of his thumb. The smoke clouded his face for a moment, then it diffused.

"There are many ways to reach Fisherman," he said.

"I had a taste of your methods in Washington," said McWade. "It was very clever, the way I was drawn into this."

"I am interested in your version," said Kerzhentseff, as if he knew the truth and was only curious about the refractions.

"The one who called herself Zofia Medera," said McWade.

"You have seen her?"

231

"She contacted me," said McWade. "I informed Ross, of course."

"Somebody was using her."

"She's built for the purpose."

"A common slut," said the Russian. His voice barely rose. "She is of no importance."

"She was to me," said McWade.

"I'm afraid I do not share your taste."

"I mean she's the reason I'm on the outs."

"Interesting," said Kerzhentseff. "Michael Ross is a subtle man."

McWade did not hesitate to resist the implication. Anyone with his training would be expected to, if only because when a man directs the eye one way, a practiced observer looks the other. Kerzhentseff, of course, knew the reflex. It was always possible that he was pointing at the very thing he did not want McWade to see.

"It might have been Fisherman who set me up," said McWade. "It might have been you."

"She is out of my hands now."

"Out of mine, too," said McWade. "She vanished."

"Fisherman obviously thought she would drive you to him."

"Or scare me away."

"You were on your way to visit his agent when we picked you up."

"Maybe I've had second thoughts."

"Fisherman is testing you," said Kerzhentseff. "He wants you to feel threatened. Turning a man always requires a certain amount of torque."

"He has been looking into the death of one of our agents."

"His interest has not exactly been a well-kept secret. His boy has been putting out the word."

"The Czech woman said Fisherman had something to do with it," said McWade. "She also mentioned you."

Kerzhentseff shook his head as if he were dealing with a student who was not applying himself. Then he stubbed out his cigarette in an ashtray, making sure that every glowing ember was dead.

"You shall do what Fisherman expects of you," he said. "You shall finish what you had begun when we interrupted. The man wants you to respond, and you shall not disappoint him. You might even take some pleasure from it."

"Under your orders," said McWade.

"There is only one way for you to come out of this unpleasant situation whole, and that is to destroy your accuser. I believe I can supply you with the means."

McWade let this hang in silence. It was not necessary to accept or reject it.

"I assure you," the Russian went on, "that what I can provide you with against Ross is genuine. It will stand up."

"So I will be serving my country, and you will be serving yours," said McWade, "a happy convergence."

"Ross is an impediment to me. He has certain contacts in my government, and he is able to reward them in ways that are inimical to my interests."

"You want to ruin the arms talks," said McWade.

Kerzhentseff held out an open palm. McWade could see the hardness of the skin, the way he must have worked to compensate.

"The talks have a life of their own," said Kerzhentseff.

McWade stood up and took a step toward the door.

"I'd be giving you something you could use against me for the rest of my life," he said.

"It is not so one-sided as that," said Kerzhentseff. "You will have a secret that you can use against me as well. I offer mutuality. We will both be holding loaded guns. Deterrence is something we can live with, no?"

But there was no suggestion of mutuality in his manner now. The guns were all on his side.

"What am I supposed to do?" said McWade.

"We will provide you with everything you need."

"I need to know what exactly you're offering."

"I'm afraid that would be imprudent. You must be committed first. When you have been in contact with Fisherman and have reported his frame of mind, that will be soon enough."

"And what am I supposed to tell him?"

Kerzhentseff was slow in answering. He stood up and moved next to McWade.

"You are a resourceful man," he said. "You will think of something."

The ride back to London took more than two hours by McWade's watch, but it did not seem as long as the trip out. The thugs let him lie down in the back seat rather than sit doubled over. They treated him with a certain amount of courtesy and allowed him to remove the hood once they had entered the city.

At the hotel the car pulled up under the awning. As he climbed out, McWade satisfied the doorman with the coins that his driver had thoughtfully pressed into his hand.

19

The maid had lined up several goodnight mints on the table next to his bed, one for each evening he had been gone. The lock of his suitcase was set the way he had left it. Inside, he found his travelers' checks, an envelope of cash and an open ticket back to Washington on top, untouched. The passport was still under his handkerchiefs. He opened the blue cover and flipped the pages until he found his photograph. He did not look at it long.

Back in the lobby, he proved his existence to the desk clerk by making good the mounting bill. He did not wait for a receipt. "I trust you," he said, putting the rest of the money into his breast pocket and tapping it as if he were swearing an oath.

A group of overdressed ladies and their men whisked through the revolving door before him. He stepped past the doorman and into a taxi. As they approached the flat, he had the driver pull up short at the spot where he had been snatched.

The lights were on upstairs, the shades drawn, just as they had been before. He watched the taxi turn the corner, and then he entered the vestibule. The buzzers were easy to decipher, two to a floor, front and rear. McWade pressed the button and held it until the tiny speaker came alive.

"Yes." The sound was distorted, but it was a woman's voice.

"Is he there?"

"Who is this?"

"Leggatt. Joseph Leggatt."

"He is out."

The speaker fell silent. McWade touched the buzzer again and held it until he heard a hollowness that meant she was listening.

"Can I come up?" he asked.

"Who is this?"

"An old friend."

"I'm going to have to call a constable."

"Now why would you want to do that, love? Don't you remember Tony Rogers's sweet voice?"

"You're drunk."

"Cold sober, darling. I need to talk."

"Is it really you?"

"The one and only," he said.

"Go outside. Let me have a look at you."

He stepped back out the door and stood on the curb bowing, arms outstretched, like a player taking a curtain call. The shade upstairs rattled and pulled away from the window, but he could not see her face.

When he got inside again, the buzzer was squawking. He pushed into the stairwell. She was waiting for him in an open door at the top landing. The angle made her as tall as a statue, her arms crossed under her breasts, the long red hair cloaking her shoulders. He climbed the final steps, and when he reached her, she put her hand on his arm and leaned up to give him a small, chaste kiss on the cheek.

"My God, Tony," she said. "How long has it been?"

"I haven't kept track."

"I've thought of dropping you a note a thousand times. But I didn't know where to send it."

"Aren't you going to invite me in?"

"Have you seen any of my articles?" she said as she stepped back to let him pass, not far enough that he could avoid touching her as he did.

"I don't read as much as I should."

Apart from the fancy view, the flat was a rather typical agent's accommodation, decent but incomplete, a half-lived life. He recognized a few things on the shelves. Jane had a taste for African art. There were ebony masks and woven shields. They had bought some of them together at the galleries.

"You seem to have settled in," he said.

"We both come and go. I still have my other place."

"I was hoping to find him alone."

"You aren't feeling wounded?" she said.

"Why should I be?"

"You'll behave then?"

"Like a schoolboy."

"I suppose I ought to be reassured," she said. "But I'm not sure I am. Schoolboys have very active imaginations."

She was smiling as she crossed the room and sat on the couch, leaving plenty of room for him. He took the chair opposite instead. It was close enough that their knees almost touched.

"What happened to you, Tony?" she asked. "Dropping out of sight like that."

"I was reassigned."

"They told stories about you."

"Leggatt did?"

"The wire service types. Dark things about your past. I didn't believe them for an instant."

"I'm flattered you cared."

"You knew me at a bad time," she said.

The slightest quaver of affection came into her voice, and he did not know how to evaluate it. Whatever the imposter had given her for a script, she was playing her part very well.

"What about Leggatt?" he asked. "What did he say?"

"How do you know him?"

"It was when you and I were still together," he said. "We have shared many things."

A natural woman would have wondered whether they had talked about her, and what kind of intimate things were exchanged.

"He never mentioned it," she said.

"That's odd," said McWade. "You'd think he would have some feelings, wouldn't you?"

She untucked her legs from under her and settled her silk robe.

"What's this all about?" she asked.

"A coincidence, I guess," he said.

"You're just the least bit jealous, aren't you?" she said, one foot rising slightly on the toes.

237

Jealousy wouldn't have been the word he would have used going in, but it wasn't such a bad one now, seeing her again.

"Imagine my surprise when I heard."

"It's a tight little community, Tony."

"And you were on the rebound."

"Not exactly. There were others first. They were not so hard to leave."

"Anyone I know?"

"Something had happened to you," she said. "I still don't know what it was."

McWade leaned forward and touched her hand. For a moment, he wanted to apologize and tell her it was not right that she had gotten caught up in this, whatever the hell it was. She deserved better than Leggatt, either of them.

"Maybe it was a stupid idea to come here," he said.

"Everyone thinks of starting over," she said, "if there has been any feeling at all."

"Tom Segal sent me," he said.

She stiffened.

"What did he want?"

"I'm not sure," said McWade.

"He's not like you," she said. "He doesn't know when to give up."

"He said he's worried about you."

Jane pulled her robe tight around her then moved to the arm of McWade's chair.

"Did he say we had been together?"

"I was able to guess," said McWade.

"It didn't last long. He had an insatiable curiosity about you. He couldn't get it out of his mind that I'd go back to you someday."

"He asked me to come and talk sense to you," said McWade. "He thinks you are involved with a spy."

If Jane had been acting, she would have let some little thing show. But she simply stood up and went to the sideboard where they kept the bottles.

"He says you'll ruin your career if you keep it up," McWade said.

She poured two drinks and then moved back and put his on a coaster. But she did not return to the arm of his chair.

"He warned me about you, too, you know," she said. "It seems to be his favorite form of courtship."

"You didn't believe him," said McWade.

"By then it didn't matter."

"I think this time he might be right. I understand Leggatt likes to talk."

"I never found silence all that attractive."

McWade accepted that as nothing more than he deserved. When he had been struggling to keep Leggatt from taking over his life at the end, he had not had much to say. Eventually it had reached a point where, except in anger when Leggatt gained the upper hand, he could not get through to her at all.

"I know him, Jane," he said. "He's a weak man."

"You keep saying that you know him, but you don't say how."

"I knew a lot of people back then."

"Spies?"

"Among others."

"He'll be back within a week," she said. "Call ahead next time so I can be sure to be gone."

"I do have business with him. That was true."

"It would have been so lovely if you had found him here tonight. You could have played the wounded party. Or is it the third man?"

"I need to talk to him soon."

"Give me a number where he can reach you," she said.

"Where is he now?"

"Off to Berlin," she said. "Don't raise your eyebrows. He's a writer, or didn't Segal tell you that? People will believe anything if you set it in Berlin."

"You write what you know," said McWade.

She went to the door.

"I think it's time you left," she said.

"I need an address," said McWade. "I wouldn't threaten him."

"That's obvious," she said.

20

It did not take McWade long to get a line on Greene once he reached Berlin. He was surprised how many familiar faces presented themselves, ready with answers, no questions asked. And the rates were more than reasonable, what with the dollar so strong against the mark.

Word had it that Greene had been in and out of the divided city a dozen times in the past year, always staying at an Agency safehouse overlooking the Wall. It was close enough to the checkpoint that the upper floors could be used to observe the ins and outs, such an obvious location that if it hadn't been occupied by Langley, the other side would have wanted to know why.

McWade went there on foot, past the ruins of shame that Berlin preserved with a kind of pride: the bombed-out shell of the Gedächtniskirche, its spire shattered half-way up, the boarded-up embassies of the Axis powers, the facade of the Anhalter Bahnhof rising from an unmowed field, flowering weeds and fat, amputated cherubs. The triumphant Brandenburg Gate, of course, was inaccessible and heavily fortified, a monument to irony.

The safehouse was not far from Potsdamer Platz, the old center of the city that now lay wholly within the barren, mined strip between the outer and inner barricades. The Wall blighted both sides of the perimeter. A few new buildings had been constructed on the free side, styled in the architecture of defiance. Commerce did not grow here naturally, unless you counted the tourist stands where the most popular items were huge, grainy posters of people who had been shot trying to escape.

Once McWade had walked past the safehouse to remind himself of the layout, he circled back to a spot where he could blend in with the tourists. A row of benches gave him a clear view of the front entrance. He shared the bench with many different people while he waited, but none attempted conversation. The Wall made free men and women hold their tongues.

At dusk the lights came up along the frontier. Before the stands closed for the night, McWade bought himself a pastry and a cup of coffee. It was not long after the last tour buses departed for happier precincts that Greene finally emerged from the safehouse. McWade threw the cup and paper sack into a trash barrel and hurried to catch up to him.

As Greene reached the intersection that led to the checkpoint, McWade began to worry that he was going to cross over into the East. He stopped at the corner near the entrance to the U-Bahn and glanced at his watch. McWade hoped he would go down the stairs to the subway, but instead he darted across the street toward the floodlit yard of the checkpoint where an American flag snapped in the wind. To McWade's relief, he got into a cab. When it had pulled away, McWade jumped out of the shadows and hopped into the next in the queue.

"Follow," he said in German as the driver started the engine and punched up the meter. "Hurry."

"You can talk American, pal," said the driver. "It's fuckin' music to my ears."

"That way," said McWade, pointing. As they turned the corner, he caught sight of the other cab again and sat back in the seat.

"If you got to play cat and mouse," said the driver, "this is the city to do it in."

Greene was sticking to the backstreets, and soon McWade had lost track of which way was east and which was west.

"Let them get farther ahead," he said. "I don't want him to see me."

"I used to do this kind of thing in the Army," said the driver. "Bumper tag with Ivan. The mope won't have a clue."

Eventually Greene's taxi pulled into a busy thoroughfare and shot up it toward the Ku'damm.

"Piece of cake," said the driver, turning halfway around to give McWade a grin.

"Wait," said McWade. "He's pulling over. Go right past him and let me out half a block up."

McWade waited until Greene was on the sidewalk and his cab had pulled away before he settled up the fare. The driver fumbled with his money then switched on the interior light.

"Turn that off," said McWade.

"Got to see what I'm doing."

"Just keep the change."

Greene might have lost himself in the crowd if he had been in any kind of a hurry. But instead, he stopped here and there to look in store windows. The duskier ones made good mirrors. McWade stayed a safe distance behind.

Finally Greene turned in at a big outdoor beer garden that spread from the sidewalk into the shadows under a lattice strung with tiny lights that gave no more illumination than the stars. Greene took a table where he could be seen. McWade circled around and found one in the shadows.

It was not long before Greene gestured to someone at the entrance. She wore jeans that showed her figure off nicely and some sort of turtleneck on top. Greene did not rise when she reached him, but he did pull out the chair and accept an ambiguous little kiss on the cheek. The two of them lingered at the table only for a moment. McWade put money in the ashtray and followed them out.

As they walked down the sidewalk the woman spoke to Greene as excitedly as a schoolgirl. Now and then she touched his arm to draw his attention to something in a window. Greene indulged her enthusiasm, and McWade wished he could see her face.

He got the opportunity in the next block when the two of them entered a small boutique. McWade was able to stand back near the curb and watch them at an angle through the window. The woman turned out to be much younger than McWade had expected. She held a blouse on a hanger up against her front, modeling it for Greene, who smiled as easily as a father might. Finally, the girl settled on a colorful scarf, which she tied around her neck as Greene took out his wallet to pay. Then she took him by the arm lightly and gave him a lovely smile.

McWade backed off as they concluded the purchase, confused about what he was seeing. The girl was barely of college age, if that. And she treated Greene like somebody perfectly safe.

From the store they went to a U-Bahn station. McWade followed them cautiously down the stairs to the clean, crowded platform. He had no difficulty keeping out of sight until the train pulled up. Only the girl seemed interested in her surroundings. Greene was so preoccupied with her that he did not even use the reflection from the train's windows to get a look behind him before he boarded.

McWade got on the next car and stood near the connecting door where he could see them. The girl did all the talking as the train sped from stop to stop. When they finally alighted, they had to pass McWade on the way to the stairs. He feigned a sneeze and covered his nose and mouth with a handkerchief. Only the girl looked his way, and her glance did not linger.

When McWade reached the street he found himself in a neighborhood where the working class tenements were as drab as those on the other side. As if in parody of the Wall, the concrete was splashed with graffiti: liberation slogans, curses, jeers. Some of the windows were boarded up. Others were decorated with scrawny plants, children's toys, porcelain mementos of a better day. The doors were indistinguishable and most did not even carry numbers, but Greene picked one without hesitation and held it open for the girl.

Once they were out of sight, McWade reconnoitered the entryway and took down the names from the buzzer list. Then he moved back across the street and stepped into an alley to wait.

Less than an hour passed before Greene came out of the

tenement alone. Tinny music came from one of the windows, the sound of a quarrel from another, voices rising, the clatter of pans.

"Over here, Leggatt!" McWade shouted.

Greene took two steps then stopped, searching for the sound. McWade stepped from the alley into a dusky circle under a streetlight. They stood on opposite curbs, staring at one another. It was Greene who finally made the move to cross.

"I heard you were in town, Ike," he said. "Ernest said we'd get you to come to us sooner or later."

"He might be surprised at how you spend your time in Berlin," said McWade. "If he knew you'd taken some poor girl under your wing like a Dutch uncle, he'd begin to wonder whether you were the man to fill Leggatt's shoes."

"You mean the dolly in there?"

"It was touching to watch."

"She's just somebody I know," said Greene.

"Don't tell me she's one of your assets. She's too young to have anything to sell."

Greene gave a guttural laugh, as if McWade had told a dirty joke.

"She's one of Leggatt's better conquests, don't you think?" he said.

"She's a child."

"Don't pretend to be shocked, Ike. You created the role."

McWade felt a surge of anger, and he did not know whether the impulse was conscience or revenge.

"Forget about the dolly," said Greene. "She doesn't mean anything."

"No more than Jane does?"

Greene smiled like an accomplice.

"You scared the shit out of her the other night," he said, putting no more weight on it than he would on any other fact of life shared between men. "She called me as soon as you had left."

"She was lucky she caught you in," said McWade.

"I'm surprised at you, Ike. Did you really think it was smart to accuse me?"

"I didn't tell her the half of what I know."

That finally seemed to reach Greene. He turned and started to walk off. McWade caught his arm. Greene twisted away.

"Let's get out from under the streetlight," Greene said.

The alley opened out onto a playground at the other end, but they didn't go that far. The jungle gym cast long shadows on the pavement, like the bars of a cell. A light suddenly flared as Greene touched a match to a cigarette.

"You smoke, don't you?" Greene said, offering him the pack.

"Leggatt preferred cigars."

"People change."

"But they usually keep their vices."

"You're not still talking about the dolly, are you?" said Greene. The glow of the cigarette lit his face. "You know, I'd always figured you to be a pretty sophisticated guy. But then I researched the book on Leggatt. You made him a regular cliché."

"Looks like you fit it pretty well."

"I'm not saying I didn't find compensations," said Greene. "At first I couldn't make out what you saw in Jane. But then I learned to get a little rough, and she came around. These German smokes taste like shit."

He stabbed the cigarette out against the concrete block wall, and the sparks dropped dying to the ground. McWade forced himself to take a breath, then another.

"Leggatt's operations were all rolled up," he said. "He was played out."

"You might be surprised. There's a little juice left in everybody if you squeeze hard enough." Greene put his hands in his pockets and leaned up against the building. "Nothing personal, Ike. But it seems to have worked."

"You've been going out of your way to be seen," said McWade.

"The opposition must have told you that."

"Half the people in Berlin were ready to sell you."

"I was hoping you'd be in a buying mood."

"All Fisherman had to do was to call me," said McWade.

245

"I told him from the beginning that I would do what I could."

"Maybe he wants you to do what you thought you couldn't." Greene swung himself away from the wall. "You need a friend, Ike."

"Like Leggatt?"

"You could do worse. Maybe you have already. I hear some very nasty stories about who you've been dealing with."

McWade was fairly sure that Greene didn't know more than what he'd shown. That was the way Fisherman set up his operations, compartments within compartments, each one of them airtight. He had obviously given Greene a hint about the contact with the Soviets, but just enough to give his threats an edge.

"What if I told you I can't deliver Ross? What if I don't have what Fisherman thinks I do?"

"Maybe you can get it if you try," said Greene.

"Where?"

"That's up to you and Ernest."

"And if I agree?" said McWade.

"It would explain a lot. Why Ross turned on you. Why you lit out. It would make you clean."

This was where McWade was supposed to begin to give. Let him muscle you a little, Ross had said. He'll expect you to be afraid of your own shadow. But now it did not feel right to yield. Maybe it was only because of his anger, but he didn't believe Fisherman would value what he got if he didn't have to pay for it.

"Give Ernest a message for me," he said.

"He isn't inclined to bargain," said Greene. "He expects me to deliver you, signed and sealed."

"Tell him that if he wants Ross, he's got to give up Leggatt."

"I don't follow you," said Greene.

"He will."

"Who are you talking about?"

"You, my friend," said McWade. "I'll deliver Ross to Fisherman if he delivers you to me."

McWade was already moving away when Greene shouted.

"He's not going to be happy, you trying to push him around this way."

"I think you might be mistaken," McWade said over his shoulder. "I think he'll be amused."

21

The next move came so quickly that McWade had to assume that Fisherman was in Berlin calling the plays. As soon as McWade ventured out of his hotel the next morning, he noticed a heavyset man in an ill-fitting blue suit following him. Just to be sure, he turned into a public restroom and waited. The man entered behind him and opened the door of every stall before stepping up next to McWade at the sinks.

"Here," he said, handing McWade a piece of paper.

McWade unfolded it and read the instructions.

"Tell Kerzhentseff I'm not ready," McWade said.

The man turned the water on full blast and leaned so close that McWade could smell the morning schnapps on his breath. "We saw you last night with the errand boy," he said. Then he dried his hands and left.

For the sake of form, McWade tore the note into small pieces and flushed them down the toilet before returning to the street. The man was nowhere to be seen, and McWade hurried to a U-Bahn station where he jumped aboard a train, rode it one stop, then crossed over and caught another going in the opposite direction. By the time he finished clearing his path, anyone who might have been watching him would have thought he was about to do something he didn't want anyone to know about.

That accomplished, he made his way on foot to the S-Bahn, the commuter line run by the East Germans through both zones. The high, filthy windows of the station made it look like something abandoned by Krupp. When the old train came, there were many vacant seats.

No matter how many times McWade has crossed over the fault line, it always gave him a chill: the grinding tension where East and West collide. But this time something else haunted him, not division so much as invisible connections, as lethal as an electrified rail.

At the Friedrichstrasse terminal, the train emptied out slowly. The old pensioners returning home were in no hurry, and even the tourists seemed to hang back. McWade followed the crowd through the corridors into a big room used for passport control. A barrier of steel cut it in half, with a series of doors opening into ten-foot chutes through which every traveler had to pass.

McWade waited at the gate as a garrulous woman with a British passport tried to engage the guard in conversation. He was sitting behind a thick window at the midpoint of the chute. He told her in clipped German that she had to be out by midnight. Cinderella, she said, giggling. A buzzer sounded. The lady pushed the rear door open and disappeared.

McWade entered next and handed over his papers. The stern young man held the passport up against the glass and looked back and forth between the photograph and McWade's face. His uniform shirt was sharply creased, and the epaulettes stood out at his shoulders like vestigial wings. He picked up a black telephone, turning away to speak, so McWade could not see his lips shape the words. Then he hung up and pushed the passport and visa slip through the slot.

"Welcome," he said.

McWade put the papers in his pocket and, when the buzzer sounded, pushed on the rear door, which swung open easily.

After changing the required number of Westmarks for the weightless coins of the East, he made his way to the street. The day was overcast and exhaust fumes hung close to the ground. His instructions directed him up Friedrichstrasse away from the public places and showcase shops along the Unter Den Linden. A few blocks from the station he heard running footsteps behind him. Then he felt a tap on his arm.

"Are you American?" said a woman's voice.

He turned and faced her. Though she did not look

German, her clothing did. It wasn't hard to tell visitors from natives here, if only by the quality of their shoes.

"Do you know the way to the Brandenburg Gate?" she asked.

"I'm afraid you're turned around," he said. "It's back that way."

"Will you take me there?"

"Sorry," he said. "I have an appointment."

"They follow Americans, you know," she said.

"They follow everyone."

"I could show you around."

"That isn't necessary. I know my way."

"Americans are supposed to be generous."

McWade noticed a uniformed policeman watching them from his post on the corner.

"But Americans do not come to East Berlin looking for a good time," he said and turned away from her.

Though it was still early, he walked at a brisk pace. A few blocks up the street he caught her reflection in the windows of a bus. He turned at an intersection, raced down a block, turned again and ducked into a doorway to wait. She did not show herself. He waited five minutes by his watch and then poked his head out. The only people in sight were some folks queued up for a trolley and a policeman standing watch at an unmarked building down the way.

Still, McWade took no chances. He proceeded up the sidestreet and then turned into an even narrower one where he found another doorway to hide in. While he waited, he pulled out a tin of Dutch cigars, the kind Leggatt favored in his more prosperous moments. The smoke was harsh in the humid air. He caught himself inhaling; it went down raw.

He moved out again before finishing the cigar, and within a few minutes he had reached a small, ugly square surrounded by gray tenements. A few children and their mothers were out. They played easily despite the choking pollution and heat. McWade found an empty bench. His cigar had gone out, and he ground it flat on the pavement with his shoe.

In other circumstances, he would have kept circling until the appointed time, but here it didn't seem to make much sense to bother. He took off his suit jacket and folded it over the back of the bench. His shirt was damp. In the distance the children chased one another around like sworn enemies as their mothers cast wary looks at the stranger. McWade did not see his stalker again until she was upon him.

"You're a long way from the gate," she said, coming up from behind.

"What do you want?"

"Follow me."

"I'm spoken for," he said.

She pushed a curl of frizzy hair back from her temple. She was not so terribly young, about the same age as Zofia Medera when he first met her in Prague.

"It is not what you think," she said.

"I don't think anything," he said. "I'm just a visitor."

"Oh, you are more than that, Mr Leggatt," she said.

"Who sent you?"

"He is not far from here," she said.

She led him across the street and into a courtyard. The rusted gate was unlocked, and behind the facade the walls were made of cinderblock, unmarked by the graffiti that you found everywhere on the other side. He followed her into a doorway and up a flight of steel stairs, footsteps ringing and echoing against the stone. On the second landing she knocked on a wooden door that carried no number. Kerzhentseff opened it.

"Very good," he said in German, dismissing her.

McWade stepped into the room and closed the door. The furniture was modern, all wood and leather, but every bit as fine as the more traditional pieces at the Russian's English country house. Most of it must have been brought over from the West.

"Having her call me Leggatt," McWade said, "what was that supposed to mean?"

"A kind of symmetry," said Kerzhentseff. "Between Fisherman and me stand two Leggatts."

"There's only one, and he doesn't count."

251

"Fisherman seems to have reposed some confidence in him," said Kerzhentseff.

McWade sat down in a comfortable Eames chair. Kerzhentseff took a place on the couch across from him. Between them on a teak table lay a briefcase, an ashtray and a copy of the *Herald-Tribune*. McWade picked up the newspaper and opened it to the sports page. The Brewers were only out by a game and a half.

"I'm having trouble figuring out your tastes," he said.

"For certain of us," said Kerzhentseff, "your papers are required reading."

"Those in whom a lot of confidence is reposed," said McWade. "Or was."

"I am more interested now in the news you bring."

McWade laid the paper down.

"You can't believe everything you read," he said. "Why, it says here that a summit is virtually assured."

Kerzhentseff took the *Herald-Tribune* and folded it under the briefcase.

"These great matters respond to the underlying interests just as our smaller concerns do," he said. "If there is a reason for the leaders to talk, they will surely do so, regardless of what happens to Michael Ross."

"Espionage is a funny line of work for somebody who believes in history and not in men."

"We also believe in contradictions," said Kerzhentseff.

"Like the idea that you and I have a common interest."

"Travelers to different destinations warming themselves by a single fire."

"I'm afraid I'm lost here," said McWade.

Kerzhentseff leaned forward.

"A long journey," he said, "begins with a single step."

"I thought you weren't supposed to believe in Mao."

"There is often virtue buried in the heart of error."

"You make espionage seem like theology," said McWade.

"Excluding God, of course. It was a Russian who said that without God all things are possible."

McWade was becoming impatient with abstraction. The

mysteries that enveloped him were all very much of world.

"The man who wrote that wasn't talking about counter-intelligence," he said.

"We take a certain pleasure in turning sentimental ideas on their heads," said Kerzhentseff, obviously satisfied with the dialectic. "I am sure you will be able to find some virtue in what I offer."

"But I'm afraid I have nothing to offer in return," said McWade. "Last night I sent Fisherman a message. I told him I wouldn't deal with his boy, Leggatt."

McWade admired the Russian's understated show of surprise, the way he preserved the lie that he and Fisherman had not already compared notes. Kerzhentseff could have fit right in at the Nest, playing by London rules.

"I'm afraid I don't see the logic in what you did," Kerzhentseff said.

"Maybe I had personal reasons."

"If I believed that, I would have to say you are a fool."

"Then just say I don't want to ruin the arms talks."

"Suppose I were to show you that the American side had already been compromised," said Kerzhentseff, touching the briefcase, as if it held some talisman that would make everything that was wrong suddenly turn right.

"Then it would not be in your interest to jeopardize the Soviet advantage," said McWade.

"Only if I believed the talks had any real importance," said Kerzhentseff.

"Fisherman apparently does. Some people think he is only interested in Ross as a way of preventing a deal."

"Then they do not understand him," said the Russian. "He is a realist. He knows that law cannot contain the instinct for survival. I think it is time for you to be realistic, too. Keep in mind where you are."

"And whether I have anything to lose."

"There is always something," Kerzhentseff said coldly.

But then his expression softened. He put the briefcase on his lap, snapped open the latch and withdrew a file jacket.

"Once you see this, you will want to bring it to Fisherman," he said. "And he will forgive your transgressions."

"I think I know him better than that," said McWade.

"I know him, too," said Kerzhentseff, "the way a man knows his limitations." He touched his dead hand lightly. "The facts he cannot deny." Then he lifted the folder again. "Facts. And how we turn them to our purposes."

"How can you be sure I won't take the package straight to Ross?"

"Fortunately," said Kerzhentseff, "I do not have to depend on trust. You see, while you are the most obvious conduit to Fisherman, you are by no means the only one. If you do not go to him, I will transmit the document by other means. Then it will become a weapon to bring you down, too. There is no way out for Ross. And for you there is only one."

"Fisherman could destroy me for dealing with you."

"And I can destroy you if you refuse," said Kerzhentseff. "It is Ross that Fisherman wants. And if you are able to give him what he needs, he will protect you. As to your sources and methods, you will say you had suspicions. Ross found out about them somehow and cut you in order to protect himself. You took heroic measures. Everyone will respect that, even Fisherman."

"I think you may underestimate him," said McWade.

"There is not much danger of that," said the Russian.

McWade leaned forward in his chair and rested his hands on the coffee table. When he lifted them, he could see a damp imprint of fingers and palms.

"Let me see what you have," he said.

Kerzhentseff slid the file folder across the table. McWade recognized the markings on the document inside, the code word classification, the familiar signature at the bottom and the initials that showed it had been to the Oval Office. He had never seen the document itself before, but he knew what it was. He had spent hours working through the numbers with Ross.

"Where did you get this?"

"A potent question, is it not?" said Kerzhentseff.

Some of the points the Soviets could easily have inferred

from the negotiations themselves, where Ross and Simpson had balked, where they had moved. But others represented unexplored alternatives, roads not taken. The memorandum told the Kremlin exactly how far the American delegation had been authorized to go.

"This had to come out of the White House," said McWade. "It was not circulated."

"You did not prepare the document, I hope."

"Ross did. I did some staffing. But he put it in its final form."

"Who had access beyond Ross?"

"I don't know that anyone did except Simpson and the President."

McWade read through the document again; there were variations from the positions he had prepared, tighter limits on a few key variables, for example. That could have reflected the President's input, reigning in Ross's desire for maximum latitude.

"I will need to know when this came to you," McWade said.

"That is not the important date."

"It will be to Fisherman."

"I myself obtained it quite recently, in fact. But my government had it early enough for it to be of considerable use. By the time it was shown to me, the purpose was only to demonstrate that others were able to provide better information than I. It was presented to me in the form of a rebuke."

"And you believe Ross gave it to someone on your side."

"I am certain of it," said Kerzhentseff. "Those walks in the park. He had ample opportunity."

McWade gathered up the papers and put them back into the folder.

"This can't be proved," he said. "Fisherman will see your motive."

"I acknowledge the nature of my interest," said the Russian. "I need to regain my monopoly over useful intelligence by eliminating a meddlesome source. You may tell Ernest as much. But from your point of view the matter is simple. You have a chance to root out a traitor who has put the Americans at a considerable negotiating disadvantage. And by happy coincidence it happens to be someone who is a personal threat to you as well."

"I'll need to take this," said McWade, holding the file folder an inch above the table as if it would leave a mark.

"Use the briefcase," said Kerzhentseff.

"What am I supposed to say about our contact?"

Kerzhentseff stood up and went to the window but did not look out.

"Say whatever you must."

"Ross may have an explanation."

"Of that we can be sure," said the Russian. "Everyone has an excuse. For you it will be duty. The self in all its lovely guises."

PART FIVE

McWade Alone

22

The passage out of Tegel Airport was smooth. The man at the gate made McWade open his bag and the pair of briefcases. He explored the contents until he came upon a pint bottle of whiskey. With great sternness he unscrewed the top and took a whiff. Then he said, "*Sehr gut,*" and smiled. He did not even look at the file folder, which could bring down a government but not an airplane. Another man waved McWade into a cubicle, closed the curtain and searched his person. There was nothing accusatory about it, just common hospitality in an age of bombs.

The boarding went quickly, and soon the jet was climbing up over the frontier. Beyond the wire the farmland stretched out as far as the eye could see, broken only by small towns at the crossroads, each with a tall-spired church just like the villages west of Manitee Bay. If McWade hadn't known where he was, he would not have guessed that the rolling plains below were collectively owned. The farmers plowed and planted in contour against erosion, and every field was marked with unique angles and whorls, like the print of an individual thumb.

At Heathrow he passed customs through the gate for those with nothing to declare. Then he went to the bank window and changed his traveler's checks to pounds sterling. He did not want to leave a trail beyond this point. As he signed his name again and again on the line at the bottom of the checks, it became more stylized with each repetition, letters dropping out, double a and c of Isaac merging into a smooth, indeterminate line.

On his way to the Underground he stopped at a pay phone and made a call to the answering service to leave a message for Stockwell to summon Ross to England immediately. The obvious meeting place was Bath. McWade did not go into detail in his message. Ross would

259

remember the choreography from their last rendezvous there.

When McWade emerged from the tube station at Piccadilly Circus he hailed a taxi and ordered it to drive straight ahead. After it had clocked two pounds, he paid and alighted. Across the street he jumped into another, which he took in the direction it was heading until he found a promising store on Regent Street.

He did not pause to shop. And if he looked as though he did not know exactly where he was going as he pushed through the crowded aisles with his bags, it was because the whole point of the exercise was to move without any explicable pattern. The rear exit placed him on a narrow, curving sidestreet which happened to lead to a decent looking hotel, the choice of it as unpredictable as a roll of the dice. Against Fisherman's deductions, randomness was the only place to hide.

The hotel was undergoing renovation. A sign at the door apologized for any inconvenience. The woodwork was already carefully restored, the crystal chandelier sparkled just a bit too much, and the smell of paint hung in the air. McWade registered as Fred Granger, shaping every letter round and distinct in an unnatural hand. To avoid showing a passport, he listed as his address a place where he and Jane had once taken a holiday, a charming village called Castle Combe.

"Beautiful country that," said the clerk, tapping the registration card.

McWade paid a week in advance in cash in lieu of a credit card.

"They filmed a movie there," said the clerk. "One of those children's things, wasn't it? The one with all the chattering animals. Must have created something of a fuss."

McWade was afraid that if he got into a conversation, his American accent would show.

"Quite," he said.

The room he was given was ample enough, but it seemed to close in on him as soon as he shut the door. He did not dare to be seen now, so for the next several days he took most of his meals at his desk. His cover story was that he was a writer, secluded against interruptions and the temptation to avoid the empty page. And for the most part he kept to his discipline, watching endless hours of sport and talk on the Beeb.

Only one night did he go out to prowl the streets. The whore he found was accommodating.

"You can put it wherever you please, luv," she said, "just as long as you keep it wrapped."

But when they reached her flat, he balked. She did not complain once she understood that he would still pay full fare.

He was jumpy when he left her. He wandered until he came upon an arcade. The children of England in their spiked hair and leather were busy at row after row of video games. The beep of exploding targets and the whine of electronic guns filled the air. Only one machine was vacant. It stood in a far corner, obviously out of place. McWade played it for more than an hour, pitching and batting and sending baserunners around the brown infield as the figures shagged a white video baseball on the green video grass.

When the day of the meeting finally came, McWade left for Bath well before dawn in a rented car. Ross was in the Pump Room at the appointed hour, sitting there as inconspicuously as a banker down from the City or somebody whose idea of risk was putting money in a pool at Lloyds.

McWade asked for a table on the other side of the room and chose a chair that exposed his back to Ross, who was dawdling over *The Times*. After letting a decent interval pass, Ross paid his check. McWade gave him a few minutes' lead before following. This way he could check to make sure nobody was following, a textbook maneuver when you were caught without the resources to do the thing properly.

The sky pressed down, threatening rain, and the park was nearly empty. McWade approached Ross from a stand of trees. The last time they had met here, the distance between them in the hierarchy had magnified Ross's presence, the sun on the far horizon. Now under all the clouds, Ross was reduced to human scale as he paced along a bed of flowers, checking and rechecking his watch. But still, when McWade emerged from the woods, Ross made no move to meet him halfway.

McWade put out his hand. Ross did not take it.

"You should have known better than to use a freelancer," he said.

"That is the least of our problems," said McWade, hoping Ross would notice that he had used the first person plural and would take it as a renewal of a commitment.

"Who was it?" Ross demanded.

"A friend."

"What does he know?"

"No more than he told you."

"I'm in the dark," said Ross.

Not likely. Ross belonged to a privileged species that casts its own light.

"I've come up with something," said McWade, edging over toward a bench. Ross stepped off in the opposite direction toward one farther down the way and then sat down and waited for McWade to join him.

All right, McWade thought. All right.

"I'm vulnerable in Washington now," said Ross as McWade approached him. "It was not convenient for me to leave. I pleaded fatigue. Personal responsibilities. A short holiday to the south of France with Emma. I'm to meet her tomorrow. She would thank you if she knew you were responsible."

"I hate to spoil your vacation," McWade said.

"Emma has grand designs."

Ross was ready to elaborate, but McWade cut him off.

"I know what Fisherman has been looking for," he said.

"She expects us to have a lovely rest," said Ross. "Small dinner parties every night, and during the day the reviving sun."

"He's on the verge of finding what he wants."

Ross gave out a single, sharp laugh and turned toward him on the bench.

"So he took the bait?" he said.

"I haven't even seen him yet."

262

"He's maneuvering into position," said Ross. "That tells you he isn't quite ready."

"I did meet his errandboy," said McWade. "I told him I wanted him to take the fall."

"That's going to make it more difficult when you make your move toward Ernest."

McWade sat back against the slats of the bench and rubbed at the paint where it was beginning to crack.

"It's funny how everybody keeps telling me I have to go to Fisherman," he said. "Talk to him, they say. Go see the man. I can't even ask a guy the time of day without being directed to see what Fisherman says about it, as if he's Greenwich Mean."

"You're afraid of him," said Ross.

If it had only been a statement of fact, McWade might have accepted it. But this was an accusation. And it was way out of line.

"Maybe you don't appreciate the stakes," McWade said.

"I didn't come here to hold your hand."

McWade's fists tightened. But he distrusted his anger, if only because Ross seemed to be inviting it, as if to drive McWade away.

"I've been in touch with Kerzhentseff," said McWade. "He's lined up against you."

"Now there's a stunning discovery," said Ross. He reached into the breast pocket of his jacket and, after rooting around for a moment, withdrew a crumpled five pound note. He threw it on the bench, where the wind lifted it and blew it to rest against McWade's leg. "For your troubles," he said.

McWade stood up. The bank note fluttered to the ground.

"They're all in it together," he said. "Fisherman, Kerzhentseff, Leggatt. You might as well count the Sisters, too, because Fisherman's wired. You have one friend left in the world, and you're looking at him."

Ross did not exactly express his gratitude. He stood up and took a step closer to McWade until they were near enough for an exchange of blows.

"If you've been dealing with Kerzhentseff, then you're

the one with the problem," said Ross. "I don't know if I can protect you in a thing like that."

"He thinks he has recruited me to bring you down," said McWade, lifting the briefcase off the bench and holding it out. "You'd better read what's inside."

Ross withdrew the folder and dropped the case negligently to the ground. He opened the file and turned quickly through the pages until he reached the one with the signature and initials. Then he closed the folder and handed it back.

"It was stupid of you to take this," he said.

"Kerzhentseff said he got it from the delegation that met with you in Moscow. He said they knew every move you were going to make."

A raindrop touched McWade's hand where it gripped the file. He bent over to pick up the case and then secured the documents inside. The sidewalk broke out in a pattern of spots. Neither man made a move for shelter.

"Nobody is going to believe you," said Ross. "The simplest explanation is that you took it from the White House yourself."

"I didn't have access," said McWade. "The first I saw of it was in an apartment in East Berlin."

The rain tapered off as quickly as it had begun. McWade wiped the slats of the bench with his hand then gently set the briefcase down.

"It doesn't hold up," said Ross. "If Kerzhentseff had this, what did he need you for?"

"To get it to Fisherman."

"There are a thousand ways."

"I was the one he chose," said McWade.

And now, he thought, for some reason you are trying to make me choose him instead of you.

"You're planning to turn this over to Fisherman," said Ross.

"I didn't say that. Tell me how they got it."

"So you're going to interrogate me now. Is that it?"

"I've got to know what I'm dealing with."

Ross reached inside his jacket and straightened something in his pocket.

"It would hardly be responsible," he said, "to share anything with a man who has just confessed that he's working with the Soviets."

"Is that the way it's going to be now?"

"I don't like being threatened," said Ross.

McWade picked up the briefcase again.

"Would it have been better if I hadn't shown you this?"

Ross pushed it away.

"Do whatever you have to do," he said.

"I'd destroy it if I thought that would help. But you said it yourself. He has a thousand ways he can get another copy to Fisherman. And then we lose control."

"Your loyalty is unrelenting," said Ross. "Maybe you've been to Fisherman already. Maybe he put a wire on you and sent you against me."

"You know I wouldn't let him do that."

Ross moved back away from McWade and spoke slowly, as if he were dictating a memo to file.

"That document could have come from anywhere. They're setting me up. It's transparent. I'm surprised, Ike. Fisherman is usually so much more clever."

"Then just tell me what you want from me."

"You're a fool," said Ross. "Fisherman must have seen it a long time ago. That's why he pushed you on me, because he knew he could use you some day."

Ross slipped his hand inside his breast pocket again then withdrew it, a mannerism McWade had never seen before, a nervous tic.

"We have to work something out," said McWade.

"Fascinating what people think they can get away with," said Ross. "What is it that you want exactly? Money? My job?"

"Stop it."

"I suppose you're going to tell me now that you're only interested in doing the right thing."

"I'm ready to help you."

"I don't deal with traitors," said Ross, reaching into his pocket again.

Whatever he had in there was tormenting him like an itch. He could not keep his hands off it.

"You're wearing a body mike yourself, aren't you?" said McWade.

"I've taken certain precautions."

McWade reached out, and Ross backed away.

"Why?" McWade demanded. It wasn't only the faithlessness but the way Ross had drawn attention to it.

"You're on your own," Ross said.

McWade did not reply. He had already incriminated himself enough. He turned and walked away. The rain began again. The briefcase slapped against his leg with every second step.

23

Back in London the next morning McWade put a call to Greene, who readily agreed to meet before lunch at a used bookseller's on Charing Cross Road a short walk from the hotel.

The shop was a warren of narrow corridors and niches. Shelves reached from floor to ceiling, displaying row after row of faded bindings and broken spines. The poetry and novels were up front near the desk where a pale young woman in a turtleneck added up the prices on an old-fashioned machine. McWade moved farther back into the secluded sections devoted to the physical and human sciences, biography and autobiography, history and drama.

When Greene arrived, he joined McWade at the shelves and pulled out a volume of the *Oxford History of England.*

"You surprised me in Berlin, Ike," he said.

"I wasn't thinking straight," said McWade.

"Fisherman didn't buy your threat, you know. He said it sounded like you were starting to slip."

"Nothing personal," said McWade. "Leggatt against Leggatt."

"Look, I'm a little uncomfortable talking in here," Greene said. Then he replaced the book and led the way back through the maze.

"Fisherman's given you a lot of leash," he said when they got outside. "He could have jerked you around pretty good after what you did."

"Was that your vote?"

"I was kind of hot," Greene admitted. "You went too far."

"We both did."

"It doesn't matter now." Greene waved away the bygones, a little too easily, McWade thought.

The traffic was heavy, and the sidewalks were crowded. There was construction blocking them at Cambridge Circus, so they had to make nearly a full turn of it to get onto Shaftesbury Avenue.

"Did you ever hear of a guy named Jerry Birch?" McWade asked.

"Name doesn't mean anything to me."

Past the roundabout there were trees, and under them the wind was chilly enough for a coat.

"Birch was a GI," said McWade, "Army-type. Straight as a rifle. Everybody's kid brother. He got involved with Fisherman somehow. Not that Birch knew it. He thought he was working for somebody else, but Fisherman had his hands on the keys and his foot on the bellows. He was the one who was making the whole thing whistle and hum."

"Sounds about right," said Greene. "He gets uncomfortable dealing with amateurs. Likes to have somebody else actually run them."

"Fisherman put Birch in an impossible position and left him to fend for himself," said McWade. "The kid ended up slitting his wrists."

Greene did not miss a step. There were only so many ways these stories ended.

"Some guys break," said Greene. "I don't know what it is about them. Something about the way they're wrapped."

"He was just a small town boy who only wanted to serve."

"It's always a shame when Tom Trueheart catches a bullet."

"I'll need some guarantees," said McWade.

They emerged from under the trees into the light again and turned onto New Oxford Street.

"You'll have to work that out with Fisherman."

"I want him to know where I'm coming from," said McWade.

"I imagine he knows all about where you've been."

They were heading now into a crowded commercial strip up past Tottenham Court Road tube station, with stores selling cameras and stereos and what were modestly described on the signs as sexual aids.

"Tell him I'm too young to retire," said McWade. "I kind of like my work. A lot of travel. You meet interesting people. That sort of thing. Tell Fisherman I want to be placed."

Greene paused at a sex shop. The windows were painted pink so passersby only saw their own reflection in the glass.

"This city's going to hell," said Greene.

"I mean well-placed," said McWade.

"He doesn't have a lot of slots on his roster anymore."

"He'll get his budget back when this thing breaks. They won't be able to do enough for him."

"People are in line," said Greene. "He won't want to disrupt his staff."

"I want to be the hero of the story. I want my share."

"There'll be plenty to go around."

"Sometimes the whistleblower gets burned."

"Not if Fisherman doesn't want him to be," said Greene. "Look, the papers are going to eat this story up. You'll go out in a blaze of glory."

Greene began to walk again and McWade quickly caught up to him.

"Tell him that's not good enough. I want to stay."

"He expects to see you tonight," said Greene. "You'll have a lot to talk about."

"I've got something he might find useful."

Greene did not ask what.

"The Hardcastle," he said. "You know it?"

"That was Ben Wheeler's club."

"Dinner at seven. He wants to do business."

"Tell him my terms."

"You want to save your ass," said Greene. "I think he'll understand that."

They were finished with the agenda as far as McWade was concerned, but when he suggested that they go their separate ways, Greene for some reason thought it would be better to stick together for a few more blocks. And so they wandered toward the British Museum. Greene stopped in front of a store on the ground floor of a stately townhouse.

"No hard feelings, I hope," he said.

"No feelings one way or another," said McWade.

"Maybe we were a little rough on you. But he had to bring you around."

Greene seemed to expect some kind of response, but McWade did not know what he wanted. Good sportsmanship? A handshake across the net?

Greene looked into the window, avoiding McWade's eyes in the glass. "You haven't told Jane about the dolly in Berlin, have you?" he asked.

"It hasn't crossed my mind," said McWade.

"I'm really very fond of Jane."

McWade had just enough feeling left to laugh.

"Don't think it doesn't show," he said.

"All right, Ike. Fair enough. I can see how you might resent what happened. I can even understand your wanting to protect her."

"She got what she deserves."

"Don't take it out on her," said Greene. "That's all I'm asking."

"I don't give a damn about your sleeping with her. She didn't owe me anything."

"But you think I did."

"Look," said McWade. "If Langley had a need to know, I would have reported what the Bulgarian thug did to you that night. It didn't cost me anything to cover for you. I didn't expect a thank-you card."

"Maybe you expected me to return the favor."

"No wonder Fisherman chose you to play Leggatt. He knows what people owe and how they go about repaying."

"Just leave Jane alone," said Greene. "I don't want her hurt."

"That's up to you."

"Then we understand each other."

"I suppose we do," said McWade.

And as they moved off in opposite directions, he realized that it had been a mistake to have taken his anger out on this man. Greene wasn't the real Leggatt. He had never been.

The Hardcastle Club was in an old building on a shadowy sidestreet that would have been brighter if it had been lit with gas. At one time the structure might have been a private mansion, the kind they cut up now for fashionable firms that want to flaunt a piece of tradition. But thanks to the dues of the members, this bit of architecture had been preserved in its original configuration, and it displayed the threadbare elegance the British seemed to love, the aristocracy of the fraying collar and rundown heel.

Just inside the door a man in a dark jacket and gray vest sat behind a carved wooden partition that went only halfway to the ceiling. Dandruff salted his shoulders. His face had a painful red flush.

"May I inquire your business, sir?" he asked as McWade shut the big, wooden door behind him.

"Miserable rain," said McWade, sweeping the moisture from his trenchcoat with the palms of his hands.

The doorman came out from behind the partition and positioned himself next to one of the marble nudes that stood on either side of the stairs. They had none of the lightness of classical stone. The curves were just a bit too voluptuous, imagined as function rather than form.

McWade stripped off his damp coat and shook it out.

"Should've brought an umbrella," he said. "Coats still go in the little room over there? The one with all the hooks? If you don't mind my saying so, you ought to consider proper hangers someday."

McWade slipped into the cloakroom, which was not much more than a closed-off hallway. When he returned to the foyer, the doorman had moved up to the foot of the stairs to defend the summit.

"Whom may I announce?" he asked.

"I'm here to meet one of your members. Or at least I assume he's a member."

"May I be favored with a name then, sir?"

"He usually goes by Ernest Fisherman."

An expression of relief came over the doorman's face, and he removed himself from McWade's path.

"Sorry about the formalities, sir," he said. "Interlopers are a problem. They come here because they've heard about the club's collection of oils. Forgive me, but the

Americans are the worst. They seem to think they have some sort of right."

"As opposed to knowing what is right, which is a British speciality," said McWade.

"He's expecting you. In the Green Room. Up the stairs and to your left."

"I know the way."

"Of course, Mr Rogers," said the doorman.

Fisherman was waiting at a table so secluded that it might have been put there to meet his specifications. His napkin tucked into his collar above the tie, he was bent over a soup bowl when McWade slid in across from him.

"I see you had no trouble finding the place," Fisherman said.

"I used to come here regularly."

"Then I won't be able to entertain you with all the quaint stories connected with it."

"I've known other members," said McWade.

"The rules do not exclude Americans. There are a certain number of spaces set aside for us. They still call them the colonial seats. I was offered membership during the war. They couldn't do enough for us in those days. I got Ben on the rolls some years later, after it had become a bit more difficult. Your drink is Scotch?"

"Heavy on the soda," McWade told the waiter. "Do you still keep ice?"

"It can be arranged, sir."

Fisherman put down his spoon and sat back in his chair.

"I've taken the liberty of ordering dinner for both of us," he said. "The game this season is said to be quite good."

McWade glanced around the room. Every available space on the high walls was hung with portraits of former members.

"A man has to be dead for a half century before the membership first votes whether to hang his likeness," said Fisherman. "Like the quality of literature and fine wine, character only reveals itself to history. At least that is the Hardcastle faith."

The waiter brought McWade his drink and a bowl of

oyster soup. A few tiny bits of ice danced atop the bubbles in his glass.

"I have always regretted," said Fisherman, pulling the napkin from under his chin, "that there's no place like it in Washington. But the people there will not support any institution that withholds immediate judgment."

"It's all very civilized," said McWade. "I might even enjoy it under other circumstances."

"There are always distractions."

"Like wondering what you want and what you're willing to exchange for it," said McWade.

"Have some of your soup before it gets cold."

The oysters squeaked as McWade bit into them. The broth tasted of milk and salt.

"I've always respected your analytical ability, Isaac," said Fisherman. "But I am not so confident that you know what is best for you."

"It hasn't ordinarily been my first concern."

"In the past it probably didn't need to be," said Fisherman. "Now suppose you give me a briefing. Bring me up to speed, the way you used to when you worked for me."

He folded his napkin before him and waited. The man could have been a Handholder, if he had been interested in that kind of secret. He was the kind of person who could bring you back to your senses or drive you mad, whichever was required.

"You've been under pressure," McWade said. "They've tried to cut your budget. Even your best allies haven't been able to help you this time. You need to deliver something that will reestablish you as irreplaceable and at the same time remind everyone of the risk of crossing you. That's why you want to do in our mutual friend, Michael Ross."

"Acute as always," said Fisherman. "But I hope you will move on to something I did not know."

"That may be difficult. You're a hard man to shop for, Ernest. The man who has everything."

The waiter cleared the soup and put out the main course — some sort of fowl in a sauce of berries. McWade was the first to taste it.

273

"Did you know that Richard Harper came to me?" said Fisherman.

"He does get around, doesn't he?" said McWade. "I imagine you know about the night he showed up in my living room unannounced. It was the same night I phoned you and offered to help."

"Harper was quite concerned about you, Isaac. He had heard that you were going to strike at me in some way."

McWade allowed himself a smile.

"He assumed that I would miss," he said.

"I suppose he told you about the unfortunate Sergeant Birch."

"I didn't get the whole story."

"It was a nice touch for you to use Harper the way you did," said Fisherman. "At first I wasn't sure what you were hoping to accomplish."

"Just throwing a little smoke. You were trying to draw me into the open, so I put up a screen."

"What exactly did you tell him?"

"I had the impression there was blood on somebody's hands," said McWade.

"He blames me for the unpleasant events that led to the eclipse of his career," said Fisherman. "He is not like you, Isaac. He is a coward. That has always been my problem with him."

"The way I get it, he was right about what you did to his boy, Birch."

"That's what made it so peculiar when he came to warn me about your activities," said Fisherman. "I could only believe it was because you pushed him somehow."

"When he came to my house that night," said McWade, "it was to enlist me against you by persuading me that I had to bring you down to save myself. And so when I was getting ready to leave the country, I wanted him to believe that his plan had backfired. I hoped he might run to you to try to cover his ass. I got word to him that it wasn't you who was out to get me. It was Ross."

"Nicely done," said Fisherman. "He told me the opposite, of course. I might even have believed him if I hadn't had a bit of independent knowledge."

274

"You always do."

McWade ate a bite of vegetables. They were overcooked, but he did not have much of an appetite anyway.

"I'm afraid I've led you off on a tangent, a rather unimportant one at that," said Fisherman. "Suppose you give me your observations. What you have seen, both during the time that you were in Ross's favor and now that you have apparently fallen out of it."

"You put me on his staff so I could be your eyes, didn't you?"

"Actually, I had no clear purpose," said Fisherman. "Though you might prefer not to believe it, Ross came to me. I agreed to your transfer, of course. You were restless anyway. You were tiring of my work."

McWade did not examine this assertion deeply. It did not matter whether he believed it or not. The question of how he had ended up where he was fell in the category of interesting but idle conundrums, like the value of i or the undecidability of the proposition: This sentence is false.

"One thing I could not help noticing," said McWade, "was that you were not at all interested when I called up and offered to help you. Then you went to a lot of trouble to discredit me and draw me back overseas. Obviously you did not believe I had the information on Ross that you needed. So you arranged for it to be provided."

"I am afraid that you have mixed up imagination and observation, Isaac," said Fisherman. "You've gone wide of the mark somewhere. Perhaps you should backtrack and try again."

"What else am I supposed to make of Steven Greene? The name you had him use."

"That was harsh, but useful."

"To make me feel threatened. To get me in a position where I could be manipulated."

"It wasn't for your benefit," said Fisherman. He finished his meat and pushed the plate away. "For Brits, they do serve a creditable meal."

"Who else could Leggatt have been meant for?"

"An interesting line of inquiry."

"I am ready to give you what you want," said McWade.

"It is always a mistake to rush these matters," said Fisherman. "Let's review the bidding."

"I need certain guarantees. That's all."

"Who told you Leggatt was on the loose?" asked Fisherman. He exhaled the question with his chin slightly lifted, as if the words were smoke.

"The woman you ran against me in Washington," said McWade. "That was really very shrewd. You worked on all the weaknesses, even some I thought belonged exclusively to Leggatt."

Fisherman listened politely, but without taking any apparent satisfaction.

"And when did you decide to come looking for him here?" he asked.

"When she made a fool of me. It was a lovely setup. It lost me my job."

"Ross was understanding, I suppose," said Fisherman. "He encouraged you to find out what it was all about."

"I told him what I had learned of your investigation."

"Of course," said Fisherman. "You were right to think that you were caught in certain elements of my devising. But the woman in Washington wasn't mine. She was almost certainly deployed by Ross. And as for my role, it is true that I revived Joseph Leggatt. But he was not designed to draw you out. It was for Ross, you see, to force him to act."

"You don't need to make the case against Ross."

"The name of Leggatt had the desired effect. It led Ross to set you in motion. He knew I was interested in Ben Wheeler's death."

"Wheeler!" said McWade. "For God's sake." His voice soared out over the chiming of the silver and the hush of conversation. "Haven't we gone beyond ancient history?"

"Everything has its antecedents."

"The Czech woman told me you were responsible for the killing," said McWade. "Maybe that was why I was careless at first. I didn't see through the legend you wrote for her, Ernest. I thought she was going to deliver you up. You knew I'd want to believe that."

As the headwaiter approached the table, Fisherman leaned toward McWade.

"My only assumption," he said, "has been that you would go the way the facts drove you."

The headwaiter stood off at a decent interval until Fisherman had finished speaking, then he stepped up and whispered something. Fisherman nodded his approval. At a snap of the fingers, one of the helps appeared and set a third place at the table.

"I have asked a friend to join us for dessert," said Fisherman.

He turned, and McWade followed his eyes to the doorway, where a man in a tight sportscoat and a dated tie that must have been provided as a convenience by the club was slouching into the room.

"Stockwell," McWade whispered.

"When Rufus had his troubles," said Fisherman, "I took the opportunity to turn the situation to good use. What is more plausible than an ex-agent with a grudge? Especially a grudge directed against me."

"He's working for you?"

"You should feel vindicated," said Fisherman. "You had argued all along that he should not be discarded, and he has always been grateful to you for that."

"Hello there, chum," said Stockwell when he reached the table. "Nice place, Ernest."

The headwaiter pulled out the chair, and Stockwell cast a suspicious eye at him over his shoulder as he sat down, as if he thought the man might try to yank it out from under him.

"I could use a drink," said Stockwell. "They have American Bourbon in a place like this?"

"I think you'll find them attentive to your thirst," said Fisherman. "Shall we order dessert right away? The fresh berries are always lovely."

"I'm not hungry," said Stockwell. "Ike looks like he's off his feed, too."

"I'm afraid Isaac may be feeling a little done in," said Fisherman. "I haven't explained everything quite yet."

"You want to do the honors," asked Stockwell, "or shall I?"

"Rufus came to me as soon as you contacted him, Isaac," said Fisherman. "It was his first instinct to walk away from the situation rather than play you double. But I persuaded him that if he turned you down, you might find someone else who might not have been as solicitous of your interests."

"If you'll excuse me," said McWade, rising in his chair.

"Please sit down," said Fisherman, "so Rufus can tell you where he's been."

"You made it so goddamned easy," said Stockwell, "that I thought that maybe you'd caught on. I just keyed on Ross going in because I didn't know the precise location of your rendezvous. I wasn't in on it the last time you met with him in Bath."

"Ah yes," said Fisherman, "that first meeting in Bath. A fascinating historical point. We'll have to remember to come back to it at some stage." As if he ever forgot.

"I watched his back," said McWade. "You're good, but not that good, Rufus."

"When you made the pass in that fancy tea room, I left him and picked up on you. I figured you might be looking for somebody tailing Ross on the way out. And anyway, I wanted to make sure there was nobody else on you."

"I'd thought of sending in a surveillance team," said Fisherman, "but Rufus didn't want it. If he had been seen, at least there would have been an explanation. He was your cutout, and so it was natural that he might be covering you."

"I had a hunch, Ike," Stockwell said. "I wanted to see who else Ross had on his appointment calendar. So after you finished your visit, I tracked him halfway across the fucking island. To a place just outside East Jesus.

"He finally pulled into a country place and disappeared inside. After a couple hours he split. I followed my gut again and sat tight until the other bastard finally showed his face."

"Tell him who," said Fisherman.

"The guy they call Zapadnya."

"Quite a coincidence, no?" said Fisherman.

"World of wonders," said McWade.

"What did you tell him, Isaac, that he had to rush off and give Kerzhentseff a fill?"

"I told him the same thing I told you," said McWade. "I asked about the terms."

"An auction then," said Fisherman. "Tell me, what did he bid?"

"Nothing," said McWade. "Apparently he didn't think he had to."

Fisherman finished his berries and wiped the juice off his spoon before setting it back down on the tablecloth.

"Show him the photographs, Rufus," he said. "We seem to have a skeptic at the table."

Stockwell reached into his pants pocket and withdrew two creased prints. The first was washed out by the sun, and the other was much too dark. They both showed the front door of a big old country house. The daylight shot caught Ross coming out. The one at dusk could have been Kerzhentseff. It could have been anybody.

"The property belongs to Ross," said Fisherman. "If I'd been bright enough, I would have discovered the purchase years ago. When he was in his glory at the Agency, he had a substantial contingency fund. There were any number of large expenditures, but nobody questioned them. The dividends were so high then that it was not prudent to quibble."

"A safehouse for the NARCISSUS operation," said McWade.

"For any purpose Ross saw fit," said Fisherman. "You don't recognize it, do you, Isaac?"

McWade studied the pictures again, but it was impossible to tell much from them. His memory was blind.

"I thought perhaps during your long absence from London," said Fisherman, as McWade handed back the photos, "before your departure for Berlin. We've had some discussion of the possibility that you'd gone on a retreat there."

McWade was silent.

"Come on, chum," said Stockwell. "Loosen up. You don't owe the sonofabitch. What'd he ever do for you except set you up? Listen, if you help us now, you've got it knocked."

279

"I guess I'm supposed to thank you," said McWade.

It was bitter, but Stockwell did not seem to hear.

"Again, Isaac," said Fisherman, losing patience, his voice going hard. "What did you tell Ross?"

"I showed him what Kerzhentseff gave me in Berlin," said McWade.

"So you've been flirting with Zapadnya, too," said Fisherman.

"He wanted me to bring it to you, but I went to Ross first."

"To see what kind of arrangement he could offer."

"To see if he had an explanation," said McWade. "Look, before we go any further, I have to know what you've got in mind."

"There's no mystery about that," said Fisherman. "Are you concerned about the purity of my motives? Yes, I expect to be rewarded. Perhaps that makes me a sinner in your eyes."

"I mean what you've got in mind for me."

"So it turns out we are all sinners in the end," said Fisherman, bridging his fingers before him. "I know this isn't a particularly attractive situation for you. You're afraid that if Ross falls, he'll take you down, too. There will be a certain amount of resentment in the White House, of course. But they can be made to see your value and compensate your discretion."

"They won't be able to trust me," said McWade.

"Trust," said Fisherman, smiling. "In my experience trust is never an adequate basis for a relationship. It wobbles. It cracks under strain. Better is fear, which grows in adversity."

McWade could see that Fisherman had made his best offer. It was a buyer's market.

"Kerzhentseff gave me a copy of Ross's fallback positions for the Moscow talks," said McWade. "He told me the Soviets had them in advance."

"The genuine article?" said Stockwell.

"I'd never seen the original," said McWade. "But I worked on the early drafts, and the document was roughly consistent with what I know."

"We'll have to prove where they got it and when," said Stockwell.

"Not every item in the negotiating instructions was actually explored in the talks," said McWade. "But as you will see, the Soviets knew it all."

Fisherman's attention seemed to have wandered. His hands were flat on the table top, as if he were communing with something unseen.

"You have the paper now?" asked Stockwell.

"Not here."

"But access."

"Certainly."

"We ought to have a look at it," said Stockwell. "Can you get your hands on it tonight?"

"No need," said Fisherman.

"The sooner we get started," said Stockwell, "the less time Ross will have to cover his tracks."

"You told Ross exactly what you had, Issac?" said Fisherman.

"Yes."

"And he was unimpressed."

"He threatened me," said McWade.

Fisherman leaned forward across the table, his hands spread wide.

"You were playing the innocent, Isaac," he said. "He had to force you to act on interests he could predict and, to that extent, control. You see, they want to take you out. I don't know why yet, but they do. The document is almost certainly a fake."

"Ike thinks it's real," said Stockwell.

"How were the final positions arrived at?" asked Fisherman.

"A meeting between the President, Simpson and Ross," said McWade.

"So they might have changed considerably from what you believed them to be."

Fisherman sat back in his chair and lifted his water glass. The liquid glittered in the light of the candle.

"Kerzhentseff will want confirmation that you have told

me about the document," he said. "When he comes to you, tell him that I do not believe his tale."

"You want him to come up with more," said McWade.

"I want to find out what you know that makes them so afraid."

"Maybe you should just ask him," said McWade.

"Give him this message," said Fisherman. "I need to talk to him face to face. Tell him to contact me at this number." He wrote it on a cocktail napkin and passed it across the table. "Assure him that otherwise I will not take any action against Ross."

"He's going to be wary," said McWade.

"He's going to be terrified," said Fisherman.

24

As soon as McWade got away from the club, he ducked into a tube station and found a pay phone. When the call went through, he identified himself and explained the situation in an improvised open code. The man on the other end of the line did not seem to have any difficulty understanding, especially the sense of urgency. It was McWade's idea to make the rendezvous near Greene's flat.

When he was finished on the phone, he had time to kill to give the Russians a chance to get there. So instead of taking the tube, he walked the distance, lost in a daze of possibilities: that Ross had fed secrets to the Russians, that Fisherman and Kerzhentseff had teamed up to ruin Ross, that Ross and Kerzhentseff had conspired to do in McWade because of something he knew.

Something he knew. That was a good one. The only thing McWade was sure of was that no matter how the thing went down, he could easily be pulled down with it. He'd been in contact with the Soviets, and everybody knew it. The only explanation he could give for his actions was that he had no idea who was who.

The car was waiting for him when he arrived. He went directly to it. There was no purpose to be served now by evasion. He had absolutely no avenue of escape.

"You know the procedure," said the man in the back seat as McWade slid in beside the driver. The black hood was on the cushion next to him.

"Is this really necessary?"

"Please slide down out of sight."

McWade pulled the hood over his head. The fabric was cool against his face.

"Maybe you will sleep."

"That would be pleasant," said McWade

"A lever on your left. Do you feel it?"

When McWade pulled it, the seat gave way behind his back. He put his weight on it until he was nearly flat.

"Will this do?" he said, his voice coming back to him muffled by the cloth.

"You see, it is different this time. We take care of the comfort of our friends."

The road rumbled beneath him. He rolled to his side and curled up, surrendering himself to silence and darkness, the distance he had to go.

When they finally pulled up, he struggled to rise in his seat. His arm was numb. It gave way under him, and helplessly he fell back. But then he felt himself being lifted upright by the shoulders. The door opened and, quite gently, a hand coaxed his head down to protect it as he slid out.

"Can I take this off now?" he asked, his fingers at the hem of the hood.

"Seven steps," said the man, taking his arm. "Now three upward."

When he was inside, the hood came off.

"This way," said the Russian.

McWade followed him to the sitting room where he had first met Kerzhentseff.

"Please be comfortable," said the man.

Once McWade was alone, he went to the windows and parted the drapes. The rest of the house was obscure from this vantage. All he could see was the gravel path, which glowed an eerie gray under the moon. The driver was trudging across it, hands in pockets, a cigarette pasted in his mouth like a running light. Beyond him McWade could make out a dim, flat expanse. It was impossible to tell where he was, which he assumed was why they let him have access to the glass. It would have worried him if they had been too lax. In that respect he had been grateful for the hood. He wanted them to fear him, but not too much, because fear always had two edges: it cut against the way it drove.

284

He let the drapes fall back into place and began to investigate the room. He was examining the contents of an end table drawer — some blank paper, a pencil, a deck of cards — when Kerzhentseff appeared in the door.

"Solitaire?" said McWade, holding out the cards.

Kerzhentseff stepped forward and put his good hand on McWade's shoulder. It was heavy there.

"So you finally paid a visit to your old mentor," he said.

"I told him about what you had given me," said McWade. "He didn't believe a word of it."

"He will believe the document."

"He didn't even want to see it," said McWade. "He has some idea that you are trying to walk me into one of your famous traps."

"You?" said Kerzhentseff. "Why would I bother?" But then he softened. "I have no reason to cause you harm. Fisherman is being overly protective. You were his protégé. I suppose he might believe your failure would reflect badly on him."

"I don't think he's overly invested in me," said McWade. "A man in his position is known by whom he defeats."

Kerzhentseff took the deck of cards from McWade and fanned them like a conjuror.

"What was his objection?" he asked.

"It seemed to be enough that the document came from you."

"I would have the same reservations, of course," said Kerzhentseff, "if I were in his position."

"That's one of the things that has been bothering me," said McWade. "You seem to think so much alike."

Kerzhentseff's fingers deftly cut the deck. Then he took the top card, looked at it and replaced it in the stack.

"Perhaps it is only an illusion," he said. "Or perhaps we are able to read one another's minds after all the years of competition. Think of what Fisherman and I might have accomplished together. You Americans do not know how to appreciate a man like him. He is a much worthier opponent than Michael Ross."

"You might be surprised about that," said McWade. "Ross is safe if Fisherman won't make a move."

"But he will," said Kerzhentseff. "The objective conditions are too promising for him to turn away."

"He thinks the document you gave me was a fake."

"Faked by me or by Ross?"

"He doesn't usually provide full explanations."

"Embellish it for me then," said Kerzhentseff, putting the cards in his pocket. "What purpose would I have in deceiving you?"

"Maybe to destroy me."

"I think you are overestimating your importance," said Kerzhentseff. "But what about the other possibility, that Ross himself masterminded an ingenious bit of disinformation?"

"He might have been authorized to plant it with your delegation, to lead them in the direction he wanted. Or maybe he was trying to discredit Fisherman's investigation."

Kerzhentseff picked up on the logic and followed it out with some amusement. "If Fisherman used the document to accuse Ross and it turned out to be false," he said, "then Ross could turn the accusation around. Make a fool of him."

"And I'd have to come forward and explain where I got it. It would not exactly look good on my resumé."

"So you did not vouch for the document's authenticity when you told Fisherman about it?" said Kerzhentseff. "You were afraid to commit yourself."

"I'm not even sure you can be confident of your own people, the ones who gave the document to you. There are any number of ways that Fisherman could be right."

"My hand," said Kerzhentseff, holding out the clawed, withered thing before him, "it could someday suddenly come back to life. I could be a great pianist. The weak could inherit the earth."

"He wants to talk with you," said McWade.

The hand dropped back to Kerzhentseff's side.

"He offers to meet on neutral ground," McWade said. "Principals only. You and he alone."

"Where?"

"A place to be mutually agreed upon. I have a number for you to call."

"And between us we will work out the ruin of Ross," said the Russian. "I'm afraid it does not parse."

"Then walk away from it. And so will I."

"What is the number?"

McWade withdrew the cocktail napkin from his pocket. The figures were smudged but legible in Fisherman's distinctive script.

"It would be amusing to speak with him, I suppose," said Kerzhentseff as he took it, "just to see what he proposes. You will wait here, of course."

"I'd just as soon go back to London."

"That would not be convenient."

"I'm to be a hostage then."

"In the classic sense of the word: a person given over to an adversary to guarantee the good conduct of his lord."

"I don't belong to Fisherman," said McWade.

"You belong to whoever holds you," said the Russian.

To prepare Agency men for captivity, part of every training cycle was devoted to lessons in how to resist the Stockholm Syndrome, the tendency of a captive to begin identifying with his jailer. The Handholders were more than willing to provide theoretically minded students a full course of jargon, from transference to regression. But now, as he was led from the sitting room back to his well-appointed cell, McWade realized that you didn't need fancy words to explain it. Kerzhentseff was right: possession was nine parts of the law.

He switched off the lights, lay down on the bed and stared up at the dark ceiling. The wind blew a high note on some loose boards outside. Otherwise it was silent. He did not know what direction the wind came from or why it blew. He did not know the meaning of the sweat that broke out on his brow. He felt as though he were in motion, high above the clouds, toward a secret destination. It was not long before he heard the birds outside and realized that somehow he had slept.

Breakfast came, but he was not hungry. When he called for his tray to be removed, he asked the little old man if there was somewhere he might be allowed to watch television to pass the time. This was obviously beyond the man's authority, so he got one of the Russians, the silent one who had driven the car the night before.

"TV?" he said.

"Yes," said McWade. "*Da*. TV."

The Russian shook his head and pushed McWade back into the room. The lock clicked shut. McWade pounded with both fists on the wood.

"Come back!"

When he stopped pounding, he heard footsteps ascending the stairs. Then the door swung open and the Russian stood in the opening.

"You will c-c-come with me," he said slowly, as if he were reciting.

Downstairs the other Russian was sitting in a small, wood-paneled den off the living room. On the television, they were replaying the decisive strokes of a snooker match.

"Stupid game," said the English-speaking Russian. "You play?"

"It's like billiards," said McWade.

"That one," said the Russian, pointing to the younger fellow who was lining up his shot. "He is winning."

"I am for the other."

"The underling."

"Dog," said McWade, and the Russian started to rise in offense. "Underdog. Not underling. I'm for the underdog."

"I am for the victor," said the Russian.

They sat watching the screen as the snooker gave way to an unfathomable cricket match and then a report on weather conditions from Cornwall to the North Sea.

"Did your boss say when he was going to be back?" asked McWade.

"Don't worry." The Russian said it like a command.

"It isn't that I don't enjoy your company."

"Company," said the man. "You work for the Company."

288

"Actually I'm between jobs," McWade said.

"Maybe this is a trick," said the Russian.

"You mean it's the kind of work a person never really leaves."

"Except," said the man, making his finger into a weapon and firing it at point blank range. "Pow!"

"We work a little differently in my country," said McWade. "We are a nation of laws. We bury men under pensions."

"Strange," said the Russian.

Just then McWade heard the sound of an automobile, its wheels spinning in gravel. One of the Russians went to the window and parted the drapes. It did not take a linguist to tell that the word he spat was a curse.

"Kerzhentseff's here," said McWade.

The two Russians exchanged excited whispers.

"Maybe I'd better get back upstairs," said McWade.

"Do not move."

The guards left the room and McWade heard someone entering the house, footsteps on the creaky wooden floor, muffled voices.

Then a big voice roared, "Idiots! You left him where he could see me."

A moment later Ross appeared in the doorway.

"Spare me the wounded countenance," he said.

"Fisherman was right," said McWade.

The guards came up behind Ross, keeping a wary distance, as if they were afraid that something McWade might say would anger him and he would take it out on them.

"You would naturally see it that way now," said Ross, "since you have decided to march under his flag. I don't think you're going to like where it leads you."

"That depends on how Fisherman and Kerzhentseff get along."

"They are fated to be enemies, I'm afraid."

"They're meeting together right now. That's what I came here to set up."

"You are a fool," said Ross. Then he looked to the guards. "Take him somewhere and lock him up."

McWade did not put up a fight. The guards supported him by the arms as they led him out of Ross's presence. They were just mounting the stairs when the front door flew open. One of the guards reached for his pistol. But then he thought better of it. Rufus Stockwell stood there with a dozen men armed with rifles and shotguns, a picture of overwhelming force.

25

McWade was not permitted to participate directly in the interrogation, even though he had as many questions as anyone to ask of Ross. Stockwell drove him to a safehouse that was little more than a bland suite of white rooms in an office complex on the outskirts of the city. As he was being shown into a makeshift control room, a technician was bringing Ross into focus on a TV monitor. McWade nodded to him and sat down. Fisherman's voice came over the speaker.

"Are you ready, Michael?"

"You've really stepped in it this time," Ross said. "Do you realize the damage you have done?"

"Perhaps you will tell me," said Fisherman.

He began by asking Ross to describe the circumstances under which he had first come into contact with Kerzhentseff. To McWade's surprise, Ross showed no inclination to resist. In fact, he seemed to enjoy telling the tale.

"I suppose you've heard Kerzhentseff's version by now," he said.

"We talked of more current matters," said Fisherman.

"He and I go back a long way," said Ross. "You remember the way we felt just after the war, Ernest. By heaven blessed."

"I'm afraid I don't recall those days so fondly."

"I was new to the service, of course," said Ross. "My assignment was to run a net of Polish partisans. Kerzhentseff had been involved in the repatriation and internal exile of Soviet prisoners of war liberated by the Allies. We had heard he had become disgusted with the work."

"It was not a good time for men of delicate sensibilities," said Fisherman.

"When the possibility of meeting him arose, I leaped at it."

"On your own authority?"

"I suppose you think I was headstrong."

"I wasn't there."

"Oh, but you were, Ernest. Everywhere I looked I saw the achievements of men like you who had been given great challenges during the war that made them grow in stature. I suppose I wanted to prove myself.

"But as it turned out, I walked right into a trap. Kerzhentseff did not come alone. I found myself surrounded."

"It was just about then that he shifted jobs," said Fisherman. "Unless I am mistaken, he inherited the responsibility for snuffing out your partisans."

"That was the odd part. He never questioned me about them."

Fisherman cleared his throat and rustled some papers out of sight of the camera. The technician in the control room with McWade slid the earphones off his head and turned in his chair.

"You ever see the old man work before?" he asked.

"Many times," said McWade.

"He's anybody's match."

Then Fisherman's voice came over the speakers again, flat as a broken bell.

"Didn't you think it was odd for him not to press you after such a show of force?"

"Sometimes a man will make a move when he shouldn't," said Ross. "It happens to the best of them."

"A skilled interrogator usually has a design," said Fisherman, "even when it isn't immediately apparent."

"If he's smart, he'll look for some way out before he gets in too deep."

"A man like Kerzhentseff would only deal from a position of strength," said Fisherman.

"If he understands his situation," said Ross, "he'll realize at some point that he has to yield."

Ross's face suddenly disappeared from the screen. The technician was ready to zoom back to find him, but it wasn't necessary. Ross was just shifting his weight to get more comfortable in his chair.

"You did have a discussion with Kerzhentseff that day, I take it," said Fisherman.

"Quite a fascinating one in fact," said Ross.

"Could you summarize?"

"He said he was interested in opening a channel of communication that might be of mutual advantage during the difficult days that everyone could see lay ahead."

"And you agreed."

"I was intrigued."

"You reported the contact, I assume," said Fisherman.

"I may have been somewhat vague about the details," said Ross. "But it was a busy time; no one was reading reports about dogs that didn't bark or bite."

"He recruited you," said Fisherman.

Ross broke into a smile.

"As it turned out," he said, "I recruited him."

The chair scraped as Ross leaned back in it.

"Surely you figured out from the NARCISSUS files that Kerzhentseff was TANGO," he went on. "That he was also LARYNX and ROGUE."

"You will have to excuse me for a moment," Fisherman mumbled.

Now McWade knew why Ross was so confident. They had blundered right into the heart of the NARCISSUS operation.

"Did you hear him, Isaac?" Fisherman said excitedly as he entered the control room.

"Kerzhentseff was Ross's mole," said McWade.

"Undoubtedly the relationship will prove to be a bit more complex than that," said Fisherman.

"It means Ross had a reason to be in contact."

"The point is that he felt he had to reveal it," said Fisherman. "There is something he is so afraid of that he had to clad himself in the past." He went to the monitor and gazed up at Ross's face. "He will show us more."

The technician reached over and touched a switch on the control panel.

"You want me to read his voice for stress?" he asked.

"That won't be necessary," said Fisherman. "He's not lying yet."

"You'll tell me when he starts?" said the technician.

"Our friend here will," said Fisherman. "Isaac ought to know."

When the interrogation began again, Fisherman took Ross through a long series of questions about mundane details. How often did he meet with Kerzhentseff? Where did the meetings take place? Dates and times. In the trade this was known as collecting shells. The purpose was to find one that could later be detonated.

"Why did you eventually bring in assistance?" asked Fisherman.

"After I took the assignment back at Langley, it became difficult to break away regularly enough to service him properly."

"Your success with NARCISSUS played a substantial role in getting you a promotion, as I recall," said Fisherman.

"At the time you were doubtful, Ernest."

"Of the source. Not of you."

"I was concerned about it, though," said Ross. "In fact I chose Ben Wheeler as a partner precisely because of your respect for him."

"I take it Ben only acted as a go-between," said Fisherman. "Kerzhentseff always knew you were his control. And that he was your principal asset."

"Wheeler had a few other sources, Czech mostly. All low level. We occasionally threw odd bits from them into the NARCISSUS reports just to make it more difficult for anyone to infer Kerzhentseff's identity."

"And he provided information only to you and Wheeler."

"That's correct."

"What did you give him in return?"

Ross was obviously prepared for the question.

"Whatever I had to," he said.

"Money? Information?"

"Both."

"On your own authority?"

"When necessary."

"But always purely in the national interest," said Fisherman.

For the first time, Ross showed some irritation.

"Whose authority are you acting on, Ernest? Did you get a formal tasking to jeopardize the arms talks?"

"We all press the limits," said Fisherman. "Some with more success than others. Your relationship with Kerzhentseff, for example. It helped advance both your careers."

"He made good use of what I provided."

"So the Soviets had their own NARCISSUS operation, too, and you were its source."

"It was advantageous to have Kerzhentseff highly placed," said Ross, getting suddenly formal. "Langley concurred in principle. You will discover a finding to this effect in the restricted files."

"I have seen it," said Fisherman. "And if I could gain access to the KGB's records I fully expect that I would find a similar memorandum about you."

But the Kremlin files were closed even to a man with Fisherman's resources. And you couldn't bring someone like Ross down with conjecture. You had to have something hard.

"I'm interested in the period when NARCISSUS shut down," said Fisherman. "I'm rather surprised the DCI allowed it."

"I presented it as a *fait accompli*," said Ross.

"And with Wheeler dead, there was nobody else he could turn to as your replacement," said Fisherman.

"Wheeler was killed somewhat later, actually," said Ross.

Fisherman suddenly excused himself again, pleading an old man's bladder.

"I hope you have been following closely, Isaac," he said when he reappeared in the control room.

"It is always fascinating to hear living legends reminisce," said McWade.

"Apparently you missed the significance. NARCISSUS was closed out before Wheeler's death."

"What difference does it make?"

"Be ready to join us," said Fisherman. "And please try to be more attentive. When the time comes, I believe you will be able to tell me precisely what it is that Ross has been so afraid you will reveal."

He shuffled out the door, and McWade turned back to the monitor. Ross seemed as relaxed as if he had spent his life before the cameras instead of avoiding them.

"Forgive the interruption," said Fisherman. "I'm not the man I used to be."

"The need for consultation becomes more urgent with age," Ross said.

He sat back in his chair, and the technician had to zoom in to stay tight on his face.

"When exactly did you decide to revive your relationship with Kerzhentseff?" asked Fisherman.

Ross leaned forward, his eyes filling the screen.

"When you came to me, Ernest, asking for help in the matter of that fellow . . . what was his name? . . . was it Birch?"

Fisherman chuckled.

"I hadn't realized your lines of contact to Kerzhentseff were that direct," he said. "But you had nothing to offer him then. You were in exile."

"A favor," said Ross. "Perhaps we both had confidence that times and my circumstances would change."

"You dealt with him regularly after that?"

Ross seemed totally in control of the facts and the way they drove.

"Not until the arms initiative," he said. "As Isaac will tell you, all avenues were explored."

"I take it that you intend to credit the progress of the talks to NARCISSUS."

"You aren't going to find much sympathy for what you have done. I can assure you of that. The back channel was vital."

"Kerzhentseff told you how far his side was willing to move," said Fisherman, "and you repaid him in kind."

Ross drew back again. His expression was no longer easy. Ernest had obviously crossed over into territory where Ross was unwilling to go.

"I am not prepared to disclose the details of the runup

to the Moscow talks," he said. "You are not cleared for it, I'm afraid."

Ross, of course, was well within his prerogatives. It could have even been argued that Ross had an obligation of silence. Suddenly McWade had the sickening feeling that he had let himself be caught out on the weaker side.

"You had an enormous investment in the outcome of the arms talks," said Fisherman. "A satisfactory agreement would have meant succeeding Simpson at the NSC."

"I will say this much," said Ross. "My writ was to avoid impasse. You do not have to strain to find other motives."

"And the President was fully aware of your means?"

"You should have worried about my tasking a little earlier, Ernest. I had all the authority I needed. You are the only rogue elephant, I'm afraid."

The man at the controls looked over at McWade as if to ask whether Ross was lying yet. But McWade still had no idea what Fisherman expected him to find in Ross's answers.

"The document you had Kerzhentseff pass to McWade," said Fisherman, "that, too, you believe was authorized?"

"You were moving into a very dangerous area. I had to try to deflect you."

"So it became your duty to try to discredit me through disinformation."

"When you continued to press your unfortunate inquiry."

"And more particularly to discredit McWade."

"He was a messenger. Nothing more."

"This is what perplexes me, Michael," said Fisherman. "You had no reason to believe he would be disloyal to you. And yet you constructed a situation that could hardly fail to make him look ridiculous or worse. You forced him away from you when all he wanted was to serve."

"I hated to have to sacrifice him," said Ross.

"You drove him into a conspiracy with me against you so that everything he might say would be discounted. It can only be that you were afraid of what he would reveal about Ben Wheeler's murder."

Ross seemed distracted, his attention lapsing.

"You've gotten pretty far afield," he said.

"McWade had investigated that case," said Fisherman.

"It is my understanding," he said, "that his investigation was unsuccessful. It came to nothing."

"Perhaps we should ask him," said Fisherman. "Isaac, won't you join us?"

If Ross had been more careful about how he had described the conclusion of the murder inquiry, McWade might never have seen the flaw in his account. But now he did.

The technician led him to the interrogation room and opened the door. Ross met his eyes as he entered. McWade was ready to face him. He did not balk.

"Ben Wheeler never turned," he said. "You lied about him to get me off the case."

"If I were you," said Ross. "I'd begin reassessing my position about now."

"When you summoned me to Bath to give me that story about Ben's gambling debts, it wasn't real. There hadn't been any investigation of Ben's habits. No incriminating evidence. Wheeler was clean."

"I've read all the files," said Fisherman. "They are quite bare of any challenge to Wheeler's integrity. In fact, they were so utterly unrevealing that I was sure the key had to be something that wasn't there."

McWade stood over Ross, who did not even have the decency to avert his eyes.

"You had Ben killed," McWade said. "He found out that you'd been giving Kerzhentseff at least as much as Kerzhentseff gave you. He threatened to expose you, and you silenced him."

"Actually," said Fisherman, "I doubt that there was any threat. Wheeler was killed to protect Kerzhentseff. That was the reason, wasn't it, Michael?"

Ross did not answer. He did not even stir.

"Nobody listened when Michael warned about the danger of the purges," Fisherman said. "But he believed that if the leaks claimed a life, this would turn the situation around. Choosing Wheeler as a target also had the effect of reassuring Kerzhentseff, who must have been terrified to see Langley hemorrhaging secrets. It eliminated the one other person who could testify to precisely who NARCISSUS was and what the operation had involved. There is a lovely symmetry to it, actually. I imagine that when Kerzhentseff ordered the execution, he strengthened his own position with his superiors by telling them that he was doing it to protect an agent in place at Langley, the key to the Soviet's own NARCISSUS operation, Michael Ross."

Fisherman put down his papers and lifted himself wearily from his chair.

"That is the way it worked, isn't it, Michael?" he said.

Ross lifted a glass from the table at his side and took a sip of water. His hand was perfectly steady.

"I think it is time to start discussing our options," he said.

PART SIX

After Action

26

If McWade had been able to accept Swain as a barometer, he would have considered the outcome of his venture abroad an unrivaled success. Swain's reading was unequivocal: "Ross came after you, and you took his goddamned job."

McWade, good soldier, did not confirm or deny, though it galled him to learn that Emma Baron had been spreading the word that Ross had been ill-treated. It was in the very nature of the endgame that McWade could not disclose to Swain or anyone else the source of his dissatisfaction. But the fact was, despite his promotion, he had not had enough influence to get his way.

The decisive meeting had been held in the Situation Room with the President's Chief of Staff presiding. Justice was represented by the Deputy Attorney General. George Watling of the FBI was along to take notes. The Director of Central Intelligence attended, as well as a representative of State. The lines had been drawn in preliminary conversations, and it came down to McWade against Fisherman.

McWade was given the floor first. His position was simple to state: Ross had violated the public trust and should be punished to the full measure of the law.

"We all know how bitter you must feel about the personal betrayal," said the Chief of Staff.

"This isn't a grudge," said McWade. "Michael Ross was passing secrets to a Soviet agent. That, I believe, is the legal definition of espionage."

"As I understand it," said the Deputy Attorney General, "he was getting useful intelligence in exchange."

"We don't know how much of it was disinformation," said McWade.

"You ever notice how they all get to sound like Fisherman after a while?" said Watling under his breath.

"Isaac is not speaking of motive," said the DCI, quite neutrally, considering. "He is speaking of procedure. Whatever one thinks of the calculus of interest here, many of Ross's decisions were simply not his to make."

"Let's not forget that he had an American agent killed," said McWade.

Fisherman sat at the end of the table, fingers laced across his tie.

"Many men have had to make tragic choices," he said.

The remark was Delphic, but McWade thought he understood. Fisherman was reminding him that Leggatt had been known to make choices, too.

"The evidence of murder may be difficult to mount," said the Deputy AG. "At a minimum we would need the Russian's testimony. And the defense would have a field day with his credibility."

"The charge is espionage," said McWade. "That much is provable."

"If it walks like a duck and quacks like a duck . . ." said Watling.

"An ancient principle of law," said the Deputy AG.

"An old canard," said the man from State.

The Chief of Staff was showing some impatience. He pointed his pencil across the length of the table to where Fisherman was sitting.

"Ernest," he said, "you have some observations of a non-judicial nature, I believe."

"I am concerned, as you are, about the arms talks," he said. "Powerful elements in the Kremlin will seize on any accusation by us as a reason not to proceed."

"Not to mention the Senate," said the man from State, "if it finds out that our side was represented by a mole."

"For the record," said the Chief of Staff, "the negotiating positions have been comprehensively reassessed under Isaac's direction, and there is no dispute as to their soundness."

"The senators won't be interested in parsing the sentences," said Fisherman.

"They'll have their guns drawn," said the man from State.

"To shoot the wounded," said Watling.

At that point the Deputy AG handed a note to the Chief of Staff, who read it, then folded it up and placed it under the yellow legal pad in front of him.

"I believe we all can agree," he said, "that it would be utterly inappropriate to decline a prosecution in an espionage case for fear of what the Soviets or the Senate might think."

It fell to Watling to make the obligatory post-Watergate remark.

"It would be wrong, that's for sure," he said.

The survivors of that period in the room were the only ones who dared to laugh.

"As I understand it, Ernest," said the Chief of Staff, "you are offering other grounds."

"The real crime," Fisherman said, "would be to fail to take advantage of Kerzhentseff."

"I thought he had been thoroughly compromised," said the Deputy AG. "How can we even be sure he isn't already in the Gulag somewhere?"

"There are ways," said Fisherman.

"We have taken certain steps, have we not?" said the Chief of Staff.

For starters, Fisherman explained, the Agency had run an elaborate damage control effort that made it appear that the compromise had been all in one direction, that Kerzhentseff had controlled Ross down to the roots of his teeth.

"You want to turn him into hero of the revolution," said Watling.

"It is a subtle business, George," said Fisherman. "They'd distrust anything too obvious, of course. But a shakeup in Washington, beginning with Ross's resignation for personal reasons, would be credible. The Soviets understand about personal reasons."

Though Kerzhentseff had been allowed to flee, Fisherman went on, the Soviet guards at the safehouse had been detained. Moscow had made a private protest and been firmly rebuffed. Meantime, the guards had been persuaded of the advantages of life in the United States. They would not be any more of a problem than the Czech woman. Ross had been the one who sent her up against McWade in order to drive him to Europe where he could be compromised. She was the only other outside person in a position to reveal the extent of Kerzhentseff's cooperation. Fisherman had rolled her up in Washington as soon as he played out his hand in Britain. He had known exactly where to find her, because Stockwell hadn't really lost her when she left the motel. Looking back on it, McWade realized that he should have known. When Rufus was on somebody's tail, he did not make mistakes. Unless you counted being vulnerable to a beautiful piece of bait. That had lost Stockwell his job at the Agency, and it might have cost McWade his career as well if Stockwell hadn't been watching out for him. McWade made no protest to Fisherman's proposal that the Czech woman be allowed to defect and be given a new identity. She had deceived him, but she had never known him as anyone but Leggatt. Legend against legend. You could not be punitive about that.

"As you can see," said Fisherman, "we hold all Kerzhentseff's strings."

"And I assure you, gentlemen, that this time the procedures for handling him will be orderly," said the DCI. "Ernest will have operational responsibility, reporting directly to me."

It was a perfect match, Fisherman and Kerzhentseff, two dinosaurs from the era before *glasnost*, feeling threatened by the change in the climate.

No one questioned the wisdom of the arrangement or the matter of Fisherman's own exposure if Ross made a public issue of the death of Jerry Birch. The notes of the meeting only showed that after serious consideration the judgment was made that the cost of abandoning Kerzhentseff as a defector in place was too high to risk bringing Michael Ross to trial. There was only one dissent.

The President quickly accepted the recommendation and used the occasion to make a number of other key personnel moves, including the replacement of the Secretary of State.

On the day he was to announce his decision, he invited

McWade to a private lunch in the Oval Office. McWade took the opportunity to tell him about Ben Wheeler. The President pushed his plate aside and leaned his elbows on the desk.

"He was a good man, was he?"

"You could depend on him."

"Damned few like that any more. Men like Ross are from a different mold."

"You know where I stand on that, sir."

"Hell, son, I'd like to string him up by the balls. But I'm not going to."

"I was hoping to turn you around on that."

"The man took a shit on that rug over there, and I'm gonna have to give him a pass."

"He'll claim he has access," said McWade. "He'll make a lot of money."

"Don't worry about him," said the President. "We're going to make you the big winner."

"I'm talking about the truth," said McWade.

The President seemed to find that thought amusing.

"I used to worry a lot about that myself," he said, "until I discovered that in matters like this the truth is whatever I say it is. And I say you did Ross in. You cut off his nuts, son. You wanted his job and you took it. People are gonna start getting out of your way."

"I'll play it however you want," said McWade.

"Well, Christ, at least enjoy yourself a little. Thirty-five years in public life, and I've only learned one thing for sure. Being in on the joke is ninety per cent of the game."

After his promotion, McWade moved into Ross's splendid office in the Old Executive Office Building. When he placed a telephone call now, he rarely had to leave a message. For McWade, nobody was in conference, nobody had just stepped away from his desk. The uniformed guards at the White House gate did not even glance at his identification anymore. They just waved him through. And his secretary was always waiting with a bouquet of pink phone slips that showed him how much he was loved.

One day, not long after the shakeup in the President's

national security team, she presented him with a message from Richard Harper.

"When did this come in?" he asked.

"First at eight. Then again a few minutes ago."

"Get him on the line."

By the time he had hung up his suit jacket, she was buzzing him. He let Harper rest in the limbo of hold while he arranged the papers on his desk, flicked some lint off his pants and picked up the *Post*, tossing the sports section and other diversions into the trash.

"I heard about your promotion," said Harper when McWade finally punched in. "I also understand your colleague got his budget restored."

"Friends in the right places," said McWade.

"And if they play along, they do seem to move up briskly."

"Is that what you think?"

"Still Fisherman's fair-haired boy."

McWade switched the receiver from one hand to the other.

"You went running to him yourself," he said. "Don't tell me about standing up to him."

"I bear no animus," said Harper.

"Just regrets that I didn't have the decency to slit my wrists."

"A thing like that," said Harper, "could only have happened to a very simple man."

McWade's hand cramped where it held the phone.

"Funny, though," Harper went on. "I always gave Rufus Stockwell more credit."

"Leave him out of it," said McWade.

"I guess you and Fisherman took care of that."

McWade's eye flitted around the office from one familiar object to another without finding a place to light.

"Rufus takes care of himself," he said.

"If you don't know the story," said Harper, "you ought to ask Fisherman what happened to Stockwell. It would be interesting to hear his account."

"The next time you want to fight with Ernest," said McWade, "keep me out of it."

Harper sniffed, as if the idea of neutrality left an odor.

"I don't think you're going to have much choice, my friend," he said. "He'll come after you just like he came after me."

All day long McWade strained against his calendar. Even with the President out of pocket at Camp David, the schedule bound him so tightly that he didn't have time for anything beyond a telephone call between meetings. Now that there was a new team at State, the planning for the next round of talks in Moscow was being staffed out the way the newspaper sages always said it should be done, and that meant endless rounds of meetings to get everyone pulling in one direction, as each department did its damnedest to get a hold of the helm.

But he could not keep his mind on the matters at hand. He put his first call shortly after hanging up on Harper and then tried again at every break. There was no answer at Stockwell's number all day. Late in the afternoon he tried the message service he had used in London and found that something had come in.

The message had been left weeks before when McWade was still in England. Stockwell apologized for not being able to look in on him and reported that he was off to Berlin on an errand for Fisherman, "just making sure our mutual friend got back to where he belongs." As the young woman read the note, she sounded as if she was working at the limits of her literacy. " 'No hard feelings, chum,' " she said. "Is that the word, love, or am I reading it wrong? Anyway, it goes on to say, 'I was working for you all along.' Does that make any sense?"

McWade's final meeting ended a little before five. When the last of the participants had gone, he surprised his secretary by telling her she could go home early because he was calling it quits for the day. She mentioned a few calls that seemed urgent, but he said they could wait. He did not have her order a car. He did not want his evening's travels entered into the motor pool log, especially his trip to Fortune.

The bar was open, but there was no one up front, and

the passage to the back was locked. McWade took a seat at one of the rickety tables and waited. The inflected, nasal sound of Asian rock and roll on the tape deck and the smell of sweet sauces were like the memory of many things at once. Eventually the inner door rattled and Lan poked out her head.

"You go," she said as she stepped into the room and closed the door.

"I just got here."

"No good. Number ten. You go."

"Don't tell me Blackie's taken away my privileges just because I got myself a little more rank."

"I no understand the reasons, Mr Isaac," she said. "But I hear him talking. He gets very angry. Go, please. Before he sees you here."

McWade leaned back in his chair and put his hands in his pockets.

"I've got a reputation as a very stubborn guy," he said. "Ask my old friend Stockwell."

Something flickered across her face as she backed away. Before she reached the door, Blackie pushed it open from within.

"Leave the girl alone," he said.

McWade did not rise. Blackie towered over him.

"You want to tell me why I'm not welcome anymore?" McWade asked.

"I own the joint," said Blackie. "That means I don't have to explain."

"Were you asshole buddies with Ross or something?"

"That skyliner? I don't want to be near any of you guys with the big profiles. You just draw fire."

"I had a job and a half the last time I was here," said McWade. "It didn't seem to bother you then."

Blackie stepped forward and took hold of McWade's arm at the elbow. McWade had little choice but to let himself be led toward the exit. But along the way he said what he had come to say.

"I need to find Rufus."

Blackie halted, and his grip tightened until it began to hurt.

"Not funny, pal," he said.

"I need to talk to him."

Blackie let go and pushed McWade back to where he could see him whole.

"A guy called me up," said McWade. "He made some remarks that got me worried. When I tried to get in touch with Rufus I came up blank. Except at a message drop we used in London. He left me a note there, but it was weeks old."

"That's a long time. A lot can happen."

"He said he was on his way to Berlin."

"That's where he ended up," said Blackie.

"You've heard from him?"

"He's dead."

McWade might have showed something, but it was a very little. He was operating again by London rules.

Blackie went to the window and took down the Open sign. He returned to the bar and poured himself a drink.

"I figured you burned him," he said.

"His message said he was delivering a guy."

"An errand for you?"

"For somebody else."

"They found him face down in a ditch," said Blackie. "One bullet in the back of the head. Close range. They'd gotten right on top of him."

"A set-up."

"Rufus would have kicked up a fight if he had half a chance," said Blackie.

He poured a little more Bourbon. Then he got another glass and measured out a couple of shots of Scotch for McWade.

"Nobody ever got behind Rufus," he said. "You didn't see him unless he wanted you to or else somebody told you where to look."

"The invisible man," said McWade. He raised his glass, as if in a requiem toast.

"If you didn't do him," said Blackie, "who did?"

McWade was not prepared to make the case that Stockwell was another man sacrificed for Kerzhentseff's credibility. But this much was clear: Rufus was perfect for the role. The Soviets would have figured him to be operating under deep cover. By having Stockwell killed, Kerzhentseff would have demonstrated that he had to take drastic measures after the Americans discovered what a fool he had made of them over the years. But from the American side Stockwell was virtually anonymous. He had been operating without portfolio, so his death went down as nothing more than another soldier of fortune meeting an untimely end abroad. It was the kind of thing that happened so often that news of it had not even shown up in the morning intelligence log.

"I was the guy who got him back to Europe," said McWade, "but I didn't send him to Berlin."

Blackie lifted the Scotch bottle back to the bar.

"Europe ain't such a dangerous place, depending on who you're dealing with. Here. Have another drink. On the house. But from now on, take you business somewhere else."

"I'd like to come back from time to time, just to find out what you've heard."

"Maybe you had something to do with wasting him, and maybe you didn't," said Blackie. "It ain't up to me to decide. But a lot of my regulars are going to draw their own conclusions. A thing like this just ain't good for the trade."

When he left Fortune, McWade headed back downtown. If the appointment had been with anyone else, he would have cancelled, but he did not have the heart to do that to Sarah.

The place she had chosen was as far from her office as it was from his. They both had to go out of their way, and this gave the rendezvous a furtive quality, as if even in attempting to find some civil ground on which to complete their parting, they had something to hide.

She was waiting for him at a table in the corner. The room was small and pretentious, but it was too early for a crowd. She smiled when he greeted her, and he felt a tug at the edge of a wound.

"How are you, Isaac?"

312

"Bearing up, I guess."

"You were gone a long time."

"Press of business."

"When I couldn't reach you, I got worried."

"There was nothing to fret about," he said, "unless you count my midlife crisis."

"That isn't the truth, is it?" she said.

The waitress came and took their orders before he had to respond. Sarah asked for something light with ice. McWade took soda plain.

"Is everything going to be all right?" Sarah asked.

"They tell me it is."

"I've read about your new job."

It seemed sad to him that she was still keeping track.

"I'm secure for the moment," he said.

"I'm glad about the prominence. Now you'll never be able to go back."

"To the Agency?" he said. "It would be a scandal if I moonlighted for Langley now. People like to think they know who they're dealing with."

"I appreciate the feeling."

McWade took a sip of soda and ran his finger over the condensation on the glass.

"There were a lot of things I couldn't talk to you about," he said.

"It wasn't that."

"But it didn't help."

He met her eyes and it was as if this was the first time he had ever really seen them as they were. For once he was not trying to find himself reflected there.

"The new job," she said. "It's what you wanted, isn't it?"

"Don't listen to what they're saying."

"Are they telling tales?"

"Some are," he said. "Swain's been spreading it around that I pulled a fast one to get Ross out of my way."

"Did you?"

"I was an innocent bystander," he said.

"You won't tell me, will you?" she said.

He chose his next words carefully because no matter

313

what the official account was supposed to be, he was not prepared to defend Michael Ross.

"If a person doesn't like what he sees, he has a duty to stand up," he said.

"You've always been big on duty," she said, but it was not nearly as bitter as it might have been.

"I neglected you," he said. "I admit that."

"And said that some day you'd be able to explain so that I would understand."

"The time might have come," he said, "if we'd stuck it out."

"If I hadn't cheated, you mean."

"One thing leads to another," he said, because he did not want the talk to turn to the other man. "I'm not saying what came first."

"One day I looked up, and I couldn't reach you anymore. Eventually I stopped trying. That came first. Then the lies."

"You don't have to give me reasons, Sarah."

"But I want to," she said. "I need to be sure."

"That it was right for us to go our separate ways? If it helps to hear me say so, I will: I think it was bound to happen some day."

"Maybe there was someone else on your side, too," she said.

It startled him to hear her say this. Unfaithfulness was one thing he never expected to be accused of. Lies, yes. Anger. Coldness. But he had always been loyal, and sometimes blind.

"I'm not seeing anybody now," she said, folding and unfolding a cocktail napkin until it finally fell apart. "It didn't last a week past your leaving. I always knew it wouldn't. Maybe you won't believe this, but I think I drove you away because that was the only way I could be free to get you back."

McWade felt something vital in him slipping. It was wrong for her to take the whole burden of their failure on herself. Eventually she would hate him if she did. Regret would turn to resentment. If they were to part with any decency, they had to share the blame.

"You're right," he said. "There was somebody else for me, too."

"Is she still with you?"

"Does it make any difference?"

"Well," she said, pushing herself unsteadily back from the table. It wobbled, and the wine and soda in her glass spilled over the rim. "I guess I've made a fool of myself again."

He reached over to touch her hand, but she withdrew it. Now he regretted what he had said. Every lie cut you off, even the ones you meant as kindness.

"I'm the only fool at this table," he said.

She put her handbag back down on the floor and pulled her chair forward again. But the look on her face was not forgiving.

"I could always tell, you know," she said. "When you were hiding something, I mean. I should have realized that it was foolish to think that just because I am alone again you would be alone, too."

"Sarah," he said. "Don't turn it against yourself that way."

"The funny thing is, I came here thinking that maybe we might find something."

"I'm not the person you want me to be," he said. "The boy from Manitee Bay."

"All our foolish ideas of ourselves," she said. There was no cynicism in it. Maybe they had at least that much in common now, how much they valued what they had lost.

"I thought you'd found some earlier, better self in me," he said. "I wanted you to breathe him back to life."

"Maybe I didn't try hard enough."

"It wasn't that. I was trying to be too many people at once. At Langley they expect you to put on and take off legends like suits of clothes. But now I've simplified my life. I am who I am. Nobody else. And even though that's not as good as I might have wanted, at least maybe it isn't as bad as I feared."

Sarah took a sip from her drink and put it back down on the shiny tabletop. She did not look at him.

"I came here to tell you how sorry I was for what I did to you," she said.

"Ike McWade wasn't what you needed. You sensed that early. It took me longer."

"I want you to come home, Isaac," she said.

It was so sudden that his first impulse was to hide.

"I promise not to be jealous of your secrets," she said.

"My many affairs," he said.

"Maybe I'd better go."

She stood up, steady this time, her fingers holding the table still as she rose.

"Please stay," he said.

"I thought maybe I could make you understand that I did what I did for wanting you."

"I wanted you, too," he said. "But I'm not sure I can have you honestly."

"My eyes are open," she said. And when they came his way, they did not distort him.

"I'm not a particularly strong man," he said. "I have always had somebody powerful to defend me. But now I'm on my own, and there is something I have to do that will keep me living the life you hate."

"Don't explain," she said.

"I have to," he said. "Maybe not everything. But this time you'd have to know what you're getting into."

"I can't say I won't be afraid," she said.

"I can't either," he said. "I have to go up against a very dangerous man."

She laced her fingers around the glass and looked at it for a moment as if it had become a ritual cup. Then she raised it to her lips.

"Then I guess you'll need an ally," she said.

When they parted it was only for a little while. She needed to pick up a few things so they could prepare a proper meal together. He had to make a stop at his office.

He entered the White House grounds by the Pennsylvania Avenue gate and took the long sidewalk that crossed the lawn. The spotlights were on, and they lit the facade like a proscenium, flat against the starless sky. In his office,

316

he sat for a moment before picking up the green phone. The encipherment machine whirred and snickered as it made the connection.

Even the Director of Central Intelligence was willing to take McWade's calls on the first attempt these days. McWade skipped the preliminaries and got directly to the point. He asked whether there was still any sentiment for ridding the Agency of Ernest Fisherman, and he was not put off by the equivocal answer.

"I believe I know a way," McWade said.

In the DCI's careful response he heard the slightest suggestion of interest and then the pure silence that, for a man of McWade's training, was all he needed to hear.

JACK FULLER

OUR FATHERS' SHADOWS

Everything should be going Frank Nolan's way. He's got a good career as Assistant District Attorney, he has an adoring family and a wife he loves. So, why isn't it?

Old Sam Nolan is dying slowly of a rare disease; Frank's wife has retreated into her music; Frank knows what she wants but he can't give it to her and isn't about to tell her why. As if family troubles aren't enough, there's been a particularly nasty child murder on the block. A horrific case but they've got the guy who did it and the case is all wrapped up. Or is it? Something isn't hanging together just right for Frank. It's a matter of a faint hint here and there, but enough.

As Frank draws closer to finding the real solution of the Susan Tatum case he learns about the nature of his own family and finally works out how he can emerge from his father's shadow.

'Brilliantly explores and develops substance and shadows'   *Manchester Evening News*

POSTA LITTLE HAPPINESS

Post·A·Book

A Royal Mail service in association with the Book Marketing Council & The Booksellers Association.
Post-A-Book is a Post Office trademark.

TED ALLBEURY

DEEP PURPLE

Defectors come in two sorts and conditions. One sort is the plain dealer with a story to sell and the other is the false flag job. Hoggart and Fletcher are MI6 defector graders in the Cleveland Square safe house furnished with electronics. There they go to work on two very different Russians telling remarkably similar stories. Belinsky is the charmer, while Yakunin is the prickly man.

Find the Achilles heel is the name of the game. If Eddie Hoggart's is the wife he almost rescued from the Soho sex industry, it seems British intelligence might have an even more dangerous link in its security chain.

Hoggart's judgement may be getting cloudy, but unless both defectors are lying, the KGB have someone placed hazardously high in the echelons of MI6 . . .

'What a relief to turn to *Deep Purple* . . . The plot is tightly controlled and the writing excellent. There is no self-indulgence but genuine feeling comes through'
Douglas Hurd in the Daily Telegraph

'No one since le Carré has mapped the lonely lunar landscape of espionage better than Allbeury'
The Observer

HODDER AND STOUGHTON PAPERBACKS

MORE FICTION TITLES AVAILABLE FROM
HODDER AND STOUGHTON PAPERBACKS

JACK FULLER

☐	48764 X	Our Fathers' Shadows	£2.99

TED ALLBEURY

☐	52087 0	Deep Purple	£3.50
☐	40574 5	The Choice	£2.95
☐	48772 5	The Crossing	£3.99
☐	05851 4	The Judas Factor	£2.99

All these books are available at your local bookshop or newsagent, or can be ordered direct from the publisher. Just tick the titles you want and fill in the form below.

Prices and availability subject to change without notice.

Hodder & Stoughton Paperbacks, P.O. Box 11, Falmouth, Cornwall.

Please send cheque or postal order for the value of the book, and add the following for postage and packing:

U.K. – 80p for one book, and 20p for each additional book ordered up to a £2.00 maximum.

B.F.P.O. – 80p for the first book, and 20p for each additional book.

OVERSEAS INCLUDING EIRE – £1.50 for the first book, plus £1.00 for the second book, and 30p for each additional book ordered.

OR Please debit this amount from my Access/Visa Card (delete as appropriate).

Card Number ☐☐☐☐☐☐☐☐☐☐☐☐☐☐☐☐

Amount £ ....

Expiry Date ....

Signed ....

Name ....

Address ....